War Girl

Leah Fleming was born in Lancashire of Scottish parents, and is married with four grown-up children and four grandchildren. She writes full time from a haunted farmhouse in the Yorkshire Dales and from the slopes of an olive grove in Crete. For further information on Leah Fleming, please visit www.leahfleming.co.uk

Visit www.AuthorTracker.co.uk for exclusive updates on Leah Fleming.

War Girl

LEAH FLEMING

avon.

Published by AVON
A division of HarperCollins*Publishers*
1 London Bridge Street
London SE1 9GF

www.harpercollins.co.uk

HarperCollins*Publishers*
1st Floor, Watermarque Building, Ringsend Road
Dublin 4, Ireland

This paperback edition 2022

1

First published as *The Girl from World's End*
in Great Britain by HarperCollins*Publishers* 2007

A catalogue copy of this book is available from the British Library.

ISBN: 978-0-00-847126-2

This novel is entirely a work of fiction. The names, characters and incidents
portrayed in it are the work of the author's imagination. Any resemblance to
actual persons, living or dead, events or localities is entirely coincidental.

Typeset in Minion by Palimpsest Book Production Limited,
Falkirk, Stirlingshire
Printed and bound in the UK using 100% Renewable Electricity
at CPI Group (UK) Ltd

MIX
Paper from
responsible sources
FSC™ C007454

This book is produced from independently certified FSC™ paper
to ensure responsible forest management.

For more information visit: www.harpercollins.co.uk/green

AUTHOR'S NOTES

You will not find Windebank or Scarperton on any map of the Yorkshire Dales for they are fusions of many villages and townships in the Craven area. My story and its characters are entirely fictitious but I have based some incidents on local events before and after the Second World War.

I am indebted to the following for sharing their stories of their farming lives: Anne Holgate, Olive and Joe Coates, Elizabeth Hird, Gordon Sargeant and Dick Middleton but especially to the late Mrs Edith Carr for the loan of photographs. I have drawn inspiration from her detailed account of surviving the winter of 1947 from her memoir: *Edith Carr – Life on Malham Moor. A mini-biography* by W.R. Mitchell, Castleberg Publications (1999).

I also drew ideas and inspiration from local exhibitions at the Folly Museum, Settle, and Victoria Hall, and from local publications: *North Craven at War: A Collection by the North Craven Historical Research Group*, Hudson History publications of Settle (2005) and *How they lived in the Yorkshire Dales* by W.R. Mitchell, Castleberg Publications (2001).

The incident with the barrage balloon was inspired by an anecdote in *Sheep, Steam and Shows* by Gerald Tyler.

I am indebted to North Yorkshire County Libraries for always finding my obscure requests, especially the Settle branch for showing me the *Craven Herald and Pioneer* articles and the local archive of the Giggleswick total eclipse in 1927.

Most of the information on the secret Auxiliary Units of the Home Guard came from www.auxunit.org.uk My hidden bunkers in the Dales are fictitious. I'd love to know if there are any still extant.

This story was sometimes written to the accompaniment of Edward Elgar's *Introduction and Adagio for Strings, Opus 47*: the background music to Barry Cockcroft's inspirational Yorkshire TV documentary, *Too Long a Winter* (1974).

Many thanks to my editor, Maxine Hitchcock and the team at Avon, to Judith Murdoch, my patient agent, Elizabeth Gill and Trisha Ashley of the 500 Club and Diane Allen for their constant encouragement and support.

A special thanks also to Jenny Hall, Joyce Price, June Parrington, Kate Croll and the late Kathleen Firth for their friendship and enthusiasm and to David and all my family for just being there.

In memory of Kathleen, who loved these hills.

. . . grief has no wings. She is the unwelcome lodger that squats on the hearthstone between us and the fire and will not be moved . . .

Arthur Quiller-Couch
Armistice Day Sermon, November 1927

Part One
A Change of Sky

1

West Riding of Yorkshire, 1926

A girl of about eight sat swinging her legs to and fro to keep them from going numb, watching the sky growing dark above. The weak December sun dipped behind the high moor and soon the cobbled streets would be crusted with frost. When was Father going to come out of the Green Man and take her home? The church clock had struck half-past four. Soon the mill hooter would buzz across the rooftops and the clatter of clogs would deafen the streets.

It had been a grand afternoon: one of the good days when Paddy Gilchrist woke up by himself, whistling and promising her a ride on a tram to Bradford to look in the shop windows and hear the Christmas brass bands. They had got as far as the park, where he'd pushed her on the swings and slides, but then they'd made a detour through the back streets of Scarperton.

'I'll not be a minute, Mirren. Time for my

medicine – just a wee nip to keep me warm,' he laughed, his dark eyes pleading as he saw the little blue ribbon on her coat lapel and the wince of disapproval on her face.

She was proud of that badge and the signed certificate from the Band of Hope that said not a drop of liquor would ever pass the lips of Miriam Ellen Gilchrist.

'Don't be long,' she pleaded, trying not to pout as her lips trembled. 'You promised me a ride up to town.'

'Aye, I know, lassie, but you don't begrudge yer dad a little comfort now, do you? You sit tight and I'll buy you some sweeties when I've had my snifter.'

She had sat on this bench so many times, dreading that the father who went in standing would be the one who'd come out on all fours. The Green Man was that sort of pub.

Paddy and Mirren didn't live alone. There was a master in their rooms: one who ruled over them night and day, whose presence lurked like a ghost in the corner of the compartments of the disused railway carriage that was now their home. He was a magician, full of piss and wind and wild schemes, who could turn her dad into John Barleycorn, the drunken sot who needed a guiding hand to round the corners on his way home, knocking folk off the pavement as he sang out of tune at the top of his voice. Sometimes she opened the latch and he fell through the door, stiff like a board.

John Barleycorn had stale breath and leaking pants. He stole her father's hard-earned wage and the food from their table, shaming her before school pals playing in the street, who would look up and snigger as she and her demon-possessed father wound their way down the ginnels from the pub, Mirren staggering under the weight of him. She worshipped her father – he was tall, handsome and strong – but she hated John Barleycorn, the drinker who was so weak and silly.

Demon Drink was not like the pantomime devil with horns and a forked tale, all red and black, shouting from a stage, or the wily tempter from the pages of her Sunday school prize book, with forked tongue and goatee beard. He came and went for no reason.

Sometimes he disappeared for weeks and gave her back the father she loved: the Paddy Gilchrist who had wooed and won young Ellie Yewell away from her farming family in the big Yorkshire Dales farmhouse, the railway navvy with his squeeze-box and fancy dancing and Scottish charm, who promised her the moon, sun and stars if she would be his bride. Then he went off to war, leaving his new bride with a bairn, Mirren's angel brother, Grantley, and with no family to support them until he returned wounded right badly in the leg.

If only Mother and little Grant hadn't died in the terrible sickness that came when she was a baby, leaving her motherless. How she wished they were all together, snug by their fireside of an evening, not freezing to death outside a public house.

Now the lamps were lit and Mirren was fed up of waiting. He'd forgotten she was there again and at the mercy of rough lads, making fun of her for being 'Jill all alone'. Soon Woodbine Winnie would be touting for business and taking men in mufflers down the alleyway to lift up her skirts – to do quite what Mirren wasn't sure, but it was something sinful.

At last Mirren recognised one of the men coming out of the pub as Mr Ackroyd, who lived in one of the far carriages that made up their row of houses in Chapelside Cuttings; old rolling stock being the only homes left for returning heroes from the war. Some wags laughingly called them 'the Rabbit Hutches', but Dad shrugged off the gibe and so did she.

Living in a neat line of compartments with steps up to their railway carriage was better than living back to back, up a steep hill with no garden to play in. She could sit for hours watching the engines shunting up and down the line, engine drivers waving and hooting. She knew the names of all the great iron boilers puffing and snorting out of the station on their way to Scotland and London; *Duchess of Hamilton* was her favourite.

Dad was a ganger on the line repairing the track. When he was in work there was always plenty of coal for the stove and treats. When there were lay-offs they still had vegetables from the allotment and eggs from the chicken coop, but money was always a worry. Granny Simms, who lived next door with her son and his one leg, cooked for them and took in the washing in return for coal and treats, baccy and beer for Big Brian, who hobbled about the town on crutches, begging.

In Mirren's life Granny Simms was a guiding light like the moon peeping through clouds. A neighbour who was mother, friend and comforter, she would know what to do. On nights like this Mirren could always knock on the window and Granny would open up, wrapped against the cold in the faded shawl she wore summer and winter, the long printed pinny with rubbed-out patches. Her face was leathery and lined with soot, hair scraped back in a knot, and she wore iron clogs, which rattled on the wooden carriage floor, and rolled-up stockings. She would take the little girl in and shove a fat rascal bun in her hand, spicy and full of currants.

It was Granny who taught her to knit, to peg a rug and bake bread, railway slice and dumplings. She saw that she got a proper schooling at St Mary's and was turned out neat to all Sunday school treats going in the town.

'He can't help himself, Mirren,' Granny Simms would sigh, showing empty gums with two yellow cracked front teeth. 'Drink is a terrible thing. There's many a red nose makes a ragged back in this town. It's a pity the Paddy Gilchrist what came back from France was not the young lad who went to war, nor the man yer mam wed. A wild-eyed stranger he returned, not able to keep down a job, but she got him straight again. But when the Spanish flu came to visit us, it went through the town like a dose of Epsom salts. Yer dad just couldn't get his head round that carry-on. He did his best with you, but men are useless when it comes to babbies. It's a terrible temptation to drown yer sorrows, lass.'

These words made Mirren sad, for she knew her love would never be enough to mend her father's heart. What he needed was the Word of God in his life, like the pastor in Sunday school preached, but Dad just laughed at her pleas for him to go to church.

'Where was God when we needed him in the Battle of Arras? Where was he when the Angel of Death knocked at our front door? Ask your preacher man that!' he would scoff. She had learned not to talk to him in drink but to hide in the little bench bed, under the quilt and blankets, pretending she couldn't hear his sobs and rantings, praying that he would be in time to go to his work in the morning. Without work there was

8

no rent money and no rent money would lead to the workhouse and pull them apart.

Then, without explanation, the sun would rise in the morning, bright and dazzling, full of promise when her real dad rose, bleary-eyed but ready for work, unaided, bringing home gobstoppers and fish and chips. She would dress quickly and take his hand before the clouds came back.

On such days Mirren could go to school and learn her tables and not worry about him being sent home. She liked to bury her head in a reading book and pretend she was the Little Princess in the attic or one of the Railway Children. On such days Dad would swing her round to 'Charlie Is my Darling' and call her his 'own wee darling', telling her she was pretty like her mother and what a lucky chap he was to have such a beautiful, clever daughter. When he held her hand and whistled to himself, she felt so safe until they stopped by the pub door and her heart sank with fear.

Now, tonight, was going to be another of the bad nights.

'Is my dad still inside?' she asked the old neighbour, Mr Ackroyd, as he passed.

'Aye, lass, stuck to the bench a while yet. There's some as never knows when they've had enough. Better get off home now. It's no night to be out in the cold. Happen you'd better come along with me.'

'Thank you, but I said I'd wait,' she smiled, torn

between wanting the warmth of Granny Simms's iron stove and the need to see her dad home safely. Why should she wait when he didn't care? Why should she believe any of his broken promises? He deserved to slip on the ice and crack his head but then he wouldn't get to work on time and would be laid off and soon it would be Christmas and she had seen a little doll in the window of Bell's Emporium with a sticky-out skirt and real hair.

But what was the point? He'd already spent his wages supping with his cronies. It was always the same palaver: he'd be ashamed and crawl home to sleep off the drink when she wasn't looking, and then pretend none of this had happened.

Why should she wait a minute longer when there was someone at hand to guide her through the dark streets?

'Wait, Mr Ackroyd, I'll come with you . . .'

She spent the night at Granny Simms's, sleeping in the chair. When it was morning, and there was no sign of Dad's return, Mirren thought he would be lying snug in one of the refuge huts on the side of the railway track, hiding until he was sober enough to face her sullen anger. So she went to school with a heavy heart and thought no more about it.

She ran home at dinner break, hoping there would be smoke coming out of the carriage, but there were strangers waiting on the doorstep with

Granny Simms, who nodded gravely as she saw her. There was a funny look in her eyes as Mirren approached more slowly.

She recognised Constable Fletcher, who was kind. He took off his helmet as he spoke.

'You'll have to be brave, lass. There's been a terrible accident. Yer dad got knocked over on the track.'

Mirren shook her head, not wanting to hear what was coming next, wanting to run, but her legs had turned to jelly so she shoved her hands over her ears. It was Granny who put her arms around her shoulders and held her tight.

'He wouldn't've known a thing, love. He fell asleep on the line. He must have taken a short cut and slipped.' Her eyes were full of tears.

Mirren couldn't believe what she was saying. 'Dad'd never cross the line at night. He said I must never do that. Where did it happen? You've got it all wrong. The track's miles from the Green Man.'

'I'm sorry, lass, but he must have been taking a short cut down the line in the early hours. He was hit on the down line – the night sleeper from Glasgow and him Scotch-born and all . . . Let yer granny make you a cup of tea,' said the constable.

'She's not my granny,' Mirren screamed in fury. 'My real granny lives up the dale on a farm.' At Christmas there was usually a parcel of clothes from Grandma, which never fitted, and a printed card from the Yewells of Cragside Farm. The rest of the year there was nothing.

'I want to see my dad.'

'That'll not be possible,' whispered the constable. 'There has to be an investigation.'

'I have to go and see if it's him. It might not be him,' Mirren said, not listening. This was all some strange nightmare she was living in and soon she would wake up. How could her dad be gone and have left her all alone?

'Come on, Mirren, you've had a shock,' Granny Simms whispered, ignoring the earlier betrayal. 'She'll stay with me until such times—'

'But it's all my fault,' Mirren cried out. 'I should've waited and brought him home.'

'Now how do you make that out, young lady?' said the policeman, kneeling down so close up she could see the hairs sprouting out of his nose.

'I should have stayed on. He told me to stay outside on the bench, but I was cold and came home. He needed me and I wasn't there. It's all my fault.' The hot tears began to roll down her cheeks. 'I want my dad. I have to tell him I'm sorry.'

'Now none of that, child,' said one of the strangers, a man wearing a clerical collar. 'Mr Gilchrist was a grown man and should've known better than to leave a child alone in the dark outside a pub,' he tutted in her defence, but his words gave no comfort.

'I'm afraid there's many as does round here,' answered the constable. 'The child was right to go home. In his befuddled state, Paddy wouldn't know what time of day or night it was. Don't fret yerself, lass. It were an accident and a cruel one at that, just before Christmas.'

'That remains for the coroner to decide,' the parson replied. 'The railway line is always a temptation, an easy way out of life's troubles.'

'Not in front of the kiddy, sir,' snapped the constable. 'She's got enough to bear as it is, without putting that burden on her.'

But the words were spoken and a seed of doubt sown in turbulent soil. Mirren had sensed early that a force greater than her childish adoration always drew her father towards danger. He'd once lived in a world of soldiers. When he sat in the Green Man there were old pals from the war who supped and sang that 'It's a Long Way to Tipperary' song that made him cry. Once she had rooted in his tin box of papers and found a likeness of him, standing so straight in his uniform, his dark hair plastered down and his moustache waxed. He looked so strong and handsome, but when he caught her staring down at it he almost slammed the lid on her fingers.

'Put that away. There's nothing in there for you!'

'Is that you?' she'd asked, looking at his kilt.

He'd stared down at the young man and shook

his head. 'Never seen him afore.' His voice was cracked and his breath smelled of stout, his skin was grey, his shoulders stooped as he fought the demons she was too feeble to conquer. She never opened the tin box again because it was where he kept his wounds and pain, out of sight of a child's prying eyes.

'It is good to see this child Miriam has signed the pledge.' The parson pointed to the badge on her lapel. 'A weakness for strong drink is bred in the bone. Do you belong to the Band of Hope?' He was changing the subject, trying to make polite conversation.

'Yes, she does,' Granny Simms interrupted. 'She's a regular at their banner parades and treat in the summer. She wears that blue ribbon all the time.'

'Good. That's a start, young lady, and next we must get the Welfare to sort out accommodation. She can't stay here alone,' he added.

'She'll bide with me tonight. This lass's not budging from where she knows best,' Granny said, holding her tight. Mirren's eyelids were drooping, her mouth was dry, her head whirring as her legs buckled. 'Look at the poor mite. She needs a mash of sweet tea. There's friends enough round here to see to the poor bairn in her sorrow.'

They stumbled up the steps and into the fug and clutter of Granny Simms's compartment, where Brian sat dosing with his dog on his lap. He didn't know yet. He hadn't heard the news.

For a second, life was as it always had been, bread and dripping on the table as if her world had not been turned upside down and she left alone.

If only she'd stayed with Dad, if only it was yesterday all over again. But the mill buzzer hooted at dinner time as normal. How could something terrible happen and the mill chimneys went on smoking just the same? She started to shake and couldn't stop.

Granny shoved something bitter on her lips. 'Sip it slowly, lass. It'll calm you down,' she coaxed, but Mirren spat it out.

'It's spirit. I know that smell. Don't make me break my pledge.'

'Bugger the pledge . . . It's the only medicine for shock.'

'What am I going to do?' Mirren cried, feeling the hot whisky slipping down her throat. It tasted bitter. How could anyone pay good brass for such poison?

'First things first. We'll see yer dad buried good and proper and you kitted out to do him proud. Everything else can wait until then. Yer a good lass and sharp as a knife, but you've not gone far to find your sorrows. Happen something will turn up for you.'

'I'll have to go in the orphanage, won't I?'

15

Everyone at school knew of the orphan kids, in their grey uniforms and cropped hair, who walked in lines around the town and had no parents to care for them.

'Over my dead body! You deserve better and, as you said, I'm not yer real kin. It's time them as are got to know what's happened,' Granny Simms smiled. 'I'm no good with lettering but we'll get someone to write and get them down here fast. It's time they took up their responsibilities. Yer mam would have wanted that.'

'But I'd rather stay here with you.'

Granny shook her head. 'Be that as it may, there'll be nothing but bad memories for you here. You deserve better. Happen it's time you were changing yer sky!'

Adeline Yewell was too busy finishing off the Christmas pig to see the letter that George, the postman, delivered to the kitchen table at Cragside Farm. He would be wanting his forenoon drinkings and a bit of gossip with Carrie before he headed across the moor on foot to the next farm.

The farmer's wife had trapped Myrtle, the brown pig, against the wall so she squatted on her fat rump. Then Adeline shoved a ball of oatmeal down the pig's throat and gave her a sup of good buttermilk from the bucket to swallow. 'That's a girl, stuff thyself!' She wanted some fat sweet flesh on this porker before she got seen to with an axe, strung up and bled off. At least her pigs died happy and belly stuffed. No place for oversentiment on a farm, she thought.

There was so much to see to before the big day and she didn't want George holding up Carrie Sutcliffe from her chores. They were getting a bit sweet on each other, them two. She hoped that didn't mean another live-in domestic giving notice. It was hard to get girls and lads to stay overlong up on the tops. They wanted to be in nearer the town.

Oh, what it was to be love-struck and silly! She could still recall the time when she'd made eyes at Joe Yewell at the Christmas dance, nearly forty years ago. It's a good job she had collared and bagged him by the New Year stir-up in the village hall as he stomped across the wooden floor in his shirtsleeves, before the fiddle and the stamp of dancing feet became Satan's snare.

Once he got 'saved' in Brother Handel Morton's tent he hadn't time for worldly gatherings, only preaching and chapel meetings. She'd caught him just on the turn, and her being Church not Chapel, it could have made things impossible.

The two didn't mix in Windebank village, never had and never would, but love conquers all, so they say. The two of them went their separate ways each Sunday morning.

If only he could have made Ellen, their daughter,

see sense when she fell for that Scotch navvy Gilchrist. They both felt it was a grave mistake, but the lass burned her bridges good and proper, and paid the price. They'd not even gone to her funeral for fear of catching the flu and passing it on up the dale.

That act of cowardice had never sat easy on her; cost many a sleepless night. To abandon their own daughter was not something either of them was proud of but Ellie'd made her bed and all that. It was her choice to go rushing up to Gretna Green making a fool of them all, having a bairn not six months afterwards. It was not easy to stomach having a thankless child.

Adeline'd done her bit for the kiddies but had never seen the last one nor wanted to, but her father being a Catholic and fond of drink was a worry. Sometimes she lay in bed and wondered if the girl had Ellie's fair hair or the blue Yewell eyes renowned in the district for the distinctive dark ring round the iris, making them sparkle like sapphires. It was those blue globes that had drawn her to Joe's side. When he gazed into her face she was lost.

'Get a grip o' thyself,' she sighed at such memories. There were geese to be plucked and sent down to market and the butcher. She hoped the prices held up for Christmas as it had been a tough year for farmers and workers, what with the General Strike and lay-offs.

She must parcel up a few bits for the Gilchrist lass down in Scarperton. She wasn't sure whether Miriam was six or seven, but Mildred at the haberdashers always set aside a few items that hadn't sold for her to parcel up. Time flew past so quickly. Where had the years gone?

There'd be many cutting corners this Christmas, making do with a cheap joint or scraps down in the market town. Joe would have to temper his chapel sermons; a little less hellfire and a little more goodwill to all men, she hoped. He could get so carried away when he got in that pulpit.

'Remember those good women have scrimped and saved to put a Sunday meal on the table for their kin. Don't you go spoiling their Yorkshire puddings with your rantings. Have a bit of Christian charity.'

'You're a hard woman, Adey! Come with me and give me a signal.'

'Never,' she would laugh. 'I like my pew comfortable and quiet, with beautiful words and no bone shaking. The vicar gives us ten minutes' pulpit talk. That's enough for me.'

Joe would be out on the moors now, foddering the sheep, reciting the good bits of his sermon to himself, rendering choruses from *Messiah* and making sure none of his flock strayed too far, for the weather looked set for a blow-in of snow. He was a good shepherd to his flock through and through. He was for sheep and she was for cows so together they made a good team.

Cragside Farm sat on the slope of the fell, tucked into the hillside with windowpanes looking south and west to get the best of the sun to warm the stone a treat. Once it was thronged with children, dogs and yard boys, but now it was quieter as their son Tom farmed higher out at Scar Head, and his brother, Wesley, was a teacher in Leeds with no interest in farming at all.

This perch was fine while they were fit and strong, and Yewells were long livers, but come the next few years Joe would have to slow down a bit. Things were tough for farmers now and getting tougher, Adey thought as she sat with Carrie plucking the goose feathers into a sack. Nothing must be wasted.

'There's a letter come from Keighley,' Carrie said, shoving the envelope across the table. 'Who do we know in Keighley? Happen it's a Christmas card from Paddy and the girl. What's her name again?' Carrie was fishing; always curious about the prodigal daughter and her infamous family who never darkened the door.

'I've never had a card from him nor the girl, and she's called Miriam, after Joe's mam, as well you know. Little good that'll do her. I'm surprised she didn't get Theresa or Maria or some fancy saint's name.'

Adey stared at the handwriting, curious for a second. The address was written in a neat copper-plate hand. It looked official and it was addressed to both of them.

'Aren't you going to open it?' Carrie was at it again, rooting for information, but Adey wasn't going to give her satisfaction so shoved the letter in her pinny pocket and promptly forgot all about it. That was the trouble with girls who lived in: they got a little too nosy about family affairs. It was none of her business who was writing to them.

'Now what's all this about you and George Thursby?' It was Adey's turn to go fishing.

'He's asked me if I'm going to the Christmas hop in the village hall. What shall I wear?'

'Clothes would be a start if you don't want to stir them all up,' Adey laughed. 'I'm sure you'll find something to dazzle him with, but I want you back at midnight and no hanky-panky. It's a long walk up that hill in the dark. Let him wait for his favours.'

Carrie was blushing, her neck a circle of pink weals. 'Mrs Yewell, what do you take me for?' she muttered.

'As silly a lass as any in the dale, as daft as a brush when it comes to a handsome face and clean shirt, but with a canny eye for a good bargain,' she replied. 'You could do worse than one of the Thursbys' lads. They're reliable, sturdy and don't squander their brass. His mother is that careful she'd skin a dog for its fleas.' Carrie laughed at her joke but her eyes were far away.

'Mind, I was young once: only the once and look where I landed up: plucking geese, scouring pigs, mucking out and general farm dogsbody stuck on the moors in all weathers. At least George won't make you tramp with him. It's a good job in the Post Office, steady and secure in hard times. You could do worse. Take our Tom. When's he ever going to get himsen wed? He's over forty and too set in his ways.'

Adey had been hoping her son might have taken a shine to this girl himself but he was tongue-tied when he came into female company, preferring to go his own gait and a game of darts in The Fleece, much to Joe's dismay. If he didn't get a move on there'd be no grandsons to take over the tenancy and run the family farm.

He was a good catch. The Yewells were a family of standing in the district. Joe was a lay preacher in the Methodist Circuit. She was a Boothroyd from a farm across the Ribble valley: two of a kind. It didn't do to marry off the moor, like Ellie. You never knew what you were getting or what sort of stock they came from, its strengths and weak points. Better to be in full knowing of the facts before signing up for life, she thought.

All in all she'd had no regrets. It was a pity you couldn't choose yer own bairns. They all needed kicking with a different foot: Wesley was all brains with no feel for the land; Tom was all brawn and no business sense; Ellie, well, she was bonny and bright but as stubborn as they came, wanting to go her own road into a town. Bradford was no life for a country-born girl, especially in the war, with rations and shortages and two babies to rear and a husband away fighting.

If she'd come home for a bit of fresh air they wouldn't have turned her away from their door, but she didn't because a Yewell was too proud to admit a mistake and they were too proud to go running after her. What a carry-on for good Christian folk!

As the morning wore on Adey was too busy to dwell on what-might-have-been. There was the farm lads' dinner to line up in the large stone-flagged kitchen, the chicken coop to see to and the ironing of shirts. She wanted to get the oven range hot for a bit of special baking: spice bread and ginger cake to put away for when company came calling. Joe would be wanting his tea before his last rounds, and tomorrow was the slaughterman's day when Myrtle would give her all. They would be at the butchering until midnight.

It was after eight before she sat down to the basket of mending by the half-finished peg rug. No rest for the wicked, she smiled, and then remembered the letter in her pocket.

'There's summat come from Keighley. Shall I

open it or you?' she asked, seeing Joe was half asleep in his big leather chair. He grunted as she opened the page, then opened his eyes when there was silence from across the table.

'What's to do? Give it here . . .'

She shoved the letter across the table. 'You'd better read this,' she muttered.

He fumbled for his spectacles and gave it the once-over, paused and then searched the flickering flames as if looking for a reply. 'By heck, that's a turn-up. I shall have to get on my knees to the Lord about this. Poor lass . . . and just before Christmas, but it's too much for us to take on at our age.' His eyes were pleading with her to agree.

Adey read the letter then she too searched the flames, trying to blot out the image of Ellie's likeness that lay face down in her dressing table drawer. This was their own flesh and blood they were assigning to an orphanage, their only grandchild, named after their own famous kin, Miriam of the Dale, who had rescued children in a blizzard at great cost to herself.

If only it weren't Christmas, with stories of wandering strangers and no room at the inn. How could you turn your back on a bairn at such a season and look your neighbours in the eye?

Joe stood up and stomped around the room. 'The daft happorth! Crossing the line in the dark, getting torn to pieces by an express. It don't bear

24

thinking about. I've seen what engines can do to a dog trapped on a rail. Railway sidings are no place for a kiddy.'

'It was good enough for two of ours, Joseph Yewell.'

'And look where it landed them. Ellie and Wesley are backsliders and town dwellers,' he argued, not looking his wife in the face; not wanting to see her anguish.

'We were hard on Ellie. Miriam's not to blame for her parents, now is she? Do we turn our backs on her? What good reason is there for that? Answer me?'

'We don't know anything about her,' Joe snapped.

'Would you turn out one of yer own stock for running with a tup in the wrong field?'

'That's just an animal.'

'We're animals too when it comes to looking after our own. Whether we like it or not, she's one of us: a Yewell with yer own mother's name. What sort of life will she have if we say no to their request? Can you live with that 'cos I can't, not now, knowing what we do . . .' Adey flushed with heat and began to snivel.

'I shall have to pray over it. It may not be the Lord's will.'

'I don't know where you dreamed that one up, preacher man. Doesn't the Good Book say, "Suffer the little children to come unto me and forbid them not"? If it's good enough for the Master then happen it'll be good enough for us too.'

'Adeline, you've no idea what you're taking on . . . she's someone else's child.'

'Our daughter's child, mind; a motherless lamb. How many of them have we mothered on in our time?'

'Let's sleep on it and see how it feels in the morning. I'm off to check the byres,' Joe said, anxious to be out of the room, far away from this unexpected request.

Neither of them slept much that night, tossing and turning, pulling the bedclothes this way and that. In the morning the slaughterman would be about his killing business. There'd be no time for private discussions until late.

Adey rose and lit a candle, opening her private drawer, the one that held stuff that was women's business: douches, sponges, pads and belts. Soon she would be at the end of all that palaver, but to start again with a kiddy and a stranger to a farmhouse? Whose fault was that? It was too much to ask of them.

But as she lifted Ellie's portrait, those Yewell eyes pierced her through like a spear straight into her heart. 'Don't abandon my child,' they cried out.

She closed the drawer and dressed ready to face this bloody day.

2

Miriam sat in the railway carriage, stunned with the suddenness of being torn away from everything and everyone she knew. Dad was barely laid in the hard ground and already his face was fading from behind her eyes. Now she was going to live with strangers in a foreign land like Ruth in the bible story. The lawyer said she was a lucky girl to get this change of sky but his words weren't sinking in.

Her new relation was sitting across from her, bolt upright, staring out of the window, but every so often Mirren caught her snatching glances at her face as if she had snot on her nose end.

Grandma Yewell had appeared in the lawyer's office when Granny Simms packed a little parcel of clothes and took her down to Keighley on the tram.

'Now you be good for yer new gran. She's come a long way to fetch you. Remember your Ps and Qs and don't fidget,' she whispered as they sat in the corridor waiting for the door to open to the old man's office.

'Now, Miriam,' he said, when they were admitted, pointing to the lady in the seat. 'I want to introduce you to Mrs Yewell, mother of the late Ellen Miriam Gilchrist, who's your grandmamma now. She's kindly agreed to take you back to the family's farm for a little holiday in Windebank.'

Mirren bobbed a curtsy like they did to the managers of the school when they came visiting. Her tongue stuck to her teeth.

'She's tall for a seven-year-old,' muttered the woman before her, in a thick tweed coat, brown felt hat and with a dead fox round her neck. She eyed Mirren up carefully.

'I'm eight and a half,' Mirren piped back.

'And sharp with it!' said the woman.

'You're a very lucky girl that your grandparents are offering to take full responsibility for your welfare. Needless to say I hope you will repay them with good behaviour, diligent service.'

'But I don't know them,' Mirren cried suddenly, realising that she must leave with this lady, and clinging to Granny Simms.

'Now none of that, young lady,' the old man with the whiskers down the sides of his face continued. 'You have a whole train journey to get acquainted . . . It's as much a burden for them to have to take you in as it is for you to make minor adjustments to your change of circumstances. You were not left in any position to support yourself, my dear. If these kind folk hadn't offered—'

The lady cut his words off, saying, 'Come along, lass. We've a train to catch or your grandfather will be left standing at the station. It doesn't do to keep a farmer waiting.' She smiled with her eyes and Mirren picked up her parcel, knowing there was no other way. She hugged Granny Simms, who wiped tears from her eyes.

'You've got a good 'un there and wick as a weasel, just like her mam, a real lady . . .' Granny Simms told Mrs Yewell. Then she was gone.

Why had her gran and granddad never visited her before? There was a big bust-up, Mirren knew, a falling-out over her dad, long before she was born. She knew nothing about farms except that they were smelly places full of cow muck and horse dung. They once went on a Sunday school trip to one up on Howarth Moor, which was a right wild place where some lady had written a story called *Withering Hats*.

She smiled now, looking at Mrs Yewell's hat. It was withering at the edges, all floppy with feathers that looked faded and frayed. It must be windy at Windebank. How would she live up in the wilds? She stared out of the window, trying not to snivel as her eyes filled with tears.

There was nothing but green fields and stone walls flashing past the window, walls running in all directions, making strange patterns over the hills: squares, oblongs, triangles and curves, and in the middle were dotted sheep like balls of cotton wool.

'Are we nearly there?' she asked. 'When do we see the farm?'

'All in good time,' whispered the woman. 'Be patient. Everything comes to them as waits . . .'

Mirren sighed and turned back to the window. She had never seen so many walls and sheep, men on carts and not a mill chimney in sight. This was a funny place to live, all strung out on your own. Where were the streets and the crowds?

Adey couldn't take her eyes off the child opposite. She was the spitten of her mother at that age: the same long sandy plaits and those blue Yewell eyes. If she'd walked past her in the street, it would've been like seeing a ghost. How could she have gotten her age so wrong? Miriam must have been born at the war's end. The son died as a baby. They ought to have visited but farms couldn't run on their own and bridges had been burned when Ellie ran away.

The truth was she couldn't bear to see her daughter living in the rough, running after a navvy into goodness knows what conditions. No wonder she . . . but this lass would get her chances even if she did have Paddy's wild blood inside her. There was a spark to her eyes and an edge to her tongue, and she was quick to defend herself like all the Yewells.

So they called her Mirren not Miriam, the Scotch way, the old Granny had whispered. The lass had a right to her name but the Yewells were proud of Miriam and doled it out to their first-born daughters for generations. Ellie had done the same for her daughter and that was touching.

Adey had to admit she was warming to the bairn even if she could see a few battles ahead with stubbornness. Mirren was a town child and not easy to settle up the dale, not used to shutting gates and doing chores. They were used to shops and dens of iniquity round every corner, cinema houses showing bare flesh as if it were decent. The child'd need watching and fattening up; all legs and elbows and bony knees. The kiddy was sitting in a dark serge coat two sizes too small, with her skirt hem showing and her stockings in need of a good darn: more holey than godly. Heaven only knew what was underneath. Full of fleas no doubt, but a good scrub would sort that out.

'Do you like the country?' she asked, trying to interest the girl away from picking her nose.

'If you've seen one sheep you've seen the lot,' Mirren sighed.

'Oh, but that's where you're wrong. Every one

of them is different and some of them have names, just like children, no two alike. The shepherd like the Good Lord Himself, knows them all. There'll be a lot for you to learn, but farming's in your blood so you'll soon catch on. Your grandfather will walk you round the fields and introduce you to his flock so they'll come to you,' she added, hoping he would take to the child as she had done.

Joe would be shocked when he saw this mite standing, the image of their lost daughter. Why had they kept away so long? This child had been allowed to run wild into all sorts of danger just because they were too proud to bend a little. Now they must make up for lost time.

The man who came in the cart to collect them was like a giant with a sandy moustache and tufts of sandy hair coming out of his nose. He stared at her.

'So this is our Ellie's bairn, skinny as a lath but bonny with it? We'll do summat with this one, Mother,' he laughed, eyeing Mirren up like a prize calf.

'No guessing she's one of ours, Joe, is there?' said his wife.

'Oh, aye, right enough, but not in front of the lassie . . . So what did you think, coming all this way on a steam train?' he offered, thinking she'd never been on a train before.

'I've been everywhere with my dad . . . Leeds,

Bradford and to the sea once at Filey,' she answered politely. 'This one was a bit slow.'

'I see we've got a right little wanderlust here but I bet you've never lived on top of the world before,' he said with a wink. She stared back, not sure if he was teasing or not. He was so tall and broad, like a giant in fustian breeches and big leather boots. His jacket had patches at the elbows, and from his waistcoat hung a real gold chain.

'Now don't go upsetting the lass. It'll all be strange to her at first,' said the woman.

'All aboard then, and let's be getting back, young lady.'

They seemed to be climbing uphill for ever, past grey stone village houses, past a small church with a stubby tower, past a duck pond, up walled tracks, higher and higher to the top of the hill where jagged white rocks jutted out and sheep scuttled past on bare grey hillsides. Down in the valley Mirren could see more stone walls and fields of sheep grazing, greens and greys and blue sky. A damp wind mopped her cheeks and she felt dizzy at the sight of such strangeness. It was another world with no people, no buses, no lines of houses lining the road, no smoking chimneys.

Then they turned off the track to the left towards a large white house with windows shining, sparkling like eyes. It was a house grander than she had ever seen before and this was Cragside, her new home.

This was where Mam had lived as a girl. How could she have ever left such a dwelling for a railway hut?

Perhaps it was the marble pillars in the hall, the clack of her clogs on the tiled floor, or the high ceilings with piped icing corners, the large square rooms off the hall or the fact that the back of the house seemed to be tunnelled into the rock, but Mirren thought that Cragside wore a frown, not a smile, on that first viewing. It was like walking into the town hall or the Wesleyan Chapel and asking for the lavvy. She was dying for a pee but too shy to ask.

A kind girl in a white apron, called Carrie, showed her into the parlour, which smelled of lavender polish and woodsmoke, and she crossed over to the long window, staring out at the view. You could see for miles and miles, right down to the river and the railway line.

'The sheep have all got coloured bottoms,' was all she could think of to say. 'Why?'

Nobody answered, but Carrie smiled. What had she said wrong?

This might look like a palace but at that moment her grandmother looked stern and forbidding, and Granddad looked awkward.

'Go with Carrie into the kitchen and she'll find you some tea,' her grandmother ordered as she flopped down on the big armchair, pulling off her withering hat with relief. 'It's been a long day.'

'I need the lav,' she whispered to the maid.

'The what?'

'The lavvy. I'm bursting . . .'

'Oh, the nessy . . . outside in the yard, or you can go to the water closet upstairs but it'll be a bit high for you to pull the chain,' said Carrie.

Mirren didn't wait for an answer and shot out into the cobbled yard to look for the toilet.

From what she had seen so far, this was one of those fussy houses with ornaments to knock over and photographs to admire. There was a shawl over the big piano that might come hurtling down if she caught it and then she'd smash all the glass. She must remember to walk slowly and not make a noise on the flag floors. The kitchen smelled like a bakery and she felt hungry for the first time in days.

If only this was just a holiday it would be wonderful. If only Mam and Dad and Grant were here visiting together, playing in the fields and then going back home on the train, back to Scarperton and her friends . . . But this was for ever and ever, amen, and they were her family now, strangers who called her by the wrong name, who lived in a cold house and spoke different.

Mirren sat on the lavvy seat and howled. She was Jill all alone and it was all Dad's fault, but she couldn't be cross with him because he was gone. They were all together now without her in heaven. It wasn't fair!

35

3

In the days that followed Mirren's arrival at Cragside Farm there were a whole new set of chores to be learned. Carrie took her in hand to feed the chickens, to rummage for precious eggs and clean out the huts carefully, and look for holes in the fence where Brer Fox could get in. Mirren wrinkled up her nose at the smell of chicken dung but knew the score.

Uncle Tom, her mother's big brother, showed her how to sweep up properly and take water to the cattle in the winter barn. The yard boy helped her scoop oats for the big Clydesdale horses. There was so much to learn and being busy made her forget about starting the new school down at Windebank.

Sometimes in the evening they gathered round the piano and Granddad placed his fingers up and down the keys to find a chord and smiled, showing her a set of gleaming teeth that Carrie

36

said Granny had given him as an early Christmas present. He played tunes without even looking at his fingers. '"Just a song at twilight, when the lights are low . . ."' His voice was rich and deep, but Granny got upset.

'Don't sing that, Joe . . . George used to sing that in the chapel concert. He was your mother's brother, Mirren, but he never came home from France. They never found him; so many lost boys. At least you're a lass and won't have to face that carry-on.' She sniffed, pointing to the photo of a soldier in uniform in the black frame on the mantelpiece. 'That's yer uncle, God rest his soul. Thank goodness some were spared, but there's one or two round here who're not the men they once were; the schoolmaster for one. I've heard that Annie Burrows has a lot to put up with these days.' She lifted her hand as if she was swallowing something from a bottle. Then she saw Mirren watching and put it down quickly. 'I'm glad to see you've signed the temperance pledge. Joe's a Methodist so we don't drink.'

'Was my mam a good singer?' Mirren asked.

'She could render a good *Messiah* chorus when pushed but no solo work. George was our baritone. He's sorely missed. They don't do concert parties down Windebank any more. There aren't enough men to go around now,' she sighed.

'Can I learn the piano?' Mirren asked, hoping

to be able to accompany herself singing like Granddad.

'We'll see when you've done your chores. Chores first and foremost, lass. The farm must come first, then making meals, sewing and mending, church, of course, and if you're quick about them all, happen you'll pare off a slice of time for a bit of music but only after you've done your homework.'

So that was how Mirren got her piano lessons, driving them mad, thumping out the wrong notes with hammer fingers until she got the knack of placing them correctly, which wasn't easy. She soon got bored with scales, preferring to read all the books left on the shelf: *Boy's Own* adventures that were full of derring-do and excitement. Getting lost in a book was one way to shut out the noisy comings and goings of the farm and the strangeness of her life high on the hills, but most of all the dreariness of Windebank school.

The school in Scarperton was large. There were hundreds of children, from infants to part-timers at the mill. They drilled like soldiers in a barracks, lining up with masters and mistresses to the sound of the bell, the whistle and the booming voice of the headmaster, who eyed up his pupils with interest and shoved Mirren into the class above because she could read well and help others. There were marching songs and country dancing, singing hymns and object lessons about nature and stars.

The school at Windebank couldn't have been more different. There was one master, Mr Burrows, and his assistant, Miss Halstead. It was a mean matchbox of a building with windows high up on the wall. A big coke stove at one end belched out fumes. It had railings round that smelled of dirty socks and wet wool, and wet knickers now and then. Everyone was mixed up together on benches; the quiet and serious ones with rough boys in holey jumpers and thick boots that stung when they tripped you up.

Miss Halstead took the littler children into another tiny classroom out of the Head's way after assembly. Mirren went to the front on her first morning to be registered, eager to show off how well she could read and write, but Harold Burrows barely gave her a glance.

'That'll do,' he muttered while she was finishing the page. His breath smelled like Dad's had done. He pointed her towards the back bench among tall lads who couldn't read or write much. Everyone stared and then giggled at her accent. At playtime the other girls crowded in a corner but didn't make friends, just stood staring at her.

It was too far to walk home at lunch so she sat on her own, eating her pasty and apple, trying not to feel miserable.

'She's one of them posh clever clogs, a townie,' sneered Billy Marsden in his jacket with his shirt hanging out of the elbows. 'My mam heard she was living in a railway hut when they found her.'

'No . . . it's a bungalow,' she lied.

'It were a railway shed, fit for donkeys on our farm,' laughed another lad.

'Shut up, dumbo. At least I can read,' she shouted. 'It was a special carriage all on one level so it *is* a bungalow.'

'Who does she think she is, bloody offcumden!' Billy was not for being outfaced by this newcomer.

'My granny lives at Cragside and I'm a Yewell, so there!' Mirren hated being singled out. She just wanted to have a friend and be left alone.

'So what're you doing living in a railway hut? Mam says you're not a proper Yewell. Her mam was a whore who ran away and had a bastard!' He put his hands on hips, waiting for her to get out of that insult.

Mirren didn't know what a basted was, or a hoor, but she sensed it was rude and when everyone started laughing she leaped up and flung herself into Billy's face, scratching his cheek accidentally. 'Shut up, numpty! You're as thick as shit!'

Mr Burrows was standing in the doorway of the school. He'd heard none of the teasing and saw only her take action. Everyone stepped back, seeing the look on his face.

'Gilchrist and Marsden, my desk, this minute. Not another word!' he screamed, cuffing them both round the ears, not listening to Mirren's attempt to explain.

'I don't want wildcats in this school. If you want to behave like an animal, you can go and amuse the infants in their room. Get out of my sight, Miriam Know-all. You're too cocky for words, with your town ways and impudence. Hold out your hand.'

The cane struck her palm, bringing tears to her eyes but her mouth was drawn tight, wincing as the next blow hit the palm, biting into her flesh. She was not going to let him see her pain. She took five strokes but Billy Marsden got off with a caution. It wasn't fair.

She was banished to the infants' cupboard with her face to the wall. Her hands were stinging and cut but she turned her face to hide her tears. The silent battle of wills with Harold Burrows had begun.

He ignored her in class when her hand was raised to answer a question. She sat sullen and unresponsive to anything he offered to the class as a whole. Billy Marsden left her alone. In fact the whole school pretended she wasn't there, avoiding her after lessons. It got to the point where there was no point in attending school any more but no one at Cragside had any idea of her unhappiness. If they found out, she might be sent away to the orphanage.

Every morning she waved them goodbye and set off for the track down to the village but once out of sight she veered off on another route. In this way Mirren got to know every nook and cranny of the Yewells' fields and gullies, becksides and hidy-holes. With her pasty and bottle of milk to sustain her, she could amuse herself for hours. If it was raining there were hidden caves and boulders to shelter under, like the sheep, outbarns full of hay to hunker down in and read the book she'd hidden there at the weekend.

There was this wonderful book called *Scouting for Boys*, all about making dens and campfires and signalling. It taught her how to lurk out of sight of shepherds and workmen. For days on end she stayed up in the hills but knew soon she would have to return to the school with some excuse of sickness in case the Welfare man came calling to see why she was absent.

December was not the month for staying out too long. The first flurries of snow sent her scurrying for cover but it was better to have frozen fingers than be caned and bullied and ignored. There was more to learning than sitting on a hard school bench.

In the fields there were hares to watch and foxes to follow, gullies and waterfalls and leaping fish. There were birds she'd never seen before, berries to identify and mushrooms that she was warned not to eat.

As long as she wrapped up in her new thick

wool coat with a flannel lining sewn in for winter, a hand-knitted scarf and beret like a cloche helmet, thick stockings and leather boots, she was warm enough if she kept on the move.

Now the sun was low in the sky, making long shadows. Mirren sensed by the way the sun moved when it was time to head back down to the track as if she was coming from school. The last bit of hometime was the worst, having to creep through the dark copse in the shadows where the tawny owl hooted and sometimes the eye of the fox glistened as the moon rose at dusk. It was dark by four thirty.

It was such a relief to leave the wood behind and watch for the twinkling lanterns in the yard and farmhouse windows before they closed the shutters. They always waited until she was home before doing that, while she sat with a slice of bread and dripping, making up stories of her happy day at school.

Two weeks before Christmas the snows came; flutterings of goosefeathers at first, turning to ice and then rain on the sodden ground. The wind turned to the north-east, making puddles into skating rinks and icy slides. Mirren decided to make a quick recovery just in case there were lots of Christmassy things to do at school but she needn't have bothered for there was not even a string of paper chains or Nativity play to enliven the season, and no part for her in the carol service in the parish church. She was Chapel, after all.

Mr Burrows had forgotten she was on the register by the look he gave her over his half-moon glasses. 'Back in the land of the living again, Miss Gilchrist? We thought you'd gone back to town.'

She stuck it until dinner break and told Miss Halstead in the playground she felt sick and could she be excused. The teacher looked concerned, felt her forehead and packed her off with a wave.

The sky was purple and grey, but nothing to worry about as she sneaked off over the track, glad to be away from the sticky sweaty smells of the school hall. The fact that everything on the hill-side was going in the opposite direction never struck her as odd.

Sheep were heading down, butting and nudging each other like the kids in the playground queue. They sensed a change in the weather. Cows were bellowing from their stalls, no bird chatter in the tree tops, as if the silent wood was waiting. She was so intent on getting away, Mirren didn't notice the darkening sky above her.

Yet it all looked so sparkly, ice like tinsel on the stone walls, sugary tree trunks. The air was sharp at the back of her throat, nothing to warn her of the storm ahead, but she pulled her tammy over her ears.

The snow came speckled at first, the wind

pushing her forward. Then it slowed her pace as she rose higher and it got thicker and whiter, the feathery flakes sticking to her coat and chapping her bare knees. Only then did she realise she was too high and must turn back.

Sheep passed her by like walking snowballs. They were taking shelter behind the bield of the stone walls and so must she. Her coat weighed a ton, stiff like cardboard, and her cheeks were stinging with the chill. Miriam sensed she mustn't stop, but finger her way along the stone walls, hoping to find the shelter of a barn. This, however, was new territory. Her eyes squinted at the whiteness that disguised where she was, her fingers ached in her mittens and her boots were like lead weights.

It was then she realised how stupid it was to be wandering alone in a snow storm. She had no strength against the wildness of these moors, being just a silly, disobellient little girl who was lost. There was trouble in the wind and no one to help her.

The fleeting warmth of her tears was no comfort. This was her own doing and her own fault, and now she was going to freeze to death and no one knew she was even missing. They thought her safe in the schoolroom. She would be found frozen like a dead sheep with its eyes pecked out by rooks.

The thought of that fate stirred her into one last effort to find a gate or a barn. 'Help me . . .'

she cried, but there was none there to hear her, yet her stubborn spirit was not going to give in without a fight.

No use turning back, for the trackway was covered and she could stumble down a gully and be stuck. It was forwards or nothing, and she wasn't going to lie down without cover. Slowly she edged forward, following the wall end. The effort took all of her strength and she felt herself struggling.

Just when she couldn't go another step, she saw an outline in the whirling white, a jagged line of high stones, walls and a chimney stack. Her eye fixed on that marker with hope in her heart that she'd found a farmhouse or a barn. Listening for the bark of a dog or the bellow of a cow, she made for the shelter. The silence, stillness and swirling snow like a veil hid what was before her but she knew there was something there if only she could get her legs to work properly. To be so near and yet far . . .

'Help me,' she called again, but no one came.

Those last few yards were like agony, carrying a load of ice on her shoulders, but she fell into the stone porch with relief. It was already half filled with a snowdrift. She shouted but no one answered. Desperation fuelled her arms to batter the oak-studded door and it yielded even to her puny weight. How she yearned for firelight and the glow of a storm lantern, the smell of bacon or an open fire, but there was nothing, just an empty shell.

Part of the rafters were stove in and she could see snow falling through the gap in the roof, little drifts piling up, and it was just light enough to see the old stone fireplace behind a great arch of stone spanning the width of the room. Inside there it was dry and sheltered. There was even old straw bedding on the flagged floor, musty and dusty where it was dry, old cattle bedding. There was a broken ladder to a small loft but she daren't risk going up there.

Through another arch she spotted the cold dairy with slate shelves. The storage holes were empty of jars. No one had lived here for years. There were a few bits of broken chairs, nothing else but four bare walls.

The disappointment rose up like bile in her throat. No fire, no welcome. There was not even a lucifer to light a fire, not even a beast to warm herself by, but it was shelter from the blizzard outside and it was getting dark.

'Be thankful for small mercies, child,' came her Sunday school teacher's voice in her head. Looking around in the gloom, she had to admit that there was everything here for her to ride out the storm.

If you were silly enough to do what she had done then this was about the mercy she deserved, she decided. She was safe and this would have to do. Outside the wind was roaring up a gale. Bits of roof rattled and clanked but stayed put.

Mirren gathered up the driest bits of straw she

could find to make a nest under the stone arch. She sat in the grate, trying to be brave. There was snow to suck on and she still had her store apple to feast on in her coat pocket. Every bite would have to be savoured slowly and eked out as if it was a proper meal, skin, pips, core, the lot.

Where she was, she hadn't a clue, but it was high up above Cragside. The chimney breast smelled of old soot and woodsmoke, and the straw itched. She thought of mangers and cheered her flagging spirits singing 'Away in a Manger'. She was away in a manger but no one knew where she was and there'd be hell to pay when they found out.

She heard little rustlings and scratchings beside and above her: night creatures scurrying into the walls. At least the house had other things here, mice and wrens seeking shelter . . . maybe wild cats, foxes, wolves . . . No use scaring herself with fairy tales. For one night she'd be glad of company, whatever it was. She was one of them, trapped, penned in, safe enough. The house will look after us, she sighed, and curled up in a ball to save heat.

Down in the valley Windebank school would be dismissed early. They had a snow drill and roll call, and children would have been collected. Others would be forced to stay by the stoves and stay the night in Burrows' den, poor buggers! She could swear out loud and there was no one here

48

to tell her off. This was better than being stuck with that hateful man. This was all his fault . . .

Mirren woke from a deep sleep feeling numb, legs aching with cramp. She scoured around hoping there might be a provender sack, something to stuff with straw to keep her teeth from chattering. There was a small store under the ladder stairs with a pan and a brush, and to her joy some rotten sacks. Once more the little house had come to her rescue. If only there was enough kindling to get a flame going.

It was then she remembered the scouting book. There was a section on lighting fires with sticks of wood and bits of cloth, making sparks to smoulder into kindling. She wished she'd read it more carefully.

Just thinking about it gave her courage to ferret in the darkness. The sky was clear and the moon was up high enough to be a lantern if she opened the window shutters. Her eyes were getting used to the half-light. It was better to keep moving than to freeze, so she packed the straw into the sack to make a little mattress, and pretended it was a feather quilt and she was the princess in the pea story. Then she gathered up any bits of wood she could find, scliffs from the stairs.

There were holes built into the inglenook, crannies where things were kept dry like the one in the old bit of Cragside for salt, and a bread oven. Feeling her way into the holes with fear in case a rat jumped out of its nest, like one had in the chicken coop the other day, scaring her half to death with its beady eye, Mirren tried to be brave. Inside was dry and she touched something hard and jumped back. It didn't move. Her fingers found a cold metal box about the size of a baccy tin.

Please let there be lucifers inside, she prayed. The tin was rusted and hard to prise open, all ridges and bumps in fancy patterns made of brass, and her fingertips were numb. In frustration she banged the edge on the hearth and it fell open.

Inside was a kit of some sort. Dad had one of these on the mantelpiece to keep his pipe bits in. It was an old comforts tin for soldiers, he had told her, once full of chocolates and cigarettes. This one had the face of the old Queen on, but nothing inside but a bit of rag, some chalk ends, a peppermint lozenge and two dry lucifers. Two chances to make a flame: another prayer was answered.

How did they do it in the scout book? She had to have some dry cloth. Her clothes were damp – even her knickers were wet where she had leaked – but she did have a thick vest and liberty bodice though she couldn't cut them. Then she found the hanky rolled in her knicker pocket, full of snot but dry enough now.

She must make a little triangle tent of straw and bits to catch alight but she needed stuff to put in the fire too, wood and bits to keep it going. Dad once told her that poor people used cow dung to heat their fires. Dried dung didn't smell, he said when she turned up her nose. There was plenty of that scraped along the walls, if she searched hard enough.

She piled everything she could and tried to light the lucifer, but it flared and went out before anything smouldered and she threw it away in disgust and frustration.

She set out her little fire again and hovered over it as she struck the last match. This one flared and dropped onto the tinder. As it smouldered she recalled she had to blow it gently, adding little pieces with trembling fingers, just like Granny Simms did when her fire wouldn't catch.

Slowly the little fire grew from a few twigs to a flaring ember of warmth and needed feeding with fresh stuff to burn. Just the sight of it made Mirren feel warm. If only there was a candle somewhere. Back to the storage holes and a fingertip search in case there was something there, and there was: just a stub, but a candle for company.

Up the stairs she went gingerly, in search of kindling and bits of plaster laths.

'Thank you, house,' she whispered into the walls. 'Thanks for shelter and firelight but I need more wood. Where can I find wood?'

Then a strange thing happened. It was as if she

could hear her dad's voice in her head for the first time since the accident.

'Mirren Gilchrist, use yer gumption, lassie. It's all to hand.'

With her candle end she crawled up the ladder and saw the broken laths lying around the walls, a pile of dry kindling. She must chuck them down onto the flags and make a pile. This was dusty work but it kept her mind off the roar of the blizzard and the piles of snow gathering from the hole in the roof.

Downstairs was warmth, a feather bed, a lozenge to suck if she dared. Water could be heated in the brass tin over the fire and she popped in the lozenge to give it taste. This was using her gumption too. Whatever happened, the fire must be fed in the hearth. No one would come in the storm, but perhaps in the morning . . .

Waking at first light shivering, Mirren smelled smoke and smouldering embers. Her hoard was well and truly exhausted but there was a good supply upstairs. Time to melt more snow in the tin. Through the gap she could see blue sky and a few drifting flakes. She opened the shutter to a mysterious white mound, strange shapes, no walls or barns or rocks, just great waves of snow, in peaks like whipped cream. The devil wind was whipping up new shapes. Her tummy was rumbling with hunger and her legs were wobbly but there was nothing to eat here.

It was warmest sitting right by the fire, hidden under the archway, and when the blackened tin was hot she wrapped it in a sack to warm her feet like a hot-water bottle. The stones were now hot and if she stayed tight she was thawed enough to tingle, but the fire was the only thing being fed. She was feeling dizzy.

What was happening at Cragside? Had they discovered she was wagging off school? In some ways she was glad to be found out. Wasting schooling was doing her no good.

'Whatever you do in life, lassie, get an eddy-cashun,' her dad once said when he was sobered up. 'You dinna want to end up like me. Even a girl needs a schooling.'

It had been easy in Scarperton, but this school was teaching her nothing and the teacher didn't care. He was useless and smelled of whisky. How she hated that smell.

Up here it was peaceful, safe between thick walls. Someone must have lived here once, but who? If only she could live here with Mam and Dad. They could keep stock and make butter and cheese, and she could show Dad all she'd learned from Granddad.

Had Mam played here as a little girl? Was her spirit watching over her now? Mirren hoped so.

It was hard to be a motherless lamb with no memories of her mam, just a snapshot in a print

53

dress. The mother of her imagination would be tall and pretty, with golden hair, and clever and sparkling, but no one at Cragside ever talked about her much when she asked questions. They clammed up and looked the other way when she pestered for more.

Did they own this house or did it belong to the bigwig in London who came for the shooting at Benton Hall? Why was it left to rot, unloved, abandoned?

Mirren made for the door, thinking if she kept in a straight line she might just make her way down like the sheep. Her courage failed when she opened the door on to a mountain of snow. She was trapped, fast in, as they said round here. Time to bank up the fire and pray. She was no match for the devil wind and the snow giants.

She sipped her hot water, pretending it was cocoa laced with the top of the milk. Mam and Dad would have loved this house but they weren't here now. They were gone and she was on her own again. If someone didn't come soon she would starve. How quickly night-time fears flee when the sun shines, but she sat like Cinderella at the hearth, too weak now to move.

When would they come?

4

Adey took one look at the sky and knew school would be out early. They must send a cart to see the child got back safely. Country kiddies took shelter in bad weather. They knew to lie low until it was safe, but Mirren was different and secretive these days and she might not do the right thing. Adey sent Joe to collect her just in case.

Now they were used to having her around the place, grown accustomed to her noisy chatter and questions. Questions. She was a bright one and her piano playing was coming on. All she lacked was practice and concentration, but she was little Miss Head-in-a-Book. It would be nice if she got to the girls' secondary school like her mam. Her coming had brought life back to the place and no one could say she didn't help out . . .

Then Joe blew in from the doorway, covered in snow.

'You're back, praise the Lord. Thanks for getting

her, Joe. Where's her ladyship?' Adey searched for the child behind him.

'She wasn't there, Mother. Burrows said summat about her going home early and that's not all. I had a word with Lizzie Halstead at the door. Mirren's hardly been in school at all . . .' he muttered.

'The little minx, wait till I get my hands on her. What's going on?' Adey was all worked up with worry and fury.

Carrie was lurking at the stove and she turned pink. 'Perhaps I should've said something earlier, Mrs Yewell, but our Emmot says that Mirren hates school and got the cane for fighting. They've been calling her names and Burrows makes her go in the baby class so she's been off sick.'

'Now you tell us!' snapped Adey. 'How long has this been going on? Oh, my giddy aunt, she's out in that snow. Send for Tom. We'll have to get up a search party.' She felt the fear and panic rising and went for her coat.

'Hang on, Mother. What good'll that do in this wild darkness?' came Joe's predictable reply. 'She could be anywhere by now. She's a sensible lass even if she's stubborn with it. She'll have found cover. Tom and the village boys will look for her in the morning.'

'We can't wait that long. She'll catch her death,' Adey was shouting back. 'Wait till I see her, scaring us half to death. You'll have to take the strap to her and teach her a lesson.'

'Wait on, Adey. Lass's in enough trouble as it is, gadding off into the hills. She doesn't know the lay of the land and not the size of tuppence ha'penny. We should have kept a closer eye on her ourselves. We used to be able to sniff out trouble with our lads but we've got out of the habit, and she's a deep one, at that.'

'You could take the dogs out with a storm lantern,' Adey pleaded.

'Don't be daft. And have two of us lost in the snow? We'll do the job proper with a gang stretched over the moor. Mind you, she's a right devil running off from the schoolmaster. I thought only lads did that,' said Joe, scratching his head.

'We've got to do something,' screamed Adey, pacing up and down the kitchen, clattering her pans.

Carrie started to cry. 'I'm not a tale teller, as you know, but I reckon Burrows had made her life a right misery. Emmot says she's top of the class but she has to sit at the back and shut up or teach the dunces to do their letters. That's not right, is it?'

'Poor lass has had a right miserable time but never thought to tell us,' said Joe, slurping his tea in a way that always got on Adey's nerves.

'We didn't bring her all this way to lose her in

the snow,' Adey sighed. 'Happen we should never have brought her here in the first place. It's not like living in a town. She never said a word . . .'

What if Mirren was already lost? What sort of Christmas would they have in mourning? How would she ever forgive herself? The girl'd been taking her bullying in silence and that showed courage, and to put up with Burrows in the state he was in nowadays. He ought to be reported. Were they such ogres that she couldn't tell them her troubles?

If she came out of this alive, they'd have to think things afresh, perhaps put her in a private school, but where would they find the cash for that?

'Dear Lord, keep the child safe for one more day, temper the wind to the shorn lamb,' Joe prayed, and they bowed their heads in the kitchen. 'Show us the way . . .'

Outside the wind roared and the blizzard raged but no one got a wink of sleep that night. They were helpless in the face of the storm. It was out of their hands now.

The fire was still crackling with more broken-off laths but Mirren was now weak with hunger and fear. Why didn't they come? Would they ever find her? Perhaps they had given her up for lost?

Outside the door a cruel silvery world shimmered with icicles cascading down from the roof ends but she was too tired to wonder at the beauty of it all. She wanted to be home with Gran in Cragside kitchen, back with Carrie making faces, back sneaking titbits to Jet under the table.

It was melting, though. There were drips plopping from the hole in the roof, but no other sound. Then she heard the faint bark of dogs in the distance. Her heart thumped with relief. Someone was out there searching for her.

'I'm here, over here!' she squeaked, but her voice was too quiet. She couldn't open the door for the weight of snow and she was desperate. What would the Scouts do now?

Uncle George's book had served her well so far. There was a chapter on camping and sending signals, but she'd skipped that bit. If she was high up perhaps they would see her smoke.

Mirren piled on more laths. The only thing to hand was her new winter coat and she was in enough trouble as it was, so she grabbed a smelly sack and tried wafting it over the flames but it caught alight and she had to throw it onto the fire. Perhaps the blue smoke might be visible.

She sat down, exhausted and tearful. Come on old house, she prayed, help me one more time and I promise, on my blue temperance badge, I'll pay you back.

There was always the hope that the kindred spirits who had once lived here would come to her rescue. She opened the one working shutter and yelled until she was puce and dizzy.

Then a tall boy in a peaked tweed cap, carrying a proddy stick, climbed over a drift and waved.

'She's here! Over here! Now then, young Miriam, let's be having you,' smiled a pair of dark brown eyes. She'd never seen him before in the village. He was about fourteen.

'Who are you?'

'Jack Sowerby, from The Fleece. You must be wrong in the head to go gallivanting up World's End . . .'

'It wasn't snowing when I left,' she answered back. No wonder she'd never seen him. Yewells didn't go in pubs. They were Satan's houses. 'Anyway, the house found me and kept me safe.'

Her rescuer didn't seem interested in her explanation but kept on whistling and shouting.

'She's alive, up here!' he called, and suddenly there were dogs sniffing at her, faces peering under sack hoods with burning cheeks, and she was pulled through the window to safety.

'So you spent the night at World's End,' laughed Uncle Tom, shoving in her hand a flask of hot soup, which burned her throat. 'Sip it slowly. You're a lucky blighter to find this ruin and hole up like a lost sheep. Happen you're a Yewell through and through. Now, young lady, don't you ever do such a daft thing again. You have to treat these hills with respect or they'll take your fingers off in a few hours and your life by nightfall. Mam and Dad are going mad with worry at Cragside. Don't you go putting lives at risk again . . . silly mutt!' Uncle Tom stared at her with cold eyes and she cried.

'Now what've I said?' he muttered. 'Don't take on. Drink yer soup.'

It was creamy broth with bits of meat and veg in it, the most wonderful soup in the world at that moment, but she still felt dizzy and floppy.

Uncle Tom had never shouted at her before. The lad, Jack, peered in through the window. 'She's got a fire going . . . She's canny enough, Tom, to think of that.' He turned to her with smiling eyes. 'I reckon we've got another Miriam o' the Dale here. How did you think all this up?'

'I read Uncle George's book.' At least Jack Sowerby didn't think she was stupid. 'I tried to do smoke signals but it didn't work.'

'That's grand. They'll be right proud of you when they find out,' he said, but Uncle Tom was scowling.

'No they won't. She's for it when she gets back, if the look on my mam's face is anything to go by. She's lost us a day's work.'

'The snow did that for you. We can't blame her for a blizzard. The poor kid's half starved. Do you want a piggyback?' Jack offered.

But Mirren shook her head. 'No thank you, I'll walk. I've caused enough bother. I don't suppose you've done anything as daft as me?' she asked them both.

Uncle Tom suddenly roared. 'His mam says Jack ran away on the first day at school 'cos he couldn't count up the cardboard pennies so he hid in the cellar of the pub and she and Wilf were run ragged trying to find him.' He lifted her up as she was struggling and her legs had turned to jelly. He carried her down to the waiting sled, to the warmth of a horse steaming, then homewards over the snow.

It was a cold crisp morning with a weak winter sun, but the journey down was like bumping over ice and the poor horse slithered. How could she have wandered so far uphill – and to the end of the world, they said?

She turned to say goodbye to her house but it had already disappeared from view, hidden and secret once more. One day she must come back and thank it properly.

They were all lined up waiting in the kitchen as she was carried in and inspected for frostbite. Someone had blasted off a gun to give notice that she was safe. Two blasts and it would have meant she was a goner, so Carrie whispered.

'You've given us such a fright, Miriam. Whatever were you thinking off?' said Granny, rubbing her dry with a towel.

'Not now, Adey,' said Grandpa Joe. 'She's frozen through. Get her in that zinc tub and warmed up. Plenty of time for a sermon when she's come to. Carrie can see to it.'

Soon Mirren was soaking in the warm tub, her hands and toes tingling, and then Carrie was towelling her dry.

'Weren't you scared all alone at World's End?' she asked.

'I wasn't alone. There were animals sheltering in there, and when the fire was lit, I heard—'

'They say that ruin is haunted. You wouldn't catch me up there for love nor money,' Carrie added.

'It's a kind place. I didn't see anyone. The walls are thick and warm.'

'You're a braver lass than me . . . World's End is unlucky for some. That's why it's been left. It belonged to one of yours years back. They said his wife was a witch but I never believed it . . . your great-granny, Sukie Yewell. She never went to church. They say . . . but I shouldn't be putting ideas in your head. You've had a lucky escape. We thought you were a goner. The snow's taken many a soul off these moors. They know about you skipping school, by the way. I had to tell them.'

'That's all right,' said Mirren, splashing the water with her foot. Carrie was wrong. World's End was a kind house. It had sheltered her and saved her life. Now she must get dressed and face the grilling downstairs.

Soon everyone in Windebank knew the child was safe, found in the old ruin at World's End. George Thursby, the postman, brought an update straight from Cragside lane end, telling Miss Halstead how the town child was found. Soon it passed from cottage to shop and pub that Mirren Gilchrist was a truant from school on account of her beating by Mr Burrows. He was called by the managers to account for such rumours and reprimanded for taking whisky bottles into school. Only his war record prevented his dismissal. His wife went to her mother's on account of her health. The village was agog at the gossip, but Mirren was to know nothing of all this.

She was trying to be extra good for her grandparents, keeping her head down, waiting for the moment when she would be summoned to make an account of her behaviour. And so near to Christmas too.

'Why does nobody like World's End?' she asked at the dinner table.

'Don't talk with your mouth full, child,' said Gran. 'I don't know.'

'Carrie said it's haunted by a witch,' she replied.

'Nonsense, she's making a cake out of a biscuit again. There's nothing wrong with that place that a bit of repair wouldn't sort out but it's too far out to be much use to us, especially in winter. You did well to find it.'

'It found me, I think. Can we mend it?'

'Of course not, lass. There's no money for that sort of whimsy.'

Grandpa was taking his tea into his study to do his sermon for the Christmas carol concert. Being a preacher was important and he was not to be disturbed when she passed his door.

Carrie began brushing Mirren's hair out. It crackled on the brush.

'Ouch!' she cried as the lugs were combed out.

'We should be paddling your backside with that brush, young lady, not pampering your vanity. Disobellience in one so young is a black mark. Truanting is what boys do, not nice girls,' said Gran.

'She's learned her lesson, haven't you?' said Carrie, pulling Mirren's hair so she nodded meekly.

'Spare the rod, spoil the child, the Good Book says,' sniffed Gran.

They all lined up against her two days later – Gran, Grandpa and Uncle Tom – and she stood as if a culprit before the constable.

'We're really disappointed in you, Miriam. If you were unhappy you should have told us instead of wagging off like that. You could have fallen in the waterfall or in a bog and no one would have known where you were. We are led to believe you're a clever girl not a dunce . . . We never took you for a quitter.' Grandpa Joe wagged his finger like he did in the pulpit when he spat out about the fiery furnace waiting for sinners. 'What have you to say for yourself?'

'I hate it there. I want to go back to St Mary's school,' Mirren sobbed.

'That's no answer,' he said, ignoring her outburst. 'It's bound to take time for you to settle in. Tomorrow you will go down and apologise to Mr Burrows, and knuckle down to be a good scholar.'

'I won't,' she snapped back. 'He hates me. He won't teach me anything.'

'You will do as you're told, young lady. I give the orders in this house. You must learn that when you do something wrong you take your punishment. Write a neat letter of apology in your best handwriting and I will check it over. You've got to get back to study. We'll help you with that bit and that'll be the end on t'matter. As for punishment, I'm sure you realise that there'll be no pantomime trips or Christmas treats for you this year. Father Christmas doesn't bring gifts to naughty children. There'll be no outings until I'm sure you'll not let the family name down.'

'I hate you all,' Mirren screamed, and Gran cuffed her around the ear, a right sidewinder. It stung her cheek and she stared, shocked. The room fell silent.

'Out of my sight, you rude ungrateful child. You put other lives in danger and shamed us before the village. I will not speak to you until you show due remorse. Go to your room at once.'

Even Miriam knew she'd gone too far and pushed Gran into clouting her, but she would not go back to that boring classroom to be caned and humiliated all over again.

The next day she sidled out of the side door, down the cinder path from the yard to the little summer hut where, she'd been told, on sunny days Grandpa sat outside, smoking his pipe and looking down the valley at the view, dreaming up words for his preaching.

It was just a wooden shed with an open front and railings round, and a bench inside out of the breeze. No one would find her there, she thought. She needed to calm her thudding heart and think of what to write to Burrows.

The bench was icy, and icicles hung from the roof like lollipops. How she wished she was back up on the tops at World's End, far away in her own fireside. If she was grown up she would run away for ever and make that hidy-hole safe from prying people; somewhere to get away from meddlers.

She sat hunched up, trying to summon up courage to go back in, when she sensed at the corner of her eye someone standing to the side, hovering, not knowing whether to cough or not. It was Jack Sowerby. She glowered at him, hoping he'd slink away.

'Hutch up,' he said. 'In a bit of hot water, I hear. Tom was down at The Fleece telling Mam all about it. I thought you might need a friend.'

'No, go away!'

'Pity. I sort of wondered if we could find a way round the bother at school. It's not a bad school.'

'It's a rubbishy school,' Mirren snapped. 'I hate old Burrows'.

'Why?'

'I just do, and he smells of whisky,' she replied, sitting with her arms folded in defiance of Jack softening her up.

'Let me tell you a story about Harold Burrows. For one, he's not old, just over thirty. For two, he's a brave man who won medals in the war. For three, he saved many men's lives and he was injured in the head. For four, I'm told he gets terrible headaches that make him scream out in the night with pain. The whisky gives him heart. Shall I go on?' Jack paused, searching her scowling face.

'So what? He's caned me for nothing and doesn't teach me anything.' Mirren stared at him.

'What do you do to help him?' Jack stared her back, his dark eyes piercing into hers. She looked away into the distance, not sure where all this was leading. Teachers were there to drum stuff in. Mirren had never thought of them as having headaches and homes and pain, just like everyone else. 'What do you mean?'

'Come on, you know how to be helpful, fetch and carry, look interested when he's talking. You could be quite pretty if you smiled more.'

'Thanks for nothing,' she quipped, but was interested just the same.

'There you go, thinking of yourself. You've got the brains, so use them. Work it out like arithmetic. Don't sit there feeling sorry for yourself. Give him some hope by passing the blessed qualifying exams. Show him you're a winner. If you get stuck I'll always help if I can.'

Why was Jack being so kind? Was it something to do with the fact that Uncle Tom was visiting his mam a lot?

'Is World's End haunted?' she asked, changing the subject.

'What do you think? You're the one that slept there.'

'I wish I could go and live up there like a shepherd, and go for walks and keep hens and not have to go to school,' she sighed.

'By the time you're ready to leave, it'll have fallen down. It's like an eagle's eyrie up there, but very lonely,' Jack smiled, showing a line of white teeth.

'We mustn't let it fall down. It's my friend and I want to live up there one day,' Mirren replied.

'Don't be daft. Whatever could you do up there? It's a poor living off thin topsoil. Even I know that.'

'I don't care. They mustn't pull it down. Uncle Tom could mend it.' Then she remembered that she was in the doghouse and Uncle Tom wouldn't do anything if she didn't go back to school.

'Why should he help you when you won't go back to school?' Jack had read her thoughts.

'If I go back and behave, will he mend the roof for me?' she smiled.

'Well, that's a start, but you'll have to ask him yourself and he's got other ideas in his head at the moment. He's courting my mam, by the looks of things.'

'Do you mind?' she asked, not sure what courting meant.

'Nothing to do with me . . . Mam's a widow. As long as he doesn't want me to be a farmer. You've got a few bridges to mend before you ask any favours off anyone.'

She looked at Jack, her hero, with growing admiration. He was already at the boys' grammar school, and if he was on her side the battle was as good as won.

Her battle was yet to come in going down to Windebank with her tail between her legs but if it meant a new roof on World's End, then it was worth it.

That night on the moor had changed everything. She knew now she was part of these hills like her ancestors before her: Miriam and Sukie and Adey and Mother.

Sitting in the twilight of that icy December afternoon, Mirren knew that one day she would make this farming way of life her own, but how she wasn't sure. Tomorrow she must make her peace with Mr Burrows. That was enough to be going on with . . .

In the days that followed the snow fell hard and there was no school, no chance to find a path to World's End. By the time New Year came and went, she was much too busy with lessons to think much about it again.

5

29 June 1927

The total eclipse of the sun was going to be the most exciting event in Mirren Gilchrist's life since that snowstormy night at World's End.

Granny Yewell was throwing a leaflet from the council on the table, telling them the hours when they must dowse their fires, so as not to spoil sightings of the sun with smoke. 'If I hear one more word about this blessed eclipse . . .' she called out to Grandpa Joe, who was kicking off his boots in the back porch and then knocking over his mug of tea on the clean tablecloth.

'There, look what you've done,' she snapped. 'What a fuss about nothing. You'd think it were the end of the world!'

Poor Gran got so flustered and crabby when the farm workers invaded her kitchen, but there was always something warm waiting for Mirren on the table after school: a pot of broth or warm oven-bottom teacakes dripping with rhubarb jam. Adey Yewell had taken a great interest in her schooling ever since she'd marched down to Windebank with her hackles raised on her granddaughter's behalf and tore a strip off Mr Burrows.

'We can't have our lass wasting that brain of hers trying to knock some learning into lumps o' lard like Billy Marsden. You should be grateful to have such talent. I want no more nonsense. She's taken her punishment from us so just you treat her right or you'll have me to deal with!' Of course, news quickly spread and the whole village was agog at Adey's stand. Mirren felt so proud of her.

Now that Mirren and Mr Burrows had come to an understanding after she wrote her own letter of apology, and the vicar had stepped in as referee with the family over the runaway episode, school was not so boring. She was going to be put in for a prize scholarship. The Head was giving her extra coaching and he didn't have whisky breath any more. A new girl called Lorna Dinsdale arrived in Mirren's class. They became best friends and they were both trying for the scholarship together: no skiving off for Mirren with Lorna chasing her heels in class for top marks.

One of their projects was to study the total eclipse of the sun, due that summer, and the vicar brought in lantern slides to explain the 'fenominer' and how their dale was to be honoured with the best view in the whole of England. It was the centre of Totality. The sun was going to be eclipsed completely right above Mirren's head.

No one in the village could talk of anything else because every farmhouse, cottage and hotel was going to be booked up with visitors. There was brass to be made.

'Aye,' Joe replied to Adey, mopping up the spilled tea, giving his wife and granddaughter one of his twinkling looks. 'Who knows what the Good Lord in His mercy, who sets His firmament in the sky and causes the sun to go down at noon, has in store for us? It's all there in the Good Book. I shall be taking mesen off to the highest spot to stand before my Maker. I'll be nearer heaven should I be taken up to glory and you should all be doing the same.'

Grandpa Joe was of the old school of local preachers; just like the preachers in the Band of Hope at Scarperton, well drenched in the Holy Bible, never considering he had done service to his Lord unless he had his congregation whipped up into a frenzy of enthusiasm, making their Sunday roast dinners dry out in weariness by the length of his preaching, but she loved him dearly. There was always a sweetie in his pocket for her and a twinkle in his eye.

'Now then, none of that talk afore the lass,' Gran said, seeing Mirren's wide eyes on stalks. 'I'll have

74

enough to do making breakfasts for all them folk thronging the hillsides for a good view. It'll be all hands to the pump, Joe. I want that yard spotless.'

Mirren knew they'd put their names down on the Eclipse Committee to provide field parking, hot breakfasts and some overnight accommodation when the world came to Windebank. All this work for a little extra brass in the kitty would be useful come the autumn when she must be kitted out far winter: clogs, shoes, uniform. Her legs just kept growing out of things. There was a limit to how far the egg money would stretch, but she would do the work and collect the takings. That was what this coming eclipse was all about.

They had seven bedrooms and she must go in the attic while Grandpa Joe could kip in the stable loft for one night and the family visitors would sleep in the upper parlour on a camp bed. Gran would charge ten shillings a night for the privilege of sleeping in her best rooms and full breakfast.

Organising parking in the fields would be Uncle Tom's job with Uncle Wesley's boy, Ben, from Leeds, but they were all moaning about the wetness of the spring and the awful summer so far, and Tom didn't want his fields poached or the lambs disturbed by vehicles.

Gran suggested they open the fields for campers, tents and cyclists, and charge at least a shilling per person. It was only for one night.

'You're a hard woman,' Joe smiled, sipping from his refilled mug of tea with relish.

'Someone has to be in this house,' she argued. 'You're as soft as butter with yer head either stuck in a milk pail or in another world, on yer knees night and day waiting for the call to glory. If thousands of mugginses want to traipse up here for a clear view, then let them pay for it, I say.'

'That's hardly the spirit, Mother, of a good Christian woman,' he tried to tease her, twinkling those blue eyes, but she was not for soft-soaping.

'Life's shown me that you don't get owt for nowt in this world. We've a bairn now to feed and clothe. You have to take yer chances, as well you know, and this event won't happen again in our lifetime right slap-bang in this dale. The minute the shadows are over, I'll stoke up my fire and make a hundred breakfasts if I have to. Think of the brass.'

'There's more to life than brass, Adey,' said Grandpa Joe.

'My name's Adeline, as well you know, but it's brass as polishes the silver, keeps us all fed and clothed. We live off our wits and off our land. The land can give us a bonus this year, that's all,' she answered. 'The girl'll have to do her stuff too and earn her keep.'

Mirren sensed that her gran got tired of having a boisterous child around when the rest of her family was grown up. She tried not to show it but it sort of leaked out at the corners. The coming of the city hordes was a worry to her, not being used to throngs of people.

'I don't like offcumdens wandering where they will, knocking down walls and leaving litter, frightening and stealing. I shall keep out of their way,' Adey added.

'They'd not want to meet you on a dark night with yer dander up. No need to put up any sign "BEWARE OF BULL" but "BEWARE OF FARMER'S WIFE",' Grandpa laughed, but Gran was not amused.

They were always arguing and bickering, and sometimes forgot she was there, but they were kindly and welcoming so that the sad life in the Rabbit Hutches seemed a long time ago. She wished she could remember her own mam. All she had of her was the photographs in her father's tin box, but being here she could imagine her as a little girl on the farm and wonder how she could ever have left such a beautiful place.

Sometimes they sat her by the fire and quizzed her about life in the Hutches but Mirren only told them the good bits. The bad times were hidden at the back of her head and not for sharing.

Cragside was a house full of men with Grandpa Joe, Uncle Tom, the yard boys and shirts to iron. Mirren helped Carrie where she could but Uncle

Tom, up at Scar Head, was in want of a wife to do all his laundry, and needed regular pies and bread to keep him stocked up. The news that he was courting was a great relief, but Florrie Sowerby worked in The Fleece, which didn't go down so well.

Grandpa teased Mirren that she was growing into the bonny bairn of the dale, the bobby-dazzler with golden curls and bluebell eyes, fringed with long lashes. She'd rather be a boy and race around the school playground with a football, never sitting still, scourge of the Sunday school trying to catch up with Jack Sowerby, who ignored her when he was with his friends. She palled up in mischief with anyone who'd let her join their gang. The village girls gave her a wide berth but Lorna stuck to her side.

No one seemed to fuss much over appearance but Uncle Tom knew the way to her heart and sometimes brought her ribbons and crayoning books from the market. Sometimes he brought Florrie's son Jack to help out on the farm. They would all be coming to help out with the parking and cooking.

Mirren's hair was bobbed short now. It was easier to manage than plaits. Grandpa Joe complained she looked like a lad, which pleased her no end.

Gran was not one for titivating her appearance to please her man. She preferred sludge colours, plain shirts and pinafores with her greying hair scraped back.

Farm cooking was plain and simple with 'no frills and fancies'. They baked rabbit pies and rib-sticking milk puddings, food to fill bellies and stave off hunger until the next feed. There was no time on a busy farm for fancy baking and showing off, Gran declared, so each week's menu followed a regimental order: roast, cold, mince, pie, hash, stew. Who needs a calendar when you can tell the day of the week by the dish of the day? Mirren thought. The days of bread and dripping and what her dad called 'push pasts' with Granny Simms were long gone.

As they went about morning chores, Gran was barking out lists and orders for the coming invasion. This kitchen was her world and she ruled it like a sergeant major. Sometimes Mirren caught the sharp end of her tongue and wondered why Gran was being so hard.

It was Uncle Tom who told her the tale of Adey's parents, who were farmers up the dale, who'd killed a cow for their own use and then when others fell dead and anthrax was discovered, it was too late for them to survive. Gran was boarding with an aunt near Settle and banished from any contact. She never saw her parents again or got to say farewell, and never went back to visit the spot. The farm was boarded up and the land useless. It would never be farmed again in her lifetime. She was the object of curiosity and pity for a while. Who wanted a child of anthrax victims on their land?

This made Mirren sad too, for she knew how it felt to be left alone in the world at the mercy of strangers. She was glad that Grandpa Joe had made Gran happy and she, in turn, ploughed all her love into running her side of the dairy, butter and cheese making and housekeeping as efficiently as she could. No one could ever say Adeline Yewell was a shirker of duty who let dust settle, or a lazy mother whose lads wore grey shirts not white, or one who kept a poor table and empty cake tins. Just when she was due a rest, along came Mirren to spoil the show.

Now Gran was going to make sure that the money pot on the mantelpiece would be stuffed full of brass by the end of this eclipse but she'd not be giving this sun dance a second glance herself.

Mirren loved Cragside. No one had a house as big or grand as this one. Only Benton Hall was bigger and it had been a hospital for the soldiers in the war who couldn't walk or talk. In her eyes Cragside was a fairy castle high on the hill. She was the princess in the turret, huddled under the goosedown quilt as the wind whistled around, the candle flickering in the draught, while Jack Frost painted ice pictures on her window. She felt safe here, the house wrapped its arms around her, shielding her from ghosts and ghoulies of the night.

Sometimes she thought she heard the voices of children laughing and playing across the landing but when she got up to find them there was only silence and creaky floorboards. Here she was queen of all she surveyed. This was her world and she'd never leave this kingdom.

Now the valley would be flooded with visitors. Tomorrow the world would come to her kingdom and she was afraid, not of the eclipse for they had done that at school for months, but of having to share this space and give up her room.

She loved the magic lantern and slides show with the blinds down, showing pictures of the moon eclipsing the sun and how the light would be blotted out for twenty-three seconds. It would go very dark and she was not to be frightened because Jack said the light would not be destroyed.

Jack's class in the grammar school were doing the topic, and he knew about everything and kept going on about 'the Totality' and that was why everyone wanted to come to Cragside to see it all.

Very important people were setting up tele-scopes at Giggleswick, down the dale, and the Prince of Wales would come to see it if he could. Grandpa Joe said they must all pray each night for a perfect viewing with no clouds to hide the sky or no one would see anything.

Uncle Tom was busy, and Florrie Sowerby was running round with a pink face shouting at Mirren to shift this, shove that, and tidy everything away. She looked so pink all the time, trying to butter up Gran into liking her.

Jack had plans to go car spotting, for there would be thousands of motor cars and motor bikes heading in their direction. He could not imagine there being so many cars in the whole world. Only the squire and the doctor had a car in Windebank.

When the first few cars began to scrunch their gears up the hill, Mirren and Jack were sitting on a five-barred gate that shut the road from the young lambs on the moors. It was Jack who opened the gates for the driver in goggles and a leather helmet. Mirren waved at them and the ladies smiled. Then the man held out a penny for Jack so they shut the gate behind them carefully and scrapped over how they would spend it.

There were three such gates at strategic points across their stretch of the moor track from Windebank village. They sat on one apiece with Uncle Wesley's son, Ben, who'd arrived on the train from Leeds. He was ten and nearly as tall as Jack. There would be pennies galore to collect if they smiled and opened the gates.

What started as a game soon was a deadly

endeavour to see each gate stayed closed, opened, and then reclosed after each vehicle. Cyclists were happy to open their own gates, nodding to the children but giving nothing. Motor bikers with side cars were not much better, but it was the large stately cars that yielded the richest pickings.

Mirren'd never possessed so much brass in her life. Pocketfuls of halfpennies and pennies, three-penny bits and even some silver sixpences were thrown at them by ladies, who patted her shiny bob as she curtsied, in case any of them were real lords or ladies.

By the evening of the Tuesday night there was a steady stream of cars heading to spend the night on the hills, waiting for the 5.30 a.m. start of the eclipse.

It was Jack who decided they would make most money during the night, guiding motorists up towards the parking fields with lanterns.

'But it's our secret, right?' Jack whispered. 'We'll go to bed no bother and sneak out later, but it won't go dark until nearly midnight. Don't go blabbing owt to yer gran, Mirren.'

Mirren had never been up at midnight before. She was a little afeared of the darkness, but she'd do anything to impress Jack and Ben. Everyone knew there would be great revels in the valley: eclipse dances and cinema shows, cafés open all night, midnight parties. The newspaper was full of notices of events and Grandpa Joe read them all out with a sad face.

'This's no way to prepare for the Lord's coming, in such drunkenness and dancing. They should be on their knees in prayer, asking the Lord to be merciful to sinners and temper His wrath. Much is expected of us, children,' he exhorted.

Mirren was that wound up with excitement she stayed wide awake in the attic, watching out of the window as their visitors arrived by the front porch to stay in the grander rooms at the front of the house. Gran and Florrie were decked out in their best checked pinnies and hats, and never noticed Jack and Mirren in their lookout tower.

Mirren didn't like the thought of strangers using her jerry pot under the bed in the night but Gran'd clipped her ears and told her not to be cheeky to visitors. It was only for one night.

Where were they going to hide all their pennies? She was dreaming of the sweetie shop down the village with a shelf of jars: rainbow crystals, liquorice straps and dolly mixtures, sherbert dabs and chocolate drops. She spent her money ten times over in her head, slavering with delight. For the first time in her life she was going to be rich beyond her wildest dreams. How she wished Dad could be here to see it all.

At last she fell asleep, dreaming of cars dancing across the sky and coins falling like rain.

Jack woke her with a start, shouting in her lug hole, 'Gerrup! Time to get cracking . . . out of the window.'

Getting out of the attic window was not for the faint-hearted. Jack had done the old sheet rope trick as best he could but it didn't stretch down far enough. He just jumped the rest, falling on the grass and waving Mirren on.

In the half-light she was terrified but tried to be brave and climbed down backwards, feet touching the stone walls until she ran out of sheet and had to let go. The jump took her by surprise as she fell on her side, cracking her elbow. Tears welled up in her eyes but Jack pulled her up roughly and she winced.

'Hurry up, slow coach . . . follow me,' he whispered, but Mirren was struggling to keep up in the darkness, trying not to cry as they made for the barn loft to meet Ben, guarding the lanterns, which Jack knew how to light.

'I can't carry one now, me arm . . .' she cried, pointing to her elbow. Jack yanked the lamp off her.

'Give it here and make for the gate,' Ben offered, and she trundled on, watching Jack every step of the way.

Out on the fellside they could hear sheep bleating at the noise of harmonicas and gramophone records echoing out into the night air. There seemed hundreds of twinkling lights dotted around the fields: campfires and the flickering of car storm lamps. It was as if the hills were alive with an army before some battle. Uncle Tom would go mad at all the mess in the fields.

There was a snaking light along the river road in the valley, cars edging their way north to see this great show. If only her arm didn't hurt so much, Mirren thought, but Jack kept rushing her to do gate duty.

'I can't open the gate, Jack. Me arm hurts,' she said.

'Don't be a girl's blouse,' Jack snapped. 'We should never have let you come.'

'Am not! Look yerself, it sticks out funny,' she snapped, swallowing her snot, trying to be brave.

'We'll have to do it together then, but yer not having my share of the brass.' Jack glanced at her arm. 'This was my idea.'

'It's not her fault she can't use it,' said Ben with concern. 'Why couldn't you both have used the back stairs?'

Mirren was glad someone understood. It was hard trying to stand her corner but the pain was yelping now.

Jack ignored her protest and did the best he could, but the takings were down without the full workforce.

Mirren knew she was letting the side down but

even Jack could see her arm wasn't right.

'It's sticking out funny. You'd better go off home,' he yelled. But both of them knew if she was caught out of bed she'd be for it and in trouble for taking money from strangers in the dark.

'Better stay put here,' said Ben, pointing to the old barn, 'until first light and we can pretend we got up early.'

Mirren was so tired all she wanted was to curl up and sleep if she could lie comfortable. She crept behind them to the shippon. It was a fine warm summer night and excitement grew as dawn broke over the valley. The day was clear and promised a good view. She lay on the tussocks of hay sheltered by the stone wall, letting Jack and Ben deal with the stragglers. Her eyelids dropped and soon she was dreaming of a wonderful eclipse.

There he was making a fool of himself as usual, thought Adey, watching Joe at his antics. He was sitting on the high ridge at World's End, marvelling at the sight of such a throng of people now assembled on the slopes, just like the Sermon on the Mount. He had it on good authority that only a miracle would open the skies for he had been to the open prayer meeting that night and heard about the Reverend Charles Tweedale, Vicar of Weston, who had attached himself to the Astronomer Royal's party at the Giggleswick Observatory in order to make sure that they would have a pure viewing of the corona.

There was no stopping him when he was on one of his missions. He'd sent word for all Christians to kneel down and pray for the parting of any clouds, for he had dreamed that a great black cloud would obstruct the view if left to its own devices. He'd decided the least he could do was to hold a vigil on this side of the hills to back up any emergency should it arise on the other, where the Anglicans were gathered. Better that Chapel and Church should work together for the good of all, for a change.

He'd tried to get Tom roped in but he was far too busy calming his restless cows. It was rumoured that animals could run amok at the first signs of shadows and darkness.

He should have had more sense than to get Adey out here when she was busy up to her elbows in flour, baking baps with the last heat on the range. She might be hard as flint on the outside but he knew her heart was warm. She'd never got over losing George, and Ellie running off like that, and blamed herself for being a bad parent.

Sometimes it was hard to fathom why Joe had taken to her so strong. The Yewell boys were known for being one-girl men. She'd not let him down, running the farm on tramlines. He couldn't fault her housekeeping but even she knew she was laced up too tight. No one ever saw her sit down to count the daisies, allus on the go. There was never a grin on her face. Perhaps a bit of laughter would do her good, crack the enamel on that stiff mask into something close to pretty.

If Adey stood still she would flop down and be a limp rag. It was better to be on the go. But Joe had dragged her high up the fell. The ridge might have a great view but there was nothing else going for World's End but the old ruins that had saved the child last winter.

She surveyed the sky. It was nearly 5.30 now and already light. She hoped Florrie had dowsed the fire but she could see in the distance a bank of cloud gathering that might scupper their view. Soon the clouds were playing hide-and-seek with the sun.

Joe was looking at his fob watch. It was 6.10 and one black cloud was progressing ever closer to the sun. The eclipse was beginning to happen and the crowds on the hillsides were ready with their spectacles and smoked-glass eye shields.

Even Adey was peering out anxiously. Everyone was willing the clouds to break. Then she saw her husband fall on his knees and throw out his arms, heedless of the curious looks from bystanders. It was time to wait upon the Lord as the cloud moved ominously on.

'O Lord of the Heavens and Earth, open our

eyes to the wonders of the Firmament. Just budge that cloud a little lower down,' he was pleading, a single voice in the silence of anticipation and dread. Suddenly the sun stood alone with the moon creeping to its position through a window in the sky. Joe got up and came rushing over.

'Come on, Adey, leave yer fiddling, come and see the miracle,' Joe yelled from his perch. 'Come up here and see the eclipse.'

'Leave me be, Joe. I ought to go down and see to things,' she snapped, but he strode over and grabbed her by the arm roughly.

'For once you'll do as yer bid. There's more to life than griddle cakes and bacon. The porridge'll keep. Have a bit of soul, woman . . .' He pulled her towards the edge facing east, overlooking the fells where people now crawled like ants in the gathering gloom.

Have a bit of soul indeed, she thought, as she stared up at the broken cloud watching the shadow pass across the sun. Suddenly there was a chill of air, and darkness was falling fast. The silence was unnerving. She was glad Joe was watching by her side.

A hush fell over the crowds. A silence you could cut with a knife, so sharp and powerful. Then came the racing shadow over the fells like the wings of some black angel brushing across the earth, an eerie shadow of death passing over their heads.

Adey watched the black moon devouring the sunlight. Joe shoved the smoked glass in front of her and she glimpsed briefly the sight of the corona of fire and bowed her head.

All the songbirds were silent and the chill made her shiver, for she felt the whole world was wiped out and for a second she felt such panic. How many of their ancestors had stood and watched in terror as this mysterious act was performed in front of their eyes? They would have looked with fear and dread at this unexpected darkness.

She thought of Mam and Dad, George and Ellie, and of the terrible war. All that grief and suffering, and for what? She was flooded with grief, and tears welled in her eyes. It was all there in that black shadow blotting out life and warmth and happiness, all the shadows of her own life rolled into one.

Yet even this shadow could not blot out the sun's rays and fire. It was an illusion of time and circumstance, just an illusion. The sun's life burned regardless, the crown of fire would win through with power. Each of those twenty-three seconds seemed like an eternity of suffering burned up, devoured in the heat of life.

Would the sun ever return them to brightness? What if Joe was right and this was the end of the world? Was she fit to meet her maker, this sad, shrivelled-up, old-before-her-time woman? More than anything she longed for it to be over, for colour and life to return, for the warmth to touch her very heart as it had when she was a child so many years ago.

She turned to look at Joe afresh, her husband, her boys, Tom and Wesley safe, this farm, her life, and young Mirren, their second chance. This was what mattered now, not the past lives.

Suddenly the Totality was over and the shadow slipped away. Light was beginning to return. The clouds raced in, closing the curtain on the sun. There was nothing to see.

Huge cheers went up, a stirring of relief and excitement as the dark moment passed. The moors began to clatter with the roar of vehicles and engines revving up. Normality would soon return, but Adey was transfixed by what she had witnessed; something so unexpected, so personal, enlightening.

It felt like a message just for her – as if scales had fallen from her eyes and she saw all things anew. How small the world below looked from this perch; how magnificent were the hills around them, grey and green. 'I will lift up mine eyes unto the hills,' she sighed.

There was such a vivid green to the fields, a sharpness to the grey walls, a freshness of the breeze on her cheek as she raced down the slope towards the outline of Cragside. She noticed the white blossom dripping from the hawthorns, their scent wafting up her nostrils. She looked up at the frontage of their ancient farmhouse as if seeing its grandeur for the first time. This is my home, my family, she thought, though Joe might be standing in his midden clothes, still smelling of the farmyard, scratching his head at all he has seen, no doubt thinking his prayers have opened the skies.

She saw Jack and Ben strolling among the crowds, eyeing the girls with interest. It was good that those two were becoming friends, but where was Mirren?

Mirren woke in the hayloft at the sound of cheering, her eyes crusted, and she wondered where she was. Then she felt the pain in her arm and heard voices whispering down below.

'Tom, behave yourself! I've got the breakfasts to do!' giggled Florrie Sowerby. Mirren leaned over to see more. Tom was on his back pulling Florrie into the hay, fooling around, tussling her. What were they doing? He was jumping on her like a tup at a ewe. They were kissing and making silly noises. Wait until she told Jack.

She was leaning so far out to see more that she rolled off the edge, falling between them with a scream. Uncle Tom lay back at the sight of her, laughing, scratching his head in surprise.

'Look what's jumped out of the hay.'

'I've hurt me arm,' she sobbed.

'I'm not surprised,' said Florrie, trying to examine it. 'I don't like the look of this, love . . . It'll need a looking-at and some of Dr Murray's bone-setting liniment and plaster of Paris.'

The two lovebirds straightened down their clothes and made for the door. Jack came tearing across the yard and in through the barn door.

'Did you see it, Mam?' he said, looking up at them all with a cheeky grin on his face.

'Of course,' Florrie smiled. 'It were that grand it made my eyes water. It makes you think . . .'

Mirren began to howl again, great rasping sobs that brought all her family running.

'Does it hurt that bad?' Uncle Tom asked.

'I missed it,' she sobbed. 'I missed it all. I were asleep and they never waked me.' She stared hard at Jack, one of her darkest glowers. It was then that Uncle Wes took a snap of her holding her elbow and scowling with his little box camera.

Gran gathered her up to comfort her, trying not to touch the sore bit. 'Don't fret on it, lass. Happen you'll be young enough to see it again,' was all she could offer. 'I nearly missed it myself and that would have been a great pity, Mirren. There'll be no second chance for me.'

If only she'd stayed in her own room and out of mischief but she had to go following Jack Sowerby. It was all his fault and she wasn't ever going to speak to him again; not never.

'Look at the mess!' shouted Uncle Tom, surveying the litter over the fields. No sooner had the world and his wife departed, and the farmers mopped their brows and counted the cash, than the real price was there to see. There were makeshift camps and fires, broken bottles, tyre marks and ruts and spilled petrol cans.

'The dirty buggers!'

'Thomas! Not in front of the children, please,' shouted his mother.

Before the day was over there was news of other farms where lambs were caught and roasted on makeshift spits over fires.

'Never again!' sighed Tom.

Mirren had had to have her arm set in plaster down in Scarperton and that meant a trip on the bus and more expense, so she offered her cash and then out it came about Jack's little scheme. Gran was not impressed.

'I can't leave you lot, five minutes . . . Now there's doctor's bills to pay and the house to clean out. Those mucky beggars from Bradford left the bedrooms in a tip. They've broken crockery, and my fancy towels are missing and the little china horse that belonged to Great-Aunt Susannah. Don't go asking me to take in lodgers again, not so much as a please and thank you, and them with a car and a chauffeur.'

'Oh, don't take on so,' said Grandpa Joe. 'They're

only things. They can be replaced. Pity the poor devils who've to go back to soot and smoke and toil. Town folk don't know how to behave in the country. They think it's a big park to play in. They forget it's our livelihood, but no mind . . .'

Mirren emptied her pockets of coins and put the whole lot on the table with a scowl.

'There's three shillings in coppers and two shilling pieces and sixpence . . . You can have that, Gran, for my doctor's bill,' she sighed. The furry sweets she was keeping back in her pocket. No one was having those.

'We'll put it in your piggy bank for a rainy day,' Gran said, siding it all away. 'I have to admit it was a grand do seeing such wonders in the sky.'

Mirren scowled again. 'But I didn't see any of it, it's not fair . . .' She turned for sympathy but none was coming.

'You can take that look off your face, young lady. Life's not fair and the sooner you learn that lesson, the better.'

Adey reckoned there were three miracles delivered on that June morning. The first was the easy one: the opening of the clouds to let them have the only clear view of Totality in the entire country. But the second was much harder to quantify. It was as if that eclipse brought such a change in their household and in herself that even she couldn't understand. It

96

wasn't so much as if she got in the habit of cracking smiles more often or bothering a bit more about what she dolled herself up in, it was more as if she were one of them pictures that got itself hand-tinted with a bit of colour wash. Her knitting patterns were a bit brighter and her pinnies took on a bit more of red and blue and brightness.

She distempered the walls of the parlours with warm earth colours. Flowers found their way into vases and in the winter she and Mirren sat hooking a great rug for the hall, made up from fabric cut from old clothes from the attic. The design was a great sun with a moon half across it, then full on and then passing over.

It was to make up to Mirren for missing all the excitement and to rest Adey's ankles and back a bit more. The sky didn't fall if you sat down and rested up a while.

Mirren's elbow was a bit of a mess and needed trips to the infirmary. The child was sad to have caused extra expense but Adey shook her head and laughed it off, saying, 'I told you the money from the eclipse would come in handy one way or another. What matters most is getting you straight again, young lady.'

What mattered most was the coming of this unexpected gift to Cragside, this second chance, this miracle of God's grace, as Joe called Mirren, proof of His forgiveness. Hard work had its place but without joy and time to count the daisies, what was the point? Adey had learned her lesson and would pass it on.

Mirren wasn't Ellie, nor could she ever be her replacement. There was much about her that needed licking into place but her coming had brought new life and joy to their old age and for that Adeline Yewell would be forever grateful.

The third miracle was that Tom was getting wed at long last. Wilf Sowerby's widow had said yes and there was going to be a wedding in September.

Praise the Lord . . . no more washing Tom's overalls and smelly socks and feeding his hollow legs. Perhaps then she could rest up a bit for she'd been feeling a bit off, of late.

After the wedding breakfast Jack, Ben and Mirren climbed the path to World's End, stuffed to the gills with ham salads, trifles, curd tarts and wedding cake. Mirren had been pestering the boys to come to find it again.

'Isn't it grand?' she said. 'What do you think?'

'You've brought us all this way to see a ruin?' said Jack, eyeing the old house with disdain. 'It's just a shepherd's hut and perishing cold.'

Ben was being tactful and said nothing.

'The walls are thick and strong,' she argued, wanting to defend her secret place, wishing she hadn't brought them now.

'But there's no roof left; it's all collapsing.'

'But with a new roof on . . . I'm going to rebuild it one day.' She could see it all done up in her mind's eye.

'You're not a roofer. You couldn't lift one of those sandstones,' Jack laughed.

'But we could help her,' offered Ben.

'If I can survive a night in a blizzard, I can put a roof on a house.' She could see the place with paned windows and gleaming glass, a new front door.

'Look, you can see right down the valley to the railway and the river. I bet the Brigantes held out here long ago.' Ben was into history and battles.

'We could camp up here and it could be our secret den.' Mirren was trying to impress Jack, to no avail.

'No, thanks, none of your mad ideas. I've enough of my own. Ben can come in the holidays and you can play hide-and-seek,' Jack scoffed.

'That's not what I meant,' said Mirren. 'This is a shepherd's house and I'll be a proper shepherd with my own flock, so there!'

'Girls can't be shepherds!' Jack laughed again. 'Your cousin is soft in the head,' he said turning to Ben.

'You'll be going to grammar school soon,' Ben smiled. 'How'll you manage to do both?'

'I can try,' she replied, feeling dumped.

'Well, you won't catch me chasing sheep up a mountain. I want to be an engineer,' said Jack. 'You've got Cragside and we've got Scar Head. How many more places do you want?'

'I want a place of my own one day,' Mirren told him.

'Suit yourself,' said Jack. 'Let's get cracking. This place gives me the creeps.'

It was at that moment, standing on the edge, looking out, queen of all she surveyed, that Mirren sensed a flicker of excitement. World's End was hers and hers alone. She had found it and it was her destiny. How could those silly clots not see its magic?

Part Two

Darkening Skies

6

'You're going to have to rest up a bit more, Mrs Yewell,' said Dr Murray, taking his stethoscope from Adeline's chest. 'That ticker of yours is showing its age.'

She pulled up her underslip quickly and got dressed. After the last dizzy do, Joe insisted they call the quack out to the farm.

'It's a tonic bottle I need, not a lecture. That'll get me right enough,' she smiled.

'Adeline Yewell, like it or not, you're no spring chicken and those puffy ankles tell me the pump's not working as it should. I'll give you some pills. You farmers' wives are all the same, up from dawn to midnight and no proper holidays. Let that young lass of yours take up the slack.'

'Miriam's got her studies to do. We want her to do well and not waste her chances shovelling muck of a morning . . . She does her share.

Happen I'll take things lightly for a few days.'

'Days won't cure this, Adey, and you know it! Perhaps I'll have a word with Joe downstairs,' the doctor threatened.

'You do that and you won't get any of my brass again. Just give me the pills and I'll try and put my feet up. Joe's enough on his plate with all the rules and regulations coming in. I don't know what the world's coming to, setting us up for another war, sending sons out as gun fodder again . . . You'd think we'd learned summat after the last packet.'

John Murray shook his head, having lost his only son at Gallipoli. 'We have to stop this madman in Germany,' he sighed. 'I'll be too old to do much, though it has to be done.'

'I just wish they'd get on with it after all the shillyshallying. How can I rest up with all the rules landing on our doorstep?'

'If you don't, I can't vouchsafe for your strength holding out, tough as you are.' The doctor patted her wrist. 'Get some extra help in and bring Miriam back from college for a while. Think on.'

'So be it then. The world'll just have to get on without me. Mirren's staying put.'

Where had the years gone since Ellie's child arrived in rags at their doorstep? Now she was a strapping lass, full of plans to be a teacher. She'd not been a spot of bother in her in-between years, always up at the ruin at World's End with Lorna and Hilda Thursby, camping out with the Girl Guides or at the Young Farmers' dances with Jack and his gang, when she hadn't got her head in a book.

She was good with sheep and bred some ewes and tups for showing. Now her world was going to be turned upside down by war and there was talk of single girls having to be sent to work like in the Great War. It wasn't fair.

Adey hoped for peace in her old age, not another dose of worry and hard work, but another war . . . It was bad enough losing George, but now there was Ben and his brother, Bert, Jack and the girls to worry about. How could it have happened all over again? This Mr Hitler was too big for his boots and needed taking down a peg or six, shouting and screaming on the wireless.

There was talk of billeting strangers out in the country and with the spare rooms in their big house she'd be first in line to take them.

The last time she'd had lodgers for one night at the eclipse it was bad enough. The new live-in, Elsie Paget, was a hard worker but there was too much to do.

Adey didn't want Mirren coming home just yet. She was a bit too stuck on Jack Sowerby, and Adey wasn't sure what to make of that harum-scarum. He'd already joined up; give credit where credit was due. Florrie confided that she was worried about him.

They would have to take young Ben up on his offer to come and help out. She didn't need the quack to tell her that she was always out of puff and that tired when she crawled into the four-poster bed of an evening her legs ached all night.

Perhaps these pills would do the trick for a while, but she didn't want Joe worried. He'd fuss and make her go to bed. If war was coming she would do her bit whatever the consequences.

Two days later there was a letter from Mirren saying she was coming home at the end of term for the duration. 'You'll need me when the farm lads get called up. Teaching can wait, Gran.'

Adey wept to herself with relief at the news. Miriam was a good lass, like her mother at that age, the runaway daughter who'd never got a chance to prove them wrong.

How mysterious are the ways of Providence in giving us a second chance, she sighed.

Reuben Yewell whistled to himself as he set about filling the gap in the wall. There was no other life for him from now on. He had left Leeds without a backward glance. This was the life. He loved setting out his stones, hand and eye working together in the ancient art of knowing which stone to place where, finding the exact one or dressing another with a chisel to fit into the shape. It was like a giant jigsaw puzzle. They never went back the way they had fallen.

From the top field he got a grand view of the dale. Its greenness never tired his eye. It was hard work for little more than his keep but he was where he wanted to be at long last.

Walling couldn't be skimped if it was to last for centuries to come; his wall reshaped and strengthened, one upon two, two upon one in the old pattern, with big through stones placed evenly as the wall rose and narrowed off. A good wall could see them all out. If only other things in life could be so certain.

Uncle Tom trusted him with jobs, especially with sheep. He trusted him over Jack because he sensed that Yewell instinct in him. He might be a plodder but when he walked the fields he did it with care and a sharp eye. Tom had shown him how to spot a ewe in trouble, to listen to see if she'd lambed and was making the right noise, pointed out the signs of weakness and strength in a new-born lamb, how to skin a dead one and mother on an orphan.

Grandpa Joe pointed out how weather came in mostly from the west, how to spot rain clouds, haze and sun dogs, how the wind changing direction was important. There was so much to learn and now that war was coming, he knew he'd made the right choice in helping them out.

What would happen to Cragside if all the men

left? Someone had to keep the nation fed and the land safe. Bert had gone into the RAF, Jack was in the army, but he knew his job was right here. Mirren was at college.

He was glad Jack was off. He always made him feel a bit of a clodhopper. Jack had never been keen on farming. He cut corners and had no feel for the animals. Mirren was more like him. She took time to do things properly. She was a nature girl, interested in flowers and birds and knew the Latin names of everything. He'd been hopeless at Latin.

He'd lived for the weekends and school holidays to come and help out at Cragside for years. Now he had a chance to pay them back.

He'd learned to fish down by the river and walked the paths with the river warden, knew the lie of the land and once took Jack out to poach a salmon from the river, which he'd then not had the nerve to sell on. Jack had whisked it down to the pub and pocketed the cash.

Jack bought a motor bike and offered to teach him to drive but he preferred slower things. He was a good horseman now.

'Boring old Ben,' Jack teased as they eyed up all the girls at the Young Farmers' dance. Jack got the best partners in Windebank: the glamour girls with painted faces and long nails, who loved riding pillion on his bike.

Mirren's girl friends, Lorna and Hilda and Aly,

were grammar school girls and he was wary of them, a bookish, giggling gang and always whispering. It was best to keep out of their way.

He and Mirren were offcomers, townies on the surface, but both of them now were country through and through. His dad had smiled and told him to go and do his war service in the dale. 'At least we'll know one of you is safe,' he quipped, making out it was an easy option. Ben almost went the opposite way with Bert for a while but the pull of the land was stronger than any other service. His ancestors might have been on the muster roll for Flodden in 1513 but he was going to stay put and put his back into the war effort. He was going to keep the nation fed.

7

In the weeks following the declaration of war, Mirren felt as if the whole of the dale was cranking itself up for a fight. Boys from the grammar school suddenly appeared in uniform, parading themselves proudly in blue, navy and khaki. Jack went into the Royal Engineers. Uncle Wesley's Bert joined the RAF, and his brother, Ben, came to work with Uncle Tom. It was good to have him around and he lodged with Uncle Tom at Scar Head.

How Auntie Florrie sobbed when Jack left the farm. For all his wild gadding about he was good to her, fetching errands from town, teasing her rotten when she tried a new hairdo, playing tricks to get her flustered. Who could ignore Jack when he was so suntanned and bronzed from haytiming, making the most of his last few days on the farm helping Uncle Tom?

They'd spread picnics in the fields for everyone

and held a hop in the barn as a farewell party for Lorna's brother, Freddy, and Jack's friends from Windebank. The fiddler kept them dancing over the stone flags until dawn.

Mirren felt so grown up in her checked dirndl skirt and voile blouse, and Jack had twirled her round and made a fuss of her.

Mirren wasn't going to be left behind teaching, and volunteered for the Women's Land Army. She was based at the unit down in Scarperton but got a dispensation to work at Cragside in the place of young Derek Sumner, the farm lad who'd disappeared one night to join the navy.

Grandpa Joe, in his fustian breeches and outdoor clogs, was eighty, still upright and fit enough, but his rheumatics got to his back in damp weather. Grandma Adey had shrunk to nothing but had a will of iron when it came to keeping the farmhouse stocked and sparkling. With Tom and Ben's muscle they made a good team.

Suddenly farming was on a wartime footing with the War-Ag Ministry breathing down their necks, inspecting fields, ordering quotas, issuing demands for extra yields in all their food production.

The Yewells paced over their bottom fields with heavy hearts, knowing some of their best pastures must be ploughed over and sown for oats, barley, kale and root crops.

'It's a waste of time,' said Joe, shaking his head

in disgust. 'This land isn't meant to grow arable. They'll not get owt off it, you'll see. Who's going to plough it over?'

'I am,' Mirren piped up. 'We're bringing over a tractor tomorrow, just the job; I've been practising on it for days. I'll have those furrows as straight as tramlines.' They all looked at her as if she was mad. Ploughing was man's work but she'd show them!

The past weeks of training were taken up with lectures and demonstrations, visits from advisors round the farm giving out orders. The villagers were busy extending their allotments and hen coops, pig arks sprouted in back gardens. Florrie and Adey were sewing up blackout curtains, grumbling that no one could possibly see into their small windows until the ARP warden told them that torchlight could be seen from the air and they must cover every opening.

Granny cursed old Josiah Yewell for building such fancy front windows for show. Ben boarded them up with wooden shutters and the house felt dark and gloomy.

'We'll never hear any sirens or whistles up here,' Florrie wittered every time she came to visit. 'We'll be taken in our beds!'

'Happen the cellar or under the stairs will have to do the job for us. There's always the big rock hole in the field to jump behind,' teased Mirren.

'And get ourselves shot trying to run across the grass?' Florrie snapped. 'You can't go anywhere off the track. There's tanks and shooting ranges on the moors. It's not safe to wander too far out. They'll be roasting our sheep if we don't watch out.'

'We'll all be roasting our sheep if they get a broken leg,' winked Uncle Tom, quoting the new regulations that did allow lame sheep to be slaughtered as food.

There was a big searchlight being built at the back of Windebank looking down over the valley, hoping to catch night raiders taking a short cut across Yorkshire.

The village seemed full of strangers; children evacuated from Leeds and Bradford billeted around the green, climbing trees and splashing in the beck. The Fleece was packed with soldiers off duty from the moor, according to Uncle Tom and Ben, squeezing locals from their benches by the fire.

Not that Mirren went anywhere near, being strictly teetotal. She'd never forgotten what drink had done to her father. It was like pissing away hard-earned brass to her, but it was supposed to warm chilled bones and some of the strangers weren't used to the sharp damp air yet.

On the morning of their turn to use the Fordson tractor, she crawled up the narrow lanes, praying no cart would be coming in the opposite direction

113

or that the gateposts weren't too narrow. Some of the girls had had to demolish posts before they could get through to do their work. She felt like a queen on her chariot, smart in her fawn corduroy breeches, green jersey and turban, riding high overlooking the stone walls with her instructor, Reggie Pilling, who could plough blindfold, backwards, without a wobble.

She was going to show those Yewell men just what a hot shot she'd become, but her heart sank when she saw them all lined up waiting for her to crunch the gear box and stall the engine.

With her chin stuck out, her eyes glued to the task ahead, she didn't want lanky Ben smirking or Uncle Tom making silly faces. Tractors were rare treasures in this part of the dale and everyone would want a go when she was finished. Grandpa Joe waved her on, shaking his head. Ben was all for horses, not machines. Hercules and Hector were his finest Clydesdales. He would be hard to impress.

'We'll do Honey Mires first and then Stubbins and then Top Meadow,' said Reggie, looking at his papers. 'They'll be sown down to oats.'

'Will they grow this high up?' Mirren asked, knowing how cold and wet it could get even in summer.

'That's what the War-Ag have decided. Only time'll tell if it works. Doesn't have to be top quality;

it's only for cattle feed. Oats have been the staple diet up here for centuries,' he added, seeing the look of scorn on her face.

'Yes, but this is sheep country, not arable.'

'Don't argue, lass. Ours is not to reason why,' he laughed. 'Just get on with it! You've got an audience.'

Mirren set off determined to keep a straight line, up and down without a hitch, turning the pasture brown side up, the meadow where clover and rattle, buttercups and rich grasses scented the air in June. All those wild flowers ploughed in. It was a good field for keeping bees. The loam was rich and moist, and weeds would sprout with the oats. It would be her job to weed and keep an eye on the crop until the stalks were ripened off.

Up and down she trundled, hoping everyone had got on with their own jobs by now, but just as she was turning round the bottom end a blackened-up face leaped up and screeched, 'Geronimo!'

It was Jack, back on leave, up to his old tricks, giving her a surprise, scaring her witless, making her laugh and lose concentration. She wobbled and her line went to pieces.

'Firm up!' yelled Reggie, not amused. 'Get that bugger out of the way!' The giggles had got hold of her and she was all over the place, seeing Jack clowning around.

'Now look what you've made me do!' she yelled

at the dashing young soldier. 'Just wait till I see you proper. Don't you know there's a war on . . . ?'

She wasn't going to stop, even for him. This was her war work and she mustn't shirk. He'd ruined her line but there was always the next.

Jack always made her laugh and her heart flutter. Mad Jack, the demon biker who drove Florrie wild when he brought his engines into the kitchen and spread them all over the floor, who roared round the narrow lanes as if it were Brooklands race track. He never seemed to take anything seriously. Uncle Tom had hoped he'd take to farming but not a chance.

'What do you expect?' Granny sniffed. 'Florrie was a Kerr before she wed Wilf Sowerby. Kerrs don't make good farmers, not bred in the bone. He'll do fine for hisself as long as he keeps moving. They like to wander, do Kerrs, allus have and allus will.'

So how come Florrie had stayed put with Uncle Tom? Mirren thought. She was always good for a laugh and could bake better than any Yewell.

Jack had stayed on at the boys' grammar school, as she had at the girls'. He'd even been abroad to France on a school trip. He could speak real French while she struggled with Latin and German.

Now he was training down London way, something to do with mines. He'd always looked out for her like a big brother should but they weren't related in any way. The girls had drooled over him when he met her off the school bus and gave her a lift. How could she admit to them how much she looked forward to having him to herself? The sun came out when he came around.

It was something to do with him rescuing her when she was little, laughing her out of her sulks with his antics. You never knew what Jack would do next, and he was a great ballroom dancer, lifting her off her feet at the end of a dance. Sometimes he looked at her and made her blush.

'You're special, Mirren. Don't you forget it. I shall have to keep my eye on you.'

Sometimes he took her out to the cinema and held her hand, other times he just left her alone. Lately he'd made her feel a right country bumpkin and she wondered if he was mooning over some flighty London piece with lipstick and kiss curls. If Lorna or Hilda ever tried flirting with him she felt jealousy flash through her body. That's when she knew she was smitten. He made them all feel so girly and giggly, with his dancing black eyes. Cragside wasn't the same when he went away. Florrie took her aside once when she saw how upset she was getting.

'I can see how you feel about our Jack but don't let him see it too much. He's like my dad and doesn't like to be cornered. Leave him be and he'll come to. He's not one for settling down, love, but if ever he did, you'd be the one. He's got a tender spot for you.'

Mirren blushed at the warning so kindly given. She'd been in love with Jack Sowerby since she was nine. It was too late to change any of it now.

She rushed through the rest of the ploughing and got on with her other chores. There'd be just time to wash and change before she set off to Uncle Tom's at Scar Head to hear all Jack's news.

In the months that followed the ploughing, everything was sown and prepared but the winter of 1940 was grim and they were fast in with blizzards and snowdrifts. Windebank waited for war to begin in earnest and waited on. The evacuees went back south to Leeds and Hull, disgruntled and frozen. The Women's Institute pickled, preserved, jammed and salvaged. The Services Comforts Fund ran concerts, raffles, bazaars, anything to coax cash out of the farmers' tight pockets. Letters came from far-flung places and sad telegrams that no one wanted to read were delivered to a few unfortunate families. Bert was on flying operations and Ben was worried.

Then at the beginning of June came the news of the miracle of Dunkirk and the evacuation of the beaches at terrible cost. Jack was one of the last to be evacuated, busy laying mines in the Channel and getting strafed and wounded in the process.

He returned one night, exhausted, his uniform

in tatters, having landed at Liverpool. He slept for almost three days without waking and then ate Auntie Florrie out of house and home. Then he was posted somewhere in the south-west on special training.

On his last night of leave, Mirren hoped they'd go to the pictures but he still looked grey and weary, and spent the evening in The Fleece with Tom and Ben, enthralling everyone with tales of his escapades on the beaches, taking free pints from any who offered until he was half-cut. Then he sauntered up to Cragside, happy to wander round checking the crops with her.

As they feared, the oat stalks were leggy and the heads were small and weak. They walked on up to World's End and stood staring down at the valley below as the sun was setting pink behind the moors.

'I take back all I said about up here . . . Never take this for granted, Mirren. This is paradise to where I've been.' This was a sober sad side to Jack she'd never seen before. He was always Jack-the-lad in company, full of jokes and quips, fooling around, acting daft. Now he looked ten years older somehow. She just wanted to hug him and take the pain out of his eyes; pain and anger that hadn't been there before.

'Was it that bad?' she asked.

'Our lads never stood a chance wading into the

water. Sitting ducks, they were, and no bloody planes to defend us . . . Still we live to fight again and I don't want Herr Hitler to get his hands on all this. If we don't stand firm now, it'll be the end of everything we've ever known.' There were tears in his eyes. There was a soft side to Jack, despite all his joking. She grasped his hand, wanting to hold him to her but he shrugged off his mood.

'No time like the present, girl. Make the most of life while you've got it. I hear Freddy Dinsdale's copped it. His mam must be gutted. We were in the same class. Not much of a lifetime, was it, for him?' He stared out across the fields and down into the valley, lost in his own world. 'Eat, drink and be merry for tomorrow we die!'

'Don't say that,' she snapped, thinking of poor Lorna's brother, lost over the Channel.

'You ought to join up proper and come and join me,' he replied, not listening.

'I am joined up, or hadn't you noticed?'

'The Land Army . . . well, you must know what the lads call you lot . . . backs to the land.' He paused, seeing her look puzzled. He dropped to the ground and opened his legs.

'That's horrible.' She blushed and turned from him.

'Don't take on, only joking. You need to lighten up a bit. Don't take everything so seriously. There's not much of a war up here, now is there?'

'Oh, no? Then why are my tyres bald with biking, my hands blistered with hoeing and mucking out and then doing a shift down in Scarperton? I've never been so tired in all my life. It's up to us to keep everyone fuelled up with milk and crops and meat and eggs. We're growing everything we can. Just 'cos there's no bombs or fighting. I'm doing my best here,' she snapped. He was spoiling their last evening together, making them argue.

'I know you are, sweetheart, but you've got to have some fun too. It's nice to know I've got a girl hard at it in muck and soil who stands for everything worth fighting for,' he smiled, his dark eyes flashing at her.

'Am I your girl?' she asked, her heart thudding.

'Course you are, always have been.' He plonked a kiss on her forehead. 'And I expect letters every week with all the gossip from Windybags but no farm talk: how Lanky Ben's landed a cushy little number on the farm with his reserved occupation . . .'

'I don't think he sees it like that. He's helping us out and has joined the Local Defence Volunteers.'

'The Look, Duck and Vanish Brigade, very nice,' Jack laughed. 'Fat lot of good they'll do if Jerry ever lands. Throw a few potatoes at them? There's not a decent gun between them. They spend most of their time in the pub.'

'Oh, come on! They do a full day's work and then stay up all night guarding the railway line, making defences. We hardly see Ben. I hate it when you're mean,' she said.

'You're mighty quick to his defence. Is there something I should know?' Jack's mood could turn on a sixpence.

'Don't be daft. Ben's my cousin, my big brother. He's not like that.'

'All men're like that, given half a chance. You just watch it with all these uniforms about. You're my girl now!' He pulled her to him roughly and kissed her on the lips. 'That'll do for starters,' he laughed. 'But there'll be more where that came from when I'm back again.'

With that he jumped on his motor bike and roared off, leaving her in a total spin. Her very first kiss from Jack, such a special moment and over so quickly. Did he love her? Was she his girl-friend now? It was so confusing: all her romantic dreams were coming true. How she had imagined this coming-together on a windswept moor, but somehow it was all so rushed and tense and matter of fact. Where was the courting, the roses, the billets-doux, those passionate embraces they showed at the pictures like Heathcliff and Cathy?

Don't be daft, she thought, grinning from ear to ear. A kiss is a kiss. This is Jack we're talking about and he was always impulsive. If only he wasn't so far away now. She didn't know when she'd see him again. This war was spoiling everything but nothing was going to spoil this long-awaited exciting romance.

Jack's leave ended and, eventually, so did summer.

There was a humdinger of a September storm one night, only to be expected at the back end of summer, but Mirren thought the roof was going to lift off and sail away. The rain splattered on the windows, battering its way through the cracks. The gale drowned out any chance of sleep. She thought she heard the drone of Junkers in the night on the way to Liverpool or Manchester and pitied the poor sods manning the gun battery out on the moors.

There were alerts on the news bulletins every night to be vigilant against parachutists and enemy agents but she felt safe in their eyrie. Jack's letters were by her bedside, full of cheery jokey escapades. She was finding it hard to make her replies relate anything other than the usual drudgery but now she must get up to prepare the milk parlour when she just wanted to bury her head in the bolster and sleep on.

Taking a deep breath, she darted out of the bed and pulled on her breeches, her jumper and dungarees, man's socks, shoving her hair in a turbaned scarf. If she was quick there was time for a brew. There wasn't much morning light but the storm had abated outside, which was a mercy.

She opened the door to let the house dog out and noticed a strange shadow in the far corner of the near field where the old ash tree rose high. With horror she saw a flying ship, a Zeppelin, a monster fish, hovering over her head.

One look and she shot back into the house, yelling, 'They've landed! Jerry's here in a flying ship! Everyone downstairs ... Get the shotgun, Ben.' He was sleeping in the attic. 'Send for Uncle Tom!'

All her training went out of the door in her panic and shock. How could they send for help if parachutists were close by? What did the leaflet say: 'IF THE INVADER COMES ...'?

Stay calm, Mirren, stay put. Go about your business and tune into the wireless, she told herself. Well, that was easier said than done with just one precious battery working. The old folks must be put in the cellar and Daisy, the latest live-in helper, must be warned.

Everyone sat round the table looking grim, sipping stewed tea. Grandpa Joe's face was drawn and pale. The shock was too much at his age.

'I never thowt it'd come to this in my lifetime, Adeline,' he whispered. 'Creeping over our heads in the dead of night. What can we do but pray ... ?'

'And keep milking. Hitler might have landed

but the cows need seeing to,' Mirren said, suddenly feeling stronger. 'They're not having our eggs either.'

Ben was fully dressed, carrying a rucksack. 'I have to go!' He made for the door.

'What's up, Reuben?'

'I've got orders if . . .' His words faded away as he shot out the door. Then there was a great roar of laughter from him. 'Come outside, Mirren Gilchrist, and tell me what you can see.'

Everyone made for the door and gawped. 'Don't you know a barrage balloon when you see one?' he roared. 'It's one of ours. Panic over, everybody.'

'Then where did it come from in the dead of night, scaring me to death?' Mirren felt stupid but she must defend her corner. He was right: it was a huge inflated balloon.

'Who knows? The cables are entangled in the ash, see, and there's a funny box dangling down. Nothing to worry about, Granddad. We live to fight another day.'

What a relief; it was nothing more sinister than one of the air defences to stop enemy aircraft flying low or dive-bombing into buildings. Mirren had seen them on the newsreel at the Majestic in Scarperton, but this one was huge. Where had it come from?

'You'd better let someone know it's arrived,' smirked Ben, enjoying the red-faced flustering of his cousin. She could have slapped him one right there but wanted to hang on to the last shreds of her dignity.

There was always rivalry between them; both being town-bred children who had found their living in the country. They were always competing to be the best farm worker.

'You can wipe that smile off your face, right now!' she snapped. 'I've got the milking to do and no time to go gallivanting, so you can just bike down to the phone box and get your Home Guard up here. I'm not having that thing hovering over us all day. It's like the Angel of Death.'

Then it was back to the chores and the mucking-out, the milking and cleaning up, trying to catch the day until Arnie Blewitt came puffing up the lane with his cronies with their one gun slung over his shoulder. She hoped they'd shut the gates into the lane and not let the shorthorns out of the bottom field.

'Now then, Arnie. You've come at last to see what's up. Good job it wasn't Jerry or we'd all be dead and gone by now,' Mirren teased.

'Orders are to guard it day and night, so that's six teas, please,' he replied, eyeing her up and down.

'Get them yerself. I'm busy. That thing's going nowhere. It doesn't need a guard, or have you nothing better to do? I can find you a few jobs,' she said.

'The cables're trapped. It don't half look like a trapped whale. They're sending for a winch to shift old Moby Dick here. I'll go and see Joe and Adey. I bet they got a shock in the night.'

He disappeared into the kitchen and came out with a tray of mugs and large wedges of ginger parkin. No one took much notice of the overhead visitor but folk kept coming to the bottom of the lane to take a peek at Moby Dick. Even the school teacher brought the children up to draw the thing, and all the while Mirren was trying to get on with her chores.

Later in the afternoon a posse of lorries and trucks trundled up the lane. At last the cavalry has arrived, thought Mirren, as a brass hat jumped out of the cab and stormed across the yard.

'What are all these civilians doing here? You were told to guard this with your life!' he snapped as the Home Guard jumped to at the sight of a real soldier. 'I want the premises evacuated now. Pack a suitcase and get out of here right now,' he ordered as Grandpa Joe stood by, not taking in his words.

Ben came running up. 'What's going on?'

'I want the place cleared at once,' said the officer.

'This is a farm and there's stock to see to,' Mirren replied.

'And you are the Land Girl here?' he said, looking down at her as if she was muck on his shoe.

127

'This is our family farm. We can't just upsticks and leave. There're old folk inside,' she argued.

'All the more reason to get everyone out.' The man was resolute and he had the troops to back him up on the back of the lorry.

'But it's only a balloon,' said Ben, standing by her side.

'This is not standard issue. It was ripped from its moorings. It has certain elements capable of destroying a Junker on contact. It's primed for action. That's all I'll say,' came the reply.

'You mean there's a bomb in it?' said Ben.

'I'm not at liberty to say . . . For everyone's safety we must evacuate the premises forthwith.'

'No one said anything about bombs,' croaked Arnie, stepping back in alarm.

'Stay where you are, man, and get on with the job. The sooner the farm is cleared, the sooner we can do what we have to.'

Mirren couldn't believe what was happening. She slammed a few nightclothes in a suitcase for her grandparents, who were flustered and frightened at being hustled out the door and onto the cart with Daisy. Ben released the horses into the far field where the cows would soon be ready for afternoon milking.

'Don't worry, I'll see to them somehow,' he smiled. 'You just get everyone up to Scar Head.'

'I'm not leaving!' said Joe, but when Ben explained

that Adey and the girls were in danger, he got onto the cart with them.

'I'll come back as soon as they're settled to gather up the sheep. If there's an explosion—'

'You stay put, Mirren, or you'll have me to deal with,' Ben said.

'You and whose army? I'm in charge here,' she snapped.

'I'm bigger than you, so skedaddle!' At six foot three there was no arguing with him on that score.

As they bumped across the fells, Mirren took one last glimpse at the rooftops of the old farm. This couldn't be happening. How could one of their own defences rip apart centuries of Cragside just on the whim of the wind? She thought they were safe from war and now she knew how all those poor bombed-out people in London felt, their homes reduced to rubble, left with only the clothes they stood up in, and relying on the kindness of strangers.

She was clutching Dad's tin box in her lap, and the portrait of Uncle George from the mantelpiece. It was funny what she'd rushed to save.

They'd heard the drone of bombers in the night, saw the glow in the distance of fires and destruction, but it was all so far away. There'd been a crash on the moors: young men on a training flight who'd hit the hills in the mist. There were a few bombs aimed at the railway line but nothing more to harass their peace of mind.

Apart from all the restrictions no one would know there was a war on up here but now she did. For the first time she knew how helpless they were. If the bomb blew it would wipe Cragside off the map, and all those brave men close by. Ben was down there protecting their stock in danger too. Suddenly she knew they weren't playing war any more. This was real and the danger was real.

None of them spoke but, once they were settled at Scar Head, for the first time in months she walked up to World's End and prayed hard that all would be well.

Ben watched the demolition operations with fascination from the top field. The sixty-foot barrage balloon had drifted all the way from the coast at Barrow-in-Furness docks. It was a hush-hush job with an external device in the box now dangling precariously over the great ash tree.

The winch on the back of the lorry was attached to the cables. Every move was planned and rehearsed. The valve was released to deflate the balloon. Then the bomb squad corporal was ready and padded to climb the tree and remove the triggering device from the explosive. One false move and all that would be left of Cragside would be a crater.

For achingly long minutes life was held in the

balance, but the brave man did his business and suddenly the panic was over.

Everyone stood around in a cloud of blue cigarette smoke once the explosive box was carted off. Ben found himself handing round mugs of sweet tea, knowing Gran wouldn't mind him using her precious rations; a small reward for saving the farm.

'What a tale to tell the nippers,' laughed one of the bomb disposal squad, eyeing the farm building with interest. 'Nice place . . . Unusual architecture for a farmhouse. Your wife did well to get the old folks out so quickly.'

'She's my cousin, not my wife,' said Ben quickly.

'Sorry. Not wed then?'

'Nah, no time for all that with two farms to run,' he replied, sensing the question in the air: what's a strapping lad like you doing out of the army? 'Home Guard duties, of course,' he added.

He was not going to tell him, or anyone for that matter, the truth: that he'd been approached early on to train for special duties alongside the Home Guard. It was his cover for secret training in the Auxiliary Unit, a hush-hush platoon of locals who met under cover of darkness; men who could go into hiding at a moment's notice into their secret fox-holes underground, bunkers already prepared and stocked should there be trouble. They were men trained to hide out for weeks, sabotage, kill, and be killed if necessary; a very secret army that no one must know about.

They'd been meeting in the dark, hiding out, doing exercises and no one suspected a thing. That was how it must stay. With a bit of luck they might hold out for six months. Knowing every nook and cranny of these hills was essential and they were handpicked for just that special knowledge and for their ability to blend in unnoticed wearing Home Guard uniforms when needed.

If Tom wondered where Ben went late at night with his rucksack on his back, he never said anything and he'd have got a load of lies from his nephew about catching poachers or night exercises.

There were six of them in his cell: Podge, the gamekeeper; Evan, the Scoutmaster; Dick and Dave, farmers; and the officer in charge, all known by nicknames. Ben was Lanky. He knew the score. Survival might be only for days or weeks should the invasion come.

The fewer people knew, the better. Ben was praying their skills would never be put to the test but at least he could look uniforms in the eye, knowing he was doing his bit on two fronts just as much as they were.

It was a shame there were no women recruited, for Mirren knew the terrain even better than he, but even she hadn't spotted the bunker tucked down the side of World's End with its entrance so carefully concealed. There was just a concrete tube as a rear escape route if things got hot. He was glad all his Boy Scouting days had come to some good use.

When all the danger was over and the lorries drove off down the hill to the main road, Ben made back to Scar Head to give them the good news. He found everyone sitting around looking glum and Auntie Florrie was wiping her eyes. Mirren stood silent, her face white with shock.

'What's up?' Ben said.

'It's Jack,' said Uncle Tom, pointing to the telegram. 'The lad's had a bad accident on his motor bike . . . hit a tree in the blackout. He's in hospital. Florrie and Mirren want to go and see him near Aldershot.'

Serves him right, Ben thought but said nothing. Jack careered around corners as if he owned the road on his Norton, scaring sheep and horses. It was about time he slowed down.

'Done much damage?' he asked.

'It doesn't say, but wrapping yourself round a tree must be painful,' sobbed Mirren. 'Why does he have to tear around like a mad thing?'

Why do girls always fall for the reckless ones? Ben sighed, seeing how upset she was by this news. Her blue eyes were sparkling with tears. She'd lost the puppy fat of her schooldays and was growing into as fair a lass as any in the dale. Trust Jack to mark her card.

'He's got the luck of the Irish and a bump on the head won't stop him, you'll see,' he replied. 'They'll give him some leave once he's recovered. Don't worry, Auntie Florrie, he's tough as cowhide.'

'But I do worry. He's already come through one bad scrape in Dunkirk and now this. One day he'll run out of lives to squander. I wish he was steady like you.'

How to be damned with faint praise, he thought. Good old boring Ben . . . If only they knew what he could do with a piece of wire and rope, they'd not write him off as dull.

'Just look on the bright side, everyone,' he smiled. 'At least he'll still have Cragside to come home to. The balloon's gone and you can all go home.'

Mirren leaped up at his news and soon they were all packed and back on the cart, chattering with relief that the ordeal was over. Arnie and his troop had long gone, leaving a mound of stub ends and a pile of grey balloon lining on the mucky yard.

The women pounced on the booty. 'It'll sew up well for couch covers,' said Gran, fingering the cloth.

'We could make a suit out of it and trim it up for summer,' said Mirren.

'Florrie will want some for curtains.'

'Finders keepers,' said Mirren. 'There's enough cloth here to suit up Windebank. We'll divide it up and wash it off and see how we go . . . Pity it isn't black for lining the big curtains.'

'You're never satisfied, ladies,' said Grandpa. 'The Lord has tempered the wind to the shorn lamb, indeed. Let us pray and give thanks for a safe delivery and for Jack's recovery.'

They all bowed their heads right there in the yard and stood in silence. Cragside was restored to them. Danger was averted. Perhaps it was a good omen, Ben mused, that Hitler wouldn't come and he might just live to a ripe old age. But until victory came, he must set himself apart and keep shtoom.

Mirren waited anxiously for news of Jack's slow recovery. The weeks dragged into a month. She wrote every day, even telling him about the escapade with the balloon, against her better judgement, to try to keep his spirits up. Perhaps this accident would slow him down.

Florrie managed one visit to the hospital, taking fresh baking in a tin that got lost in the crush on the train.

'Don't look so worried,' Florrie laughed on her return. 'He's all in one piece and as cheeky as ever. His head must be made of concrete. Your letters cheered him up no end . . .'

Mirren blushed scarlet. There was no hiding how she felt about Jack from anyone now.

They'd been hard at the pig killing and now Cragside could face winter with a line of salted flitches stored in the back dairy on hooks in the beams, when George Thursby, the old postman, puffed through the farm gate as Mirren was mucking out.

'The inspector's on the warpath counting pig quotas. Taylor's rang The Fleece to pass it up the dale to get them extras hidden.'

'Thanks. Come in and get your drinkings,' Mirren winked. 'Tell Gran you deserve an extra slice of spice bread.'

No one took notice of the rules and regs that said they could only kill one pig for their use, but took liberties in the hope that what wasn't seen wasn't missed. If they were found there'd be a fine and a fuss, and no one wanted that so it was up to each farm to spread the word when the War-Ag man came to call.

Ben would have to get word now to Scar Head. They'd promised pork for Christmas to some of the families who'd helped over the summer by way of a thank you.

'Where shall we hide them?' whispered Mirren, knowing the obvious places were the first to be checked. 'The cellar's not safe or the out barns. If he creeps in there while we're not looking . . .' Then she heard a whinny from the stable, where Hercules, the bad-tempered Clydesdale, was stamping for attention.

They fetched the oat bag and tempted him while Ben carried the carcasses out of sight covered in sacks to the back of the stable.

An hour later Mr Simpson's van arrived un-announced. He was in a foul temper, having slipped on the mud and splashed his gaberdine mac, so Gran sat him down for a chat and a wodge of her best treacle parkin. Little did he know he was eating molasses from the can allowed for cattle feed, which cooked up a treat in cakes and biscuits.

'Time to get going, Mrs Yewell. Just the two carcasses, is it?' He smiled a sly smile, knowing what the score was but powerless to do anything about it. 'I'll just have a nosy around,' he continued. 'On my own, if you don't mind.'

He searched the dairy and cellar, the attic eaves, the barns, and was making for the stable block until Mirren stepped in. 'Please help yourself, Mr Simpson, but I must warn you, Hercules doesn't like strangers . . . I'd hate to see him kick you. We can't be responsible for any injury caused.'

'Really?' The inspector looked at the stable door and at Mirren's open face. 'I'm good with horses.' Her heart sank as he made to open the door but Hercules reared up right on cue and Simpson shut

137

it quickly again. 'I take your point, miss. Thank you, everything seems to be in order, but then I'd expect honesty from the God-fearing family of Joseph Yewell,' was his parting shot that, fortunately, Grandpa Joe didn't hear.

'What's that he was saying?' he asked.

'Nothing,' Mirren smiled, glad that his hearing was not what it was. 'I'm going to find a carrot for Hercules.' That bad-tempered beast had saved their bacon in more ways than one.

It was nearly Christmas and if the weather held Jack would be back on leave now that he was recovered and on duty again. He'd been knocked out and bruised but nothing to worry about, so Auntie Florrie was baking for Yorkshire just in case he made it home.

Mirren was rushing through her chores in time to get a lift to the Home Guard hop in the village hall that evening. All the girls in the hostel were turning out and they'd be dressed to kill. For once she was going to make an effort and get out of her jumpers and dungarees so as not to let them down. That meant buckets of hot water to heat to have a strip wash and a scrub to get the farmyard stink off her body and hair. She was going to wear her one and only best frock and stockings, and show off the marcasite necklace that Jack had bought her for her twenty-first birthday.

Her new outfit was inspired by the scene in

138

Gone With the Wind, when Scarlett O'Hara made a dress from curtains. Florrie had rummaged in the trunk for a length of some velvet salvaged from old parlour curtains. Gran insisted that Mirren should have something decent to wear to the party but no one wanted to waste good fabric, so they cut away the faded bits. There was enough to make a fitted frock with short skirt, three-quarter sleeves and a sweetheart neck. Jack's necklace was on show for all to see. Florrie helped Mirren sweep her hair into a victory roll at the front, leaving the rest to fall in waves down her back.

'You look a right bobby-dazzler. Those lads won't know what's hit them!' she laughed.

Mirren hardly recognised herself in the mirror. Getting dolled up was not something she'd bothered with before. It was like looking at a stranger in the mirror, but it was the brightness in her eyes with the hope that Jack would be coming home that was lifting her spirits.

If Jack came home she didn't want him to see her in all her old muck and make-do. The other Land Girls would be giving him the eye. 'Eau de Farmyard'; that pong of stale milk, dung and sweat took a bit of stomaching, and getting rid of, but they'd soon got used to it. Everyone competed to have the strongest perfumes, just in case, but all Mirren could manage was lavender water and Lifebuoy soap. She hoped it was enough.

Ben would pick her up in the farm truck and just so it looked a legitimate use of petrol, he'd tether the nanny goat in the back as if she was being taken to the vet. They all did this from time to time, stretching the War-Ag regs a little bit.

As she dressed with care Mirren wished it was Jack escorting her to the dance, but there'd been no letter for a week. She'd lost track of him since his accident and he was vague about his new posting. If only he'd get back for Christmas it would be the best ever, war or no war.

Ben took trouble to brush down his uniform for the dance and polish his boots to a glass finish. He'd washed and shaved, Brylcreemed his fair hair when he found a parting, and brushed his teeth. He didn't want to smell of the farmyard tonight, not when he was escorting Mirren in her best clobber, but he was not in the mood for dancing.

He had heard that his big brother, Bert, was missing. The telegram came a week ago and so far there was nothing else. They were praying he was shot down and captured. So many young men lost on bombing raids ended up as prisoners. It was better than the alternative, but the news was awful and he felt sick whenever he thought of it.

He'd gone straight to Leeds to comfort his mam and dad. They were putting a brave face on things but his mam's eyes were red-rimmed with crying. He'd felt so helpless.

'We have to keep hoping and getting on with the job,' she'd smiled through her tears. 'Thank God you're safe.' There was not one iota of reproach in her voice that he was in a reserved occupation but he could see it in the faces of other town folk, who passed on their condolences at the front door of their villa close to West Park.

When he saw Mirren coming down the grand front staircase in her velvet dress, with her hair half up and down, carrying her dancing shoes and looking like a ripe plum, he forgot his sorrows.

'You scrub up well,' he said, trying not to show how much her appearance stirred him. 'Better wrap up and take yer gumboots. It's right clashy weather outside. There'll be snow before long.'

She looked put out at his words for some reason and gave him a scowl but he bundled her into the passenger seat, shoving his rucksack to one side.

'Any news? How's Auntie Pam?' she asked. 'You must bring them here for Christmas.'

He nodded, not wanting to spoil the evening by thinking of the war.

'You go everywhere with that old thing – has it got your life's savings in it?' she said, starting to fidget with the strap of his canvas bag.

He pushed it onto the floor. He could tell no one that it was his survival kit. If there were a sudden warning, he would down tools, grab it and go into hiding. Inside was all the weaponry for killing: a pistol, a few rounds of ammo, a Fairburn knife, wires, tools, maps, Horlicks tablets, rations to keep him on the go until he went into his secret bunker to await instructions.

They'd done so many rehearsals now: exercises in the dead of night, recces of the camp on the moors, seizing the battery in a mock battle, laying dummy traps on the railway line, living off the land for days on end. It was *Boy's Own* stuff but in deadly earnest. Uncle Tom once caught him for being late and gave him an earful for skiving off but he took it like a man. It would have been treason to betray the truth and reveal anything.

The two of them bumped down the track to Windebank in silence, leaving the truck parked out of sight up the top lane, and tethered Jezebel to the verge to munch around. There were plenty of other revellers with the same idea, with chickens squawking and dogs barking. He could hear the trio warming up and the windows were blacked out, but it was pitch-dark with only a few white lines etched onto the street corners to guide wary travellers.

The church hall had been done up by some of the Home Guard wives; lanterns, storm lamps and candles in jars on windowsills, paper chains and bells hanging from the ceiling. There was a

Christmas tree on the stage where the Jimmy Benson Trio had set up shop; fiddle, drums and piano to give the dance a bit of swing.

Ben looked hopefully to the far end where under cloths was a Jacob's join supper laid out with the usual sausage rolls and pies, bridge rolls full of cold cuts and meat paste, pasties, fruit pies, slices of cake, all portioned out to give everyone a fair share. He was starving just thinking about the supper. There was a licensed bar but little beer to go round, pop and crisps if they were lucky. Some of the lads would be sneaking off back down to The Fleece to top up. Dancing was thirsty work and they'd be here until dawn, if it was a good do.

There were a gaggle of schoolgirls in ankle socks, trying to look grown up. Mirren's friends from the hostel eyed Ben up with interest; the lipstick and rouge brigade, smelling like a chemist's shop. A few village ladies were hovering around the tablecloth to shoo away sneaky fingers.

Ben wasn't much of a dancer: two large left feet in the waltzing, but he could swing around better in the country dances. He spotted some of his platoon lurking in the doorway, eyeing up the talent, and went over to have a chat. He felt safer in male company. When he turned round again, Mirren was tripping the light fantastic with Arnie Blewitt. She did look grand in the lamplight, full of life, her fair hair bouncing after her, neat ankles twisting and turning. She made the other girls look common and over-made-up, he thought.

Halfway through the evening, when the stir was hotting up, he wondered about giving his cousin a twirl. She might be his cousin but he'd hardly known her until he came from Leeds just before war started. Their paths had never crossed much as children, just occasional visits and the escapade when she broke her arm in one of Jack's madcap schemes.

She had looked a right tomboy in her grammar school gear and always had her head stuck in a book when they came to visit. In truth he was a little in awe of her book learning. But, like everyone else, she'd put any career ambitions on hold once war was declared, which made him admire her all the more.

It was about time he told her how much he liked her, but that would sound daft and she'd probably laugh him away. They were mates on the farm, a good team. He wasn't any good at all this romance lark and was in no position to go courting. He didn't fancy making a fool of himself on the dance floor so he hung back, content to let others swing her around the floor.

There was the usual scramble for the supper plates and Ben ended up going back and forth to the kitchen on somebody's orders. It was eleven o'clock before he plucked up courage to ask Mirren for the slow foxtrot, which was a big mistake as it was also a gentleman's 'Excuse me'.

Arnie was shuffling around, polishing the floor with his feet and clinging on to her for dear life so he decided to rescue her, butting in: 'It's my turn now.'

He hadn't realised she was so small. She barely came up to his shoulders. He could smell her newly washed hair and when she smiled up at him he went all wobbly inside. They did a few steps and he trod on her toes.

'Excuse me.' There was a tap on his shoulder and he turned round to see Jack Sowerby smirking at them.

'Jack! Oh, Jack, you made it!' squealed Mirren with such obvious delight that Ben stood back to release her, watching bemused as she hugged Tom's stepson with a little too much enthusiasm for his liking. They glided off together without a backward glance.

So that was how the land lay, he sighed. Ah well, perhaps as well. He backed off to the doorway and pulled out a packet of ciggies to join the lads. That was his last foray onto the dance floor tonight. Once was enough. He needed a smoke and some fresh air.

Mirren had no eyes for any of the other soldiers once Jack was in her arms. He looked so bright and handsome, his dark eyes flashing mischief as they twirled around the floor, dancing and dancing until she was giddy with excitement.

He was home for Christmas, for five whole days. For once, trains had run on time, snow hadn't disrupted the roads, his arm was healed; everything was perfect.

How glad she was to have made that extra effort to glam up. He'd saved her toes from being broken by Ben's size twelves. When you worked alongside someone all day what was there to say to each other except, 'How's Daisy's udders?', 'Have you set that trap for the rats?', 'Did the new lad see to the hen hut roof?' but with Jack there was a whole world of fresh topics. Where was he now? What had he seen? What's on in London?

'I can't believe you're here,' she sighed. 'Why didn't you write? I could have come and met you.'

'And spoil the look on your face when I breezed in? You can never tell with trains and I hitched a lift from Scarperton station. If you'd been waiting and I'd not shown, you'd have a face on you like sore feet. Come on, let's get out of here . . .' he whispered.

'You've brought a bike?'

''Fraid not. It's shanks's pony for a bit until I get another one,' he said as he guided her by the elbow out of the crush. 'Let's pop into The Fleece.'

'It's after hours and you know I don't go in those places,' she said.

'Signed the pledge, have we?'

'I did as a kiddy . . . I just don't fancy the stuff,' she insisted.

'Well, let's walk the slow way home then. We've a lot of catching up to do.'

They climbed the path to Gunnerside Foss and on up to World's End, holding hands. The sky had cleared and stars were dotted right across the sky, making patterns and shapes. The moon was bright but in the distance the searchlights arced over the moors.

They found some shelter out of the wind and Jack whipped off his greatcoat and sat down, holding out his hand. 'Come on, Land Girl. Backs to the land!'

'Stop that!' she snapped, and caught him on the arm and he winced. 'Sorry, is that your bad arm? Is it badly hurt?'

'I'll get worse before this war's over,' he quipped.

'Don't let's talk about the war . . . Let it wait. It's Christmas and you're here,' she sighed, snuggling into his side.

'Is that all the welcome I get?' he laughed, pulling her closer, and she kissed him with a closed mouth.

'That's a little girl's kiss,' he teased. 'Let me show you another way.'

He was kissing her so deeply, forcing open her

mouth to receive deeper longer kisses that sent shivers down her insides. His hands began to feel for her breasts and finger them roughly. Even Mirren knew where this would lead and drew back coyly.

'Not here, not now, Jack,' she whispered. Things were moving too fast and she was afraid.

'When then?' he whispered back. 'You're my girl, my only girl . . . don't you want me to . . . ?'

'I do, but it's damp and cold and I'm frozen. This is my best frock . . . if it gets stained,' she said, knowing they weren't the real reasons she was holding back.

His jibes about Land Girls being 'easy' had gone deep, making her wary of spoiling the romance of his return. She felt a novice and clumsy, not knowing what to do next. There were dangers in letting a lad have his way. One of the girls in the hostel had already been discharged pregnant and in trouble.

'I'd make it right, love. I'd never do anything to get you in trouble, if that's what you're thinking. I'll not force you into anything either. It's just I'll be going away soon and we might not see each other for ages, or ever again. You can't blame me for wanting an early Christmas present,' he said, standing up. 'But you're right. It's a bit parky up here. Funny how we always trek up to World's End . . .'

'Because it's quiet and no one comes here, and

this is where you found me or have you forgotten?' she whispered, thinking of the night in the snow.

The moment had passed and the chill was getting to both of them. Time to plod downwards and towards Cragside.

'We could have got a lift with Ben,' she offered. 'He ran me down to the hall. Have you heard about Bert?'

Jack nodded but said nothing.

She sensed his disappointment hanging unspoken like icicles, cross with herself for being so slow and calculating, but there was a warning light flashing in her eyes and a voice saying: 'Be careful, slow down. There's plenty of time, no rush to fulfil your loving.' Now it felt awkward and her excitement deflated.

'You'll be coming for Christmas? We'll play silly games and do carol singing – you will, won't you?' she asked, desperate to know she was still his special girl.

'Same old Cragside Christmas. Don't worry, Mirren, I'll be there . . . hoping and waiting . . . You're my girl.'

'Am I? You don't mind me being . . . ?' she pleaded, looking him straight in the eye.

'You looked gorgeous tonight. Every man in the hall was jealous. You should have seen Ben's face when I turned up,' Jack laughed. 'You and me're meant for each other.'

She sensed he was no virgin lover, no novice declaring his undying love. He knew what he was doing and how to go about loosening her up, but she couldn't help herself when she was in his arms. Why was it all right for lads to have fun but if a girl experimented she was a slut?

He saw her to the farmhouse door, pecked her on the cheek and walked on up to Scar Head, leaving her feeling mean and silly, confused, excited, nervous and suddenly afraid. She mustn't let Jack down. He was going to fight. He could be killed and he needed comfort. If she didn't give it perhaps someone else would.

If only there was someone she could trust enough to talk this over? Florrie was too close, and family. The girls in the hostel talked about sex all the time but she didn't live in and had no special friend there. Lorna had gone very religious since Freddy died. She would be horrified at this behaviour. The only mate she had was Ben. He was her listening ear but he was the last person she could ever tell about this.

He'd just heard his brother was missing in action. He was going to go home to see his parents again to persuade them to come back to Cragside to cheer them up. Why did this war change everything?

Even Gran was looking peaky, out of breath at the slightest rush. Mirren hated to think Joe and Adey were getting old but there was such a weariness in Gran's eyes when they sat at the peg rugging, a breathless panting as she climbed the stairs. The thought of Gran not being around made her panic. There was so much to learn and so little time.

8

Mirren was determined to put on a good show for the family. The fact that she had never been in charge of the whole Christmas dinner before didn't matter. Gran was not well and confined to bed for the morning so she must see to the goose for the first time, and organise Daisy and Grandpa like troops before battle.

She loved Christmas, the most magical time of the year, even for a farm hand, and with wartime rations it took a palaver of bartering to get enough raisins and muscatels and spices to do the pudding justice. Thankfully there were enough people who couldn't stand dried fruit in the village but wanted fresh eggs or a bit of brawn as a swap.

It was Christmas morning and Jack, who was staying at Scar Head, would be coming to sample her cooking so she must look sharpish and see to all the vegetables. The farmhouse dresser looked so festive and cards were strung up across the beams, the tinsel and holly sat on every ledge, the fire in the big parlour blazing. Now there were just the buckets of potatoes and carrots to peel. Her hands were frozen in the cold water but her heart was singing. Tonight she would be with Jack.

On the cold slab sat one of Uncle Tom's geese ready to be stuffed with Auntie Florrie's home-made forcemeat. What a blowout there was going to be. Daisy was peeling the store apples to make a sauce and there was just Gran's pudding full of grated carrot, nuts and every spare currant to be boiled in the set boiler in the outhouse: so much to think about before they went to chapel.

Daisy was to see to the range and Gran while they were out. The dining table was already prepared with the stiffest of the damask cloths, set with china and napkins. All the cutlery sparkled, and in the centre was a cardboard and plaster sleigh full of holly and the first Christmas roses, that grew in the old croft under the wall. There were home-made crackers with no bangers inside so everyone had to shout as they pulled and pretend they were the real ones.

Mirren thought she ought to stay home but it was always the tradition to go to chapel and support the singing. Perhaps Jack would turn up with Tom and Florrie but if he had any sense he would lie and make the most of the morning. She would go and pray for forgiveness for what she was about to do tonight given half a chance!

Once there, her mind was racing, anticipating lying in Jack's arms, when she was jolted awake by Ben singing the next Christmas carol, drowning out these fantasies with his rich deep voice. If only it was Jack standing by her side.

Not even Hitler could spoil this Christmas, she thought, with his bombs and threats, not here at least where the family was gathered together. Only Uncle Wes and Auntie Pam were absent – and Bert, of course. If Gran could come down for the meal then everything would be as it always was for a few hours.

'I'm ready for that goose,' said Uncle Tom on the way home, looking at his fob watch on a chain. 'Singing and a good sermon gives me a grand appetite.'

Too long a sermon gave Mirren a sore bum on the hard chapel benches with sit-up backs, but the minister had kept it short for once, and she needed to be getting back to see to the trimmings. Daisy was reliable but had to be told to do things. Perhaps she should have stayed at home after all.

There was a delicious aroma when they opened the back door. 'Oh, joy in the morning!' said Grandpa. 'I'll have to loosen my belt to do justice to all your efforts.'

'Nice not to have to cook for a change,' whispered Auntie Florrie, unpinning her best felt hat and making for the lobby. 'I'll go and see to Gran and help her dress. I see our Jack's arrived at last,' she smiled, looking out of the window at her son standing by the wall smoking a cigarette.

'I'll just see to the bird,' Mirren croaked, trying not to blush, opening the oven door gingerly to check on the roasting fowl.

Everyone had drifted into the kitchen towards the delicious smell. Ben went to fetch the ginger beer jar from the cold larder shelf, when there was an explosion of smoke and fat as the goose shot across the kitchen like a cannonball, setting everyone back on their heels. Quick as a flash Ben pulled Mirren away from the lava of fat. Auntie Florrie took one look at the mess and screamed as the hot fat bubbled over the flat tin onto the flag floor and Tom's glass of ginger beer spilled and ignited the fat into flames.

'I thowt this house was supposed to be teetotal.' He looked down with surprise. It was Ben who whipped up the rag rug and dowsed the flame.

It was like a flash flood all right, Mirren just standing there yelling, 'The goose, my poor goose! The dinner's ruined!' She looked round the room in horror.

'Never mind the goose, love, we could've all been drowned in fat and done to a turn,' laughed Uncle Tom. 'Roasted in that avalanche.'

'I'm so sorry!' Mirren was in tears.

'Didn't Daisy think to drain off some of the fat out of the tin?' whispered Auntie Florrie.

'She didn't say,' said Daisy looking woebegone at Mirren.

'Still, Adey's floors are spotless, we can eat off them later,' chuckled Ben, seeing the funny side of it. But Mirren was shaking her head, feeling stupid and shamed in front of the family.

'You've cooked your goose and no mistake,' added Jack, putting his arm round her. Everyone was smiling and laughing as if it was all some big joke not a humiliating disaster.

'No one's been injured. All's not lost, love,' said Grandpa Joe. 'Wait until Adey hears this. It'll cheer her up no end.'

Mirren rushed out into the yard, wanting to cry, taking in great gulps of air to steady her fury. How could they laugh at this disaster?

'Come back in,' shouted Auntie Florrie. 'We've called out the lifeboat to rescue us . . . You did well to get it all done on time. Don't get in a maddle on Christmas Day. If we get on us pinnies when the fat's cooled down, we can let the bird rest a while and no harm done.'

She was only trying to help but Mirren wailed, 'What about the veg? I can't get at them.'

'Dinner will be a little late this year,' said Jack, fanning the flames of Mirren's fury. 'I'm sure Mam can find a few bits to keep the wolf from the door.

We'll all muck in and make it happen, you'll see. Don't take on, it's only a bird!'

Mirren sniffed back her shame, not seeing the funny side at all. The floor was like a skating rink as they crouched down to scrape off the goose fat. What a waste of precious medicine; all those jars of liniment and chest rub piled into a lump of gunge.

As if reading her thoughts, Florrie smiled. 'Don't worry, we can render it down again.'

The goose was laid to rest on top of the range and soon the veg were ready for the table. Everyone was full of elderberry cordial, pink-faced and making merry. Gran struggled downstairs to see what the fuss was about and had a good laugh too, which was the best medicine of all even if it was at Mirren's expense.

'She didn't say,' Daisy kept repeating to anyone who'd hear, but they were all too busy enjoying themselves to criticise.

Then Tom, Jack, Ben and Grandpa put on a floor show in their pinnies, prancing about.

'You've heard about the Dying Swan,' said Jack. 'This is the dancing goose.'

The sight of them fooling around made Mirren's lips quiver and burst into a smile.

'That's better. No tears on Christmas Day.'

The goose was rich and succulent despite its strange dance across the floor and everyone fell on it with gusto. Adey's Christmas pudding was up to scratch and her Christmas cake tasty, despite being a little thin on fruit this year. Uncle Tom did his usual trick of producing a ten-bob note from his mouth and pretending to choke on it.

Soon the dining table was covered in crumbs and stains and bits of cracker and silly hats, and the old folk retired to their little snug to snooze away what was left of the afternoon in peace.

Then it was time for the next lot of company to arrive, visiting farmers and their families for a party singsong and a game or two of cards. The tale of the dancing goose was told over and over again as the women cleared away the debris to start again on preparing supper. All the tensions of the day were drifting away.

It was the usual Christmas ritual: games and a day out of time, but there was still the stock to see to. Thankfully it was the men's turn to see to them while the women prepared a supper fit for the King: rounds of cheeses, trifle with real cream topping, Christmas spice bread, cakes and cold meat with bowls of potato salad, chutney, beetroot pickle.

No one had come empty-handed. The day was going well and it was not over yet.

Mirren's eyes followed Jack around the room. It was as if some invisible thread was spinning a web around them, a strange attraction of heat and body, a feeling she had never experienced before of anticipation, an aching in her loins to reach out and touch the fine curve of his cheek, to bury his head in her breasts; a spark of sudden aware-ness that he felt the same pull of souls. Something was fizzing inside her like bubbling pop. In the bustle of busyness, toing and froing with the other women, something magical was stirring, so warm and wonderful she could hardly breathe. It separated her off from the rest of the noise and laughter. She was lost in a whirlpool of desire. All she wanted was to fall onto the rag rug into his arms and for everyone to go away so she could make the most of him. She felt like a bitch on heat.

She fingered her dress. The warm deep cherry velvet echoed her mood, shaped her body, showing off her neat waist and full bust. She might be built square but everything was in proportion. Someone wound up the old gramophone and familiar tunes took on a whole new meaning. She wanted to seal all these precious moments in a jar to take out in the long months ahead.

Jack took her by the hand and whirled her around the room until she was dizzy. She could feel his breath, and the scent of him was sweet to her nostrils. He had lost that ingrained smell of hay and farm. They glanced up at each other and smiled, a brief exchange of eyes and meanings.

159

Tonight we'll be as one. This is where I belong, she sighed, feeling the touch of his fingers like electricity surging through her body. She'd never felt this urgency before. This was no gentle courtship. This was raw naked hunger. She sensed the stirring in his body and drew back. There was more on the boil than the kettle!

If only this was Hollywood, he could be Rhett to her Scarlett, Heathcliff to her Cathy, Maxim de Winter to her Rebecca, but this was Yorkshire and romance was thin on the ground except at the Plaza Picture House in Scarperton. She sometimes skived off with the Land Girls to the afternoon matinée on market day, swooning at the fancy costumes and handsome heroes. Now she had one of her very own.

Anyone could see they were smitten, and Florrie didn't seem to mind. Jack was family but not a blood relative. Gran was too poorly to notice much these days.

It was almost a relief when everyone started to make noises about going home but not before another serving of supper and toffees. Coupons and rations were forgotten for the day. Belts were loosened, ties undone, corsets unhooked when Cragside was having a blowout. Neighbours, children, soldiers on leave squashed together for one final singsong.

Jack saved Mirren a place on the floor as

Grandpa began his ghostly monologue about the mysterious barghest, the white hound of the dale, omen of death and doom, and one of his sightings. As they crouched together she felt his hand reach out and squeeze hers tightly, his fingers caressed the inside of her palm so gently she felt herself flush with pleasure. If he had said, let's slip away now and go to your bed, rip off our clothes and make love all night long, she would have risen, meek as a lamb and done his bidding, not caring what anyone thought.

His hand brushed her thigh lightly and she was transfixed by the sensation. It was now or never. They might never get another evening together but how was it going to happen if he went back to Scar Head?

By the time everyone lingered and chatted, it was time to take Gran up to bed and help her undress. Grandpa was tired and Jack came up with the perfect solution.

'You have a lie-in in the morning,' he said to the old man. 'I'll kip down with Ben for the night and see to some chores then. I'm good at taking orders,' he smiled, winking at her.

Nothing more was said, just one brief exchange of nods as they parted at the top of the landing but she knew that for the first time in her life she would not be sleeping alone.

Lying in bed with not one wink of sleep in her,

she waited for the house to go quiet. She had checked that Ben had finished the rounds of the yard, settled the dogs. She could hear Daisy banking up the fire, climbing the stairs to her bedroom above. She waited and waited until she was forced to rise and put on her dressing gown and make for the parlour, but it was in darkness too. She climbed back up the stairs with a sickening lump in her throat. She had got it all wrong. She didn't put the light back on and sighed as she flung herself on the bed.

'Ouch!' whispered a voice. 'You weigh a ton!'

'What took you so long?' she said, not quite believing he was here at last. Her arms were around him in a second and she cradled him tight.

'I've come for my Christmas present,' he whispered. 'Hope I'm not too late?'

There was no time to reply, for he stopped her mouth with his kisses. There was no fear in how their bodies crushed together, strained to express all they felt, and what was happening was as natural as talking and breathing. Why waste precious moments in words when bodies can do such delicious things to each other?

There was no time for coyness, only the desperate seizing of the moment. All Mirren's scruples vanished in the primitive surge to mate and surrender.

Jack's breath smelled of whisky and cigarettes,

162

a heady brew. She melted under his touch as his fingers sought out her nipples and flicked them into life. His hands moved downwards until she felt her blood turn into treacle. As he entered her she felt a searing pain and it was hard not to cry out. As he moved forwards and backwards deeper into her, the soreness fell away and then he withdrew and it was all over before she had begun to settle down and enjoy herself. There was so much to learn.

'I've not taken any risks, love,' he whispered. 'I hope I didn't hurt you too much but it'll get better with practice when we're wed.'

She pretended to hit him. 'Is that a proposal?' she said, her heart leaping at his words.

'I suppose it is.'

How could something so wonderful be rationed to only those with wedding rings, she mused. Thank goodness lovemaking wasn't on coupons. They'd have used up a whole year's worth in one night, but who cared? Heaven knew when they would get some again but the thought of a honeymoon kept her awake all night.

Ben lay awake, seething. Jack's camp bed was empty and he knew where he was and he was furious, jealousy and envy all mixed up. How dare Jack come home and ruin everything with his fancy talk? He'd seen them eyeing each other up all night. He was furious with Mirren for falling for such obvious charm.

He lay in the darkness, powerless, trying not to think what was going on down the corridor. What had Jack got that he hadn't? Easy to answer that, he mused. Florrie's son had a way with girls, a confidence and patter, but he was also a man's man and could drink any of them under the table and still seem sober. He made Ben feel like a clodhopper, a homespun bumpkin with two left feet.

His mind was raging with scenarios of murderous revenge: sabotaging Jack's motor bike brake cable, ambushing him in the dark – jealous fantasies that shocked him. It was Christmas and goodwill to all men was the order of the day. Mirren had made her choice and it was none of his business.

In the early hours, Jack crept back into the room and Ben shone his torch in his face. 'Where the hell have you been?'

'None of your bloody business.'

'If you're just messing about with our Mirren . . .'

'What's it to you? She's your cousin, remember.'

'She's one of the best and deserves to be treated right. If you get her into trouble, I'll kill you,' Ben snapped.

'You'll do what? You and whose army? What do you know about girls? You're too scared to lay a finger on any of them!' Jack was mocking him.

'Shut it!' Ben leaped out of bed and pinned Jack by the neck. 'You'd better be marrying her or you'll have me to answer to. Don't go breaking her heart. I heard about you and Doris Hargrave, last summer. She went to pot when you dumped her. Tongues wag in a small village.'

'Get off me, Lanky . . . That was ages ago, nothing to do with how I feel about Mirren.' Jack shrugged and smirked, which only made things worse.

Ben grabbed him and shoved him against the door in a stranglehold. 'I mean every word. If you so much as—'

'Hold yer sweat. What's got into you, the parsnip wine? You never could hold your liquor. Don't jump the gun. As a matter of fact I've just popped the question and she's said, yes . . . so shut up. Needless to say I'll not be asking you to be best man.'

'That's all right then,' said Ben, releasing his hold, feeling sick at this news. 'I only want what's best for her.'

'You want her for yourself but I got in there first,' Jack laughed. There was a cruel glint in his eye. 'I don't need to explain, do I? First come, first served, so keep your filthy paws off her.'

'I don't think of her like that,' Ben replied.

'You're no man if you don't. Believe me, she's hot stuff under the sheets,' came the boast.

'Oh, shut the fuck up!' Ben snapped. This was not the old Jack he used to muck about with as a lad. He'd always been easy-going. There was a cold edge to his tongue now, a cruel ruthless streak Ben had never seen on display before and he was worried.

'Go screw yourself, boyo!' Jack taunted.

Ben grabbed a blanket and took himself down to kip by the hearth. He didn't want to be in the same room as Jack. His homecoming had spoiled everything and Ben wished he'd gone back to Leeds. He kept thinking about Bert, lying dead, broken somewhere, or caged up in a camp. The sofa was too small for him but this discomfort was nothing to what his brother would be suffering out there if he was still alive. It was a long restless night.

'I've got some good news. Jack and me are thinking of getting wed soon,' Mirren announced the next day as she sat perched on Gran's bed.

All the Christmas excitement had been too much for Adey and she was staying in bed for the day under strict orders not to budge.

'We want to do it quickly in case he's sent abroad soon.'

There was silence for a second as the news sank in. Gran looked at Joe and back at Mirren. 'Eeh, you've caught us on the hop there. I allus thought it'd be young . . . Are you sure? Jack Sowerby . . . Florrie'll be chuffed but it's a big step to take, lass.'

'I've known him since I was eight. We're well suited.' Mirren was surprised that Gran wasn't more excited.

'But we thought you were staying on the farm like Ben for the duration,' said Grandpa.

'What's that got to do with it?' she said, puzzled. 'Who said anything about leaving the farm? I'll be going nowhere. I'm still a Land Girl and there's a war on. It's going to make no difference while Jack's away.'

'Once the war's over, Jack'll want to be making tracks to better himself. You know what Kerrs are like. He'll never make a farmer and you'll be going with him then,' croaked Gran, her sharp grey eyes piercing into Mirren's.

'We'll see when the time comes. Anyway, that's a long way off. People change their plans. I thought you'd be pleased,' Mirren added. It was not quite the joyous reaction she had hoped for.

'As long as you're sure, love. We just want you to be happy. If Jack is Mister Right who are we to gainsay it? Marriage takes two and Jack's always been a wild 'un. Florrie will tell you that. I reckon it was not having a dad around when he was a kiddy. I allus remember him jumping off the foss straight down into that water, a right little devil with no sense of danger.'

'That's not his fault. I didn't have a mother,' Mirren snapped.

'I know, but happen a wedding will help him find his roots. No one can say you aren't a solid and sensible girl. Where would we be without you now?' said Gran, stretching out her hand. 'Congratulations! We were blessed the day the Lord brought you to our door; a second chance to put things right with Ellie. Love lists where it wills, lass, we know that,' she sighed, looking towards her husband.

'Don't worry, I'm not Mam or Dad. No hole-in-the-corner wedding for me. War or no war, I've set my heart on him and a proper chapel do. He'll make us proud no matter what the future brings.'

'Then we'll have to get our skates on and get cracking. A real chapel do means a choir, sit-down breakfast in the barn, if needs be. Let no one say the Yewells don't know how to put on a show, but it'll all have to be above board, no under-the-counter dealings or any alcohol. We're not footing the bill for Satan's brew.' Gran sat up already looking brighter.

'That's more like it. Don't you worry, I'll see to it all. Ben can help me. You just get yourself fit again. A wedding is just what we all need to cheer us up!'

Ben couldn't believe Mirren would go ahead with marrying that scumbag. Jack didn't love Mirren as a man should with all his heart and soul. It was all sex. He wanted her body to keep him warm when he came home on leave. He'd make promises he'd never keep. It wasn't in his nature.

Jack was not cut out for country life. He'd been one of the first to volunteer to see the world. Sooner or later he'd take his cousin far away from everyone she loved here, far from them into towns and cities. Then he'd get bored with her and drink too much. Mirren deserved better.

Now, if it were him going down the aisle with her he'd get that little house she loved so much shipshape, reroofed and made spick and span, new windows and floorboards, a lick of distemper. He'd build her a kitchen with cupboards and they could live on the tops content. Only it wasn't him she wanted.

Not once had she looked in his direction with the sort of cow eyes Lorna Dinsdale was making at him when she called. Lorna was always hanging on his every word and lingering in the yard, holding him up from his jobs. Trouble was, when he looked at her there was no spark. It was a shame because she was a nice enough lass, nice figure, shiny hair and pleasant voice, and she'd just lost her brother in the RAF.

You don't choose who you love, he thought, stretching his long legs under the table, disturbing the house dog who rested her head in his lap. Pity!

It was time to look over Mirren's list. She might

not love him but she knew how to make him jump to her bidding.

Mirren could hardly believe how quickly they could organise a wedding once the family got used to the idea. If Jack was going to go abroad it was better that they spent some private time together before he went, they argued. Everyone could see they were in love.

Auntie Florrie was a bit subdued at first, but then got into the swing of the arrangements in the time-honoured place of her own mother. Granny was failing but was determined to attend the wedding in the chapel on 21 March: the first day of spring.

Finding enough coupons to buy a wedding dress was out of the question so Mirren found a dress-maker in Scarperton who ran her up a lovely two-piece dress and jacket in pale turquoise wool crepe. She found a sharp black hat with a feather in the side and matching gloves and shoes. The girls in the hostel gave her some dyed parachute silk to make underwear and she felt like a princess in all her finery.

Only Ben ignored all the fuss as if it wasn't happening, and every time she asked what was the matter, all he'd say was, 'Are you sure you're doing the right thing? What's the rush?' which was no help at all.

Mirren assumed his indifference was because he thought she'd have to give up her work, but there was no possibility of her leaving Cragside, nor did she want to with Gran in such bad health.

The day dawned fine for a change; the first day of spring in all its glory. Outside, the daffodils were nestling in the shelter of the stone walls, the tired snowdrops flopping and the sky set fair for the day.

Mirren lay in bed gazing up at the ceiling. As from today she'd be Mrs Jack Sowerby, a proper married woman with a husband in the Forces. She was the envy of all the Land Girls, who took great delight in plying her with lurid details of what to expect on her wedding night. She'd sat wide-eyed, looking all innocence. It was nobody else's business what they'd already been up to in bed.

Daisy helped her get dressed, fussing over the angle of her hat so it showed off her new shorter hairstyle. There was a small posy of spring flowers to carry and all the guests were given buttonholes and sprays, which Mirren and Daisy had sat up half the night putting together.

Yesterday Florrie, Daisy and Mirren set out the trestle tables with white starched linen cloths in the Chapel Hall for a stand-up buffet. No one was allowed to sit down to eat in case there was an air raid! Gran was overwhelmed with gifts of ham and pies and home baking. The wedding cake was a plain sponge sandwiched together with jam and frosted over with butter cream. It was the best they could do at short notice. Mirren was going to give Jack an old family signet ring and she was making do with a second-hand wedding band as gold was scarce.

This upset Florrie for some reason. 'I hope you're not tempting fate,' she whispered. 'It ought to be a new one. You haven't even got an engagement ring.'

'There is a war on,' snapped Mirren, tired with all the preparations. What did it matter if someone had already got some joy out of the ring? It was the best Mr Soames, the jeweller, could offer at short notice.

She drove down to Windebank in Mr Bennett's ambulance saloon cum taxi with Grandpa looking dapper in his preaching suit and Gran with her fox fur tippet and best hat. Lorna was the bridesmaid, wearing a borrowed tweed coat and hat and a new dress underneath. It wasn't the most stylish wedding party in the dale but it was going to be one of the happiest.

It was a lovely family wedding. Jack brought a soldier friend, Eddie Minshall, to be his best man. Uncle Wes and Auntie Pam came from Leeds. They had heard that Bert was captured and safe at long last. Ben looked splendid in his Home Guard uniform, towering over everyone with a face like thunder. The reception went without a hitch until some of Jack's mates got a little tipsy by tripping over to The Fleece to top him up. Grandpa was on his feet to toast the couple with elderberry cordial.

'Raise your glasses to this brave couple setting out on the most exciting journey of their lives. May the Lord grant them the blessing of a happy hearth and the patter of tiny feet in due course. May He bring our Jack safely through the dangers to come.' He turned then to Gran with a wink. 'If they're as happy as we've been these fifty years, I shall be content, eh, Mother?'

Mirren thought her heart would burst with joy and love. All she loved were sitting around them wishing them well. If only Paddy and Ellie, her parents, were here to share this precious moment . . . When she turned towards Jack she thought her heart would burst with pride. We're so lucky, she smiled to herself. Soon it would be time to toss her bouquet, say her goodbyes and suffer the blizzard of confetti when they went to catch the train up to the Lake District for three nights in a hotel by the shores of Lake Windermere.

She tried to hold on to every second of those magical days, knowing that in the months and years to come it would be the one precious unsullied time when they lay in bed all morning, walked in the hills in the afternoon to see the famous daffodils, and then dining by the lake.

Jack was gentle with his lovemaking and took her slowly, waiting at first, but she could never quite catch him up. There was an art to this malarkey that neither of them had quite got the hang of yet, but it was wonderful to be lying in his arms so close. In that chilly hotel bedroom there was such a heat and energy when they came together, and for those few nights the war went away.

Mirren wished she could stop the clocks and that they wouldn't have to separate at Carnforth station, but Jack was due to report to a base in Scotland for yet more hush-hush training. Who knew when they would meet again?

Once back at Cragside it was as if it was all some dream. The cows didn't know she was married, or the sheep, which were soon due to lamb. By April she knew she mustn't go near them for a while. Ben would have to see to them and she would concentrate on the dairy for a while. He was furious at her desertion and wanted to know why.

'Can't you guess? An expectant woman doesn't risk being close to the lambs just in case . . .' she replied, not able to look him in the face.

Auntie Florrie was ecstatic and got out her knitting needles. It was all round Windebank in hours that there'd be a Christmas baby at Cragside.

In the months that followed Mirren's whole life was turned upside down. Jack sailed to somewhere hot and dry. Gran was looking tired.

Uncle Tom and Ben took over the farm, with Mirren and another farm hand trying to salvage the oats and barley that were flattened by storms. The stooks flopped over and wouldn't ripen off. All that effort for a poor yield, just as Grandpa had said, and they all bemoaned the waste of prime pasture.

Suddenly she felt very alone. New life was growing inside her and she ought to be excited but Jack was so far away and his letters were few and far between. He took the news of their honeymoon baby with delight but insisted that there were to be no more family names; no Jacks or Miriams, Reubens or Toms.

'No disrespect, Mirren, but it's time for a change. Our baby will have a modern name, one all of its own.'

She knew the Yewells would be disappointed as there was a tradition in the family to name the first girl Miriam. The old carved box, handed down from Miriam to Miriam, was in her possession but Jack, being a stepson, wanted to start traditions all of his own.

These thoughts gave her hope that in years to come they could live out their lives up here with their children and watch them grow and prosper once this wretched war was over. Until that joyful day, she would light the home fires, pray for his safe return and do all she could to keep the farm prospering.

9

Ben caught Gran in the wash house struggling to turn the mangle and fighting for breath. 'You shouldn't be doing that, you've not been well. Mirren and Daisy can do it later . . .'

'I'm not wasting a good dry breeze. Here, peg these out for me while I find one of them pills the quack gave me. Good money after bad, I reckon. They don't seem to be doing me any good,' she muttered.

'Shall I get Grandpa?' Ben was anxious. Her face was ashen.

'He's down the far end at Cowside.'

'I'll send for the doctor . . .'

'You'll do no such thing. I've had worse than this in the night. Just leave me be, son, and see to your chores,' came the order, but the voice was weak.

'No I won't. You'll just do as you're told for once and get up those stairs to bed if I have to carry you myself. Rest is what you need.' He towered over her with a steely look in his eye.

'If you put me up there I'll never get out of it,' she whispered.

'Nonsense, a good sleep and you'll be fine.'

'I'll be getting that right enough, the long sleep . . . Now promise me you'll see the farm right, and Mirren and the babby. I'm relying on you to hold the fort until Jack comes back . . . if he comes back,' she muttered as they inched their way slowly up the stairs.

'What do you mean?'

'I've got a bad feeling about it . . . just a twinge now and then. It's not going to be easy for them love birds. Promise me you'll lend a hand. She's so like her mam, falling for a roving bloke, it's worried me.'

Ben flushed, sensing her meaning but not knowing how to respond. Why was Gran spilling all this out now?

'I'll do what I can but you'll be fine, just you wait and see.'

'No I won't see, Ben, that's the trouble, I'm fagged out. I've tried to keep going but the spirit's willing and the flesh's weak. It's time I was taken home . . .' she sighed and flopped onto the bed.

'Don't talk like that, Gran. Come on, let me get those shoes off. Then I'm calling Grandpa and the doc. He's a right to know . . .'

The days all melded into one after that as they tiptoed round her bed, one by one, trying not to tire her. Dr Murray shook his head. 'She's a stubborn old mule but it's beaten her this time and she knows it . . . I told her to rest up.'

Grandpa Joe sat patting her hand, not wanting to leave the room. Daisy brought up endless cups of weak tea that no one could drink. Tom, Ben, Florrie and the yard boys kept the farm going while Mirren walked down to Windebank to send a telegram for Ben's parents to get on a train fast.

'I can't believe she's going to leave us,' sobbed Mirren. 'She won't see our baby. It's not fair, and Jack far away.' She flung herself into Ben's arms unabashed and he smelled the farmyard in her hair, the earth on her dungarees, felt the bump she was carrying, and he held her gently for fear of spoiling the moment.

'We'll manage, all of us, and Florrie will help you. It's Grandpa who'll need minding. They've been wed for over fifty years. He looks so lost, just standing staring up at the hills. I've never seen him so yonderly.'

'I can't let her go, Ben, I'm not ready to let her go,' Mirren wept.

'We can't stop her, love. She's tired out and it's her time. She wants to go to sleep and we must say goodbye as best we can and she knows you'll take over her role. You'll be champion. Remember

179

what she used to say: the eye of the mistress is worth two of her hands. She's taught you well and you'll carry on just as she carried on when Joe's mother died.'

'How can I follow her?' Mirren looked up and he so wanted to kiss away the tears and fought his demons to stay calm. She relaxed in his arms and he felt like choking with joy.

'You will do right by Cragside – we both will. We'll see it through and make her proud of us. The world's a sadder place for Gran going but we'll manage somehow,' he said, and looked out of the window. The sky was darkening and soon it would rain. Time to be up and doing. Farms wait for no one.

Mirren sat holding Gran's bony hand. How quickly she had shrunk into the bed, but she was peaceful, half awake and then fading. She lifted the birdlike claw with its tissuey skin and marvelled.

This was a hand that had laid fires at dawn, swept floors, scoured pots, a hand that turned the hind quarters of a lamb in the womb, planted crops, pickled onions, plucked goose feathers, wrung the neck of hens, rubbed saltpetre on beef until her skin was raw. This hand had soothed beasts and bairns alike, grasped the reins of a bolting horse, steered wheels through blizzards, whipped up the best of cream sponge cakes and the lightest Yorkshire puddings in the district, and now this hand was still. It had done its last job, gently plucking at the bedclothes, which Florrie said was a sign that the end was nigh.

How can I let you go? Who will care for me as you have done? She felt the baby turn and put her hands on her own belly. Please God I live to be a good mother myself.

In that second of her distraction, Grandpa cried, 'She's gone, she's passed over to her eternal reward.' They all bowed their heads and Daisy opened the window to let her soul fly free out onto the hills.

Mirren felt the chill of autumn whisk around the room. The women left Wes and Tom and their father alone. Gran's day was done.

Ben watched his cousin get slower and slower, more cumbersome, her swollen belly marked out on her apron, rubbing against flour and coal. He watched her waiting for the postman, only to be disappointed when news didn't come.

He saw her absentmindedly setting a place at the table for Gran, only to whip it away with tears in her eyes. They sat glued to the wireless with its one precious battery, waiting for weather and news. Sometimes she sat in the big parlour at the piano, fingering the same tune over and over again and then banging down the lid in frustration.

They had their first batch of evacuees, a private

arrangement. The family came for safety into the country and the husband came at the weekend to visit them when he could. They were polite enough when he was around, but the mother spoiled them and they ran riot in the farm, teasing the dogs and leaving gates open, tormenting the chickens until Ben yelled at her to keep them in check. The mother had no discipline.

If this was what it would be like with a kid around the place . . . but no, Mirren would not let her baby grow up like this lot.

She was too busy being in love with the idea of being the farmer's wife, a married lady and mother-to-be, lost in a world of her own that excluded him.

Perhaps it was time to spend longer out of her way at The Fleece, take out one of the Land Girls or even Lorna Dinsdale, anything to get away from her.

They were busy harvesting the last of the vegetables. Mirren and Daisy were pickling onions and crying tears into the bowl. Mirren's legs were aching with standing and it was time for a break. Grandpa had brought in a sack of spuds from their veg plot. He had aged in the past months and got so thin.

'I'll just go and see to my sermon for Sunday,' he shouted. 'I'm preaching at Gunnerside Chapel

Harvest Festival and they like a bit of hellfire there but they'll get the usual "plough the fields and scatter the good seed". I reckon it's the carrot that shoves the donkey, not the stick – or happen both,' he laughed. 'Praise goes a long way further than punishment. I'm softening in my old age. I used to be all rant and now I prefer a gentler way. I'm learning sense in me old age.'

'You go ahead and I'll bring you your tea when it's mashed. You look done in,' said Mirren, ready to sit down herself.

'My, it's warm for the time of year. Yer gran loved the back end. I can't believe she's been taken,' he said, wiping his brow.

'I know, but she's here in spirit, making sure I don't overboil the jam, just behind my shoulder sometimes. I can hear her voice: "Now think on, Miriam, keep yer mind on t'job." They both laughed and Mirren turned back to the cooking range.

Somehow the tea got stewed and it was nearly five o'clock when she took in his favourite slice of ginger wodge. He was sitting at his desk, looking out the window with a beam on his face. Mirren called his name and reached out so as not to startle him but his eyes were glazed and his hand was already cold.

How could they be sad that within months those two had found each other again? The whole dale turned out to pack the chapel and schoolroom to sing praise to Joseph Yewell.

'They don't make 'em like that any more,' said the minister.

'Behind a man like that was some hell of a woman,' said another to Mirren with a wink. 'Adey was a stickler but she had a heart of gold.'

'I know,' she said through her tears. To have known their love was the biggest gift of all, not the grand farmhouse or the beautiful scenery. It was love that mattered and she prayed that she and Jack would find that steady love when he came back to her and their little one. Her time couldn't come soon enough now.

10

December 1941

'I think you're mad to be going out in that state,' yelled Ben from the back door. He'd finished the milking for her now that she was too big to bend. Mirren was determined to get to the rehearsal down in the village. It was the last one before the concert on Saturday. She wanted to go out while she still had the freedom. Soon the kitchen would be full of nappy buckets and bibs, all the paraphernalia of a new baby in the house.

'It won't happen tonight,' she yelled back. 'The midwife's called in and felt around.' Mirren was in no mood to be cooped up like a pregnant sow or listen to another of Ben's lectures.

How easily had she fallen with this baby, but the terrible thing was now she was getting nervous and wished Jack was close by. He was in North Africa and heaven knew when they'd be together again. Like so many couples separated by this war, it was

185

time to keep busy and not fret. Jack wrote hoping for a son and kept nagging her to take care, convinced they were about to sire the next captain of Yorkshire County Cricket team. His letters were always a precious distraction. When they were delayed her blood pressure went sky high with worry.

All that mattered was that the baby was healthy. Boy or girl, it would be a reminder of Jack. It was taking her all her time now to do her chores, lumbering as best she could, like a beached whale, waiting for the waters to break. But not tonight, she hoped, because she needed a good sing.

Rehearsals for *Messiah* were the one chance to open her lungs and let all the emotion out, all the worry, the uncertainty. There was something in that music that swelled her ribs with pride, stirring her uneasy soul, giving her some peace from this turmoil of eternal worry about Jack. Worry stalked her night and day; always at the back of her mind was the terrible fear of how she'd cope if he didn't come home. Tonight she was going out, baby or not. It could jolly well wait its turn.

There was a part of her that wished the lump would stay put and melt away somehow, but Tom and Florrie were that excited. She'd tried for a baby for years but to no avail. It was going to have the finest layette in the district.

Once he had got used to the idea even Ben fussed over her like a mother hen. It was quite touching, him treating her as if she were one of his pedigree ewes, one of his best breeding stock, which, she supposed, in a funny sort of way she was. The family were looking to her to continue the bloodline. The first of the few so far, she feared.

Poor Bert was going nowhere, and Ben was hopeless. She'd set him up with dates at the hostel, lovely girls interested in farming, perfect farmer's wife material, but he took them out and then nothing. He could be so stubborn. It wasn't fair to them to be mucked around. Then she recalled how his Uncle Tom was a late starter. Perhaps Ben was another slow burner and it ran in families.

There was no one in whom she could trust to confide her growing fear of giving birth. Everyone seemed to assume, being a farmer, she knew the score. She'd seen enough to know things could go wrong: calves got stuck in the womb and needed rope to be pulled out; lambs needed turning and her hands were too big sometimes to do the job. What if the bump didn't budge?

Perhaps wartime was not the right time to bring a bairn into the world. No one knew the depths of her fear and not having a mother was a real burden to her. Auntie Florrie did her best to help her but she was worried about her son too.

I should have thought of all this when Jack and I were on our honeymoon, she mused to herself. The decision was out of her hands now.

If only it was not the Christmas season, when the post was full of letters and parcels and cards from friends. There was one letter and photo from Jack. How she had pored over every word, giving it pride of place on the mantelpiece. If only she could tell him how she was feeling, but by the time he'd get her news the baby would have arrived.

'I hope you know what yer doing, going out on a night like this,' said Ben, watching her putting on her coat that gaped in the middle over her bump. 'It's a cold night and happen there's frost on the tarmac. I don't want you driving on ice in the dark. I'll give you a lift. If you must go, stay at Peggy's in the village for the night. She'll see you right, but why you want to go gadding in the middle of winter . . . What's wrong with your own fireside?' he said, his blue, blue eyes piercing her own.

Why was he so hostile? What she did was none of his business. They used to be friends but now they snapped and snarled at each other and she didn't know why. Sometimes she couldn't look him straight in the face for fear he would see how angry and hurt she was by his attitude. It was all to do with Jack somehow. He was making it plain he didn't rate him much as a husband and that got her all worked up.

'There'll be plenty of nights by the fire when winter sets in and I've a bairn at my breast so I'm letting myself run in the meadows while I can. It's only one night,' she snapped.

'We'll be that worried,' Uncle Tom added, supping tea at the kitchen table, and she loved him for it. 'Do as Ben says and stay overnight.'

'Then I'll take a pigeon in a basket and let it out with a message in the morning, if that'll set yer mind at rest,' she said, patting her bump. 'This one's in no hurry to come, I tell you. It's a lazy lump and doesn't kick much.'

There was no answering that one since they had no telephone and it was their usual way of communicating when someone left the dale. Pigeon post, they called it.

Messiah night was the one time she could be assured of a bit of female company, a bit of a crack along the line of altos as they waited for the others to arrive. Hilda Thursby, as she now was, and Lorna would both be there. It was a combined choir of all the village chapels in the district, much famed in the area for its rendition of the 'Hallelujah Chorus'.

Why was it that *Messiah* was never sung, it was always rendered, she mused, like plaster on walls? Every year, Handel's oratorio made its appearance in the first weeks of December and somewhere throughout Yorkshire there must be a rendering of *Messiah* every night of the week. Most of the singers knew it off by heart for they went from chapel to chapel to help out.

As she sat in the pew waiting for the choirmaster to gather up his baton, the soloists to limber up, she felt the wooden seat digging into her back. She had brought a cushion but that didn't seem to be doing the trick. They stood to sing, and what a blessed relief. It had been a jostling ride down into Windebank that night and now she was paying for it.

It was one of those stop-start rehearsals that never seem to get going. Everything was wrong: the basses were late with their entry, the sopranos were out of tune, but looking at the ages of some of them it was not surprising. They kept parting company spectacularly with the male parts.

'Talk about "All we like sheep have gone astray". Ladies, please, watch my beat,' shouted the choirmaster, the veins of his temples bursting with exertion. It was not going well but they weren't the Huddersfield Choral Society, just a bunch of mill workers, farmers' wives and teachers, quarrymen and a few Land Girls and soldiers padding them out. All were wrapped up against the draughts, and ancient village worthies, willing to have a go, had brought hot-water bottles for their feet.

Somehow they struggled together, sang themselves hoarse, letting the power of the music raise their meagre voices to dizzy heights. The B flats were cracking and there was the odd screech in the wrong place, but Mirren was putting her heart into the rehearsal with gusto.

In that moment, in that music, she could forget all her worries and let rip, but the ache in her back got no better. She was feeling so uncomfortable by half-time that she went for a stroll across the green just to straighten up. Perhaps she should have stayed at home after all and put her feet up as Ben suggested but she was desperate to get away for a few hours' change of scene.

Sitting in the chapel only reminded her of that Sunday a year ago and the dancing goose, the Christmas dinner and the look of bemusement on Grandpa Joe's face. She felt like bursting into tears at the sweet memories of Jack's kisses but swallowed her nostalgia and made for her pew, trying not to grimace during the great rumbling 'Amen' chorus, but a huge contraction gripped her by the belly and made her sit down.

Now that wasn't wind or the fish pie, that was for real, so she took some deep breaths and thought about the latest craze for mind over matter. I'm going to sing 'Worthy is the Lamb' if it kills me, she decided, standing to give the chorus some passion.

By the end of the chorus, she was limp with emotion and sweat, and the sickening realisation that this bairn was not going to wait for the end of the rehearsal to make its appearance. Birth was supposed to take hours. Was this one just protesting wildly at her singing efforts, preferring to shove its way out rather than hear her screeching?

She whispered to Hilda and they shuffled out, collapsing through the chairs and into the vestry followed by half the married females as rumours spread of something interesting going on, all wanting to give advice and not a midwife among them.

Someone went to the kiosk to phone the doctor while someone else ran for Nelly Fothergill, who had had thirteen children and lived by the green.

'I don't think Mr Handel quite expected such spectacular effects from his "Hallelujah",' she gasped between contractions, knowing any second something bloody and messy was going to shoot out onto the polished vestry floor.

There was a plaque on the wall to focus on until she saw old Josiah Yewell's name, one of the trustees, one of the founders of the chapel. Can't get away from flaming Yewells, she cursed at him. Men, what do they know?

Was he the rascal who had two wives but became so religious in his old age that one of his missus had thrown a pillow down the farm stairs one night, telling him to go and sleep in the blessed chapel if it was more important than her, or was it someone else? She was too tired now to think, getting fuzzy with pain.

She was taken over by strange grunts and primitive noises, not in the least musical, groanings rendered on the floor among the cushions and army blankets and newspapers scattered as the impatient baby shoved its greasy head into the world for its first breath. It was a girl, a dark-haired little beauty.

Nelly made sure that the baby was breathing, and from the stunned choir in the chapel came cheers and clapping, and a stirring rendition of 'For unto us a child is born'.

Never had Windebank chapel seen such drama since the vicar of St Peter's had thrown a piss pot out of his window over the chapel band processions on Christmas morning for disturbing his slumbers, singing carols right under his window, annoying his lady wife.

The Irish midwife arrived after it was almost over, tidied the baby up and shoved her in Mirren's arms. Mirren looked down at the screwed-up purple face. She thought she could see Jack in her daughter but this child looked like all new-born babes, wrinkled and swollen, and she felt numb and exhausted.

'And what will you be calling this little princess?' the midwife asked. 'Handel?'

'Georgina Fredericka?' laughed Lorna, who was musical.

Mirren was so exhausted and shocked that she could hardly think.

'Now as I recall, December the sixth is the feast of Saint Nicholas, so it is. Nicola or Carol?' said the midwife, determined to have a name at hand.

'It'll be another Miriam, won't it, your ancestor who saved the children of the dale?' suggested Lizzy Potts, the minister's wife.

Mirren looked down on the little face, recalling Jack's wish for something fresh. The name was already decided for a girl. 'She's called Sylvia . . . Sylvia Adeline.' She was determined to give the child at least one family name too.

What a shock but what joy in this urgent delivery. Their own Christmas baby was born, a sign of hope in a dark world. Mirren would never be alone again with this little companion at her breast to love.

Love flooded over her for this tiny mite born in a rush. It all felt as if she was in a dream as she waited for the ambulance to carry them across the village to stay the night under the midwife's roof. They mustn't take any chances with this precious cargo. Cragside could wait. She thought of the messenger waiting in its cage.

Poor Ben and Uncle Tom, she sighed. They were going to get one hell of a surprise when the pigeon landed on their roof tomorrow morning.

Cragside went into raptures at the new arrival and Ben couldn't take his eyes off the tiny thing in her bassinet cot, draped in net. Her flannel nightdress and knitted jackets smelled of talc and lavender water. He thought Sylvia was the most perfect thing he'd ever seen. She was a potted version of Mirren except for her dark hair and olive skin, and when her eyes stared up at him they were like jet buttons.

Auntie Florrie couldn't keep away and decided to decamp down to Cragside for the duration to give the new mother a hand. The arrangement suited them all fine. They took on a young Italian POW called Umberto at Scar Head, who worshipped the baby and sang tenor arias to 'Bambina Sylvia' in a loud voice.

New birth was giving hope for the future – new lambs and calves and stock – but Sylvia was different. Ben'd never been close to a baby before and he cradled her nervously at first until he got used to the size of her. Her hands curled like fronds, her lashes grew and when she gave him her first smile, he was her slave.

He was glad to be out of the way at Scar Head when she squealed all night with colic and it was the women who did the floor pacing, but he stood proud as one of her godparents when she was baptised in the chapel, draped in the ancient lace robe that had served the Yewells for over a hundred years.

Sylvia Sowerby tripped off the tongue but how he wished she had a proper Yewell name. He tried

195

not to watch Mirren nursing the baby in a corner out of sight, her breast full of milk, the baby nuzzling with contentment, and he was envious of Jack all over again.

How mean it was to be relieved that Sylvia's father was far away and it was him who got the hugs and kisses of the little infant when he carried her around the fields at lambing, who picnicked with her at hay timing and pushed her pram proudly to show her progress. No one called him a girl's blouse to his face and he knew he was being unusual in making such a fuss of a girl, but he wanted her to love the farm as much as he did, to pick flowers and know their names, to treat stock with respect, to have an eye for good form and line in a beast but all in good time, he mused; Sylvia was only a baby.

He talked to her sometimes as if she was grown up, and when she could crawl on all fours she followed him around like a faithful puppy in trousers cut from Grandpa's old fustians with patches at the knees.

The activities of the secret Auxiliary Unit began to scale down and there was hope that the invasion was no longer a priority. He could begin to think there would be a future for him, but his rucksack was never far away and they still did exercises in the woods and kept the operational bunker well stocked.

News from the real front was slow but getting better, and they all plotted Jack's progress in the newspaper from victory at El Alamein in November '42.

On Sylvia's first birthday, she stood up and staggered across the hall. 'Ben ... Ben ...' were her first words, her mouth covered in precious cocoa icing from her little cake. Everyone roared with laughter and he blushed.

At Christmas he played Santa and filled her stocking with knitted toys and a wooden horse on a trolley. He had to watch where she was after that, for she followed him around at his chores and he made her a little brush to help.

Mirren seemed happy to let him take Jack's place. Sometimes he felt guilty that he was getting the pleasure of the baby but at the back of his mind he knew a time of reckoning would come and he'd have to take a back seat once more.

Jack's unit was bogged down through the fall of Tunisia to the invasion of Italy in the summer of '43. Still, the news was good and the best of all news was their entry into the South of France. Jack sent postcards from France to Sylvia. Surely the end was near.

Mirren kept pointing to his picture but the little girl had no idea who the strange man in uniform was. 'Daddy,' Mirren kept saying, pointing but Sylvia turned one morning and pointed, 'Daddy Ben!'

He blushed both at the compliment and with embarrassment. There was nothing he'd have liked more but it was never to be. Four years is a long time in the life of a child. The months and seasons had rushed by so quickly. Then the letters stopped after the agony of Arnhem in September '44 and everyone but Mirren feared the worst.

She stuck out her chin like a warrior and carried on gathering the sheep across the fells, lost in her thoughts. Ben knew better than to challenge her when she was in such a mood.

When the war news was at its grimmest and there was no word from Jack, Mirren took Sylvia up the well-trodden path to World's End, first in her arms, then on her back in a sling when she grew heavy. Now she could walk unaided, with sturdy little legs in wooden clogs, her body wrapped up in scarves and her head in a woolly hat. Florrie was her devoted slave and kept her supplied with knitted outfits. Her dark hair had grown into natural ringlets, her face round as a ball, with a beaming smile that allowed her to wind Daisy, Ben and the farm hands around her finger.

They would stand on the crest of the ridge and shout into the wind, telling Jack all their news and calling him home.

'Daddy, home!' Sylvia mimicked, not understanding as they wandered round the ruins, playing houses. No one knew of their secret visits and if they did they said nothing. It was none of their business. Mirren had to be strong for all her family now, and she drew that strength from the wind in her face and the rocks beneath her feet. There was comfort in this refuge and she wanted Sylvia to share in the joy of the place. One day she would make a home for them up here, safe from all the troubles of the world. When the war was over this would be their hidy-hole.

11

October 1944

It was the morning of the Harvest Supper and the village was trying to raise a thousand pounds to add to their big War Savings campaign so the hall was being decorated ready for the evening's concert and everyone was baking treats from their hoarded rations of eggs, butter and treacle, to be auctioned off.

Up at Cragside, Florrie, Daisy and Mirren were peeling apples from the orchard and Sylvia was getting under everyone's feet as usual. They had ten pies to bake and two sponge cakes to raffle. Sylvia needed a fancy-dress costume for the children's competition but Mirren couldn't settle until the postman had been.

Every day she looked out for letters, and just when they'd given up hope a whole pile of them came together from somewhere in Belgium. Then

200

nothing, and the news about the parachute campaign wasn't good.

Jack had transferred into some airborne division ages ago but his letters were vague and censored. They knew so little about his activities, only that they were hush-hush. He'd been away for almost four years now; four whole haytimes, harvests and lambings.

He'd missed Sylvia's birthdays, and although she kissed his picture every night and said, 'Good night, Daddy,' his daughter had no idea who he was. He'd missed all her important milestones: the first tooth, that first step, her first words, her potty training, blowing out the candles on her little birthday cake. How would they catch up when he came home?

He was beginning to feel a stranger even to Mirren. Letters were no substitutes for kisses and cuddles, for chats over tea. They had had only three nights alone together in three and a half years and it all seemed a lifetime ago.

Everyone was drabber, wearier and fed up with war. The travel restrictions were beginning to bite, petrol was short, rationing was stricter. There were more inspections and checks. Labour was harder to get as most of the young farm lads were called up. The whole agricultural effort was a disaster in the dale as the crops didn't ripen off and the ground lost quality.

Mirren was sick of war and the newsreels and the slow Allied progress into Germany. They'd hoped for a quick end after D-day and peace before Christmas but still it was all dragging on and Jack's silence was terrifying. To have gone through all he had and be lost now was unthinkable. She felt so out of touch with him. There was so much to share with him.

By the afternoon, Sylvia was overtired and crotchety, and none of them was in a mood for yet another fund-raising effort. The house was a refuge for evacuees again, these latest fleeing from the doodlebugs in London; a private arrangement with a family who were cousins of Auntie Pam in Leeds was made, bringing Margery, her mother and Dennis and Derek, two little boys who were full of mischief.

It was good to have children for Sylvia to play with but she was clingy and shy with them at first. Daisy still lived in, and Uncle Tom and Auntie Florrie too since Mirren's grandparents died. Large as the house was, it was noisy, untidy and getting shabby.

Nothing had been replaced: neither furnishings, bed linen, crockery nor pots. There were scuff marks on the oak table and up the hall stairs, a line on the walls that got higher as Sylvia grew, but there was no paint to cover up sticky finger-marks.

Sometimes Mirren wished everyone would go away and leave her in peace with her little girl but she was always glad of help and couldn't manage the farm on her own. Walking round the fields and walling were two ways to get away from folk.

Ben had taught her how to do it properly. Mirren would never have managed without his help and encouragement. More and more she relied on him as her big brother. He was patient when Sylvia clambered all over him, feeling in his trouser pocket for the sweets he saved for her from his ration.

He kept an eye on Mirren at the socials when some of new RAF boys got frisky and suggestive. She'd seen too many local girls go off the rails while their husbands were away. To her it was the worst betrayal of all; flirting and dancing was all that was needed to cheer the lads up at the hops but anything else was unthinkable.

Now it was an effort to get dressed up and she was going to give the Harvest Supper a miss if she could. The wind had got up and she shoved an old coat over her shoulders and a scarf round her head to see to the chickens. It was growing damp, another grey mizzling day half over and still no news.

She didn't know what made her look down towards the farm track, but a speck on the horizon caught her eye. Was it a horse strayed out of the field? No, it was too small. It was someone trundling up the track. There was just something in the mist that made her stop and stare and wonder. Her feet just edged forward for a better view.

There was a jaunty stride and the swing of a greatcoat and Mirren knew, she just *knew*, and her legs started to run and her heart was pounding.

'Jack!' she screamed. 'Oh, Jack!' hair flying, her arms outstretched in welcome. She ran towards him and then tripped and fell flat on her face, in a crumpled heap, and the soldier came running.

'Drunk as usual,' laughed an oh so familiar voice. For a moment time went away and they hugged and kissed and cried with joy to be together again.

'Jack! I've been so worried. Why didn't you send a telegram?'

'And have you think the worst? You know me, I like to give a surprise. How's my best girl?' he bent down to pick her up and his breath smelled of ale and cigarettes. 'Well, I have to say you look a bit of a sight in your old clobber. I thought it was a tramp running to steal my whisky. Where's the little 'un? Tucked up in bed? I'm dying to see her . . .'

They marched up the track arm in arm and Mirren's face was aching for she had a grin from ear to ear. 'Florrie! Come and see who the cat's dragged in!' she yelled.

A face appeared at the window and then there was a scream and suddenly his mother leaped on him and burst into tears. 'If I'd known you were coming, we'd have set out a spread . . . Let's be looking at you . . . You've lost a bit of weight.' There was a deep stitched scar across his cheek.

'What's that?' Mirren pointed.

'I had an argument with a dispatch bike, another bump on the head. It must be made of concrete, but this one knocked me out.' Jack laughed searching the room. 'Where's my nipper then?'

'Just out with her Uncle Ben as usual,' said Florrie, and Mirren saw a flash of annoyance cross her husband's face for a second, then it was gone.

'I'm starving!' he said, and proceeded to tuck into the sponge cake sitting on the table. He was still sitting there when Ben carried in Sylvia, who was sucking her thumb.

'She's had a fall and wants her mum,' he said, and then stopped, seeing who was sitting there. 'Now then, Jack, the warrior returns.'

'Not before time,' said Jack. 'Come here and let's have a look at you, young lady.'

Sylvia hung back and started to cry, clinging to Mirren's skirt.

'This is your daddy,' said Florrie, trying to be helpful, but the little girl hid even more and wouldn't go near him.

'She's just tired,' Mirren explained, seeing the

hurt on his face. 'If I'd known I could have prepared her.'

'Looks to me as if she's been spoiled rotten while I was away; doesn't know who to turn to,' Jack answered, ignoring the child and sipping his tea. 'She'll soon change her tune when she sees what I've brought her. I see you've got a house full,' he said seeing Margery and her boys creeping through the kitchen, trying to be invisible. 'It looks a right pig sty in here.'

'We've made a few changes,' Mirren smiled.

'So I see,' he said, and his eyes looked so disappointed that she signalled to Ben to get everyone out.

'Don't worry, we'll all get out of your hair,' said Florrie, taking the hint. 'It's the harvest do and there's a pile of stuff to go down. You'll be giving it a miss,' she winked. 'Sylvia's a bit young to be out late. Daddy and Mummy can put you to bed tonight. Won't that be grand?'

'I go with Denny and Derek,' Sylvia said, wanting to follow the evacuees.

'No, love, not now. We'll play with Daddy instead,' Mirren tried to appease her but the minx could be wilful when crossed.

'No . . . no. He go away.' She stared hard at Jack, then buried her head from him again. No one knew what to do to salvage this reunion. Sylvia was kicking and screaming, and then Mirren smacked her bottom and everyone disappeared quickly to leave her to it.

Jack got up, making for the drawing room with his kit bag, upset. 'She can wait for her present after that little exhibition.'

'Don't take on,' Mirren whispered. 'She's just flummoxed by all the fuss.'

She was caught whichever way. Better to calm down the child first, feed her and get her into bed, then let Jack have her full attention. What an unexpected turn-up! How many nights had she dreamed of his return and now he was here and she looked like something the cat had dragged in, the house was a mess and his daughter was playing up.

Sylvia needed no rocking and was tucked up without a murmur. Mirren did a quick change out of her farm muck and dabbed some lavender water on herself, brushed out her hair from her scarf and pinched her cheeks. She wanted to look her best for Jack, and tiptoed down the stairs expectantly.

Jack was snoring by the fire, flat out with a half-bottle of whisky, half empty on the side table. Poor love was exhausted and needed peace and quiet, she thought, and left him to it. She took up her mending and sat opposite, watching him sleep, the expressions flickering across his face, twitches and gasps. Let their lovemaking wait. Her husband was home and all was right with the world.

Over the next few days they pieced together his wartime travels: how he was trapped near Arnhem and escaped capture, got himself back to England with help from the brave Dutch underground. Now he had two weeks' leave before he must return to barracks.

Her heart sank at the shortness of his stay. After four years they needed months to get to know each other again, she feared. Florrie fussed over him every second she was free. They never seemed to be alone.

'You've lost some weight, lad. Just look at you, all skin and bone,' she said, shoving another ladle of soup into his bowl. He looked up, his eyes dull and his skin sallow.

'Don't fuss, Mother. I'm not that hungry. I've eaten enough broth to last a lifetime. You've had it easy here,' he sneered, looking at the pile of bread and butter, the mound of cold cuts. 'Our Sylvia's getting quite the little fatty.'

'No, she's not, she's just perfect for her age,' Mirren argued, hurt at his comment. He was so snappy in the mornings, sitting about smoking, getting under her feet as she went about her chores.

'When are this lot going home to Scar Head?' he whispered. 'It's like Piccadilly Circus in here. When are we going to get time to ourself? I'm sick of tripping over Big Ben and his farm hands. I didn't think we'd be reduced to having prisoners of war in the house. I spent enough time fighting them in Italy. Now I've got to hear a wop singing in the yard.'

'Jack!' Mirren went hot knowing Umberto was in earshot.

'Berti is one of the family and he's so good with Sylvia.' That was a mistake.

'I don't want no Eyeties fondling my kiddy. It's bad enough she chases after Ben. She looks through me when I try to play with her.'

She could see the hurt in his eyes. You couldn't force a child to warm to a stranger. It took time and patience, and Jack wasn't showing anything but frustration.

'Tom and Florrie have let out the farmhouse. It made sense with all the shortages. This house is big enough for all of us, but I'm sorry it's such a bus station.'

He did look so weary and edgy, the mischief gone from his dark eyes. The Jack who went away was not the one who'd come back. Poor man had been to hell and back and here they were living the same old life but different too. How could he not be disappointed?

He was trying so hard to woo Sylvia but the more he stalked her the more she ran from him. He'd brought her a dress that was too big and some dolls she wouldn't look at. She preferred to play with farm animals and build bricks with

Dennis and Derek. She was not the girly girl Jack was expecting at all.

'Leave her be and she'll come round,' Mirren offered, but Jack ignored her advice.

They managed some walks out together, up to World's End, and made love by the rocks and under the moon but it was a rushed and chilly coupling, not the passionate embrace Mirren was longing for. It got off to a wrong start when she insisted he wear a French letter.

'No more babies for a while, Jack,' she whispered. 'Not till you're settled. We can start again then.'

'Aye,' he agreed, 'when we get ourselves out of this madhouse and away from all our relatives. You can't breathe for Yewells on yer back.'

This outburst took Mirren by surprise. The thought of leaving Cragside never entered her head. Farming was the only life she knew and the thought of moving back into a town made her shiver, but she said nothing. This was the war talking, and his weariness, so she held him close.

'It'll all be different when the war's over,' she smiled.

'It better had be,' snapped Jack, buttoning up his trousers. 'I didn't fight a war to come back to shovelling muck for the rest of my life. There'll be training schemes on offer. We can make a whole new life down south. The lads I've met live the life of Riley down there. I didn't realise just how backward everything is up here: no electricity, tele-phones, bathrooms and indoor toilets . . . You should see London, the shops and flicks and shows. There's nothing but hills here. It's so primitive.'

'It suited you before,' she replied, seeing the strained look on his face. 'Be patient.'

'Patient! I've seen good men die for nothing. I've seen starving kids with bones sticking out, and horrors . . . Don't get me started, Mirren. I need a drink.' With that he rose and took her hand. 'Shall we go down The Fleece?'

'You know I don't go in there,' she snapped. 'Come home and I'll make you a cup of tea.'

'Tea? I'm sick of it! I need something a bit stronger than char, love. You go off and see to the kiddy. I'll go and get my medicine at the bar.'

This was his pattern, which had been going on for days. Mirren was close to tears, torn by wanting to keep him company but knowing she was needed back on the farm.

'Don't be long,' she waved. 'I'll make us a nice supper.'

All the way home she felt guilty that Jack had not got the welcome he deserved. Tonight she would make something special for him, lay the table, get Sylvia to sleep in her proper bed for once, and they could talk and be alone. Then it would be all right.

She waited and waited in her best red frock. She

had cooked a rabbit pie with her best topping, and a blackberry and apple crumble. She watched the clock crawl round to nine o'clock. She felt sick and anxious and unnerved, hurt and then cross. The supper was put back on top of the stove and she undressed, climbed into bed with acid in her throat. How could he spoil a wonderful night? She waited and waited until he crept up the stairs and fell through the door drunk, smelling of a taproom; the smell that took her back to being a child and frightened her.

'You are my Lily of Laguna!' he sang, lurching forward to kiss her.

'Shush! You'll wake everyone. Where've you been till this hour?'

'Having a good time for once . . .' His speech was slurred.

'I cooked you a lovely meal,' she whispered. 'I waited and waited . . .'

'Don't nag . . . not back five minutes and I've got a nagging wife,' he said.

'I'm not nagging. I wanted tonight to be special,' she replied.

Jack leaned over and grabbed her arm. The stench from his mouth was stale. 'Come and make your hero happy again,' he laughed, trying to ease himself over her.

'No! Not like this and you, drunk. I'm too tired and not in the mood.'

'I didn't come all the way through Europe, ducking and diving with the devil's fire bursting over my head ... enemy fire, with half a dozen bloody buzzards hovering, wanting to peck the feathers off my back, darting from hedge to hedge with guns blasting us to kingdom come ... running like hell. I didn't come all this way home to a wife who was too tired, so get on your back and do your duty for once!'

'Jack! Don't talk to me like that!'

'Like what?'

'As if you hate me. I didn't start this war. You could've stayed here on the farm. I'm so proud of you doing your duty but I've never seen you so angry. Don't blame me!'

'You'd be angry if you'd seen what I've seen ... I want to just blot it out,' he said, and for a second she saw the old Jack in his eyes: Jack who hid the kittens from the drowning bucket; who wiped her tears when Jip, her collie, died; who sat with her at World's End after Dunkirk, who'd promised her the moon, the sun and the stars if she'd only be his wife.

'But getting blathered isn't the answer,' she offered and then wished she hadn't.

His body stiffened at her reproach. 'What do you know about it?' His voice was angry and hard, the voice of a stranger, and he held her so tight that her body recoiled at his embrace. There was no point in struggling. He wanted comfort in the only way he knew. No point in resisting, and she felt used, opened up and rammed by his hard demanding sex. There was no love, no tenderness, just brute force.

Mirren lay there afterwards, shocked, trying to understand. He'd suffered and he was still suffering. She must make allowances for his drunkenness. This was not the real Jack but a wounded Jack, and he needed understanding not rejection. Why did it feel as if she was being punished? What had she done wrong?

She waved him off at Scarperton with a heavy heart, his last words ringing in her ears.

'When I come home again I want them all out, all them Yewells. If I hear that child call Ben her dad one more time . . . It makes me wonder what you've been up to behind my back!' he said, gripping her tightly on the arm.

'Oh, Jack, how could you even think that?' Mirren's eyes were brimming with tears and her arm bruised from his grip. He was so rough when he held her, as if she was his possession, not his loving wife.

'Think on . . . I need some peace and quiet, not a house full of strangers. And tidy the place up a bit. It looks like Paddy's market.'

This was not the Jack she had yearned for, this sad, angry soldier. Even his own mother said he had changed and not for the better.

'He's that sour, he'd turn milk. He doesn't listen to a word his mam says. He's not right in the head, anyone can see that. You'll have to be patient with him.'

Every night Mirren had tried to reach out to him, suffering his rough lovemaking without protest, but it had done nothing to bring them closer together. Now the thought of Jack returning for good filled her with unease. Perhaps when the war was over, with fresh air and good food, the old Jack would return once more.

As the train chuffed out of the station she turned her back on the smoke and soot with relief. Time to climb back to Windebank and normality. Six weeks later she realised she was pregnant again. This time there was no joy, only fury that she'd been caught and trapped. Christmas was coming soon; another wartime Christmas and bad weather to come. Only the thought of Sylvia's excitement gave her any incentive to plan ahead. She wasn't bothered if Jack came home or not, and that was what shocked her most of all.

It was another hard winter with blizzards and hard frost. Ben sensed that Jack's visit had not gone well and Mirren dragged herself around, not looking him in the face when he asked if she was OK to lift loads. It was as if she didn't care what happened to the coming baby.

Margery and the boys went home to London and Uncle Tom decided to return to Scar Head. Now that Jack would be home soon, it was felt the couple needed time to settle down. There were wild tales of Jack's drinking sprees down at The Fleece on his leave. Nothing escaped the gossips of Windebank: how he came out on all fours one night and jumped on someone's motor bike and left it in a hedge; how he had a fight with one of the lads from the artillery battery and left him with a bloody nose; how he was a barstool bore and cadged drinks in exchange for gruesome war tales; how he could sort out the army better than Monty himself. If only half of them were true, Mirren was in for a rough time.

War had done terrible things to Jack and Ben wished he could talk to him, but the fact that Sylvia clung around Ben's legs had not gone down well. Sometimes he thought he saw a flash of hate in his eyes. When Jack returned he was going to keep a weather eye on him.

Once they were settled, though, Ben had his own plans to leave. It was time to train himself up. They were advertising for trainers in the college near York; to find experienced workers who could get agricultural courses onto a better footing. He fancied a change away from all that held him at Cragside. Mirren needed time to lick her husband back into shape and he needed a change of sky.

Funny how he had always thought his life would be forever at Cragside, but once Jack returned he would not be welcome. Sylvia must learn to turn to her dad for comfort and treats, not him. The new baby would have a father around and would get a better start. Mirren could run the farm with Uncle Tom just as well as he could.

Two's company, three's a crowd, they said, and it was true, but he would see to things for awhile longer, make sure Mirren got her proper rest. She was her own worst enemy, always on the go, skipping meals when everyone else sat down.

He hoped Jack appreciated what he'd found in her. She was a farmer's wife without equal in his eyes. None of the girls she'd thrown at him could measure up to her standards and he wouldn't settle for less.

Mirren took her troubles to World's End, climbing high away from the farmhouse, leaving Sylvia with Granny Florrie. Most days now she felt stiff and sore, and angry inside. Nothing was turning out as she planned for her family. How she wished she could have turned back the clock to when Gran and Grandpa were alive, when things seemed simpler and Jack was Jack-the-lad, shinning down the window on a sheet, when they were all full of dreams and schemes.

Now Sylvia needed new clogs and gumboots.

There was a new coat to buy and eventually another baby to clothe. Why did she resent now having to do it all on her own?

Why did Jack now get mixed up with her own dad in her dreams? It was weird and scary. Had she married a man like Paddy, who made promises and never kept them, who spent pound notes as if they were loose change? Oh God, she was going crazy! Her stomach tightened like a drum skin and she was afraid. If the two of them did leave Cragside how would they manage?

12

VE Day, 8 May 1945

There was so much to do before the afternoon's party on the village green, and Mirren was that thronged with jobs she did not know where to start first. There was a bowl of trifle to be made for a start.

Jack was making himself useful, building the great scaffold arch out of greenery and flags that was the centre piece of the display on Windebank Green, giving a hand loading trestles and chairs onto the back of their wagon, from the church hall down the road. No doubt he'd drop in to The Fleece for a quick half before he came to collect the family for the fun and games.

He was home on leave and seemed to have turned a corner since his last visit, thrilled at the prospect of another baby on the way. There was no talk of moving away and his mother seemed to have talked some sense into him, telling her son they were much better off living in the country for the moment, with a roof over their heads and an income from the farm.

Even Sylvia was getting used to him sleeping in her mother's bed. Jack's seeing her alongside Uncle Ben always stirred things up for the worse, though.

If ever there was a young farmer in the making, it was Sylvia. In her corduroys and wellies with a flat tweed cap cut to size and a pretend crook, she looked like a miniature shepherd. So far she showed no leanings at all to wear pretty dresses, even for the afternoon party. If it didn't have four wheels or four legs she wasn't interested.

Jack looked on in dismay but held his peace, leaving her well alone, and she in turn began to answer when he called her and take his hand now and then. Mirren decided long ago not to keep her child too close to the hearth as some farmers' wives did with their daughters. They made cakes and buns together and went walking the fields but Sylvia was shared out between the grown-ups. Jack was persuaded to read to her each night.

No child of Mirren's would ever want for books and learning, girl or boy. She wanted Sylvia to be free to go to college when the time came, even if it meant fighting the Yewell family tradition that farming must always come first and foremost.

It was hard to recall she'd passed her matriculation, had attended the teacher training college in Ripon and had plans to become a proper teacher. That was another lifetime ago but it didn't stop her love of novels and biographies from the circulating library. Now the chance to teach was a distant dream. The war must have scuppered so many well-made plans, but it was over at last and her heart was leaping with relief.

Time to turn back to her task. Trifle was a fiddle to make when you were in a hurry; sponge fingers to soak, home-made custard to boil, fresh cream to skim, soft fruit to poach, and they wanted to be down in the village hall by mid-afternoon before the concert and fancy-dress parade. Her back was giving her gip again. Tiredness swept over her like a wave and she had to sit down, feeling faint.

So victory was here at long last but there was a bit of her feeling empty inside. This was a day to remember, with bonfires and bells pealing, bunting in the streets, but even though Ben had promised to help with the milking, there were still chores to do.

What a big fuss they were making down in the village. Not that she was against all the patriotism or the end of hostilities but it was making such a lot of extra work. There was the sports day to come, the pageant and gala procession, the massed school choir festival in Scarperton, the Brownie fancy-dress float, a dancing display and WI events and competitions, baking for the children's bun feast on the green and the old folk's treat, the refreshments for the Crazy Cricket match with men dressed as women and women as men, and a half-made fancy-dress outfit for Sylvia to finish before this afternoon.

Sylvia had begged for a special outfit for the day but Mirren's mind was blank until she saw a bit of the old grey cloth left from the barrage balloon. Why not dress her as her own namesake, Miriam, the famous ancestor of the dale, in a little grey frock and white Quaker collar? Florrie could make the collar and cap out of a linen napkin, and Tom would find a little lantern for her to carry. Everyone knew the story of how her ancestor kept the school children in the chimney, safe from the blizzard and fallen roof. It was quite an original idea, she mused, laying out the costume on the bed. Better to wait until the last moment to dress her up. The little monkey could get filthy in two minutes.

Ben was too busy to make the trip down to the village but there was going to be a lamb roast outside The Fleece later in the evening, and that would be more his scene.

There was a damp raw edge to the morning, and Mirren caught snatches on the wireless of the sound of excited crowds cheering at anything that moved, braving the rain with the usual British stoicism. There was no May sunshine up here. It was more like autumn than spring. What did they expect, living so high up, making do with nine months' winter and three months' bad weather as the old joke went.

As long as the kids got their party and could run off steam with sports and dancing, they would have honoured the day. If the weather did its worst then everyone would be shovelled into the village hall to put the trestle tables up there. What would they do without their patched-up gaberdines and macs, umbrellas and leaking gumboots?

The sheep and cows didn't know it was VE Day and still needed their routine, so life at Cragside Farm would go on as normal. Bank holiday or not, the stock must come first. Lambing was in full swing and there were orphans drying off in the barn, makeshift pens of suspect mothers that needed coaxing to feed their lambs, calves and piglets running amok given half a chance.

But Mirren had to admit to a tinge of excitement about this special holiday and the chance to have an afternoon crack with her friends in the grey stone village full of cottages. There was something about the way that Windebank nestled under the big hill that comforted her. Small as it was, they'd all pulled together in the war, welcomed strangers, raised a staggering amount of savings bonds, supported their shops and deserved a day off for all their combined efforts.

Her life was a predictable round of seasonal chores: lambing, clipping, haytiming, gathering, tupping, muck spreading and lambing. Anything that made a change – market day, visitors, Christmas – was always welcome.

She hoped that for Jack and her, life would be settled and more stable now. Their new baby would be born in peacetime. Her husband would be demobbed and rationing would end. Farmers would get the recognition for all the hard work they had done in keeping Britain fuelled with food; the worst of the wartime regulations would end, surely.

How much would little Sylvia remember of all this? All she could think about was the party and treats and playing with her friends. No wonder she was as high as a kite with impatience. What it is to be young, Mirren sighed, looking at her daughter with pride, with all your life ahead of you.

Down on the green it was like Merrie England at play. The eaves were draped with bunting and the flags were flying from windows. The dark clouds were holding off but Ben didn't think for much longer. There was such a feeling of relief that it was all over but not for those poor souls out in the Far East.

He had made a fruitless trip into Scarperton to pick up some milk powder for hand-feeding the weaker lambs but everything was shut and it was a waste of petrol. Jack had been holding court as usual outside The Fleece, chewing the ear of the landlord, but at least he was being a little less sharp with Mirren, in public at least.

He had to leave the couple to make up and go their own gait but it wasn't easy when he was so protective of her. There was something about Jack he didn't trust, especially when he had the drink on him. He turned into a violent bully, the charm mask slipped and he was quick with his fists. Better to get him back home before he got blathered and spoiled the afternoon, he thought, waving to him and offering him a lift back to the farm.

'I'll walk,' Jack waved back but Ben stopped the truck.

'Mirren'll need a hand with the kiddy while she finishes off,' he said, more as an order than an offer. Jack rose from his bench, pulled a face and trundled across.

They drove back in silence. Jack had already had a skinful and was just about the right side of merry. 'I could've walked,' was all he said.

When they got back Sylvia was having a tantrum, not wanting to put on the dress.

'If you don't wear your costume, there's no party for you, my lady!' said Mirren. She turned, looking to Ben, but he just shook his head and sucked on his pipe. She turned to Jack, who shook his head too.

'Do as yer mother says,' he said. 'That's her department, not mine.' And that was that, no arguing when they all put up a united front.

Sylvia reappeared in her costume and Uncle Tom found his Box Brownie and took a snap of her scowling by the barn door.

Now it was almost time to go and everyone was rushing round finishing off chores. Jack was hanging about, getting in the way so Ben told him to shift the Fordson into the barn, back it down out of the way so they could park up the truck, get the horse and cart loaded up and then he could get on with the afternoon in peace.

Ben himself would rather come down later for the feast. Kids' stuff was for parents and grandparents, not for him.

He was making for the gate when he heard Jack brum-brumming the tractor engine as if it was a racing car. He smiled. Jack was a big kid, still trying to impress everyone. One day that guy would grow up and find he had a wife and two kiddies to support, not burn good rubber. 'Cut it out!' he yelled in annoyance. It was only a borrowed tractor and not theirs to fool about with. Better to do the job himself, he thought, and turned back. He didn't want any scraped paint.

There was no one else in the yard but the tractor was parked up by the barn door so Jack was clambering down from the seat to open the big doors.

He could see Sylvia standing with her hands on her hips, watching them from the kitchen door.

'I'll do it . . . you're not supposed to leave it running,' he shouted.

Jack ignored his call and made back for the seat with that cheeky grin on his mug that seemed to charm the girls but left him cold. Tractors were temperamental and could cut out or be flooded. It was daft asking Jack to do anything. What did he know about this sort of machinery?

'I can do it, no problem,' Jack yelled back. The engine stalled and juddered.

'Jack, you're too tiddly. Let me sort it.' Ben moved up to pull him off.

'Bugger off, Lanky!' He was fiddling with the gear stick and yanking the knobs in fury, and the key was in the engine so he twiddled that too just to annoy him. The tractor roared up and then jumped back and there was a bump, shooting him with a jerk, and he couldn't stop it and was thrown sideways with the shock of it. He was sliding and clinging on but the tractor was going backwards into the wall. Ben was yelling and everyone came running, rushing past him.

It was then, when Ben turned, that he saw a pair of black wellies lying on the floor and there were legs in the wellies and a grey dress in the mud.

Mirren came running and screaming, and suddenly Tom and Ben were tugging at the wheels and taking the controls and shunting the tractor forward. There was a lot of shouting and Jack was dragged inside out of their way by Florrie. The door was slammed behind him.

Everything was in slow motion but Ben and Tom strained and strained until the wretched machine was pulled clear. How they did it, the strength they found, the pumping desperation and the sounds of Mirren screaming, he would never forget.

There was no telephone and someone had to race down to the village and raise the alarm. Tom was in no fit state so Ben backed the truck and raced off, leaving them.

Jack was sitting in total shock, unaware of anything. He kept seeing the wellies, Sylvia's little wellies. One minute she was standing by the kitchen door and then she was . . . why didn't she jump out of the way? They hadn't seen her. Speeding towards the village, Ben felt so cold and shaky and very calm. It was all his fault. If he only had left Jack in the pub and not interfered . . .

It was the sound of the argy-bargy outside that made Mirren leave her baking table and go outside to see what the fuss was about. It was the roar of the tractor when she knew Ben was in the byland somewhere that didn't feel right. Tom was there first, pulling the wheel of the tractor away from the barn door, straining with all his might to pull something free from its grip . . . one of the dogs. No, oh, no, her baby! She was trapped between the wheel and the barn door, crushed by the force and speed of the accident.

Suddenly everything went blurry, fuzzy round the edge. She could see the grey patchy sky and hear the blackbird pinking on the roof of the barn, see the straw and muddy tyre wheels, smell the burning rubber in her nostrils. Everything was alive and loud and clear and she saw herself looking down at her beautiful daughter and her muddy costume, white, grey and blood.

Florrie bundled Jack away from the scene and Ben came running, suddenly looking every one of his twenty-eight years.

'Do something, Uncle Tom,' she heard herself screaming as she looked down at Sylvia's blood-stained face, bruised and an odd colour. She was so still and silent, which was not like her at all. There was a trickle of blood coming out of her ear and Mirren began to shake and shake.

'Do something, Ben. Do something, somebody . . . please.' She was screaming so loud she thought the whole dale would hear her cry for help.

Tom's face was grey and hard. He cradled Sylvia in his arms and she saw tears rolling down his cheeks. It was the sight of those tears that turned her heart to stone.

'Ben's going for the doctor,' offered Daisy, but Mirren couldn't take it in.

'Well, don't just sit there like a statue. Bring her inside and let's get her warmed up. The kettle's boiled we can give her some tea,' Mirren bustled, suddenly alive with possibilities. 'I'll rub some life into her. Get her away from that damn tractor.'

Still Uncle Tom did not move but he looked up. 'It's too late, love, she's gone. Sylvia's been taken from us.'

'Don't be daft, she's just out cold,' she was arguing. 'Bring her into the warmth. She'll catch a chill with just that skimpy dress on. Bring her inside and we'll happen patch her up.' She could hear her own voice as if from a distance, so brisk, so cold, so businesslike.

'What do men know of these things, Sylvia? I'll soon have you up and running. You're just winded. Mum'll see you right.'

Tom carried Sylvia into the kitchen and Mirren brushed all her baking out of the way, spreading a cloth so the girl could lie close to the range. She covered her in blankets and a warm rug. Her face was blue and purple and grey in patches and her eyes were tight shut. She looked so tiny under all that bedding. She busied herself with a sponge cloth and bowl of Dettol, wiping away the gunge and grime from her head, rubbing her cold fingers

230

with all the love she could muster but still she did not wake up.

'Come on, Sylvie, wakey wakey . . . It's VE Day and we've got a party to go to,' she urged, hearing the cheering coming from the wireless. 'You don't want to miss the party, do you? Where's Jack? Why isn't Jack here to help me?'

'Switch that bloody thing off!' Tom screamed. She could see he was distraught but it didn't register. Nothing was registering, only that Sylvia was fast asleep and in no hurry to wake up.

'No, don't switch it off. Sylvia wants to listen to it. She wants to hear all the bells ringing. Turn it up.'

Then Ben was standing in the doorway, looking at her. His face was grey. He switched the wireless off and grabbed her arm. 'Stop it, Mirren, stop this. I'm so sorry, love. It's all my fault . . . She's gone and there's no life in her now,' he said.

'Don't you dare tell me there's no life in my daughter. Look, she's warm. She'll come round soon. Don't you touch her!' She was shooing them all away and still guarding her when Dr Murray came through the door, grim-faced, with the police constable carrying his hat under his arm.

'Come on, Mrs Sowerby, let me examine Sylvia.' He stepped closer and she smiled.

'I'm so glad you're here. Perhaps you can put some sense into this lot. They think Sylvia is dead

231

but she's just sleeping. There's hardly a mark on her. She wouldn't leave us on VE Day, now, would she? See, she's all dressed up ready to go,' she said shaking her head. 'I'll have to sit down. I've got a right pain in my back now with standing.'

Someone gave her a drink that made her mouth go dry and the room spin, and suddenly she could hardly keep her eyes open. The rest was a blur of nothingness. There was pain and stabs in her groin and a gush of something warm and wet in her legs. Somewhere in the fug was pain and cramps and more pain. Her belly went flat and her breasts leaked and then she knew that the baby was coming too soon, but when she looked there was nothing there, just towels and the smell of Dettol and a huge emptiness in her body. She couldn't raise her head from the pillow.

In the days afterwards she crawled out of bed hoping for oblivion, praying for the celebration day to come again so she could rearrange it differently but as each new dawn crept into the sky, she crawled down again, hoping for night never to end.

Of Jack there was no sign. He hadn't spoken a word since the accident, the terrible accident that had robbed her of two lives. The doctor had sent him into the hospital to bring him round. It was as if he had never come home.

All Mirren knew was that Sylvia was taken and

she would never see her again. She had gone to a place where she couldn't follow. One morning they were dressing up to go to the biggest party in the village and then she disappeared from them.

Florrie and Daisy had taken all Sylvia's clothes and the toys from her bedroom and stripped it bare, and the door was locked on it to make it easier for them to bear. Mirren hadn't the strength to protest. It was all she could do to put one foot after the other and creep from room to room, calling her name in case she was hiding from them.

In chapel, funereal voices whispered all around her. It was no comfort to say Sylvia had gone to a better home and only the good die young. It was no comfort that her little body was put in a box in the churchyard out of sight where it was windy and chilly. When she wanted to call out her name, someone whispered, 'Hush, don't upset yourself. Crying won't bring her back. Time's a great healer . . . You'll have other children one day.' 'How dare you say that? I want Sylvia!' she screamed out, and everyone heard her pain. Jack was too sick even to hold her up. It was Ben who kept her upright at the graveside.

It was as if Sylvia had never lived in Cragside, never kicked the banisters and got told off for picking the plaster from the wall, never sang in her bath or raced over the fields chasing sheep. There were no photographs and she was never spoken of in front of Mirren except in hushed tones. Friends passed her on market day in the street rather than face her raw grieving.

'Our Sylvia was too good for this world so she was taken, not spared. It didn't make any sense. She was taken for an angel in Heaven,' wept Florrie with a quiet voice, not looking at her.

Mirren spent hours sitting up in her eyrie at World's End, the wind battering her and rain pouring down on her face, but she didn't care. Ruins were what suited her now. The nights when sleep wouldn't come she spent looking at the photograph, the only one she salvaged, the one Jack kept in his pocket, creased with looking at: a baby shot of Sylvia smiling. She was never for sharing after that, and she hid it in Dad's tin box under her bed.

Sometimes she forgot and when it was dusk she looked for her coming down from the top field on Ben's shoulders, coming through the kitchen door full of chatter. It was hard waiting for that little voice to shout, 'What's for tea?' and her saying, 'Wipe your feet!' But it never came.

There were no words to explain that terrible moment when life's gone from a body or any sense in the death of a precious child. It took only seconds for Sylvia to leave them, ribs crushed and skull broken, and for Mirren's world to end. To bury her precious kiddy was an abomination on the face of the earth and she would never get over it as long as she lived. It went against nature. It was agony to speak even her name in company.

Her dreams were full of her child running through the house in her Fair Isle jumper and dungarees made from worn cord breeches.

Sylvia would never grow old or marry and have children, or roam the world and do as she pleased, and it was all their fault. Two men who should've known better than to mess about with engines when there was an excited child in the yard. The coroner said as much himself. She would never forgive Jack and Ben for her death.

They were named and blamed and shamed. It was an accident, one of those tragic things that can happen on any farm if people were careless. Farms were and always will be dangerous places for children. Sylvia died because she was in the wrong place at the wrong time. That is what Mirren's head was saying: not drowned or killed on the road, lost on the fell or abducted, but in her own back yard where she should have been safe and something in her died alongside her child that day.

The tractor was just a machine and should not have been left like that with the key in the lock parked at an awkward angle. The yard was too busy. Sylvia was distracted but Mirren blamed them for the loss of the baby too.

Shock had brought on the labour too early. The little lad was too small to live and didn't stand a chance, the doctor explained to her. She couldn't feel anything. They had taken him away before she'd even seen him, taken him away like rubbish in the bin, not buried decently. It was cruel, he said, but for the best. How did he know, her heart cried out, but he was the doctor and they knew best, didn't they?

The sheep, the lambs and the cows didn't know what had happened. People took over while she recovered her strength, but Dalesmen knew that hard work and silence were the best solace. So they just got on with life as best they could through the slow procession of the seasons in turn. Dalesfolk made no show of grief, or they didn't until now. No amount of repainting the barn doors would ever wipe the memory of that accursed day. Nothing would bring Sylvia back to Cragside.

Each morning Mirren took her hen bucket of grain and walked past that door. How she hated that tractor, but it wasn't hers to destroy. It disappeared one morning, never to return. She hated herself and Jack for being alive when their child was dead.

Something between them died that afternoon.

Ben drove Florrie to the hospital near Scarperton in silence. None of them had slept for weeks. His dreams were filled with the noise of the engine, his feet trying to run to help but stuck in thick mud, trapping him, a helpless looker on at a needless tragedy.

He had never seen a young man collapse so quickly into a crumpled shell of humanity. Jack was in total shock, brought on by the sight of his little girl being killed by his own carelessness. His eyes were dead, gazing far from any words spoken to him. He had not uttered a coherent word. Florrie tried to bring him round but he retreated into such strange behaviour that they feared for his life.

The news of Mirren's miscarriage tipped him over the edge to a point where Dr Murray wanted him off the farm – 'I can't vouch for his safety after this.' Now Jack was twenty miles away and poor Florrie was dreading seeing him locked up in an asylum.

Ben sat outside in the van, ashamed, but Jack's mother wanted to see her son alone. Weakness like this was not for sharing outside immediate family. Ben hadn't even time to visit his own parents.

Returning to Cragside, Ben watched Mirren's anger grow but said nothing.

'Jack's not coming near this farm when he gets out of the loony bin,' she shouted. 'He killed his baby. You tell him he's not coming back here,' she snapped.

'But he's your husband,' wept Auntie Florrie. 'He's been in hospital a month. He's not himself. He knows what he did and it's floored him. You have to make your peace with him. If he could turn the clock back, believe me he would. Don't make it any worse than it is, love.'

Florrie and Tom were in a losing battle with their daughter-in-law, thought Ben. Mirren was lost in her own guilt and loss. She wanted to lash out at all of them, and most of all at him. Her eyes were hard as steel when she barked orders to Umberto. There was no reasoning with her. This stalemate couldn't go on. It was affecting everyone on the farm.

'If you're going to be hard on someone, blame me,' he butted in. 'It was me as brought Jack up from the village. If only I'd left well alone but I thought . . . You must go and see him. He needs your help.'

'I know what you thought: better get me laddo home before he drinks too much. We all know what Jack's like when he's blathered. He can't keep away from an engine.'

'But he's sick and weary, Mirren. Have some pity. Don't do this to him. Blame me, but go and see him . . . Make your peace.'

'I do blame you. I blame everyone, but most of all myself,' she snapped back. Her eyes flashed, hard, flinty. 'How can we live here after this?'

'There must be a way,' he replied, thinking of his long-ago promise to Gran to see them both right. How he wished he could pack up and go back to Leeds, away from the bitterness, but that was the coward's way out.

There was no reaching the woman when she was in this mood. They were all hurting, going through the motions of daily routine like automatons.

It was high summer but the sun couldn't lighten the gloom over Cragside. They all needed to spread out and find some peace away from prying eyes.

Mirren was needed on the farm, but her living here every day was agony for all of them, and a cottage in Windebank was too public. What she and Jack needed was a private place to grieve and he knew just the place.

Ben looked to the heavens for the first time in weeks. 'Don't worry, Gran,' he whispered. 'I know just the place to set them right again . . .'

13

The hospital outside Scarperton stood like a fortress, set high on the moor overlooking the River Wharfe; a world of its own with high forbidding gates, a palace with tall windows with bars across them. It had taken two trains to get here. Why was she coming?

Mirren gulped. Was it to see Jack suffer? One look at the place and she sensed it was like a prison. Her husband was under lock and key and she must face him for the first time since Sylvia died. How could she look on his eyes and hair and not see the image of her own child? How could she face the murderer of her unborn baby? She would soon know.

The pills that Dr Murray forced upon her were long flushed down the pan. They had done nothing to dull her pain. They made her woozy and dry in the mouth, but she couldn't face this journey without some strength from somewhere.

In her bag was a cake in a tin from Florrie, a copy of the local *Gazette* and a little package from Tom that looked like a bottle, a bit of comfort to help him. There was no point in giving him that, she sneered. It had done enough damage. She would chuck it in the nearest dustbin.

Anger rose like bile in her throat. What was the point in giving him liquor to drown his sorrows when she couldn't drown hers with anything stronger than tea?

There was a small crowd gathered at the door for visiting time. She wished she'd asked Ben to come for support, but he was too busy, and Florrie came when she could. The visitors made a row of anxious faces as they were ushered down tiled corridors to the wards, hearts beating faster at the thought of what they must face and the smell of mopped floors and bed pans.

It was a strange subdued meeting. Jack sat there staring out the window, not even looking up when she came. His eyes were like dead fish on a slab, cold and glassy and drugged. He was in a borrowed dressing gown that was too big for him, his cheeks were sunken and he looked like an old man. She wondered if he had even recognised her. The sight of him overwhelmed her.

'Jack! It's me, I've come to see you,' she offered.

He turned, looked at her unsmiling, nodded his head and she sat down. He didn't speak so she filled

241

the gaps by telling him she'd lost the baby and had to have a scrape-out and wasn't up to visiting before, making excuses why she had put off this moment.

He listened, his face blank as if he was a stranger, fiddling with his dressing gown cord, not looking at her. She didn't understand.

'I thought you'd be glad I'd made the effort to come and clear the air,' she offered. This was hard work and it was making her angry. 'Look, speak to me or not, but we've got to have this out,' she nagged. Where had this fishwife voice come from? 'I blame you and Ben and I blame me. It never should've happened. If only you'd kept out of that blessed pub, but, oh no, you have to have your nips. Ben should have let you get sozzled and stay put, but he was interfering, as usual. Sylvie would've been with us and none of this . . .' She was yelling at him now.

Jack turned away and blanked her out as she wagged her finger at him.

'And you can stop all this funny business, shutting me out. You heard what I said. No use hiding away in the madhouse, getting folks sorry for you. It's not fair. Face what you've done like a man, fair and square on. You killed our beautiful little girl!'

'Mrs Sowerby! A moment, please,' said a man in a white coat with a foreign accent.

'I've not finished yet, Doctor. I need to get this off my chest but he won't listen.'

'Not here, not now, Mrs Sowerby. Be patient.

242

Jack's not well, he can't listen to you. He can't think straight yet but he will, given time and rest. I'm Dr Kaplinsky.' He held out his hand but she ignored it.

'But he killed our child,' she screamed, and everyone in the ward stood listening to her.

'It was a terrible accident. Your child ran into the tractor,' said the doctor with the soft voice.

'How do you know? You weren't there. I was! He did it,' she said, pulling on Jack's sleeve to try to wake him out of his torpor.

'Come,' the doctor insisted, 'let's talk in private. Jack is not listening. The war has left him with many problems. He needs time and treatment. Peace and quiet to heal his spirit.'

'But what about me? Don't I get time to recover? This nightmare will never end as long as we live. I haven't gone doolally. Someone has to get up and see to the cows, no matter how bad it gets,' she snapped at him.

'And that is the best way, Mrs Sowerby. Keep busy and keep going from day to day. Push the pain away. It's hard but I see you are strong. Jack is different,' he added. His eyes were dark and kindly enough, but what did he know of her pain?

'What is it to you?' she sneered.

'Believe me, I know,' said the young man with the beard. 'Come, sit down and rest. Just hold his hand for a while. It is good you have come.'

'I'll do no such thing. He'll have to get over it on his own. I've a bus and two trains to catch. I came to see how he was and, now I've seen for myself, he can rot in here for all I care.' Mirren stood up, put on her coat and made for the door.

'Please, wait . . . It has to be unlocked.' She stood politely while the keys turned, shuddering at the sound.

'Pull yourself together, Jack, or I'll not be coming again,' she shouted, and then stormed down the corridor, fuming at the injustice of it all. How dare he be mollycoddled and she told just to get on with it? The anger was bubbling like a kettle on the boil inside and she was that thirsty and chilled through.

She sat on a bench outside in the garden to calm down. It wasn't fair. No one cared about her and she felt in her bag for a hanky and found the bottle of whisky. What a waste of money and coupons. This was the cause of all their troubles. Wait until she saw Uncle Tom.

She lifted the glass bottle. The golden amber liquid glinted in the sun. So what does the water of life taste like? She smiled, unscrewing the top out of interest; she sniffed the fumes and saw her dad. She made to pour it away and then stopped, swallowed, and tasted some. It burned its way down her throat.

'Hell's bells, and they pay good money for this?'

She swallowed some more to warm her through. Popping it back in her bag, she took nips all the way home.

By the time she arrived at Windebank halt, she was feeling calmer and pink with satisfaction. She'd gone and made her peace with Jack. Everyone would be pleased, Ben most of all. He was being very secretive of late. Perhaps he was out courting again but why he needed his tool bag with him was a mystery. Not that she cared. For the first time in weeks she didn't care about much at all and slept like a log.

Maybe a day out to visit Jack was just the time out she needed away from this accursed place.

The visits to see Jack seemed to be doing Mirren good, thought Ben as he began the long job of repairing the roof at World's End. Down came the last of the rotten timbers and he hauled up some old but sound timbers from a barn on the sled. He had laid out all the sandstone slabs in order to put them back on the roof and sworn Tom to secrecy when he helped him out. They would fix up the cottage as a surprise for Jack and Mirren.

There was a new POW, yet to be repatriated, called Dieter Klose, who was helping out down at Cragside. He was of farming stock and useful.

Florrie said Jack still wasn't speaking, but he

recognised his wife and mother when they came. Mirren came back full of good cheer and went about her work with gusto. It was hard to put what was different about her; she was full of vim and vigour but then got tired and crotchety again as the strain of the past months took its toll.

Florrie whispered that Jack was to have some newfangled electric-shock treatment to jolt him out of his lethargy, they hoped. He would have pads put on his head and a current run through, which would give him a fit. The doctor assured them it was safe and it might just get him back on his feet again. It sounded awful to Ben.

Mirren didn't talk about her trips much. She sometimes stayed late and went to the pictures. No one begrudged her a day off, but she didn't seem that interested in the stock. Lately she over-slept and was groggy first thing until she had her brew and perked up ready to start the day.

No one had ever seen her walking up to World's End and she had no idea of the surprise they had in store. Dieter was told to ward her off the track with an excuse if he saw her going in that direction.

Now the war was over there seemed to be even more regulations and rationing as the shortage of manpower and foodstuffs began to kick in. Ben put his own plans to move away on hold. This was no time to be heading out of the dale.

He was still involved with the Young Farmers,

and drifted back under the wing of the ever-faithful Lorna, who was teaching at the village school. They went for walks together and dances. She helped him show some sheep at the Ribblehead Show, grooming their coats when Mirren forgot to turn up on time. She was good company and Ben could forget his worries when she was chattering away.

The whole dale knew about their recent trag-ellies and asked about Jack. What was there to say but that progress was slow? Ben must see more improvement in the family's spirits before he departed and there was his secret project to finish. He didn't visit Jack himself. He knew he wouldn't be welcome.

Over the weeks World's End was shaping up well; one big living room with store room and kitchen off, some proper stairs to two bedrooms above. All the upper floor was boarded with timber they had scrounged. Materials were now in short supply so it was a matter of make do and mend, and don't ask too many questions.

There was water from the sunken well and a little stone WC to the side. Mirren would soon make a home of it out of everyone's way. Somehow he couldn't see Jack being too suited but it was a start and it was better than living with his parents.

Tom and Florrie were thinking of letting Cragside as holiday lodgings in the summer. It was too big for the family now and ought to be sold off but who would want this cold barn of a house? Better to let it earn its keep.

Mirren assumed everyone would be living at Scar Head farm but she showed little interest in the plans. This indifference was a habit hard to get out of, Ben thought. Sometimes she was like her old self, busy in the kitchen and garden, going to market. Other times she was weepy and retired to her bedroom. They were all pleased she was visiting Jack but her absence when she went got longer and longer, and her timekeeping unpredictable. Funny, her being such a stickler for punctuality.

It was all part of losing Sylvia, Ben sighed. Cragside would never be the same again. He was glad Gran and Grandpa weren't around to see this change of fortune. Ben trusted that his surprise would stir Mirren and Jack back to life and give them hope for the future. The rest was up to them after that.

Mirren made sure she had the eggs hidden in her basket, safely wrapped in Jack's change of pyjamas. Fresh eggs were like gold in the town, and butter too; all strictly rationed and under the counter but her supplies were much appreciated, with customers willing to pay over the odds for farm produce. No one missed a few eggs in season.

She always packed a few sweets and buns to take

to Jack as a treat but he had no appetite. Her visits were getting shorter and shorter and she tried to avoid that awful doctor if he came in view. At least she did put her head round the door before skiving off for the day.

Jack deserved everything that was coming to him. She wanted him to be stunned back into remembering everything so he could feel the pain she was feeling and more, the guilt and anger in full measure. That thought made these weary visits worthwhile.

She was getting used to being back in a town, part of a crowd and anonymous. No one knew her history here in Scarperton. She could saunter through the streets staring at half-empty shop windows, putting off the evil hour when she must face the big iron gates and locked doors.

For that she needed some comfort and it was there waiting round the corner in the back door of Brennan's licensed grocery store: her usual bottle of amber nectar, the medicine, if taken in small doses, that would see her through the coming visit.

Theirs was an amicable arrangement. She delivered her produce and Alf Brennan produced a bottle: no names, no questions asked. It wasn't as if she was overdoing it. In truth she'd broken a life-long pledge of temperance but she was a grown-up now and knew how to spoon out the spirit, carefully sipping it slowly. It was no different from Doc Murray's pills but this medicine worked, and it was only for a while, until she felt better. Something had to see her through this terrible time.

No one knew her here, deals were strictly tit for tat, but she brought extra this week so that if she missed a trip then she needn't be without her medicine up the dale.

She had hated the smell of it at first. It took her back to Dad's breath, but now she found it strangely comforting. At first she would shut her eyes and gulp, but now she could sip it and not squirm. She didn't want to enjoy the taste. That might make her make a habit of it and end up like Dad with his 'wee drams'. Oh, no! That'd never do, but it was her little secret and it dulled the edge of her pain, her reward at the end of a tough day. It helped her sleep without dreaming.

It wasn't as if she was wasting anyone's coupons or stealing cash. It was her way of staying strong for Jack, of forgetting Sylvie's broken body. No one could deny her such comfort when her husband was tucked up safe in hospital, drugged to the eyeballs . . .

'I'll take two this week,' she smiled at the grocer. 'In fact, three might be better.' It was always a relief to have those bottles tucked down in her basket as she sat on the train heading north. It helped her face the going back to Windebank and the walk home.

'Sorry, love, two's all I can manage. I've got regulars I can't disappoint, but if you come down on Saturday I'll see what I can do. I'm expecting another supply . . . Oh, and if you could bring some bacon too . . .'

She scurried out to the street on edge. Coming out of the asylum always made her knees buckle. She needed a pick-me-up just to get through the gate. Perhaps she ought to try somewhere else or, better still, save her supplies and wait until the Golden Lion opened and have a little nip to warm her through for the journey. She could catch the bus home. The world wouldn't miss her for another hour or two. No one would begrudge her a little free time.

To step over the threshold of a public house on her own took some doing. She breezed in and said she was freezing and could she have a nip to keep out the cold. The woman at the bar, all dolled up, looked her up and down with suspicion. There was only one sort of woman who went in a pub alone and that was to pick up men. She eyed her thick tweed suit and felt hat, her sensible brogues. There was no mistaking Mirren for a lady of the night.

Soon she popped in every week and they passed pleasantries and she told them she was visiting a sick aunt in the asylum and the chaps around looked at her with pity and bought her a round. Her presence was now fully understood. 'Wouldn't catch me in one of them places,' was the general opinion.

The pub was cosy and warm and the fug of stale ale and cigarettes, soot and sawdust no longer bothered her. She chatted to the regulars and watched the old men play dominoes. She gave accounts of the imaginary progress of her sick aunt. Here she felt safe among chums, who took her at face value: just a farmer's wife down from the dale to shop and do good. There was nothing wrong in that and yet . . .

Sometimes as the nights grew darker and colder it got harder to face that lonely trek on the last bus home, walking through the copse in the dark, the wind in her face, the look on Ben's face. That 'Where've you been till this hour?' sort of look.

She got into the habit of telling tales about not wanting to leave Jack, doing shopping for him, popping back, all lies. She said she'd eaten in a café so no need to heat up any tea, and by the way she was going to pop back on Saturday to give Jack a surprise.

Sometimes Mirren didn't recognise herself, her brash lies and skin-deep answers, quick to snap at Ben if he looked put out. It is easy to lie when you are trusted, she noted with concern.

'I was hoping to get off early on Saturday. I'm taking Lorna to the pictures,' he said.

'I'm not stopping you. Uncle Tom'll cover with Dieter, and I'll do the morning milking,' she offered. 'So it's back on with you two then? About time,' she smiled, but as she climbed the stairs she felt put out and jumpy that Ben was getting his life together. He'd be leaving them soon. It didn't take long for him to forget his goddaughter.

Ben and Lorna, Jack in hospital, Tom and Florrie had each other. Who was there for her?

She unpacked the bottles carefully, tucking them deep into her wardrobe and shoving the empties into her bottom drawer. It was time for her medicine, a big swig. She wanted to sleep tonight. It was going to be a long trek until Saturday.

By Friday night she was down to the last dregs of the second bottle. The medicine was not working as well as it used to for she was awake all night watching the dawn creep through the gap in the curtains. She rose early and went in search of their secret hoard of bacon flitches. How was she going to cut off a hunk and get it out of the farm in her basket? She would need a suitcase, but Jack might need some fresh clothes. No one would suspect anything. They'd be glad he was up and about and dressed. It would mean he was soon coming home. The thought of his return made her sweat.

Ben sat through *Brief Encounter* holding Lorna's hand and trying not to yawn. It was a woman's

253

film about a housewife and a doctor having an affair in some small town. He perked up when he recognised Carnforth station in the shot, recognising the tunnel and the platform, and the music wasn't bad. Lorna was weeping buckets.

'Wasn't it sad? They were made for each other but she had to go back to her real life and do her duty . . .'

He patted her on the hand and looked at his watch. They might catch the fish-and-chip shop open on the way back. It was time he stepped up this on-and-off romance, give her a bit of attention. He'd never kissed a girl properly before, or made love, for that matter. Lorna was not the sort of girl to experiment on either. He couldn't lead her on without it being serious. She was a straightforward Yorkshire girl, a no-nonsense sort with a kind heart. He could do far worse than stick with her but deep inside, it was Mirren's lips he wanted to kiss, her body he wanted to hold. God help him if he was just a one-girl man. He was doomed.

How could he go on fooling himself that all this work at World's End was anything other than a chance to pretend that he would be sharing it with her himself? He was a right muggins.

Mirren would stick with Jack, like it or not. Lately she was so unreliable in the mornings he'd begun to think she was sickening for something.

Mirren – all he ever thought about was her when it should be Lorna on his mind.

They walked up the high road through the village, dawdling and chatting while he plucked up the courage to make a move. He could see her eager, her eyes sparkling with expectation. Be a man and get it over with, he thought as he reached for the gate to open it but a shout from the post office house stopped him in his tracks.

'Ben? Is that you? You've saved me a right hike. 'A've just had Sowerby missus on the phone. She's stuck in Scarperton, daft bugger missed the last train. She asked me to say she'll not be fit in the morning. Poor lass, and her having to go all that way to visit Jack. She didn't want you to be worried.'

'Thanks, Harold.' Ben waved his hand at the postmaster. 'I'll have to go, Lorna. You heard the gist of it. I can't have her walking in the dark. There's tramps and deserters on the run. Daft happorth, visiting finished hours ago. What's she been up to? You women and the pictures . . . all that romancing . . .'

'Well, we don't get much in these parts, Reuben Yewell,' she snapped at him.

'What's that supposed to mean? I took you out,' he said, puzzled.

'I might as well have gone myself, the interest you took. You were asleep in five minutes.'

'I was up at the crack of dawn,' he offered, knowing it was true.

'Did madam not surface again? They say she's a right lady of leisure, swanning round Scarperton, twice a week. I thought you farmers were having a rough time? She's been seen going in the Golden Lion of a night, and on market day,' Lorna added.

'Don't be daft. Mirren's teetotal and always has been,' he snapped back.

'That's not what I heard,' she sneered. 'Bold as brass through the front door.'

'I thought she was your friend,' he said, feeling his pulse racing at this news. 'After what she's been through, I'd not begrudge her a port and lemon or two . . . Who's been spreading this nonsense?'

'No one you know, but it's true so you'd better get off and rescue the damsel in distress before she wears out her precious shoe leather.'

This was a side to Lorna he didn't like. 'You can come with me if you like,' he offered.

'What, and play gooseberry? I'm not blind. Everyone knows you slaver over her like a puppy. I'm not playing second fiddle to her tune. Go on, beat it!'

'Oh, Lorna,' Ben stuttered, not knowing what to say. 'I'm sorry if I've spoilt your evening. I'll make it up to you.'

'No you won't. I'm sick of excuses, excuses. If it's not the farm, it's that ruin you're restoring.'

'Who told you about that?'

'Does it matter? Everyone knows everyone else's business in Windebank. I'm sorry about what happened to Jack and Mirren, we all are, but it's about time they pulled themselves together and didn't expect you to pick up the crumbs under their table,' she said, looking up at him with tears in her eyes.

'If that's how you feel . . .' Ben sighed, suddenly bone weary.

'Yes it is, and the sad thing is you've never noticed how I felt before and never will while yon girl from World's End is on the loose. Watch it, Ben, you may get more than you bargain for meddling with those two. Oil and water don't mix, or should I say, whisky and wine,' she said, and with that warning she swung through the gate, put her key into the front door and slammed it behind her.

Ben drove the truck slowly with the pinwheel head-lights on, peering into the darkness, trying to spot a glimpse of Mirren on the road. Surely she was not trying to thumb a lift on the main road? How could she think of such a thing unless she was not right in the head? Surely not?

He spotted her three miles out of Scarperton, barefoot, carrying her shoes and basket as if she was off to market, her headscarf was round her head with her hat plonked on top.

'Get in!' he shouted, leaning across the seat. 'What the hell are you doing at this time of night? Do you want to get run over?'

'I'm fine,' she smiled. 'The fresh air has done me good. I went to the pictures and fell asleep through the second house.' She smiled sweetly, looking at the road ahead, not at him and he knew she lied.

'What did you see?' he snapped, knowing it would be *Brief Encounter* on at the Plaza too.

'Oh, I don't know, some cowboy so boring I dozed off. The usherette woke me up. It's been a long day,' she sighed.

'Don't tell me lies. You've been in the pub, drinking.'

'Why, Ben, what a cruel thing to say. You know I don't drink. I'd never go in one of those places,' she replied without a shake in her voice.

'So how come you've been seen going in the Golden Lion, regular as clockwork?' His voice was cracked with fury.

'I just popped in to sell them some eggs, didn't I tell you? I've got quite a little round going.' She had an excuse for everything.

'Oh, you've had a round or two, I can smell it on your breath. I didn't come up the Wharfe on a biscuit tin. You stink of smoke and there's whisky on your breath, not just on your clothes.'

'I had just the one to tide me over. Jack's visits

are such a strain and I was frozen. It seemed like a good idea. No harm done ...' Her excuses drained away.

'Pull the other one, Mirren. I wasn't born yesterday, you must be tipsy to be taking a risk like this,' he said. His hands were gripping the wheel. He wanted to shake her.

'Oh, shut up! Don't be so po-faced. You sound like my Sunday school teacher. Did little Miss Lorna give you the push? Have I spoiled your evening?'

'Mirren, this isn't you talking. If you're in trouble you only have to talk to me about it, not bottle things up and drink it. Nothing good comes out of those sort of bottles. How many times've you told me? It's a mug's game,' he pleaded.

'Oh, but it does, you're wrong. It's only medicine. It calms me down and gets me to sleep and makes me forget. There's no harm in a nip or two and I'm not bothering anyone else,' she said with her arms folded in defiance or defence – he wasn't sure which.

'But you bother me, wasting petrol coming to find you. Don't you think I'd rather be doing something else than ferreting around looking for you?'

'I didn't ask you to come. Sorry, sorry, sorry. Is that enough? Now shut up and let me sleep.'

What else could he say? Lorna was right. The gossip was true. He was too stunned by her casualness, her lies to argue. She was drunk enough to be beyond reach and soon she was snoring away, flopping her head on the side window all the way home.

Ben drew up in the yard, lifted her out of the truck and carried her upstairs. No one was up. He took off her stockings, loosened her jacket and blouse. She looked so peaceful, lying there. He felt such a desire rise up but he daren't do anything. How he longed to hold her close and take this terrible pain away from her, the pain she was trying to blot out. If she had his love wrapped around her, there would be no need for whisky or booze. They would fight the demons together.

Mirren woke with a fuzzy head and a tongue like cork matting. The room spun around her and she lifted herself slowly. How had she got back home? Her clothes were crumpled up, her stockings were in tatters on the chair. She could recall going into the pub and chatting to Monica, the barmaid. Then they were chucked out at closing time and the station was shuttered. How had she managed to get back here?

There was the long black road, headlamps, a stretch of stars torching her path. It was like a jigsaw all broken up with a few corners filled in. There was an argument and a man's voice . . .

Her watch said ten o'clock in the morning. Hellfire, she'd missed morning milking again and it was Sunday. There'd be ructions. Time to pull off her suit and girdle, throw on her farm stuff. Aiming for the door, she banged her shins. Blood and sand! I'm in for it, she thought.

She crept down the grand stairs slowly, not wanting to trip. Florrie was bustling about singing hymn tunes in her best frock. Since Sylvia died she'd taken to chapel big time and would be off to the service.

'You're up then? Ben said you were unwell and he had to fetch you . . . a bit of a tummy upset, was it? How's Jack?' No further questions so all was well there then.

'He's fine. The treatment is making him remember stuff,' she smiled. Jack was slowly coming round – well, a version of Jack, not the one she used to know; a bit like herself. She was forgetting the Mirren she used to be. 'It was just a gippy tummy but I'm fine now. I'd better get cracking. I owe Ben a favour. Is he doing his rounds?'

'No, he's up the tops, as usual. I'm glad you're feeling better. He said you were right poorly in the night. Would you like to go to chapel?'

Mirren shook her head and patted her stomach. 'No, I daren't risk it,' she lied. All she could think about was making sure Ben hadn't spilled the beans. She must apologise to him and put things right, but first there was another thing she must do.

261

She crept back up the dark oak staircase to her room and rummaged in her basket, just in case he'd spotted her medicine. There was nothing there and she felt panic rising. She rifled through her wardrobe and the drawer of empties, then her knicker drawer – all her private places – but there was nothing and she began to shake.

Then she remembered the last resort, the tin box under her bed. Opening the tin she grabbed the spare bottle but not before she saw Sylvia's face in that photograph looking up, scowling, the last one they ever had, and she slammed down the lid, swallowing her whisky quickly. This was going to have to last.

It was time to get out into the field and find Ben. There must be no tales told out of school. As she trudged up the track, there was no sign of him walling, just Dieter who was waving frantically and running over, but she dodged him and took a short cut over a stone stile. Onwards and upwards to the high fells where the air would clear her head, fresh and cool. The loose limestone scree slowed her down. It was a long time since she'd visited World's End – not since VE Day. For a while it had been her refuge but lately it was too much bother. Let it go to rack and ruin, she didn't care. All the days were the same, grey, flat and empty, since Sylvia left them.

At least in Scarperton she could meet new

people and be one of a crowd who laughed and worked in the mills and shops, clocking on and off, not like farmers who never got a chance to clock off.

Perhaps when Jack came out they would have a change of sky, as Granny Simms used to say. Funny how she could hardly recall any of that time, as if there was a wall between her and her childhood with no door in it.

She panted up the hill, unused to its steepness, and then stopped in shock at the sight before her, not sure if she had come to the right place.

The ruin was no more, but in its place was a fine cottage with a roof, new windows, signs of building rubble and activity. Someone had been hard at work rebuilding World's End and they were making a fine job of it too. She walked around, stunned at the detail and effort into the little place that had saved her life so many years before.

She could hardly bear to look. No one had said anything about it being renovated but it was months since she'd bothered to come. Funny how she'd always thought of it as her World's End, but the land probably belonged to Lord Benton. The Yewells must only rent it and now it was taken back.

She trekked back down the hill disconsolate, her insides churning like a butter tub. Who would go to all the trouble? She spotted Dieter in his battledress with the yellow circle at his back. He was waiting for her, cap in hand.

'Who is building up there?' she said in school-girl German. He smiled at her effort and answered in good English. 'I help Herr Ben for his sweet-heart, I think.' He patted his chest. 'He make new home, I think, but it is top secret, I think.'

Mirren took in his information in one gulp. How dare he? How dare Ben go behind her back and take her dream and make it his own? Behind her back take Miss Goody Two-Shoes Dinsdale and live up there all cosy and lovey-dovey. It was not his World's End, it was hers!

She was so angry she forgot her mission to find him. If she saw him she would have screamed at him. Best to avoid him, the serpent, getting wed and not telling her. How could he steal her dream? The tears dripped down her cheeks but she would not give him the satisfaction of knowing she knew his little secret. All she needed was a drink. She raced back to Cragside and hid in her bedroom all afternoon, burying her head in the pillow, sick at heart. World's End had been her secret refuge and now it was gone.

'Jack's coming home for the weekend. We've had a telegram,' yelled Florrie from the foot of the stairs, rushing round giving everyone the good news. They were busy getting the beef stock ready for the Christmas fat stock show. It was all hands to the pump in the rush to make them secure in the cattle truck.

Ben watched Mirren's face drop at the news. 'It's too soon, surely. Who said he could come out?'

'The Polish chap, the nice doctor with the beard. I heard he was rescued from one of them concentration camps, poor devil. There's a few of them round Leeds doing a good job, if our Jack's anything to go by. Dr Murray says if he settles he'll come out for Christmas too,' Florrie beamed. 'It's an answer to prayer.'

Mirren shook her head. 'You and Tom'll have to go and fetch him then. We're too busy with all this palaver, aren't we, Ben?' She looked him straight in the eye for the first time in weeks. He'd begun to think she was avoiding him and he put it down to her shame at being caught drunk. They'd not talked since, but she was careful to show him how sober she was and she was back on form for the cattle show, which was a relief.

'We'll be proud to bring him home in the van. He needs a rest and feeding up. The sight of these hills will perk him up, and your cheery face, Mirren. I'm going to bake a right big sponge if I can find some eggs. I'll be wringing their necks if those hens don't do their duty. We allus seem short these days,' she sighed.

Ben looked at Mirren, willing her to own up to

her secret egg round but she looked away with pink cheeks.

Having Jack back would be the best medicine, Ben thought. Then he would show them his surprise and give them a chance to get to know each other again. No more trips to hospital and no temptation for Mirren. He'd not smelled spirits on her breath, just mint imperials, which she sucked furiously, perhaps to give her mouth something to chew on. If she was making an effort he wasn't going to tell tales.

It had been such a bad year and now she was seeing sense. The egg episode would stop now that winter was on them. Mirren was sensible. She knew enough was enough, but even he knew this weekend visit would be difficult for all of them. It was the first time Jack had faced the farm since the accident.

It was hard not to feel sorry for him. He wouldn't wish Mirren and Jack's suffering on his worst enemy. It still felt like some nightmare. They were dreading Christmas without the fun of seeing a little kiddy opening her presents and her stocking. Children made Christmas special.

His mam and dad were coming, and maybe Bert with his foreign fiancée, Irina, if he could get her into the country. They'd met when his camp was liberated. She was an interpreter. It was the talk of the district how he'd come home safe at last with a pretty foreign bride in tow. Her arrival was going to take some stomaching for some, seeing as she was German. She'd helped Bert after the war and now he was going back into teaching woodwork. Ben couldn't wait to see his brother again.

The war had changed them all but drawn them closer as a family. His mother and dad were full of Bert's adventures. He hoped family closeness would hold up Jack and Mirren at the worst time of the year.

'Come on, slow coach,' yelled Mirren. 'We'll be late. I want a rosette at least out of this lot. This is the first big show since hostilities ceased,' she laughed. 'Mind you, there'll be a few hostilities in the auction ring when the judges give their verdict.'

'That's my girl,' Ben sighed with relief, she was back to her old self. How silly he was to think she wouldn't straighten herself out, given time and some understanding.

Scarperton Auction Mart was buzzing with good humour. The white coats were parading their beasts round the ring, heifers, bulls, calves, all rippling with good meat. Local farmers in tweeds were gathered in flat caps, chewing over the entries, eyeing up the opposition. Butchers were out in force choosing their Christmas stock while the auctioneer rattled off the prices. There were stalls of produce, farm wear and fancy goods, and wives with baskets, on the prowl for a bargain.

The Yewells were grooming the last of their beefers, polishing them off to show off their haunches but all Mirren could think of was Jack coming home and having to share her bed. How would she take her medicine with him around the room?

She'd have to shift her dwindling supplies. Her nerves jangled every time she thought of him coming home for good: all of them together and no Sylvia.

She couldn't bear the thought of her lying in the ground and not jumping on their bed with glee on Christmas morning. She just wanted to forget the whole damn business. This wretched season ought to be banned.

She'd made sure in the past weeks to avoid the toy shop windows, the Christmas displays and festive decorations, meagre though the post-war ones were. To see children pointing out Dinky toys and dolls in boxes, toy prams and dressing-up clothes was agony.

She was going to need supplies to get her through the coming weeks, and there were no spare eggs or provisions to barter, just the brooch that had belonged to Gran, the one she'd have passed on to Sylvie, had she lived. What was the point now? Better to buy medicine and give everyone a hearty

Christmas. If she dulled the pain, she'd be better company, but pawning her brooch for drink didn't sit easy. Gran would turn in her grave.

She slipped away from the Auction Mart in the centre of town, down to the old second-hand shop at the back of the Town Hall where Sam Layberg sold watches, second-hand jewellery and junk. There was a discreet sign with three golden balls over the door. She slipped into the shop and produced the brooch from its box: a large amethyst surrounded by seed pearls in a gold setting.

He examined it carefully. 'Nice piece, Regency, family? I can't give you more than two guineas for it. There's not much call for big stuff.' He sighed over his half-moon glasses.

She knew and he knew it was worth a lot more but she nodded. 'Don't sell it. I'll be back for it,' she smiled, taking the cash quickly, trying not to gasp at what she had just done. It was so disloyal, but needs must . . .

'That's what they all say, young lady. Now I have a shop full of stuff I can't sell,' he whispered.

The coins were burning through her purse. It was just about opening time and if she trawled enough off-licences she might get herself a full bottle of whisky and some halves. There were one or two places to avoid, for they sold duff bottles, watered down with God knew what; she dreaded to think. She needed full strength to see her through. This time she checked every entrance to make sure no one recognised her. It wouldn't do to be caught red-handed.

By two o'clock she'd spent every penny, wrapped her purchases carefully in her shopping bag and headed back to the show. Ben was waiting with a face like thunder.

'Where've you been?' He drew close to smell her breath again.

'Never you mind. A girl has to do what a girl has to do. Haven't you heard of Christmas shopping or am I expected to buy it all here? Jack needed new pyjamas and I'd got enough coupons. I saw a little scarf for Florrie. No peeking until Christmas.' She smiled sweetly through her lies. That took the shine off his shoes. 'You thought I'd been down the Golden Lion again. Go on, admit it? You'll have to trust me. Those days are over now. We've got Jack home and we'll give him a good time.' It hurt to play-act in front of him but what else could she do?

Ben stepped back, looking relieved. 'We got a second for Gertie and a third for Horace. Pity you weren't here to see it, but I suppose you ladies have to make the most of an outing to the shops now you'll not be gadding off each week.'

Was there a warning in his voice? It was hard to tell. Ben was acting like her policeman and it got on Mirren's nerves.

'I'll gad where I like,' she snapped, 'and when I like. You're not my keeper and I'm not a child!'

'Someone has to look after you. You've got so thin and I never see you eat a square meal. I never see you pick up a book either, or peg rugs with Florrie like you used to.'

'Nothing is like it used to be, or have you forgotten? You've got your life to live and I've got mine,' she said, and walked away from him.

The sooner he got wed the sooner she could settle down with Jack and try to make a go of it. Ben unnerved her when he drew too close. There was something in his eyes that stirred up stuff. He was young and strong and fit and bursting with energy.

Perhaps she and Jack should move right away and go down south, as he wanted to. This new Jack didn't seem so eager. Once he was at Cragside he'd be fed up in five minutes and want to move on.

Mirren took her bag to the ladies' room and had a swig to calm her nerves, chewed on a peppermint and splashed on some lavender water, just in case her gaoler was on the prowl.

Now she had to think where to hide her supplies away from prying eyes. World's End would have been ideal if it wasn't so far to trek, but now it wasn't hers. She didn't want Tom and Florrie finding out her secret habit. They had enough on their plate worrying about Jack. He wouldn't care either way.

It was funny how she was getting an expert on how to find black-market booze around the district. It was as if there was a secret little network of cronies all after the same stuff and all helping each other find new suppliers, word of mouth round the pubs and shops. She'd make sure Tom got in some stuff for Christmas. Beer or brandy – anything would do to eke out her own bottles. They were not for sharing. She had to be strong for Jack and to stop Ben from nagging and get through the festive season without making a fool of herself. Christmas was an endurance test and she had to look after her own interest if she was to survive.

Ben could like it or lump it. It was none of his business. If he didn't like it he could camp out with his ladylove at World's End and leave her to get on with living her way. She still hadn't forgiven him for stealing her dream.

14

Jack shuffled through that first visit in a dream, drawn, bent and so tired he fell asleep even when they were talking. That weekend was to be the first of many and it was a strain trying to be bright and breezy, chipper and cheerful. Florrie did her best to cajole her son into eating some of her best baking but he barely had a spoonful. It was hard to make conversation with him. He didn't seem to hear what they were saying, had not a spark of interest in farm chitchat. He avoided Dieter as if he was a bad smell and just stared out of the window across the valley, lost in his own world.

'Come on,' said Mirren, trying to stay patient. 'Snap out of it. We're going to make the best of the season whatever. Pam and Wes have made the effort to come and visit. Your mam's doing her best. Buck up!'

'You don't know what it's like. I feel tired all the time.'

'But you do nothing but sit around,' she replied. 'Let's walk the fields. It's time we had a chat.'

'What about? I should think you said it all in hospital. I know you're only going through the motions. You look worse than me in the mornings.'

'That's because I'm trying to stay on top of the job. One day at a time, and I've no time to indulge myself in self-pity. What's done can't be undone,' she replied.

'Do you think I like feeling like this?'

'There you go, feeling sorry for yourself again. Buck up and come and help me muck out. The doctor said exercise would do you good.' His whining was getting on her nerves.

'Not with that Jerry on the prowl,' came his reply. 'Why did you let them bring Krauts here?'

'Because Dieter is hard-working and cheap labour and he does the job.' What had Dieter got to do with anything?

'So you prefer Jerry to me now, is it?' He stared at her hard.

'What's that supposed to mean?' She avoided his gaze.

'You've not looked the road I'm on since I came back,' he added.

'And why should I want to? You've not made any effort. You don't wash or shave unless I badger you, your armpits smell of sweat. I'm doing my

274

best trying to put things behind me . . . for better or worse, Jack. That's what we promised but it's hard.'

'You ignore me as if I'm some weak-willed idiot. I can't help how I feel,' he argued back.

'Feel, feel . . . feel. I'm sick of how you feel. What about how I feel, trapped in these hills with only memories of how it once was?'

'But you've changed, Mirren, grown that hard you'll snap. Strong you may be but it feels I'm being punished night and day, in my dreams, every waking moment, and when I see the look on your face it's like sore feet. How's a chap supposed to feel? And why's Lanky still sniffing around here? I thought he was wedding Freddy's sister?'

'He will. Give them time. Those two are on the slow boat to China, blowing hot and cold. Enough of them. What are we going to do? We can't stay here for ever, not now . . .'

'I'm not ready to shift yet, love. I've got to get my head together. There's whole bits I can't piece together. It's the shock treatment. I don't want any more of that. It burns your brains.' He fidgeted with his hair.

'Then buck up, smarten up, and we'll go down The Fleece and have a little celebration.'

'But you don't drink.' He looked up at her with surprise.

'That was before Sylvie died. I'll not refuse a

sherry or two, or a beer even. I need to get out of this place and I can't go on my own, now, can I?'

'I can't drink with my tablets. Dr Kaplinsky says I'm dried out now and better to stay off it. It was doing me no good, as well you know. Thanks but I'll give it a miss.'

'That's not like you to miss a treat. Where's that *esprit de corps*? It'll do us both good just to go down and see your pals. Come on, one won't do you any harm.'

And that was how they found themselves propping up the bar at Windebank amidst the faded tinsel and tatty paper decorations, the spit-and-sawdust brigade, listening to gossip. Everyone made a fuss of Jack and bought him drinks and he began to liven up.

Mirren slipped down as many as she decently could before the bell rang and Bill suggested a lock-up. Those who were still at the bar when the bell rang were locked in. They were still there at two in the morning.

Somehow they staggered home and into bed without too much noise, laughing and giggling like naughty schoolkids, fumbling into a drunken cuddle, snoring and waking up with heads like helter-skelters.

Now that was better, Mirren smiled. If you can't beat 'em, join 'em, she reasoned. Better to share the same hobby.

Suddenly Christmas at Cragside was nothing to fear.

'What's got into Mirren?' said Ben's mother, Pam, eyeing her at the table with concern. 'She's up and down like a yo-yo, never still and that thin, and she was always such a bonny lass. Now she's shrunk to nothing. Still, it can't be easy for her with Jack on the bottle again. Florrie's that worried. They stay out all hours. It's the talk of Windebank how they've perked up. I hope Mirren will keep him on the straight and narrow. She always was a stickler before but lately . . . I'm not sure.'

It was as if Sylvia's death hovered over them all like a dark cloud, never spoken of but always there, and those two were partying as if there was no tomorrow.

Mirren was hitting the bottle again, down the pub laughing and joking, pretending all was well, glassy-eyed, tanked up one minute and miserable the next. Ben knew the signs by now. It made him sick to watch her.

Lorna was avoiding him too, trying to play hard to get, but he didn't have time for games. There were enough games going on here.

Nothing was ever addressed. Tom and Florrie didn't want to upset Jack, and he was treading a fine line trying to hold himself together, but Mirren wasn't helping at all, taking him down to the very place that had caused his first trouble. Ben didn't understand her any more.

He caught her by the outbarn, loading hay, for the weather was set for snow.

'What's your game, setting Jack back on the booze?' he yelled, not caring who heard him. 'He was dry for months and now he's as bad as ever. I'd have thought you had more sense. I'm that worried about you, Mirren. Drink's not the answer.'

'How would you know?' she said, her eyes blazing hatred.

'It doesn't bring out the best in you. Cut it out for a while . . . sober up. Everyone's beginning to notice.'

'So what? It's my life. I can live it how I please. I will take my medicine when I like, where I like. You can't stop me.'

'Medicine – is that how you see it? Poison, more like. It's changed you from being my reliable friend into someone I can't trust any more.'

'Who says I need your friendship anyway? You stole what was mine for your girlfriend. I don't trust you either,' she said.

'Don't talk daft. When did I ever steal anything of yours?'

'World's End. I've seen what you've done with it . . . for her. Dieter told me. That place was mine first.' She stared back defiantly at him, waiting for a response.

Ben took off his cap and roared with laughter. 'You nincompoop! So that's what you've been sulking about all these weeks. I knew there was something up.'

'Don't you dare laugh at me, Reuben Yewell. There's nothing more to say if you're going to take that attitude. I hate you!' She stormed off, leaving him standing, calling her back.

'But let me explain . . .' he called into the wind.

'I'm not listening. Kettle calling the pot black, that's you!' She raced off down the track.

The stupid woman thought World's End was for Lorna, Ben smiled, and she was jealous. He could see it in her eyes, up a gumtree with fury. It was time to clear the air once and for all and show that harridan just how wrong she was. Then he wanted to see the shame on her cheeks when he showed them his gift.

'It's not a night to be gallivanting out,' Florrie advised. The sky was leaden and full of snow feathers and ice. She looked up from her knitting. 'Better to stay indoors and have a game of cards. It's icy out there.'

Mirren breezed past her. 'We'll borrow the van, won't be long. Jack's been stuck in all day long, helping with paperwork. He deserves a treat. You wouldn't begrudge us a bit of life now, would you?' She knew how to get round Florrie.

'You never used to like those places, Mirren,' Florrie sniffed, not looking up. 'Now you can't keep away.'

'There's nothing to keep us here, is there?' Sylvia was laid on the table as her trump card.

'No, well, if you put it like that, but don't be late. Tom's got a bad chest. It's your turn to do the milking.'

'When have I ever let him down?' she said, knowing full well she'd be pushed to rise by first light.

Jack was looking brighter, more his old self, more the man she married except in the bed department. They'd not managed to get it together very well yet. But she wasn't exactly Hedy Lamarr in the glamour stakes to help it on.

Ben went about like a bear with a sore head. He'd offered to take them both up to World's End to show them round but she refused politely and didn't want to hear any more on that subject. World's End was off limits until hostilities ceased. She didn't want to see the pride in his place when he showed them his love nest.

It had been a dreadful morning at the local marketplace. Lorna had snubbed her in the street. Hilda Thursby, now a mother, was pushing her pram and ducked behind the stalls when she saw her coming.

Mirren knew people were pointing at her behind

her back, saying that she was the wife whose hubby had run over his kiddy while drunk. She knew what they were thinking and she didn't care. She and Jack had each other and a bottle for company. The rest could go hang!

It was a freezing night, sure enough, and a wind had got up. They rattled down the village in silence. There was something on Jack's mind. He'd gone quiet and shut off.

'Cat got your tongue?' Mirren said, hoping to chivvy up his mood, but he looked ahead and shrugged his shoulders.

'Well, this is going to be a great night out if you're in a strop!'

'I was thinking perhaps we should go to the flicks tonight and not the pub. I'm getting fed up with the same old faces in Windebank.' This was a surprise.

'Then let's go on to Scarperton; it's only ten miles down the road. There's enough petrol to take us there and back. I know a good place there. Fresh faces to meet.' They drove down the narrow lanes and crossroads to the market town and parked up the van.

'Fish and chips or a slap-up meal at the Rose and Crown,' Jack offered. 'Then we can go to the second house at the Plaza, like old times.'

'Who needs a meal? Save your brass. Let's get straight to the Golden Lion. They do crisps. There's

281

a good fire and a piano. I know the girl at the bar – Monica, she's called – she'll make us a sandwich.'

'Mirren, we need to talk,' he said in a quiet, serious voice. 'This drinking's got to stop. It needs cutting down. We can go to the Plaza or go dancing, if you like, make a proper night out for a change,' he offered again.

'What's got into you?' she snapped, not understanding this sudden change of mood. 'It's not like you to miss a pint. Don't be a girl's blouse.'

'It's not that, love. I just think we'd better slow it down a bit. Ben was saying—'

'Oh, so Holy Joe has been telling tales, has he? Given you a warning. Take no notice of him, he's in a mood since I won't speak to him. Come on, I'm going in even if you're not.'

Mirren left him on the pavement and headed for the pub door, certain that he'd soon follow her. She breezed in, greeted the gang assembled and waited for the door to open but it didn't. It was too cold to be messing about so she went out to search for him. He was sitting in the van weeping, a grown man howling his head off.

'What's up with you now?' she snapped, irritated. This was Jack going backwards again. 'Come in and forget your misery. I want you to meet my friends.'

Jack shook his head. 'No, love. I know all about it . . .'

'About what?' She was puzzled now. His face was a picture of misery.

'What you've been up to with the bottles. I found your empties.'

'What bottles might they be?' She shivered but tried to look puzzled.

'Your medicine bottles. I was searching for some slippers and went in your wardrobe and they fell out. There were dozens and dozens of empties,' he croaked.

'So?'

'Mirren, there were whisky bottles everywhere, pounds and pounds worth of empties. What have you done to yourself?' he sobbed.

'I don't know what you mean.' She flushed at his discovery.

'Oh, come off it, you're drinking enough for two, worse than any man. I know you can't help it. I know what it's like. I used to see the army whisky swiggers, taking nips here and there. The officers were the worst. It's strong spirit. This isn't you, not the girl I married,' he whispered.

'And who beat me round the head, took me whether I wanted it or not and killed my babies?' she screamed. 'That's not the guy I married either!'

'It can't go on, not like this. It'll harm your insides. Women can't take it like men.'

'Want to bet? Come on, you've said your piece

and I've listened but we're wasting good drinking time. Don't be a spoilsport.'

'Dr Kaplinsky said I must fight my demons and drink made them worse, not better,' he pleaded again, but she'd heard enough.

'Dr Kaplinsky? I'm sick of his name. What does he know?'

'I told you before, he knows about suffering. He lost all his family in the war. They were Jews. Let's go home. I'm done in.'

'Well, I'm not, not at all. If you won't come in then I will jolly well go back and enjoy what's left of my evening. You can go home and I'll walk back.'

'Don't be daft. Like that time when Ben came to find you?' He faced her angrily.

'Oh, so he's been telling tales, has he?'

'He's your cousin, he's family, he loves you. It broke my heart to see those bottles hidden away. I want to keep you safe. You're my girl . . .'

'Don't go all teetotal on me now, Jack. It doesn't suit you.'

'Drink doesn't suit you either. It's not the answer. Together we can move away, put all this behind us, make something of ourselves, but not with a bottle between us. What would yer gran and Joe make of you going in pubs? They'd be horrified, and I've brought you down to this. I showed you the way. Please, Mirren, come home

284

with me and we'll make plans and find a way through together.'

'Leave me alone! I'm fine. I need a break, not a sermon. I'll get the last train home, I promise. You can meet me at the Halt. Go on then, on your way if you're not coming in. I don't want you hanging around. You can do the morning milking,' she laughed, but the laugh was hollow as she waved him off. What on earth had got into Jack?

He'd turned coat and gone all strait-laced and prissy. He must be having one of his turns. Well, 'Let him go, let him tarry, let him sink or let him swim', as the song went. His loss. Where she needed to be now was not in a van with a lap full of fish and chips from newspaper but through the door where there was a roaring fire and a vat of whisky to drink dry or die in the attempt. That was better. It was true that the world looked better through the bottom of a glass.

The whole gang was there, Elsie, the wild Irish market trader, ripping up and down the keyboard singing old Irish ballads. There was Mr Fisher and his mates, arguing over whose round it was, and then there were builders' boys, who'd start a fight before long and be chucked out into the chill air.

At closing time they all spilled out onto the street and someone knew a cellar where you could get stuff on the QT. Mirren's breath steamed in the frost and she drank until her purse ran out.

Elsie bought the cardigan off her back, the new one Pam had knitted for her for Christmas.

Cragside was lost in the mist. Jack was a faded argument. Here she could let rip and be herself, singing and cavorting. One by one they all peeled away until there was just her and Elsie, sitting on a bench, roaring out songs.

'Shut that bloody racket up!' shouted a voice from a window. 'You're waking my kids!' Dogs were barking. The drunks rolled up the High Street laughing. Mirren didn't feel the cold with a bottle in her bag and then she slid on the icy pavement and her bag flew off her arm and the glass broke, spilling precious liquid through the straw. She kicked the broken glass in frustration.

'Pick it all up, young lady, or I'll make you!' said a gruff voice.

'You and whose army?' she heard herself say.

'Pick up that mess yourself and get along home.' There was a pair of black boots and navy trouser bottoms in her face. Mirren looked and sniggered, and then saw the blood on her hands and knew no more.

She woke with a banging headache in a lock-up cell with grey walls and tiles covered by a blanket. Her hand was bandaged tightly and she groaned. This was Scarperton police station.

'Right, Mrs Sowerby, if you'll just sign here to

say these are the contents of your bag and purse, your watch . . .'

'Why am I here?' she croaked, her eyes bloodshot and her forehead throbbing.

'Don't you remember?'

'Not exactly. I was out with friends.'

'We didn't see anyone with you, young lady. You were insulting my police officer, and drunk and incapable. We are charging you with disorderly conduct. Is there anyone you'd like us to inform of your whereabouts?'

'My husband, Jack . . . John Wilfred Sowerby of Cragside Farm. He can come and fetch me.' The police inspector nodded and left the cell.

Oh shit! She sat in the bare cell, feeling foolish, hungry, hung over and in need of a stiff one to get her on her feet. If only Jack had come with her, none of this would have happened.

Ben had never seen Jack in such an agitated state when he brought the van back alone.

'Where's Mirren?'

'You may well ask,' came the answer. 'Just come and look at this!' Jack stormed up the stairs, two at a time and Ben followed behind. Curious. What on earth had got into him? Jack was peering into a sackful of bottles. 'This is what it's come to . . . hidden in her wardrobe. Go on, count them. She's Paddy's girl, right enough, and it's all my fault!'

Ben peered into the pitiful pile of small whisky bottles and swallowed hard. Bloody hell!

He felt like an interloper in their bedroom, with Mirren's clothes scattered over the chair, the overwhelming smell of perfume trying to mask the stench of stale whisky.

'I don't know what to do. The doc said to keep off the stuff and now she's drowning in it. I left her in that pub in Scarperton. I were that mad . . .'

'The Golden Lion?' Ben said, not looking at Jack, not wanting to see the despair on his face. He ought to feel glad that Jack was getting his comeuppance but he felt sick with worry.

'You knew about her little haunt, then? Why didn't you say?'

'It was not my place, as you'd soon have spelled out,' Ben replied. 'I didn't fancy your fist in my jaw.'

'Is that what you think? We all used to be mates. What's happened to us? I come back drinking like a fish and kill my kiddy . . . Don't look like that. It's true. Now Mirren's hitting the bottle and I'm sober as a judge. God forgive me, I shouldn't've abandoned her. I'd better go back.'

'No, I'll go,' Ben offered. It was a foul night and Jack was not fit to drive.

'It's not your problem. I'll be fine.' Jack raised his hand to fob him off. 'Just a bit out of practice with all those sleeping pills. I'll be all right.'

'What's going on?' Florrie was out of her bedroom door, wearing iron pin hair curlers under a pink net. 'You've been up and down them stairs like thunder . . . What's going on?'

'Nothing, Mam, go back to bed. We'll explain in the morning. I'm just going to fetch Mirren from the station,' Jack said.

'At this time of night? Have you two had another quarrel?'

'Nowt like that, go to bed,' Jack snapped.

'I'm coming with you,' Ben ordered. His heart was thudding with fury at Mirren for keeping them up again. Would she never learn?

'Well, I'm driving!' Jack jumped back into the van. They backed out of the yard and down the drive and track towards Windebank. Ben sat in the car on the bench seat, waiting until the steam train puffed into sight on its way up to Carlisle.

Jack stood by the platform as the last stragglers left through the side gate, walking back, his shoulders hunched. 'What's she playing at?'

'Missed the train again?' Ben shrugged. 'Hop in. I'll drive.'

'This is my shout and my wife. We'll have to go and fetch her from that flaming pub. Hutch up . . .'

He was driving like a madman, taking corners too fast, lost in his fury.

'Steady away, there's ice on the road.' Ben was

nervous. Jack's love of speed, racing round bends, wasn't funny on a night like this. 'Gently, Bentley, there's a black patch in the shadow of the wall. This's not Oulton Park! Calm down, she'll still be in there.'

'I hope so. She needs help. What a bloody mess. If only—'

'Just concentrate on the road; you're making me nervous. It's a while since you've driven in these conditions. Let me take the wheel,' Ben offered, but Jack was adamant.

'What've I done to make her like this? No, don't tell me!' He turned to look at Ben for one second and suddenly the wheels went into a skid.

'Jack! Reverse the wheel!' Ben screamed, trying to grab the steering wheel. They ricocheted off the stone wall and spun into the air. It was like some slow waltz, shaking like marbles in a tin can, the sound of splintering glass. The van door opened of its own accord and Ben was flung onto the grass verge. The last thing he saw was the wheels spinning, the van upside down.

He woke with a crushing pain in his side. There was not a sound from the van but somewhere a dog barked in the night.

The policeman came back with a cup of strong tea sweetened too much.

'Have you rung the post office at Windebank?

They'll send a message to him. He'll come for me.'

'I'm afraid that's not possible,' the officer muttered, looking at her sideways on. 'I've contacted a Mr Reuben Yewell instead. He'll be along shortly.'

'But I want Jack, not Ben,' she said, knowing it would mean more lectures and sermons from the mount. The whole of Windebank would know her business once Sergeant Bill Turnbull passed the glad tidings around, but it would appear in the *Scarsdale Gazette* anyway. She felt numb and silly now. If only she'd not broken that bottle. It was cold without Pam's cardigan, and how would she explain its loss?

Why was everything taking so long? she thought, watching the hands of her watch creep slowly round. She tried to look contrite and smiled at the young man who brought her more awful tea but he looked at her as if she was an object of pity.

It was a relief when Ben stood in the doorway still in his farming gear, smelling of dung and hay. He could at least have changed his shirt.

'At last! What took you so long?' She stood up, trying to look dignified in her dirty skirt and tattered stockings. 'You needn't look at me like that! Where's Jack? He said he'd wait for the last train.'

'Oh, he did that all right, waited and waited,

291

but you weren't on it, were you? Then, being Jack, he made his way back to Scarperton just like I did to find you, but there was black ice on the road, Mirren, the sort you don't see in the middle of the night. We skidded and crashed the van, did a spin and hit a wall full on.'

He paused, shaking his head, and she sank onto the bench, winded with shock.

'Is he OK?' she mouthed.

He shook his head again wearily. 'Mirren, there's no easy way to tell you this, but Jack is dead. He died at the wheel. It would have been quick, the ambulance man said.'

'Is this some sort of joke?' she snarled, looking at the bobbies standing in the doorway.

'No, missus, sadly not,' said one of them. 'We were called out early this morning to an incident. The A65 is treacherous. Poor man never stood a chance. This one here was lucky he fell out of the van.'

Mirren sat in the back of the police car, silent, stony-faced, out of this world, with her brows furrowing, trying to shake off her hangover. Suddenly she felt so small and vulnerable and lost. This was all some dreadful nightmare; too much cheap hooch was giving her strange dreams. There was Ben, full of bruises, telling her some tale about Jack being dead, but it was little Sylvia who was dead.

Then she was in some cold tiled place where

they were making her look under a blanket. Her eyes wouldn't focus. It was as if it were all happening to somebody else and she was looking down from the ceiling. It looked like Jack fast asleep except for the dent in his head and the strange colour of his skin. She saw herself nodding but her tongue was stuck in her mouth.

It was just like Jack when he saw Sylvia, not a tear or a murmur of regret, just an eerie silence as if she'd retreated into another world. This couldn't be true. In a minute she'd wake up and it'd all be all right. It was like the day Granny Simms had taken her in, the day her dad had not come home. How strange.

Dr Murray gave her something to make her sleep and they stood over her while she swallowed it, but it did no good and she jumped up, pacing the floor, searching the farm for her hidden bottles, searching to no avail.

'You won't find anything in the loft or the cellar.' Ben had heard the noise and opened her bedroom door. He was no comfort at all. 'I've gone on a recce and cleared them all out. You are going to sort this out once and for all. It can't go on! Jack mustn't die in vain. Pull yourself together for his sake!'

Mirren held up at the funeral, or they held her up as she walked behind the coffin, her eyes staring ahead, not wanting to look down. Tom and Florrie were in pieces but the Dale's farmers, as usual, came out to honour their own and the strong singing of 'Rock of Ages' had everyone in tears except her. Chapel folk knew how to stand together in grief. She was no part of the proceedings. It was just meaningless words and empty condolences. She watched it all from a long way off.

Jack was buried with Sylvia in the parish churchyard, and they planted bunches of snowdrops around the grave.

The day held up, being almost spring. The days were pulling out but it felt that darkness would always cover Cragside from now on. Ben had never felt so alone. How he wanted to escape, but he had promised Gran to see things through and he was not letting her down again.

'Where are you taking me?' shouted Mirren as Ben, grim-faced, dragged her up the hill, up the familiar beaten track to World's End.

'I'm taking you home . . . to the house I did up for you and Jack to live together. I'm putting you inside and locking you in until you sober up enough to see sense. That's what I'm doing!'

His words fell on deaf ears. She made to turn back, but he threw her over his shoulder like a sack of coal. He was taking no more nonsense from her.

'No you don't! You can climb out of the window,

294

jump off the ridge, if you must, but you'll be sober as a judge when you do it, right? This nonsense has got to stop!'

'Put me down! You can't do this to me! I've a farm to run ... things to see to,' she screamed, wondering why he was behaving like a caveman.

'Who're you fooling? You've not been running Cragside since Sylvia died, not for months. You've been in another world. You can do what you want up here but there's no booze, I've checked, and no pub, no hiding place. The cupboard is stacked with food. You won't starve if you ever start to eat again. I'll check on you and Dieter will guard you. He knows the score. We'll watch over you but this is where it stops, right?'

'This's barbaric. You can't make me stay here!' she yelled, feeling foolish on his back.

'Oh yes I can. I'll be behind that door night and day. You're not coming down to Cragside until you clean up your act. Tom and Florrie have enough sorrows without watching you stumbling all over the show pretending you're *compos mentis* and bringing them more grief. I've told them you need to be on your own for a while. This is your problem and you'll sort it one way or the other.' His voice was hard and angry.

'You're very hard all of a sudden. What gives you the right to be my gaoler?' she continued, hoping to cajole him out of this stupidity.

He fixed his lips, hard and mean. 'Promises I made a long time ago to people I respected and loved, and I don't want Jack to have died in vain. You owe it him. We all let him down . . .'

'But I keep telling you, I don't have a problem. I can stop whenever I choose,' she argued, but there was fear in her voice.

'So you keep telling me, so prove it. Show me that Mirren Sowerby can take her punishment. Prove me wrong.'

'Oh, go to hell!'

'It's you who'll go to hell in there, but I'm your friend and always have been. I want the old Mirren back, not this . . . walking skeleton with crazy eyes. I don't believe you any more. So go on, and get in, sort yourself out and prove me wrong.'

He threw her in the door and turned the key. She could stew in there for a few days and see how she managed. He wanted to teach her a lesson.

15

Mirren paced the flag floor of World's End, bemused at Ben's antics at first. Then she looked around in amazement. So this was what he had done for them both? She felt so ashamed.

The walls were plastered and limewashed, the old range was lit and its flue was cleared. The stone sink had piped cold water from the slate tank outside. The hearth was swept. There was a supply of split wood and kindling, old sleepers for logs and even a humiliating jerry pot and a supply of newspaper. He'd thought of everything.

Upstairs was a makeshift bedroom with a camp bed and blankets, a chest of sorts and washstand and mirror.

'I'll show him,' she snorted, not quite believing that she was imprisoned. She didn't need a nip but every time she said the word her throat and lips ached for the taste. Then she thought about Jack's sacrifice and shivered, hot and cold, shaky and unnerved by the silence. She still couldn't believe that he was gone.

Soon it would be growing dark and she felt afraid.

By nightfall she was achy and shivery and feeling sick. The joke had gone far enough. How dare he lock her up like a prisoner? Now she was going down with a chill and all she needed was a nip to warm her throat. All she could think of was a drop of something to calm her down.

Ben popped his head round the door later with a flask of hot soup. She tried to look in control.

'Get that down you,' he insisted, 'before it gets cold.'

'I'm fine.' She waved away his offering. 'I don't want your bloody soup. It's too warm. I want to go home. I promise I'll never touch a drop again.'

'Nice one, Mirren, but it won't wash. I expect there's a bottle I missed somewhere, in the outbarn?' He searched her face and saw her mouth drop. 'I thought so. I found the one in the milking parlour and the one hidden in the rafters of the nessy. You're in a bad way and need help.'

'Ben, I can't stay here. I'll catch my death. It's freezing,' she pleaded.

'I thought you were roasting a minute ago. You will stay upstairs and I will kip down here. This is the only way to stop you. Hasn't there been enough grief this year? I want to get on with my own life and not have to nursemaid you.'

298

'I'm not stopping you,' she barked, hoping he'd go away.

'Yes you are. I won't leave until old Mirren's back in charge and I see her in your eyes. There's no easy way to dry out. Doc Murray says—'

'So the whole world knows my business now?' she yelled. 'How dare you take over my life? Get the hell out of it!' she screamed, pulling off her boot and throwing it down the stairs. He ducked and it missed his cheek.

'I'm going nowhere and neither are you. This is your World's End for a while. You're going to have to sweat this out of your system and it won't be pleasant. I'm being cruel to be kind,' he pleaded as he left her alone with just the storm lantern for company.

For three nights she paced the floor, sweating, crying out with cramps and perspiration. 'Let me out of here! You can't do this, you sadist!' There was no answer from him but she knew he was close by and Dieter took turns to guard the door. It was unbelievable what they were doing to her and her indignation fuelled her anger even more.

The bedroom was indeed her World's End, her hands trembled and she twitched. She cursed and swore and lay on the bed crying as the agony of withdrawal curled her into a ball.

And all he brought her were foul-smelling teas made from dried leaves he'd bought from some quack. They smelled of carbolic and disinfectant all rolled into one, and tasted like piss.

Then came the terrible dreams that tore at her sleep. Sylvia and Dad were waving through half-open doors. When she ran to find them they were gone. Jack's bruised body was rising up to wag a finger at her. She screamed out and Ben came rushing up to hold her through the nightmare. When she lay back exhausted he disappeared downstairs.

'Hush,' he cried. 'You're doing really well. It'll pass. All this will pass.'

She screamed as the spiders crawled out of the corners of the room, creeping over her skin, and she tried to cover her body from them. 'Let me out! Oh, Ben, have pity!'

She took the last of the powders he left and sipped it slowly with a grimace. This was not medicine, it was torture by mouth. He was poisoning her and then he'd hang and she'd be glad.

By the fifth day she slept in and woke to find the winter sun filtering through the makeshift blind. Outside looked bluer and brighter and greener, with snow still hanging back in the crevices. Her tongue felt smoother and for the first time she sensed a little hunger in her belly.

Mirren peered into the wall mirror, not recognising the reflection of sallow-faced harpie, with scraggy hair, sunken cheeks and broken veins on her nose. Who are you? She blinked as if to make the horror go away but it pulled faces at her. It was real. Then she remembered all that had happened: Sylvia, Jack, her public shame to come.

It was like looking down at another person, not Mirren Gilchrist or Mirren Sowerby but a stranger. She wanted to cry out at this image and fell on the bed sobbing, rocking back and forth, trying to piece together those lost months: Jack's breakdown, the hospital visits, the Golden Lion, the police cell, funeral. How could she ever face the family again?

'Ben, Ben, let me out, I'm starving!' she cried. There was no one there but she noticed the door was ajar and she climbed down the ladder and went in search of food and fresh air.

Downstairs the fire was lit and crackling, and she recalled that very first visit here as a child, a little girl lost in the snow, saved by this ruin. Now it had done it again, saved her sanity, made her clean, rinsed the mud out of her mind. She was cured. No more whisky ever again.

How long had it taken? Days or weeks. Time had no meaning here but she felt clean inside, fresher. Ben would be pleased. She would look Tom and Florrie in the eye and apologise. It was as if for the first time in months she could see things differently and feel her own thoughts.

How could she have been so daft? How could

she bear to think about poor Jack? He would have understood her torture. He had tried to warn her but it was too late to make it up to him now. The pain of it made her wince.

She must thank Ben for being her big brother again. It couldn't have been easy, and how she'd misjudged him and all the effort he had put into her house. She'd called him every name under the sun, cursed him for imprisoning her here, but he knew World's End was her friend. It had held her and protected her, but she was better now and must get back to the real life down at Cragside, pull her weight as never before.

For the first time in months she tasted the salty bacon she'd cooked and relished the smell with fried bread and fresh eggs. It was a welcome feast. She boiled the kettle until she had a zinc tub full enough to make a bath, stripping herself down for a decent wash, soaking her hair and combing it, rubbing it dry so it smelled of soap and smoke. Mirren felt clean all over, tingling with the chill but alive.

From the window stretched the panoramic view across the valley. She could see for miles and wanted to run outside to embrace the whole hillside. The door was still locked. Ben had not trusted her enough to set her free just yet.

We'll see about that, she smiled to herself, opening the window shutters wider to squeeze her narrow body through to freedom. Just the knowledge that she could was enough. It was good to sit by the fire and listen to her racing thoughts. Where had she been all these months? The answer was plain enough to guess.

Her drinking had taken her to a faraway place, a wild shameful place, a place her father knew well, but she was not Dad and had broken the spell. She would never touch whisky again. It didn't suit her constitution. It had made her mental, like Jack. Now she could face Cragside and face the fury there. She had paid her due, done her sentence. Everyone must realise she'd never let them down again.

How thoughtful they were in letting her come up here to rest. It was basic but her woman's eye roamed over it. It would suit her well but it needed some pegged rugs and mats, some decent curtains, draught excluders, proper bedding and towels, cushions and a proper chair by the fireside. Given a little attention it could be cosy. Men never saw those details that softened the edges of a room – lace, fabric, pictures, ornaments. It could be her home with all her treasures, her carved box that belonged to her ancestor, the first Miriam Yewell.

When Ben bothered to return he'd get a surprise to see her cooking, clearing up, whistling tunes. She must thank him properly for setting her back on the straight and narrow. Now it was up to her to mend all the broken bridges and fences she'd crashed into on the way.

First she would invite Ben and Lorna for tea, and make cakes and pastries and try to heal the rift there. She'd go to chapel with Florrie and help with the Brownies and get herself out on the farm, keep herself busy so there was no temptation to pop into The Fleece for a quick nip.

No one would ever say that Mirren was not a reformed character. She'd seen the error of her ways. Now she knew better, thanks to Ben, the rest would be easy.

In the weeks that followed, Ben watched her progress with anxiety at first and then pride and not a little relief that his cure had worked so well. Mirren had done 'cold turkey' and come out the other side, and now she was more like her old self, or almost. She was cheerful and chipper, hard-working, full of ideas and plans.

He could see that World's End had worked its magic once more but it was one thing being dry in the safety of this moorland retreat. At some time she must face the stresses and strains of the real world; the reality of her now being a widow with little income, the memories of this last year, the strictures of rationing and depression.

They were all aware that it would soon be the anniversary of Sylvia's death and Mirren must get through that day; a day forever celebrated as VE Day, not a day of mourning and regrets.

He must stick close by her and help her through the worst, and make sure there were no whisky bottles to hand. There was still a bit of him unsure enough to go round checking if he had missed any hidy-holes. One sip and she'd be off again. Doc Murray had explained that there was only so much he could do and that the choice to stay sober was always Mirren's alone, but surely if he kept her safe ... He couldn't bear to think of her starting up again.

So far so good. She was sober and going about her farm business with gusto, doing extra shifts to make up for past misdemeanours. The women were heavily into spring cleaning, beating rugs, washing anything that wasn't tied down, turning Cragside upside down. Turning from winter into spring was a serious business and there was no let-up as Florrie, Daisy and Mirren scrubbed, cleared out, beat, hung out, aired and generally got in everyone's way. There was no place to sit down and then they started on the dairy and shippon and outside paintwork. Dieter had never seen such a palaver.

There was tension in the air between Florrie and Mirren, an undercurrent of blame and bitterness not easily healed by spring cleaning. Mirren decided to live alone up at World's End for a while until she felt stronger. Ben was glad that the two women were apart. She busied herself tearing up old clothes to make yet another rag rug.

If her eyes were a little too bright and her determination a little too brash, Ben felt it was just Mirren's way of getting back to her bolshie old self.

She was brave in facing the embarrassment of her caution at the police station when the inspector tore her off a strip for her unreasonable behaviour. They decided to take into account the tragedy of her past year in mitigation for her conduct. She took it all on the chin, unflinching, and he was proud of her.

It was the first time she had left the farm for weeks. Her trips to market were supervised but she didn't seem interested in socialising.

The anniversary hung over them like a black cloud. How would she get through that day? Then Uncle Tom had a brilliant idea.

'Let's give ourselves a day out,' he suggested. 'A proper day out on the train to the seaside or the Lakes – you lot choose. No use hanging around feeling morbid. It don't change any of it but it'll happen pass the time with a change of sky.'

They were all sitting down to Sunday dinner and it was good to see Mirren's cheeks filling out, the dark circles under her eyes barely shadows now.

'What do you think, Mother? Sea or lakes?' Tom smiled at Florrie.

'Oh, the sea – Morecambe or Blackpool or Southport. They have some nice shops there. I fancy a bit of Lord Street. A bit of sea air will do us all good, but it's lambing time, Tom,' Florrie said, knowing it was the busiest time of year.

'We'll see. I might have to stay back with Dieter. You do the first milking and we'll manage the rest, but you three must make a day of it. We can't take Sylvia or Jack but you'll be taking them in yer hearts for all of us.' Tom was not one for making speeches but he'd certainly come up with a solution for 8 May.

'Are you going to bring that lass of yours, Ben?' asked Florrie. 'It's about time you and her made it official.'

Ben found his cheeks flushing. 'Lorna's given me over for Harry Batty from Holly Bank. I think she got a bit fed up the way things were.' He didn't want to cite Mirren as the cause of their recent bust-up. He'd spent so much time keeping an eye on her that he'd stood Lorna up one time too many.

'I'm sick of kicking my feet, waiting for you to show up on time. This time you're free to chase the black widow, but you'd better watch your step, her with those big blue eyes. She's a wild one. She'll run you ragged, chew you up and spit you out. Don't make an ass of yourself mooning over her!'

There was nothing much to say after that outburst, for every word of it was true. He had no eyes for Lorna Dinsdale or anyone else as long as Mirren was in this world, sober or drunk. She was all he had ever wanted, but now was not the right time to share his hopes and heart with her. Every day must be a struggle for her.

Tom's little speech was the first time anyone had dared mention Sylvia's name for months; a rare treat in a house that had no reminders of her on show, no snapshots, no toys, nothing to prove she had ever existed.

Tom wasn't sure if that was the right thing to be doing. It was all beyond him. Florrie hinted it was the only way to see Mirren through the next few weeks and stop her from going 'funny' again.

In the end it was Southport that got their vote. There was almost a direct line by train that they picked up at Hellifield.

Lambing was too far on for Tom to risk coming, and Ben offered to stay back but Tom insisted he escorted the women. His instinct was to go along and chivvy Auntie Florrie into having a break. The two women together might be a strain on both of them. Florrie didn't get out much, and Jack's death had aged her by decades. Her bitterness towards Mirren was tempered by the fact that Jack had caused them problems and worries and she knew he had not been the best of husbands but he had died with honour. Now it was Mirren's turn to show she was strong.

They stopped at Windebank on the way to the station halt just to lay daffodils at the graveside. Mirren kneeled while Florrie wept. They walked away silent and separate, lost in their own thoughts and grief.

The train drew into Southport station and they waded through traffic on Lord Street to head for the beach. The sands seemed to go on for miles and the sea was not to be seen. There was still evidence of coastal defences and everywhere was shuttered and grim, but some of the big hotels were getting a fresh lick of paint. It was all a bit depressing with no bustle of holidaymakers, just a few elderly gentlemen out for their constitutional. There were flags flying, reminding them of the day.

The pull of the shops was too much for the women and they sauntered back towards the main street and its parades of classy shops. Not Ben's cup of tea at all but he had agreed to come and he was doing his duty.

To passers-by they must have looked like any young couple up from the country with one mother-in-law in tow. If only the truth were so simple, Ben sighed.

Mirren looked frozen and sullen, not enjoying herself much. Her eyes were glazed as if she was miles from the bustle of the shopping arcades.

'Why don't I leave you to go round the shops?' he suggested, knowing Florrie would like to browse. He would go in search of some rock and novelties for the farm lads. How would he explain seaside rock to Dieter; pink candy-striped sticks with writing all through?

'We'll meet up by the Scarisbrick Hotel and find a table for our dinner. We deserve a treat,' he smiled, looking up at the red-brick hotel. 'Then we can just meander until it's time for the train back.'

It was like flogging a dead horse. Mirren nodded glumly and turned away. He couldn't reach her and she was merely going through the motions.

'We shouldn't have come,' she whispered. 'I should have stayed with Tom. I can't forget. It's no good. Let's get the train home now,' she pleaded.

'But we've only just arrived,' snapped Florrie, suddenly catching on. 'I've a few things to buy while I'm here. It's a shame to waste a good day out.'

'You and Ben go off shopping then, and I'll sit here by the war memorial on the bench. I'm feeling tired,' Mirren replied in a sharp voice.

Oh no you won't, thought Ben. We'll all go together or not at all. He didn't trust that look in her eyes. 'Let's walk back down the Esplanade,' he offered.

'Not with my corns,' protested Florrie. 'You two go off and I'll take a trip round myself. I wish you'd make your minds up!' She was sensing the tension mounting. 'We'll meet up outside the hotel,' she added, trying to be cheerful.

Ben marched Mirren back towards the sea and sand, hoping the breeze and fresh air would lift her mood. Perhaps it would have been better to have stayed in Cragside after all, but this outing was only for one day.

They walked side by side in silence. Mirren was building a wall around herself with no door he could bash open. It was not the time to push her but he couldn't help himself. He was worried now, but she spoke first.

'When are you going to leave Cragside?' she said out of the blue.

'Who said anything about me leaving?' he replied, taken aback.

'I'm fine now. You've done your duty. It's time you were looking after yourself. If Lorna's dumped you, all the more reason to hit the trail,' she snapped. 'I thought you wanted to do some training.'

'I do but . . .' How could she be dismissing him out of her life?

'No one's stopping you, Ben,' she sighed.

'You are, if you must know. I just want to be

around a bit longer,' he said, not looking at her as they walked.

'You want to be my gaoler in case I've sneaked a bottle or two upstairs? Well, I haven't, not yet, but if you hang around for much longer, I will, hovering over me like a mother hen. You did your job well at World's End. We can manage without you at Cragside now we've got three POWs. Trust me, I'm a big girl, I've learned my lesson and I can look after myself.'

'I do trust you, but not in this mood. It's still early days. Doc Murray says—'

'If Doc Murray wants to give me advice let him visit me himself instead of sending you as his messenger boy and his mouthpiece. I just want to be on my own. Can't you read my lips? Leave me be!'

'I care about you, Mirren, I always have. We look out for each other and I want to see you on the road to—'

'Oh, grow up, Ben. There is no yellow brick road to wonderland when you've lost your whole world, when every time you shut your eyes you see your child lying there. I don't want you around, reminding me of it all. Jack's gone and it's my fault. That's another thing I have to live with. Why don't you bugger off out of my life?' Her eyes pierced him like icy daggers. 'Do I have to spell it out? I don't want you here!'

312

'You don't mean that. I lost Sylvie too. She was like my own daughter and many was the day I pretended she was. I loved her as my own. Don't shut me out. I loved you both . . .' His voice was raised in desperation. How could this be happening?

'Don't talk so soft. You get on my nerves. You should've married Lorna and been happy, not hanging round the farm being my gaoler. Go away and let me get on with my own life!' she shouted, pushing him away.

'Don't say that!' He shoved her back, unable to help himself.

'Is that lad bothering you?' said the man in a couple, hearing the argument as their voices rose.

'Yes, he is,' Mirren snapped, and stormed off, leaving Ben flushed, furious and lost for words. What had he done to deserve all that?

She hadn't meant to say all those things to Ben. They were unfair and cruel, but he was getting on her nerves. Mirren stormed back towards the station, not wanting to spend another moment in the town. It wasn't Southport's fault. It was just the trip was a mistake and she could smell the beer coming out of the pub doors and alleys.

She wanted to get as far away as she could from shoppers and fish-and-chip stalls and hotels and cheerful people, back to the hills where she belonged and the silence of World's End.

How did they think she could ever survive the anniversary in a strange place? There would be a train going east to Preston and from there she'd get on the first one that went towards Leeds if there was one, and blow the consequences. Florrie and Ben could have their treat in the Scarisbrick Hotel. What she needed was to be left alone.

All that hard work on the farm, the extra shifts and humble pie she'd eaten were taking their toll. If only she had the comfort of her nips. She knew that was dangerous but she needed something stronger than stewed tea to tide her along on the journey home. Not a nip, of course, but perhaps a glass of wine as a tonic. Just the one, though; she was not going down that road again . . .

Mirren sat in the buffet savouring the sweet taste of tonic wine. It was full of herbs and goodness and it slipped down easy, as did the next one and the next. It was only like pop, though. Three would have to be enough as she climbed on board the train with a smile on her face. What a relief to be heading back home. What a blessed relief to be away from their well-meant fussing.

She sat in the empty carriage watching the fields rush past. 'Peter dum dick, peter dum dick,' clacked the wheels over the rails, and she nodded off.

She woke when a guard shook her awake. 'Ticket, please?' he asked, and she rummaged in her bag for her return.

'Where am I?'

'You should've got off at Hellifield, love. You'll have to pay extra and next stop's Scarperton Junction. Better wait there for the up train.'

She staggered off the train, feeling silly and not a little fuzzy. The tonic wine must've been stronger than she thought. How stupid to have slept through her change. Then she stood and recognised just where she was: the other end of Scarperton, not far from Chapelside Cuttings. How strange to be only a few yards from where she was born. It was years since she'd been here.

Now she was hungry and feeling shaken. The wine had taken its toll. She'd have to wait for another connection, for a train going north from Leeds. It was like one of those eerie dreams when she couldn't find the way home and it was still 8 May. Oh hell!

Florrie would be furious that she'd sent Ben packing, let them down with breaking her pledge – but it was only tonic wine and only three glasses ... In for a penny, in for a pound, perhaps some more would make no difference. She couldn't face them after this so she might as well make the most of the evening.

It was as if her feet knew the old paths by heart – through the side streets, on the cobblestones, past rows of terraces with corner shops, the sooty taste of chimney smoke up her nostrils, the smell of the cotton mills and the clack of clogs on the pavements, neat doorsteps with whitened donkey-stoned steps and flags flying across the streets to celebrate the day.

In a daze of confusion and nostalgia she found her way back to the Cuttings and the line of carriages that had been her first home. The little allotments were still there but there was no sign of life at number five.

Granny Simms would've long gone. The faces peering at her through net valances were the faces of strangers, not neighbours, unfamiliar in turban headscarves. She was a country lady now, not a townie, in her summer frock and short jacket and sandals.

The child had come home one more time, she smiled, standing by the railway line, sniffing the soot and seeing weeds sprouting by the tracks.

There was Dad, picking docks to boil with nettles and oats, thickened with onions to make his special dock pudding when funds were tight. It tasted all green and slimy in her mouth but she swallowed it so as not to hurt his feelings. Why had she remembered that?

Mirren wandered past St Mary's school where she'd sat obelliently on the bench, looking up at the blackboard. It was still there, only smaller and shabbier than when she attended.

Then she saw the long low roof of the Green

316

Man. It looked now to her adult eyes like an old farmhouse converted into a public house, tucked away in what once must have been fields. How many times had she waited on that bench for Dad to come out with her heart in her mouth, waiting, waiting. She felt the tears rolling down her cheeks, tears for that little girl who waited for the man who never came, and she wept for the little girl who she'd never see again, who would never be eight or twenty or have children of her own.

In her throat rose up that familiar acid of bitterness for those lost years and all the broken dreams. Well, Mirren Sowerby, she decided, you're a big girl now; it's about time you saw for yourself what the inside of Dad's hiding place is like. What is so special about it that Dad preferred it to me?

Without a moment's hesitation she walked inside and shut the door.

16

Ben brought Florrie back to Cragside after their silent lunch. The pork was tough and stuck in his gullet. She was tired and tearful, and there was no point hanging about after Mirren's desertion. Over lunch he had tried to cover for her but Florrie was not fooled.

'It were a mistake to shift her. She's a stubborn mare, is that one, but she'll come round given time. I hope she's not done something silly. It's about time you looked to yourself, young man . . .'

Ben smiled at her concern. 'That's just what Mirren said. Time for me to move on then?'

'Mirren talks through her behind sometimes but a change of sky might do you good. No good hankering after what's never going to happen, lad.'

He could see she meant well but it was not what he wanted to hear.

'Is it that obvious?' Ben blushed and spluttered on his crackling.

'From the day you came with Pam and Wesley, all those years ago, to help out at the eclipse. She's allus been the one for you, cousin or not. You Yewell men are all the same, thank goodness, but lazy when it comes to doing something about it. Look at Tom. It took him years to pluck up courage to ask me to walk out with him,' she laughed. 'I know when Wilf went west I thought the world had come to an end, and then up pops Tom and I've been twice blessed. Pity that Jack and her were never suited. We all knew that, but folk have to go their own gait, as they say.

'There's some lovely young lass out there waiting for you so don't waste your time on what's not for you. Mirren's that twisted up inside, she's not to be trusted. Don't think we didn't know what was going on . . . It's in the blood. Ellie was a fool to follow Paddy Gilchrist. He was always a devil for his drink, so Tom says. Mirren's the same but no one can do owt about it . . . It's her show, not yours, so leave her be, Ben. You're putting good money after bad there.'

'But I tried.'

'You did your best but it's not enough with them as can't take it. Jack was finding his way through his problems with help. Going back to her undid it all. She'll have to do the same. I'm trying not to be bitter but it's hard. They were two of a kind and that didn't bring out the best in either of them.

319

Then with the war and Sylvia . . . It's in the Good Lord's hands now, not yours . . . I'll be praying she finds salvation one of these days. I wish we were rid of her but she's family. There, I've said my piece.'

Ben was stunned at this outburst.

They sat in silence in the carriage on the way home. Then, as they neared Hellifield, Florrie whispered again, 'Mirren's said one good thing, though. It's time for pastures new for you. She's letting you off the hook by her way of it. We'll manage. You've been like a son to us and seen us through the worst. We'll be sorry to see you go but you've only got the one life, Ben. Look to it and to yourself for a change. No one will think the worst of you for that.'

Ben listened with a heavy heart to yet another dismissal. Perhaps it was time to leave Cragside after all, leave all that he loved about the place, leave the stock and the hills and find other experiences, see a bit of the world outside this dale. His heart was heavy at the thought of going. Why did it feel like exile and banishment?

The inside of the Green Man was little more than a smoky hovel with sawdust on the floor, a thin fire of sorts, and old men sitting around staring at her as if she was a creature from another planet, in her cotton frock and tweed jacket, not the usual mill girl in clogs with curlers wrapped in a head-scarf.

It took a while for her eyes to adjust to the gloom, to the fug of smoke and fumes and rough coughs from old men hugging the fire. The barman stood and stared.

'Looking for someone, are you?' he said.

'Now you come to mention it, yes, I'm looking for my dad. I just wanted to see what the attraction was in here,' she replied as they all stared.

'Yer not from here, are you?' said one old man.

'Oh, but I am, number five Chapelside Cuttings ... Gilchrist, Paddy Gilchrist's daughter – you know, the one that got killed on the line a good few years back.' She saw their faces change.

'Oh, aye, Paddy,' said one old man. 'Scotch navvy on the railway. Sad do was that.' She was the object of interest now.

'Poor man missed his footing, they said,' said another.

'I heard that he lay on the line ...'

'Shut up, not in front of the lady. So where's you living now?' said the barman with the moustache and come-hither eyes, beckoning her to the bar. 'On the house.'

'Up the dale on a farm, my mother's side – and make it a double whisky,' she added. 'And no water.'

'So what brings you to this armpit of the world?' someone joked.

321

'Just passing through.'

'Nothing passes through this pub but piss and wind, pardon my French, or passes out on all fours or I've not done my business. Another?'

'I know all about that, and thanks,' she said, swallowing it down quickly.

For the price of a pint they all had a tale to tell about roaring Paddy, the Scottish soldier who could spin a yarn. She didn't recognise her dad in any of their tall tales but she let them talk on while she supped.

Someone jangled the ivories and she forgot she was a lady and told some of the filthy jokes she'd heard in the Golden Lion, to their obvious enjoyment.

Suddenly in the fug she saw him there in the shadows, laughing and joking, emptying his pockets of all his wages, lingering over the last drop, forgetting her outside, and she felt her fury rise up.

'Don't you lot have homes to go to? Children to put to bed and wives to talk to? What a waste of hard-earned brass, just going down your throats.'

Why had he left her alone? What was wrong with her that he preferred their company to hers?

'Now, none of that, young lady. You've had a skinful yourself and you can't hold it like we can. I hate seeing women drunk; they make such fools of themselves. There's the door. I reckon this lass's Paddy's girl, after all, whoever he was,' sneered the barman, and she could have hit him.

'Chip off the old block!' said another.

'No, I'm not,' she said, trying to get up with dignity.

'Just look at the state of her. Next stop she'll be out in the alley for a pee and a puke, by the looks of her. Shame on you, lass. Don't come in here tellin' us what's what!' The old men were ganging up against her now.

Mirren staggered into the street and the cold hit her. She made for the nearest lamppost and leaned on it to steady herself. She was about to turn when a middle-aged man in a grey mac and trilby came up to her.

'How much?'

'How much for what?' she replied.

'How much for the business? Just up the wall, nothing fancy, a hand job'll do . . .'

She still hadn't cottoned on. Then it clicked and she saw Woodbine Winnie, with her back to the wall and her drawers round her ankles while some man humped her up and down; the other girls pacing the pavements, looking for trade while she sat outside this wretched place.

'I've got nothing for sale,' she snapped.

'What, a looker like you, all dolled up and asking for it? How much?'

'Bugger off or I'll call the police. What do you take me for?'

'A drunken tart who's down to her last sixpence and needs a punter, or aren't I good enough for you?' he shouted.

'Just leave me alone,' she shouted, trying not to shake at the enormity of his words. Had it come to this?

She stumbled down familiar streets, feeling dizzy and sick, and then she threw up over the pavement and gasped at the danger she was finding herself in.

So it had come to this: back in the gutter where she belonged, skint, gasping for another drink, cold and out of her head with whisky. She was no different from her dad after all, just another loser, another lost cause. What was the point?

All those broken promises: everything she touched she destroyed. All her promises to be sober had turned to farce. What was there to be sober for? There was nothing worth living for.

Jack had tried to help and died in the attempt. Ben had tried to protect her from herself and she'd sent him packing. She was nothing but a useless bit of cow muck with no willpower and no pride left. One difficult day and it was back to square one. What was the point of going on?

It was still 8 May, the date forever branded into her brain. Victory in Europe. Where was her victory?

She found herself walking towards the railway

station along the side of the track, a familiar path she knew since childhood. How many times had she guided her drunken father carefully over the rails, the short cut across towards their carriage home? The one night she hadn't bothered he'd been killed. There was another life she'd destroyed but it was not going to happen again.

Like father, like daughter, better just to follow in his footsteps and get it over with, no more messing up, letting people down. She just wanted to go to sleep and put an end to the misery. No point in troubling anyone ever again. There was nothing to live for, not now, and no one cared if she lived or died. Better to call it quits and let them off the hook.

Mirren lay across the track – at least it would be quick – but the iron rails dug into her back and she shifted into a ball between the rails. Nothing came.

Perhaps it was just a shunting line. Perhaps it was easier to keep walking and be hit in the guts by one of those big black steaming monsters that scared her as a child. It wouldn't see her coming but she would hear it in the distance.

Her head was spinning and she was sobering up in the chill air. Her courage was failing.

'Oh, for God's sake come quickly,' she yelled into the darkness but nothing came. Now she was shivering and sobering fast. It had to come soon . . .

'Don't be a numpty, Mirren. Away to yer scratcher!' A long-forgotten voice pierced her head. 'Away home to yer bed, the now!' There it was again.

'Dad?' she called out, seeing him walking along the line swinging a lantern into her face. 'Away home. This is no place for yer, mo ghoil!'

'Dad? I'm here!' she shouted, running towards him.

'Who's that on my line? Get off, you bloody fool. Don't you know there's a train coming?'

The guardsman swung the lantern into her face. 'What on earth are you doing here, miss? You're trespassing. Get off at once!'

'I was just taking a short cut,' she heard herself say.

'Like hell you were . . . I know what you were up to: taking a short cut to hell, more like. Just get off this line at once and don't come back! It's me as has to scrape you off the track and I've done a fair too many of late to want any more messy jobs. Don't you have a home to go to? This is the end of the world for you, the end of the line, if you step back on.'

Meekly she hurried back to the embankment and scrambled up, shaking at what she had just been about to do, and sat down trembling. He was right. This was the end of her world. So easy to give up. No more worries. How could she even think of it?

Not now, when she was sure she'd heard Dad

calling her like he did when she was lost in the snow on the night she found World's End. She had seen it sparkling in the snow, her refuge and comfort through so many sorrows. There was another end of the world after all, she remembered. Her heart was thudding with confusion.

How could she go back and face World's End, knowing what she had tried to do? Whose was the voice she had heard? Had her father come to rescue her? She'd gone in search of him and he had found her. Her dad had stopped her in his tracks. Why? Who would rescue a girl like her? How could he think her worthy of saving after all she'd done? But he had!

She sat on the chilly grass and sobbed and sobbed. The dam had burst and the floodgates opened at long last. She wept for Sylvie and howled for Jack's needless accident and the fact that she'd never said goodbye. He tried to do his best. She wept for the woman she'd become and the shame she'd brought on her family. What a mess, what a sorry mess she'd made of everything.

'I am weak and I have no more strength left.' In a flash she knew she had sunk so low and come to the end of the line. 'Dad,' she cried out into the darkness. 'I can't stay sober on my own. I need help. Oh God, Dad, please help me. I can't go back to World's End like this. Where can I go?'

There was silence and then the clanking of iron

wheels on rails in the distance. The world was going on just the same. No matter what tragedy she'd suffered it would go on turning.

She stood up, sobered, her head rinsed clear by tears, and began to walk slowly back towards Scarperton. Everywhere was shuttered and silent. Turning away from the station a name, a place came into her head and it was not far from here. It was worth a try. This time she hoped the gates of the asylum would open and shut her in.

The telegram from Mirren was brief.

'DO NOT SEND SEARCH PARTY. I WILL CONTACT SOON. GOOD LUCK BEN. MIRREN.'

'Now what are we to make of this? Another of her little tricks?' sniffed Florrie.

'She's a funny one but at least we know she's safe and in one piece. You hear such tales these days. I never slept a wink last night, wondering where she was, but she's let us know even if it's not good news.'

Ben was packing his things up, relieved that Mirren was safe. She'd gone on the razzle and sobered up enough to keep them in touch. She was too ashamed to come home until she had got her act together so she could fool them all again. This would be the pattern for years to come and he'd never be able to trust her not to have slip-ups. It was all hopeless and beyond him. Better to get out now.

He couldn't go on mollycoddling her. It was time to let go of his dream of ever having her to himself. Florrie was right: she was a hopeless cause. Time for a change of sky.

There was an agricultural college near York that was advertising courses for practical supporters and an emergency teaching diploma. It would do him good to have a look at other aspects of farming – arable and animal husbandry. Teaching was in his blood, after all. He might try another farm or go abroad.

He would like to learn more about proper crop growing after all the blunders they had made trying to grow oats in this high altitude. Perhaps he could take in some estate management. The possibilities were legion, but his heart would always be in limestone scree and pastures, here in the Dales.

There was no point hanging about. Tom gave him a bonus and some extra. He was letting them down but there would be men demobbed soon and back in the fields. He said his farewells and made for the station. No use hankering over what would never be. Time to move on. He was not wanted here.

17

They were sitting on the grass in the shade of one of the big ash trees. The asylum garden was well tended and it was a beautiful June afternoon so the group were meeting outside.

'My name is Mirren, Miriam Sowerby, and I am an alcoholic.' There, it was said, and it was as hard as giving birth to admit those words to herself and to a circle of patients in the very place she'd visited Jack not that long ago.

Dr Kaplinsky was sitting at the back, silent, watching her first confession.

'I was teetotal until my daughter, Sylvia, died in an accident. My husband was a drinker, as was my father, but I thought I would never take to strong drink, especially whisky. But I did and it became my only source of comfort. I know now I can't take anything with alcohol in it. One drink leads to another. I've not had a drink since May the eighth, the first anniversary of Sylvia's death.

With God's help I will try to go through this day without a drink.

'To feed my habit, I stole things that weren't mine, I betrayed a loving friendship. I let my family down but most of all I let myself believe it was everyone's fault but mine for letting my child die in such a way. I blamed my husband and my cousin. There is no justice in life's events and life's not always fair or in my control. I see that now. Others have suffered like me one way or another but I must only talk about what I know.

'I thought I was alone and abandoned, and I lay down on the railway track, wanting to die like Anna Karenina in the book, but I couldn't do it. Don't ask me why. I heard my dad's voice calling me to get up and telling me off, and a man came out of nowhere and shooed me away so perhaps I was not meant to go in that fashion . . . I don't know. Perhaps I didn't end my life because I was too scared. I heard a train and I wanted to live. That's all I know. Then I decided to come here and ask for help. Sounds simple but it was the hardest thing I've ever done. I hated this place when I visited Jack here but I know I can't stay sober on my own.'

Everyone clapped.

'You chose life, Mirren,' said the man sitting next to her. 'You chose life over death. Every day you say no to a drink, you choose life.'

'Do you think so? How can I ever stay sober?' she asked.

'By doing what you've just done: acknowledging your weakness and asking for help from others, from a higher power than just your willpower. That way you're never alone, never abandoned, and if it gets too much try to keep busy with other things. You can do it but it won't be easy. One day at a time is all we can ask of ourselves,' he said, and the others nodded.

A woman smiled and added, 'There'll always be temptation but put it in the corner of the room, not centre stage. Keep busy and you'll find ways to be the master, not its slave. You can do it!'

Dr Kaplinsky edged forward. 'Have you thought that May the eighth is a good date to remember? It will always be Victory in Europe and, of course, a sad day of loss for ever. But it is also for you, Miriam. Victory over alcohol, the day when you discovered your true self and began the battle you'll have to fight for the rest of your life. Every time you choose to be sober, you win another victory. Sylvia and Jack will be proud.'

Mirren stayed in the hospital for six weeks, using her savings to pay for her stay. They had given her the latest electric pad treatment, shocked her brain, giving her such a headache and fuzzy feeling. Her mouth tasted of rubber but it was the talking with other patients that helped her most, knowing they were all fighting the same battle to stay sober that she was.

There was nobody to rely on now but herself and the support of her new friends. Dr Kaplinsky and the nurse slowly taught her to respect her own strengths, to grieve over what had gone and to let it go, to plan ways to feel good again.

Somewhere in all their discussions she had discovered some way to forgive herself for being weak, to forgive Jack and Paddy too for being human like herself – no better, no worse. It would take a lifetime to fathom it all out.

How she longed for World's End, for the peace and solitude it would give her.

In the high summer of 1946 when she returned to Cragside and got stuck into haymaking she was sad to see Ben had taken her advice and left. There was so much she wanted to tell him and share.

Tom was struggling and she stayed on at Cragside and tried to make her peace with Florrie, but it was not easy. Too much had happened. It was better just to help with the influx of summer visitors to the farm, cooking, cleaning, showing she meant business this time.

The visitors spilled out to World's End Cottage, for the income was needed now.

In September she wrote to Dr Kaplinsky, thanking him for his help and offering World's End as a respite stop for any people he felt needed fresh air and quiet to get their broken lives back together again. All they needed to bring were their ration books.

She welcomed strangers, refugees, all sorts of humanity for a few weeks to walk the hills and draw breath. The path to World's End was well trod.

She often thought of Ben, working across the county now, getting on with his life without her to worry about. She'd sent him away in a fit of pique and bitterly regretted his absence. Cragside was not the same without his cheery banter. They had said stuff she wished could be unsaid. She almost wrote to him but then thought better of it. Best to leave well alone. It was enough to get through each week sober.

Her greatest thrill was a trip to Scarperton long overdue, stepping down the cobbled street to see Sam Layberg's shop to redeem Gran's brooch. As luck would have it, the brooch was still in its box after all those months.

He stared up at her over his glasses and smiled as he handed it back.

'I said I'd come for it. Took longer than I thought,' she said.

He grinned. 'You've kept your promise to yourself, young lady, and restored my faith in humanity. Wear it with pride. It's too beautiful a jewel to be in a pawnshop, just like yourself.'

There was a spring in her step after that little remark. She crossed the road to avoid reminders of the Golden Lion, making for the Copper Kettle tearoom instead. In half an hour it would be time to catch a bus to the hospital for her monthly meeting with Dr Kaplinsky. This rendezvous was her lifeline, her hope for the future, her own World's End.

Part Three

The Snow House

18

1947

She can just see the dark head among the butter-cups, ribbons and ringlets bobbing in the wind, chasing across Stubbins pasture but the child is out of sight and suddenly there are nettles and tall burned grasses hiding her from view. She calls and calls but there is no answer.

Mirren was woken by the chill, dragged from her dreaming, dragged from the solace of chasing Sylvia. Why did she have to wake up?

> Come to me in the silence of the night;
> Come in the speaking silence of a dream;

She heard herself calling out the lines from her favourite Rossetti poem. Asleep, fully clothed on top of her bed again, woken only by the chill of the icy bedroom stabbing her back into conscious-ness, this was getting to be a habit, a lazy habit.

It was Sunday, with twenty cows to be milked, but no breakfasts to make for the men and time to please herself, she hoped, while cracking the ice in the water bowl. Had she remembered to bank up the Rayburn to keep the back boiler going?

This falling asleep fully clothed, piled high with musty blankets, had to stop. She opened the shutters to look out on the February morning.

If only the sky was not so pigeon grey, darkening from the north. She needed no weatherglass to know there was snow on the wind. The old fears were creeping into the corners of her mind, closer, closer, making her uneasy. She hated snow.

She would have to crack the ice on the water tank again with the axe. The chores were all hers for the day: buckets of water to the indoor beasts, mucking out, chickens to feed, fields to scan for sheep. Thank God most were gathered down from the fellside closer into the farm, but there were stragglers out on the tops that would need rounding up.

The lorry would not be dropping off Kurt and Dieter from the German POW camp to help with evening milking. It was church in Scarperton for them and a long trek back for Sunday dinner.

Florrie might call in for tea as usual, walking up from Windebank after taking her Sunday school class, if it faired up. They had made a truce of sorts since Mirren's return. She liked to keep an eye on her daughter-in-law, just in case. Even after all these sober months no one could quite believe she meant it.

Sunday or not, it was all the same here; udders must be emptied and milk collected up. The new live-in girl, Doreen, was visiting her parents, the cow man was courting down at Rigg village but if the weather closed in again she was in for a packet of trouble to deal with all by herself.

The snow fences needed repairing from the last downfall before Christmas, and they were getting low on fodder.

If it was bad Florrie would make straight for home back at Scar Head and she would be spared her incessant chatter about Ben's new job on a farm near York. He wrote to Florrie but not to her. There was nothing to say. She'd shoved him away from the nest and he'd made another life. Good luck to him.

Florrie found comfort in her chapel work and seemed to think it was just what Mirren needed to come out of herself and be more sociable. Once she sat down to wolf down a plate of ham and eggs, there was no stopping her. It made Mirren's ears ache, all that wittering on about having no new clothes to wear. Who had, after six years of war and nearly two more years of make do and mend?

Clothing coupons were the least of her worries.

How was she going to manage when Kurt and Dieter were repatriated? She'd fallen lucky with them. They were almost family now. They were farmers' sons and needed no training up on chores. She saw to it that they were well fed and muscled up for the job. The rhythm of a farming life knew no war zones or language barriers. It was a good arrangement.

Then Sam Lund, the shepherd, put her in a mood by going on about the ring round the moon the other week and it being Candlemas. He didn't like the signs if the sun was breaking through the clouds as it was now.

'Aye, Missus Sowerby, three circles is a bad sign. A pale moon is growing snow, I reckon,' he sighed, scratching his cap, searching the sky. 'I'd rather see a wolf running with me flock than the sun out on Candlemas morn.'

She ignored his warning. Everyone knew February could go either way: snow or rain, black or white. Only a fool thought winter was over. It mostly never started until the back end of January but they'd had such a poor summer and rough December, a mild New Year ought to even things out, but when was life ever fair?

She was glad that Christmas was behind them. Florrie wanted to do it the traditional way: visiting other farms, cards round the table and chapel singalongs. Mirren tried to make a bit of an effort, inviting their Germans for a meal now that the rules against fraternisation were lifted, killing a cockerel and boiling an apology for a Christmas pud just to show willing, but her heart wasn't in it. Going through the motions sapped every ounce of her energy.

Christmas was for kiddies and families, and a dangerous time for drinkers. The big old Yewell celebrations before the war was what Florrie yearned for, before . . . No use going over all that.

There were just the three of them now, Mirren, Tom and Florrie, with lodgers in Cragside when they could get them. World's End was deserted. Her supply of refugees had dried up for the winter. It was too grim in a cold farmhouse at the mercy of every whim of the weather.

Uncle Tom liked to feel he was in charge and gave her orders each week like some farm hand, but Mirren sometimes wished he'd stay put and leave her to get on with things her way.

'Mirren Sowerby, you're getting an old grump,' Florrie would tease. 'Just look how you're letting yerself go. When was the last time you looked in the mirror? Ben wouldn't recognise you,' she cajoled, as if Mirren was interested in her appearance.

Sometimes she felt as old as the hills with all the sorrows of the world on her back.

There was the usual selection of cast-off overcoats to pile on her shoulders: army greatcoats from the Great War, Ben's Home Guard one that drowned her, and some tattered mackintoshes at her disposal. There was always one standing stiff with frost like a guard on sentry duty by the range, others hanging on the pulley over the kitchen range to dry off. If they were all sodden then she could pile on the sacks over her head like Sam did. Sheep didn't care what you looked like in a storm.

Responsibility weighed heavy; she was no shirker of duty. This was her portion and she must swallow it.

No use looking backwards to what once was. One day at a time in soberness. That was her philosophy and it would get her up of a morning in the refrigerated bedroom. She was keeping up the family tradition as best she could. There was no other life on offer. A woman could run this farm as well as any man. No one could say she didn't do a man's job as well as most.

There were enough on the tops ready to point the finger at her drunken past, saying that farming was not women's work, but perhaps she was best kept from the town. There were enough men around the place to keep busy. Doreen might not be much help outdoors but she would give a hand with butter making and kept the surfaces clean enough.

Not that they did much of that now, with all

watched. He could hold his beer and never made a fool of himself, not like her lapses . . . They'd been a team, two work horses hitched to the same wagon for a while.

When he left she carried on, knocked sideways by her sudden need of him. She had thrown stuff back at him in anger and lost a friend.

Was it her fault that Cragside, once full of coats and gumboots and the noise of dogs and men, had fallen silent? Only the coats were left to bear evidence: Gran and Grandpa Joe passed away, Jack gone, Ben, Daisy married and away, and Sylvia buried in the churchyard. There was no future in this place now.

She had tried to fill the emptiness with whisky, but no longer. There were evacuees who came and went, refugees who lived in for a while up in the cottage, hired hands and POWs to fill the spaces left by Ben and Jack, but no one could stomach the bad winters or the isolation. You have to be born to it, she thought.

This stone house was built to withstand all that

the regulations for subsidies. It was hardly worth the bother.

She missed Ben. He'd kept well out of her way ever since their falling-out. She heard news of him through Uncle Wesley. She'd let a good friend go. No one could fault him. He was reliable and trustworthy, a good stockman who never clock-

'You come to me in dreams that I may live my very life again though cold in death . . .' No use going over the past, look forward, but it was weeks since she'd been to a meeting. Somehow it got harder to make the effort. It was time she proved she could go it alone.

Piling on the layers she went to check the water in the shippon. Milking was warm work with cheeks soothed by the flanks of her beasts, its fug of warm straw and dung. She only hoped there was enough fodder to see them through a bad spell.

Crossing the yard with the can full of milk strapped to her back from the cows in the outbarn, she felt the first flakes of snow settling on her cheeks, and shivered. The fight was on again. Sam Lund was right. They were in for another blow-in.

The sooner she did her chores, the sooner she and Jet could drop the latch and turn to the peat fire for comfort. Florrie wouldn't walk up here in snow. She'd more sense than to risk getting caught on foot.

This would mean Mirren wouldn't have to take a pan of hot water upstairs and do a strip wash, change her clothes and put on something half decent to show it was her half-day off. She needn't change the rug in the parlour for the best one, or lay the table properly as Granny Adey used to do every Sunday, the embroidered cloth with the hollyhocks in the corners and lace trim. She could make do with something on her knees in the kitchen, hugging the iron range. There she would have only dogs and ghosts for company.

The old place was full of spirits, rattling, chattering in the wind, stomping hob-nailed boots along the stone-flagged passageways. She didn't mind them. They had as much right to be here as she did. Sometimes she wished she might catch a glimpse of loved ones, of old Miriam her namesake, her guardian; of Sylvia, but her spirit was elusive. She sensed she wasn't tied to a house place but roamed free over the fields with a line of old farm dogs chasing behind.

Lately she noticed after evening jobs she was that whacked she fell asleep, nodding off by the firelight like Granny Mutch, but there was no one to tell her off for skipping her darning. Even when she was sitting, there was always mending and knitting, unravelling old jumpers to reknit into something warm to wear that fooled no one. They always held back a fleece to spin up and dye. Florrie did a whole baby layette for Sylvia.

Florrie was always trying to get her interested in sewing. Mirren was happiest left to herself, and that was taken wrong among the other farmers' wives, who thought her snooty and standoffish. She was a drunkard who by rights ought not to be running Cragside, taking jobs from the men. They were suspicious. She didn't go to the Women's Institute or to church. Her trips down to Scarperton on market days were brief and she lingered only at the library to change her books. There was always temptation to sniff the air and she might be lost again. Funny, spirits no longer had a hold of her senses. They just made her feel sad at those wasted months.

Florrie was right about her appearance, though. She must look a fright in a pair of old jodhpurs and holey jumper, but who was to know if she missed her lick and a promise, she smiled. It was too cold to get undressed. Happen she smelled of the farmyard to strangers, but could smell nothing amiss herself.

Where had all the 'golden locks' gone that Sylvia used to twist around her finger and tug when she was going to sleep? It was going grey in the wings and was firmly anchored in a victory roll, using an old stocking, flattened with a headscarf or man's tweed cap. Her cheeks were wind-burned and pink, with ice-blue eyes that missed nothing. She was still firm and full breasted, with a figure honed with lifting bales. Trousers suited her, and Ben's twill shirt and army jacket her favourite outfit. She could still smell the sweat of him. It comforted her to wear his clothes. It was as if she was taking on his mantle and trying to do all the jobs as he would have done them. He would be glad she'd made it through the wilderness months. What use had she for dresses and tweed suits?

She would never darken the door of a church again if she could help it. The consolations of religion meant nothing to her, nothing at all. If it gave comfort to others, so be it, but it wasn't for her. Her gods were closer to the hills, the old spirits of the Dales that promised nothing more than blood, sweat and tears for working this upland pasture.

On a clear day she could sometimes hear the

bells of St Peter's, Windebank in the distance, ringing out the seasons in turn. Kurt and Dieter were Catholics and went to services there when they could. Yewells were staunch Chapel, with a few renegades like Wes and Pam turning to Church when they went up in the world.

Sunday was just another day in the week for Mirren, but the one that she was allowed to spend to herself and that suited her fine. She would give last week's local *Gazette* a good going-over.

She kept peering out across the yard to the fields. The snow was building up and a strange unease crept over her, reliving the night when one of the farmers up the dale failed to return from Windebank, last winter. His poor wife was waiting with hope, searching with the lantern, calling with the men for hours, lanterns across the snow, hoping he had taken shelter, sick in her stomach as the night turned to morning and her worst fears were confirmed. The newspapers had gone to town with florid prose: 'Tragic death on Windebank Moor. Young farmer vanquished in raging storm. Gallant man loses his footings in the snow . . .' describing how the lifeless body of George Pye was found lying close to a sheepfold, only yards from shelter. What the papers refrained from saying was that he had spent the night with his cronies in The Fleece, as usual, and staggered back to be caught in a storm with half his wits sozzled, disorientated, crossing and recrossing his own tracks. It was a stupid, needless accident but she knew how easy it was to drown sorrows in drinking. That could've been her. Everyone up the dale had some tragedy to blot out.

She was too on edge to pick up the paper now or a book. The classics and poetry were her preference: the Brontës, of course; Dickens, rereading into the small hours sometimes when sleep was elusive. Where was it she had read that there were three bad things in life?

> To lie in bed and sleep not.
> To wait for one who comes not.
> To try to please and please not.

That was it. She had made acquaintance with all three in her time. Don't go down that path, Mirren, she muttered. No going there or she'd never get the evening milking done.

Ben woke in the middle of nowhere, trying to fix a point in the landscape he recognised. The train rattled on, packed with Sunday travellers, all squashed together, trying to get some kip on the long journey north.

The low sun was already flooding over the stone walls like rose-coloured silk. As he gazed over the hills he recognised that peculiar winter light like the soft hues of firelight. Even the sheep were tinged pink and gold. All the roughness of the stones, the bare branches caught up in the flame, and then suddenly the light was gone.

Transfixed by the sight and sudden recognition that this must be close to Scarperton and home territory, Ben felt a stirring, a restless surge of energy and a voice whispering in his ear, 'Go back. Pay them all a visit. Rebuild your bridges before you go off on your travels. Make your peace and sort it out once and for all. Australia's a long way in the other direction!'

He turned round to see who was talking to him but the rest of the soldiers in the carriage were nodding and snoring. This was crazy. Now he was hearing voices singing loony tunes.

It was time to make for the door. Then he realised it was Sunday and this was the Scottish express that didn't stop at all the little station halts. The stone walls were rushing by and he felt a panic. It was still light. There was still time, as his feet felt the wheels on the track slowing down, reducing speed. He tried to ignore the voice.

'Why are you sitting there? Get off right now before it's too late.'

For one brief second this crazy idea hung in the air. If he missed this chance perhaps he might never see Cragside again, never get a chance to make his peace with Mirren. He stood up, gathered his case and his bag, his coat, pulled down the belt that lowered the window, peered out as the steam and soot rushed into his face. They were slowing down near Windebank level crossing. This was his chance.

He was suddenly wide awake, alert to danger as he threw out his bags and jumped onto the bank, rolling down just before the small station platform. With one leap into the unknown he was in free fall, parachuting into old familiar territory, answering the call in his head. He knew he was finally going crazy.

'You can't do that 'ere! It don't stop 'ere!' shouted a man, running towards him, while the one o'clock from Leeds to St Enoch's, Glasgow, with its long line of maroon carriages, was already shunting out of sight.

Ben sprang up, sniffing that clean damp air up his nostrils, the welcome tinge of soot smoke. He was back in the hills one last time. It had been a long time since his last visit.

He would give them all a surprise, and Auntie Florrie would be delighted to feed him up and give him a bed for the night. There would be no other train on a Sunday in early February and the porter-cum-gate keeper was already demanding to see his travel warrant, looking up at him with suspicion as his ticket was for Port Greenock.

'Now then, I know your face,' he said gruffly. 'You shouldn't be jumping off trains, lad, but you always were a devil. It's one of them Yewells, is it?'

'Ben,' he smiled back sheepishly, straightening his greatcoat and trying to act casual. The rest of his stuff was scattered along the line.

'This's highly irregular to jump off a train. I should report you,' said the little man, trying to lift the battered case from cluttering his line. 'Happen you're a rare 'un to turn out on a day like this. Have you seen that sky? Off to see Tom Yewell up the tops?' His accent was thick but the welcome was typical. He wanted to know all his business. 'It's no day to be wandering about the fells. The nights pull in sharp up here. Any road, you've miles to hike,' he said, pointing to where the hills rose high in the distance.

The last-minute pilgrim smiled to himself. He'd miss all this – being recognised even by strangers who were curious about your doings. He was going to sail halfway across the world on an assisted passage to start a new life amongst total strangers. How he wished he could take all this with him.

He was glad he had not joined up, but taken work on an arable farm near York. He missed sheep and hills but a gang of farmer workers were setting off for the New Territories where farmers were needed and there was land to buy. Ben was free to follow his impulse, a free agent with time to say his farewells. His mother was upset, of course, but she still had Bert to mollycoddle since he returned from Germany. He and his German wife were the talk of Horsforth for a while.

Ben stood on the platform, uncertain. Taking out his last pack of Capstan from his pocket, he tapped the box several times to loosen the pack, pulled off the Cellophane and peeled back the packaging to shake out two cigarettes. He offered one to the porter, who popped it behind his ear with a nod. Then he pulled out his Ronson lighter from his trouser pocket and lit up, leaning back on the wall out of the wind. His hands were still shaking from the fall.

'I'd forgotten how grand it is up here,' he smiled, drawing in the smoke. 'I guess a Sunday is not a good time to hitch a lift, though,' he sighed.

'You're dead right there, chum. They'll all be sleeping off their Sunday dinner. I hope you've eaten?' asked the porter.

'Yip, sandwiches on the train,' Ben replied.

'It's a fair hike over the moor road. If you crack on apace, you'll happen make it by nightfall, but don't leave the road and if snow blows in find yerself a barn or summat for shelter. Don't go wandering around or you'll end up frozen in a ditch. We lost one man last winter. I'd leave yer case here. It'll be safe enough with me. Where're you living now?'

'On my way to New South Wales,' Ben replied, warming to the Yorkshire man.

'By heck! That's going it. The wife's brother emigrated to Melbourne. Is that anywhere near your place? Jimmy Ewebank is his name. He's a farmer,' said the porter, certain of finding a connection.

'I haven't a clue, but if I see him I'll tell him you were asking,' Ben offered while shoving his valuables, papers, shaving kit and some clothes into his canvas bag. It was time to take a hike. 'Be seeing you,' he waved.

He strode out on the icy road from the village halt with the wind behind his back, pushing him forward. This would be his last jaunt in the hills before he embarked for a new life.

He'd been putting off this return for months, making one excuse to himself after another. He wasn't sure if he wanted to face all that sadness again. Mirren had straightened herself out without his help but he knew how cunning she could be. Now she lived alone, taking in refugees, who knows what she was getting up to?

He just wanted to know she was OK before he left. There was so much anger at their last parting. She still might hate him but he wanted to know how she was surviving.

There was no mistaking the clouds were gathering into a purple bruise as the first flakes of snow fluttered down on his cheeks. He was glad of his old army coat, and pulled his cap down over his ears. The only way was forward. This wonderful snowy landscape would set him up for the long trek home.

It was good to be alone. '"Keep right on to the end of the road,"' he sang to Harry Lauder's tune.

The snow was speckled at first, the wind behind and to his side, not in his face. It didn't slow his pace but as he rose above the first snowline, above the village, onto the Windebank road, higher up he saw that it had been snowing for hours on top of ice. Snowflakes were building up on his shoulders, clinging to his trouser legs.

This was stuff that could build up into towers of snow whipped around into ice-cream cones, freezing limbs in hours. Ben thought about turning back but the track behind him was obliterated in this grey-white swirling blizzard. For the first time he felt uncertain, lost in a once-known landscape. He would have to move forward pretty darn sharpish.

'What a fine mess you've gotten into now,' he smiled, trying to cheer himself up pretending it was a scene from a Laurel and Hardy film.

Sheep passed him like walking snowballs. They would make their way to shelter. He snatched at the hope that the stone walls would lead to some barn.

It was the patchwork of handmade walls that always fascinated him about the landscape on his first visit; each wall crisscrossing the dales over the tops. The barns were squat and square, and plenty of them, thank goodness!

Where there were sheep, surely there would be shepherds or farm buildings, but in the dwindling light there was nothing.

He plodded on over ever-deepening snow, lifting boots that felt like leaden weights. He worked his legs like machines, keep moving, following the sheep tracks onwards and down-wards. They would know where to shelter.

The sheep were suspicious of a stranger in their midst. He hoped some of them knew his scent but it was so long since he was here. Don't stop now, keep moving, he thought. His duffel bag was topped with snow. It was easier to drag it behind him to leave some trail of his presence.

His coat was frozen like a cardboard crinoline and the wind stuck his cords to his skin. A weari-ness was overtaking him. He was lost. He was doomed unless he found somewhere soon.

Now came the battle against the wind to stay upright. It felt like trekking through a dense jungle, pushing his limbs through snowdrifts, trying to feel for the stone walls, which were fast disap-pearing. His eyes were tired from squinting at the whiteness. His fingers ached with the cold. He had fingerless mitts. His leather gloves were in his case. His cap was useless but he tied his tie over the top to rope it to his head. He must not lose more heat.

There was not a soul to be seen. No one in their right mind would venture out in this wilderness. Everything must fend for itself in this icy blast. The urge to lie down and rest was getting stronger and he knew that he must fight the impulse.

What a crazy stupid fool he was to leave the comfort of a train for this endurance test. When would he ever learn? He had no power over the wild spirits of these hills. He was at their mercy. How frail was the human body against such an onslaught; how quickly the elements can ravage skin and bone.

How many sheep carcasses had he dug out, frozen into grotesque shapes, blackened by frost. It took them hours to hack away the earth for makeshift graves. He knew what frostbite could do to limbs and faces.

There was no one to blame but himself if he died out here, alone like a wounded animal. No one but the porter knew he was on the road. They would all be tucked up safe for the night. Was this to be his last resting place, stuck in some ditch in the drowsy slow sleep of death? Like hell it was! If only he could find the old bunker, the foxhole they'd built by World's End, but it would be suicide to try to get up there. It was too high up.

Was this his reward for an impulse to say goodbye to his family, an impulse to follow a crazy voice in his head?

Death would be peaceful, lying on a downy pillow, cushioned suddenly warm as the frostbite took hold. He had heard how men dropped down, convinced they were fine when they were dying. He could see the beauty even as he struggled against it, the wind whipping the drifts into ripples like the ridges of a Marcel wave on a silver head of hair.

He could hear the bleating of sheep gathering together, more afraid of him than the weather. There was an owl hooting. Where there were owls there must be trees, a copse, some shelter, perhaps? He strained to hear it again but there was only silence.

He knew these moors blindfold and he wasn't going to peg out in a snowdrift. Get digging, Ben, make a shelter, keep your limbs moving, make an igloo, a cocoon, and wait for rescue. Pray yourself out of this mess. He was not ready to meet his Maker yet. He was too angry to pray and his anger was the only thing that might keep him alive. In his anger he would dig himself a snow house.

When it was done he sat upright, rigid, afraid to sleep or sink back into his bivouac beside a wall, numb fingers unable to open the cigarette case or burn the lighter fuel, resigned to his fate.

Then he remembered the whisky in his bag, a present for Uncle Tom. He had put it aside as a thank you. He managed to use all of his hands to fish in the canvas sack. The bottle was wrapped inside some socks. His fingers were too numb to open the top so he smashed the neck of the bottle against the stone wall and let the burning liquid trickle down his throat, reviving his spirits. At least he would pass out happy.

When your time came it came, he reasoned, but not here, on home ground with the safety of a bunker somewhere close by. It was too ridiculous for words. Yet he could sense death creeping towards him, black cowled with a stick, a light drawing ever closer. His eyelids were heavy, his arms useless. There was no more fight left in him.

Mirren couldn't settle to her mending, prowling round the kitchen, biting on her chunk of toast, restless, opening the door to check the weather. The storm blowing in from the north was abating now. How could she settle when there were still sheep out on the moor, stragglers ravaged by a wet spring and autumn, poor hay and weak lambs that hadn't thrived as they should? What if Florrie was caught halfway home in the storm like George Pye?

She sensed a gruff voice nagging her, tugging her away from the fireside. It was her father's voice with a lilt. He always had an instinct for trouble when he was sober. He could read the wind and the skies better than any weatherglass. Surely

Florrie wouldn't be so daft as to walk up? Yet she was uneasy.

'Damn and blast it! Come on, Jet. We'll happen check down to the lane end before it's overblown, just in case,' she called, dragging the greatcoat from the pulley and pulling on a cap, fixing one of the sack hoods over her shoulders like a monk. She lit the storm lantern and faced the polar wilderness outside, holding a prodding stick.

'I'm not afraid of you,' she muttered to the sky, but her voice was trembling knowing she must beat a path through the storm. Snowfall might look like falling stars but it was treacherous, a fickle friend flattering, disguising the familiar.

Snow could stop armies in their tracks, beggar a poor farmer overnight, and snow could torture and kill. One false move and you were done for.

The fields were smoking with white powder. Icy particles whipped up from the drifts stung her eyes. The sky was clear, frost clear as the wind dropped for a few minutes.

Only the loose snow danced in front of them. She knew the best bield for the sheep, the favourite walls where they would shelter out of the northeasterly, waiting bunched up for rescue, their fleeces sometimes frozen together.

Jet scampered ahead, drowning in the drifts. He was not the sharpest working dog, an average collie with sheep, but in snowdrifts he was a maestro.

He could make mischief but he could nose out trouble with the best. He wasn't a setter, sitting on his finding, waiting for instructions, like an obellient gundog. He would be in there scrambling and scratching to get at his discovery.

He was up in the corner as usual, scrabbling about as Mirren felt for the horns of the sheep and yanked its face into the air pulling it free, releasing the reluctant beast from its icy grave.

'Good lad!' she smiled. It was hard lifting them out of danger, but satisfying. Jet was in his element. He liked praise and she was glad of his company. If this was a serious blow-in it would mean foddering three times a day with the sledge into the fields, making sure her food and fuel lasted until supplies could be delivered again. She could last a week, two, three at most, but the thought of no help at hand was daunting. Surely the snow diggers would cut open the roads at daybreak?

'When the snow falls dry it means to lie' went the old saying, and this was powder fine on top of ice. She could not rid herself of an uneasy feeling and turned back on their footings towards the safety of the house.

The scene looked as beautiful as a Christmas card, complete with glitter, but it hid a coldness and cruelty. She would be living alone in a snow house like the Snow Queen with icicles in her heart, fast in, cut off at the mercy of the weather. She would just have to stomach it.

She whistled for Jet but he didn't come. She whistled and cursed the disobellient mutt. In the brightness of the snow she could just make him out scrabbling in another drift. He was only doing his duty and the sheep would need all the help they could get to survive this spell.

She stumbled across the drifts, numb with cold, aching to go back to the warmth of her peat fire and mug of Bovril. This 'Miriam of the Dale' stuff was a bit too much and she was tiring. The dog was still scrabbling away, tail wagging with excitement.

'Let's be having you!' she muttered under her breath, burying her hands to fish for more horns. She could feel something rough but soft to her touch, but it wasn't fleece. She parted the snow and shone the lantern into the snow. In her hand was a piece of khaki woollen cloth. In her hand was the hem of a coat.

There was no time to lose. Her heart lurched as more of the fabric came into view. She scrabbled alongside the black and white collie, sick with the knowledge that this was how Farmer Pye was found, frozen in the ditch without any signs of life.

'Not again.' She urged her hands to brush aside the cocoon in which the body was trapped. How long had the poor soul been stuck fast? How was she going to drag a dead weight back into the farm? How was she going to wake the dead? This was not fair, this terrible reminder of her own journey as a child. She had to do something.

At least this man had had sense enough to shelter by a wall and make some bield for himself. His face was wrapped up in a scarf, in a pocket of air. He'd done his best to stay alive but it must be too late now. Then she saw the whisky bottle and smelled the liquor. The aroma hit her like a blow, taking her back to those terrible scenes in her head and the shame. The bottle was empty, thank God!

Not another drunken sot? Not another capurtled fool wandering over hill and dale out of his wits? When do we ever learn?

She was used to tramps and bog trotters on the moors, calling at all farmhouse doors for handouts. Sometimes when it was harsh she would let them kip down in the hay barn for the night but not before she searched their pockets for matches just in case.

There were good tramps and rogues, war-scarred veterans and lazy deserters. This one looked fresh-faced, with no matted beard and foul-smelling clothes, younger than most of her visitors.

'What am I going to do with him? I can't have

him in the house. I don't think I could drag him there. He's a big man. What's he doing stuck out here at this time of night?'

She often talked to herself. It was Paddy Gilchrist's nagging spirit that had brought her out here with the dog. His prompting might yet save this man's life.

The tramp's sandy hair was matted with ice. There was something about him she recognised. The face was clean shaven, the bit she could see was handsome enough and he was still breathing. She bent close to check his breath as his eyes flickered for a second, blue eyes fringed with frosted sandy lashes. He muttered something incoherent in what she took to be a foreign language so she bent down closer, smelling the whisky on his frozen lips. There was no time to judge his stupidity. She must treat him like a frozen beast and revive him as best she could.

She rubbed his arms with vigour to get warmth into them, but straw, hot water and blankets were what were needed now, with sweet tea and hot-water bottles. She had to get him on his feet before his limbs froze for ever, but how?

'Oh, give me strength to lift him, to rouse him from his stupor. He has to help himself or he is lost.

'Stay by, Jet. Stay.' She ordered the dog to sit across his body, tearing off her sacking to cover them both, leaping in panic back over their footings. She must go to bring the sled and harness the cart horse but then she remembered the barn door was fast with snow. The muffled man would die of cold long before she reached him.

There was nothing for it but to drag him to his feet. He had to get his own limbs going, get the circulation back into his frozen body. He had to help himself.

Every second seemed to be in slow motion as she tugged and tugged at his frozen coat to release him from the snowdrift.

'Get up! Get up. You are not far from the house,' she cajoled him out of his stupor. 'Come on, last lap. Wakey, wakey! You've got to help me. I can't drag you. You've got to work your legs!' she shouted in his ear.

He opened his eyes through the slit in his frozen scarf like a drunken man, not taking in her words and yet searching her face with his eyes, unable to form words with his lips. She was rubbing his hands. It was going to hurt like hell once his numbness wore off. She had to get him into the kitchen to thaw out.

From somewhere outside of herself she felt the strength flooding into her tired body, sap rising up in a spurt of energy to get him sitting upright, pulling him on his feet, but his legs were rigid and he was going to fall.

He groaned and cried out in protest but she felt angry with frustration as to why this drunken stranger had to stray onto her land, interrupting her peaceful evening and demanding such attention.

'Lean on me,' she ordered gruffly, thinking about a sack of coal stuck on her back. At least her shoulders were used to heaving burdens. She would drag him behind her, bent double with the effort, but they would get to that fixed point where she placed the storm lantern to light their path home. She would rest and put the lantern ahead again, and drag him to the next fixed point until the outline of the whitened farmhouse came into view.

Slowly they edged ever closer to the farmyard, but there was a gate to open; a gate blown over with snowdrifts. The snow was beginning to fall again and soon there would be another blow-in. The last yards would be the worst if he didn't help himself. She could feel the cold seeping into her body.

Then she remembered the cripple hole, the gap in the stone wall where the sheep could run from one field to another. If she could only drag him through the wall, but it would be blocked by now. The gate would never open. The wind was rising and whipping the snow. She could see only six feet in front of her but nothing was going to distract her from one last effort. Her shoulders were on fire with the effort.

'What do I do now?' she cried into the wind. To be so near and yet so far from safety ... Suddenly the wind dropped and the clouds parted for a few seconds. The moon shone down, torching a path. The snow was piled so high by the farm gate that it was right over the stone wall, built up, freezing hard, a ready-made slope for her to cross over and down into the farmyard.

There was no time for gratitude, only to seize the moment; one last dragging, pushing effort. She crawled up herself and then dragged him like a sledge down the slope, laying him with relief on the snow.

'Come on, nearly there,' she shouted yanking his arm.

He made one supreme effort to stagger to his feet, his arms clinging across her chest. Together they staggered to the door already covered with thick snow, but after all she had been through kicking a path into the kitchen was nothing at all.

The warmth and light of the room hit them both. She had never been so glad in all her life to see the flag floors and kitchen fire. She smelled the peaty smoke with relish.

'We've made it,' she cried, but now the real rescue job would begin in earnest.

He was already prostrate on the floor, exhausted, disorientated and fevered. She was going to have her work cut out to save his hands and feet from permanent damage. Stripping off his greatcoat and army jacket, she found underneath a woollen shirt and thick vest. These layers must have saved his life.

They were not the clothes of a vagrant unless they were stolen from a washing line. There was a mixture of tweeds. Around his neck and face was the frozen scarf masking his face. She would have to peel it off with care or it would rip off his skin.

She was curious now. She examined him like a carcass. He was well muscled and well fed but on the thin side and very tall. Everything that was dry and warm must be piled on top of him. He needed thawing out by the range like a frozen sheep. She smiled to herself, thinking of the tune from *Messiah*, 'All we like sheep have gone astray,' and thought of Sylvie's birth in the vestry when she was young and full of hope.

There was no time to lose. Whilst the kettle was boiling it was time to tackle his feet. To her surprise his boots were well made but his socks were welded to his skin. She took the nearest towel and began to massage his toes gently. What was she doing with a stranger at her hearth, rubbing him down like a beast? Florrie would have the vapours to know what she was up to.

She placed a warm cloth over his face to release the frozen mask, curious to see who was underneath. Then she fished in his pockets for some identity.

There was only a silver cigarette case and lighter, some coins and tickets. There was a thin diary with a travel warrant stuck in one page and baler twine. His name scrawled was smudged by water, unreadable, but you could tell a lot from a pocket. Here was a farmer on his way to market, who smoked and drank with the best. It didn't add up to much but perhaps she would be safe in the house with this curious stranger, unless he was a thief.

She took away the lighter, just in case. He was in no state to be moved and in for a rough time when the numbness wore off. She would make a bed for him by the hearth with the dogs.

The wind was rattling the doors as it did when it blew in from the east. They had beaten the blizzard by the width of an eyelash. 'Someone must have been looking after this chap,' she muttered as she prepared the bowl of water. Now she must be cruel to be kind.

It was like laying out the dead, sponging him down, opening his shirt, listening to see if his breathing was steady. Jet sat by her side, interested, trying to lick him back to life. There were hot bricks in the bottom of the Rayburn. Wrapped in old cloths, they could be padded round his body to warm him through.

It felt as if she was in some strange dream: the walk in the snow, feeling the coat in her fingers, dragging the half-dead man into the safety of the house and now anointing his body with lanolin, trying to rub the life back into him.

She was exhausted with the effort, unnerved by him lying there, packed with blankets and rugs. What if he died on her?

She sat vigil until her eyelids were drooping and found herself wrapping the blankets around herself. She might as well kip down with the dogs by the hearth, lie by his side and see him through until morning, but first she must unpeel the scarf.

Bit by bit she released the material, first his nose, then his mouth and neck, and only then did she see who it was . . .

19

Ben stirred, hearing himself groaning. Was this a dream? Where was he? He lay helpless on a rug, stripped, covered over with rough blankets. There was the smell of wet dog, muck and manure and peat smoke, and he sensed he was safe. Then he felt the searing pain of his thawing body and rolled in agony, his limbs on fire. A woman was rubbing his arms, slapping life and pain back into him when all he wanted to do was sleep.

'Ben, I have to do this,' a voice whispered, checking to see if he was really awake. All he could register was pain and a pair of his own eyes looking down at him with concern. What the hell was going on? He shut his eyes to hide his agony but she kept shaking him as if he was a rag doll. Why was she doing this? Then he recalled the station and the walk and the blizzard, and being dragged across the snow with a dog licking his face. It was Jet wagging his tail in his face, and his eyes focused and he saw it was Mirren torturing him, pulling him up and making him change position. Then he saw the bowl of hot water.

'No! Have a heart! Mirren, is it really you? What happened?'

'Later . . . we have got to get your feet in the bowl,' she said, her cheeks flushed with exertion.

'My feet are fine,' he protested, trying to focus on her hair loosened from a scarf.

'I'll be the judge of that,' she snapped.

Still the same old Mirren, sharp as a knife, he sighed.

'If you're daft enough to walk through a blizzard then you risk losing your toes and fingers. Don't be a girl's blouse!'

'I'll do it slowly,' he groaned.

'Do it how you like, but just get on with it,' was all the sympathy he was going to get. 'I've made a pot of tea.'

The drink was piping hot and laced with sugar from her ration. Swallowing took his mind off the agony in his toes as they were coming back to life. He began to shiver and saw that he'd been stripped down to his underpants and vest.

'When you've finished, I'll have your head in friar's balsam. Might as well keep the chill off your chest,' she ordered, like a hospital matron.

How could he protest, face down with his head

covered by a towel, sniffing camphor fumes? His cheeks were raw and stinging.

'What on earth possessed you to come tramping up here? You were nearly a goner when Jet found you.'

'It wasn't that bad when I left the station,' he muttered under his towel, feeling naked and silly and entirely at her mercy.

'You should have stopped in the village. Honestly, you haven't the sense of a flea. I had to get you out of those wet clothes and quick.' Mirren plonked a pair of Grandpa's old fustian breeches, a thick shirt and clean vest before him. 'These'll have to do for now. I've no other spares. There's not enough hot water for a bath so I sponged you down as best I could. You'd got some smart tweeds on for hiking. Off somewhere special?'

'I was making for Glasgow; got a ticket on a ship. Didn't Florrie tell you?'

'Tell me what?' She paused from her busyness.

'I'm emigrating to Australia ... an assisted passage.'

'Are you now? Deserting the old country in its hour of need? What happened to college?' she replied, and then there was silence. Mirren left him to struggle into the breeches and long socks. His whole body was tingling and sore, but where there was feeling there was life, he thought with relief. The smell of bacon was coming from the range like perfume to his nose, and he was ravenous, gazing around the familiar kitchen with pleasure. Nothing had changed: the smooth flag floor with rag rugs covered in dog hair, custard-cream walls and ancient stove. The cupboard of china plates still fixed to the wall, a clutter of pipe cleaners, jugs and candlesticks over the mantelpiece, a glowing kerosene lamp in the middle of the deal table, two dogs watching him and Mirren's open book turned face down as usual.

Grandpa's breeches itched and smelled of moth-balls but they covered his credentials perfectly. He blushed to think of Mirren undressing him. How unbelievable that she had found him like that. It was hard to take in that he'd escaped death by a whisker.

'You're done then?' She eyed him furtively as she laid the table. 'Were they expecting you at Scar Head?' she added. 'No one said, but then I only get told what Florrie thinks is good for me these days.'

'No, it was a last-minute idea on the train. I jumped off at the Halt,' he said, eyeing up the bacon rashers, his mouth slavering.

'Why doesn't that surprise me? No panic then with Tom and Florrie. Sit down, eat up and rest a while. It's not fit to throw a louse out in this storm.'

'I don't want to put you to any bother,' he offered.

'You already have but you're family, so no mind. Get stuck in,' she smiled, and the clouds parted, the stern look on her face brightened, her full lips smiled and those sad eyes flashed a welcome. In that instant he saw her beauty again and knew he was lost.

Mirren watched him wolfing down his bacon with relish. He finished off the last bread in the bin, slurping down his mug of tea, savouring every sip, and it was like old times round the kitchen table after milking. If she hadn't got out of the chair he could have been lying in the drift, stiff as a board like George Pye for weeks. It didn't bear thinking about.

'How're your toes?' she asked, knowing he must be in agony.

'I've still got ten of them, thanks to you,' he smiled, and she had forgotten just how blue were his eyes and fair his hair in the lamplight. 'You saved my life.'

'You tried to do the same for me and I never thanked you,' she blushed, not wanting him to see how close to tears she was.

'It's bad out there. Do you want me to try to get to the barn?'

'Just get those legs going up and down the stairs, up the passage. Give them a good stretch. The beasts are going nowhere. Time you had a proper rest. Happen in the morning you'll be fit enough to give me a hand,' she paused, recalling that he had a train to catch and a ship to board and she might never see him again. Better make the most of him while he was around.

She poured hot water from the kettle on the hob into a stone bottle and passed it over. 'You know where everything is. I've aired Grandpa's bed. You can sleep posh tonight.'

She could see him wincing as he rose up and it was natural to give him a hand up the stairs with the lamp. Ben smelled of balsam and moth-balls, soap and something she couldn't quite fathom. It was over two years since he had climbed those stairs. He leaned on her and she could smell his warm breath.

The curtains were drawn and the drapes around the four-poster pulled across.

'It'll be clashy tonight. Listen to that gale blowing in, but we might get out in the morning,' she said without much conviction.

If the storm continued they were going to be stuck together for a few more days. Judging by the look of him he was in no fit state to be let loose up the dale. Why did that fleeting thought warm her cheeks? She ought to be furious with him still, but somehow now was not the time to be going into all that.

They sat in silence, only the ticking of the wall clock, the stirring of the dogs by the door disturbing this makeshift meal. For the first time since his arrival

Ben felt awkward and unnerved by the tensions still unspoken between them. He was bone weary, propping his hand on his chin to stop it from dropping onto the table, eating the tinned corned beef hash with one fork, trying to stay awake.

They had slaved like navvies all day digging out. There were just too many trapped sheep for two of them to tackle, too many buckets of water to fetch, too much fodder and mucking out. Back and forth with freezing limbs and aching fingers, the ice biting his cheeks and nose as they trudged over the snow.

Nearly three hundred sheep were bleating for fodder, sheep trapped, frantic for release. Already they were pouring milk away and it froze into piles like ice cream. It was too cold to make butter and they hadn't the strength to load the milk kits and try to make it to the lane end just in case a lorry might get through. They worked like two pairs of hands with nothing to think about but the next bale or the next bucket of water.

The storm was still howling the odds. There was no escape from its iron grip. It was going to be some battle to fodder the beasts in their stalls. Every journey was an excavation, and dangerous. How on earth would Mirren have survived without help when none of the farm hands would make it back for days? Until then he was her only hope and he owed her his life so he was staying put.

Now they sat speechless, lost in their own thoughts. Sooner or later Mirren's drinking must be brought up but now was not the time. He'd noticed the house was still stripped bare of any trace of Sylvia's presence; not even the photograph of her sitting on the bench taken as a baby, no toys or reminders. The house was sanitised and empty, not how it used to be, cluttered and welcoming. The big rooms were never used. They were too big to heat now. Mirren lived in the kitchen and in the bedroom with the little parlour off it upstairs.

It was dark by the time they staggered back after their chores. First job was to thaw their frozen coats, to hug the fire until they stopped feeling numb and only then did they look round for something easy to fill the belly: soup, porridge, scrambled egg, anything quick.

'I'll have a go at digging out to the lane end tomorrow,' Ben offered.

'Don't waste your strength. The more you dig, the more the wind just blows it back,' Mirren said. 'Can't wait to leave us?' she smiled, but her eyes were cold.

'Just thought it might help getting the milk out. It breaks my heart to chuck it out,' he snapped back, hurt that she was so quick to see his offer as a desertion. 'Any road, I'm not budging until you and I've cleared the air. I can't go halfway across the world knowing I'm not welcome here.'

'Who said that?' she replied.

'Why do you think I kept away for all these months . . . after what you said?'

'That was ages ago! We were all in shock and said stuff better left unspoken.'

'I hear you sorted yourself out.' There, it was out on the table now.

'No thanks to you this time, but you did me a favour, made me work it out for myself. It was like a madness. Drying out is never easy but I was in a safe place, in the madhouse where it all began,' she said. Her voice was clipped and her words carefully measured.

'Was it awful?' he asked.

'What do you think? Finding out you're not little Miss Perfect after all, finding things about yourself, but I had to do it for their sake. I dosed myself up to stop the pain and it was poison, just like you said, but you can't be told so you just have to find out for yourself the hard way. I have to live with the consequences and I do every day. I guess men and women do things differently.' She stopped and eyed him again. 'Is that why you're off to Aussie land, to put all this behind you?'

'Don't be daft. No . . . it's just there're opportunities there for land, to be my own boss.'

'Uncle Tom always looked to you to fly the Yewell flag here and you beetled off and left us to it.' There was a ring of accusation in her words.

'I couldn't stay after . . . Florrie wanted me to get away. It wasn't just me. You were so angry. We could never have worked together, and after Jack, well, it was not right to stay.'

'His heart was never here after the war. He drowned his sorrows. This was never what he wanted. Sylvia bound us together and when she . . . something snapped between us. I hated his drinking . . . but got hooked on it myself. It got worse and it reminded me of my dad all of a sudden, the very person I'd hated for letting me down. You know, on that night I left you, I found my way back to the line where he died when I was small and left me an orphan. I loved my dad but hated him drunk. Jack began to remind me of him, but it was me as lay on that track and wanted to end it all.' She eyed him. 'Do I shock you? Well, I shocked myself but someone stopped me and I got up and chose life. I'm not my dad, I'm me, but if I drink again I could end up back down there and I don't want to feel like that ever again.'

It was the longest speech he'd ever heard from her. She looked up at him, rising quickly. 'The war has a lot to answer for but it's over now and you've a new life to lead. I wish you well, Ben,' she whispered, patting him on the shoulder as she darted towards the door. 'I'll bid you good night. There's a hot brick in the oven. Wrap it in the towel. We can't spare water now for bottles. If you need a shave . . .' She paused, seeing his stubble.

'I think I'll grow a beard. It'll keep my face warm and the ice off my lips.'

'Pity,' she quipped. 'It'll grow red and won't match your hair. You'll look like a Viking on the pillage.'

'Who cares in this weather?' he laughed. 'You look like a walking eiderdown.'

'Precisely; anything to keep warm,' she replied. For a second there was a flash of the old banter between them. He'd heard more about her history today than in the whole of the time they had worked together. Perhaps because he was leaving she felt she could share stuff with him, trusting he'd tell no one. Perhaps she was relieved that he was off to pastures new, perhaps not; it was hard to tell with Mirren.

Yet Sylvia's name had been spoken just the once and before he left he wanted to beg a snap of his godchild from her. Surely that was not too much to ask.

Mirren lay in the dark, too stirred up to sleep. Grief never ends, she sighed and just the mention of that precious name brought back every second of that terrible day, and just that sniff of whisky in the snow brought so much back into her mind again. How easy it would be to slip, but the need was more bearable now. There was a sadness to the edge of it that softened each haunting memory.

Death is for ever, and for months she couldn't let go of the hope that it was all a nightmare and she would wake up to see her baby's dark head on her pillow. It was never there and she'd gone on living, but it was a different life, with the terrible knowledge that awful things could happen again. She needed someone to hold her together in case she fell apart again.

Jack had been too shattered to do that and she hadn't been able to let anyone else near enough. Ben was strong but she had pushed him away and now he was going to the far ends of the earth to get away from her. All that anger and blame and fear had driven away friends and family until she was set up alone with strangers, her heart iced over with hurt and fear. Ben would find love and comfort, but she couldn't risk ever letting anyone close. For the first time for months she wept quietly, sitting up in the chill, fiddling for the candle, and that was when she felt something strange again. She was not alone. The house creepers were back.

For a second she tensed but it wasn't a physical presence, more a comforting presence all around her of women: farmers' wives who had paced these floors, treading the same Gethsemane road, a company of weeping women, Rachels weeping for their own lost children in the wee small hours of the night, mothers who couldn't be comforted. It was this sharing of loss that bound her to Cragside for ever. A bit of Sylvia was here within these walls. How could she leave? She buried her head in her pillow.

Grief has its own milestones, its own sad progress, perhaps: Sylvia's birthday, Christmas, the anniversary and the ones to come. Each of these needed marking, and she had hidden all her pain away in suitcases or it had been done for her, and she had never bothered to sort out her daughter's clothes or her toys. What the eye didn't see . . . Now there was time. They were confined indoors, fast in, and Ben was the one person in the world who might help her face her fear. It would be the one last task they would share before he left. It was up to her to open the door, to clear the air once and for all.

At first she was cross because his coming messed up her solitary routine. It was duty that had dragged her out in the snow and duty that revived him, and yet the thought of him going away for good . . . He looked different, older and more care-worn. He had suffered too in his exile. Tonight his presence was companionable and welcome. He smelled of earth, woodsmoke; honest sweat glistened on his brow in the firelight.

She noticed his broad hands stretched out for warmth; farmer's hands, chapped, gnarled with wind and rain, rough and even bigger than her own spades. His palms were callused, blistered from all their shovelling, and just for one second she wondered what those hands would feel like dusting over her skin.

A frisson of shock sparked through her body. She had undressed him and sponged him down like a brother *in extremis*, but now she was curious and not a little shocked by the realisation that Ben might be her cousin and a friend, but in the fire-light he was first and foremost a man.

'Remember how Grandpa Joe used to say that a good bit of wood gave two heats?' Ben shouted as he split the logs with an axe.

'Could we ever forget? The first was in the chopping and the second when it was on the fire,' Mirren said as she was loading the logs onto the foddering sled, layered up in coat, scarf and sacking hood.

Splitting the wood, crashing blade onto bark, was strangely soothing, releasing all his tension and stiffness. The pile was drying off by the fire. The last of the fallen trees stored under tarpaulin was damp, but dry enough at the core to eke out the peat.

Day was following night, and still it snowed. Their daily routine was digging a tunnel out to the cattle in the byre, which bellowed in protest at having only half-portions. Ben looked out across an arctic landscape, snow on ice whipped into monumental sculptures. He thought of their flock still not rescued, heavy with lambs. No amount of wool would save them from this devouring monster. He turned back to his chore with a heavy heart.

There was relief in Mirren's eyes when he tackled something extra, but he felt uneasy. Something was shifting between them as if being stuck together was forcing some change. There was a tension that he couldn't explain, a restless nervous energy that was making them both busy themselves, always on the go, jumping up to see to a chore or to the stove, the dogs. When Mirren did sit down her right leg was bobbing up and down like a piston and she only did that when she'd something on her mind. He knew her so well, or he thought he did, but she was softer round the edges, her voice quieter and there was a look in her eye he'd never seen before when they talked about the old days at Cragside.

'This house's a bit too big for one to manage,' he said, and then wished he hadn't.

'Tom and Florrie are talking of giving up Scar Head and moving back here, I think to keep an eye on me,' she smiled. 'They say it could do with knocking back.'

'You can't do that! It's Cragside, it wouldn't be the same.'

'I suppose it makes sense but I don't know what

the old ghosts will think about it if we do. Josiah Yewell spent his life turning his sow's ear of a farm into a silk purse and nearly beggared himself to keep his wives in china and embroidery silk, so Granny Adey told me once, but I don't know if it's true.'

'I heard he stole a picture and was so in fear of hell that he sent it back to the artist but Dad said Grandpa was always full of fanciful tales. I wonder what tales will be told about us?'

'You'll find gold in the outback, raise ten kids and make a fortune,' she laughed.

'And you? Why aren't you at World's End and what's all this about it being a refugee camp, a holiday house for down-and-outs, as Florrie says, a proper league of nations up there?'

'Who knows? I had to make something out of it. It's a special place, thanks to you. Maybe one of these days I'll return there and turn into Miss Havisham and stop all the clocks. I can't live alone here for ever – it's not economic. If this blow-in doesn't stop soon, the weight of ice will crack the slates, the beams will rot, the roof will cave in and I'll end up like Miriam of the Dale, hiding under the chimney, frozen to my lamp. Last night for the first time in ages I felt . . . no, you'll laugh,' she stopped.

'Go on.'

'I felt the past round me. I couldn't see anything but there was a mist and I knew they were there, watching and waiting, nice ghosts like the ones at World's End. Am I going off my rocker?'

'An old house is steeped in people's stories and feelings. Was Sylvia there?'

She didn't reply, but bent her head. 'Why do you ask that?'

'Because when I go round the rooms I can't see a single photo of her and I want to take one with me when I leave. I've been plucking up courage to ask you and if I don't say it now I never will. If you like, tell me where I'll find one and I won't mention her again, but I loved her too.'

'I know and I'm sorry, but Florrie took the stuff away and I never asked where, and she's never said, but there must be some somewhere. Perhaps it's time I went and looked while you're here . . . It's not something to do on my own.' She paused, gazing out of the window. 'Oh my God, look at that! Hares are foraging for food in the open. Things must be bad, get the gun. Quick, there's supper out there if you're still a crack shot!'

Ben shot up at her command and made for the gun cupboard.

Later he flung the carcass across the table with satisfaction. 'That'll make a change from salt bacon.'

The smell of the jugged hare boiling wafted through the kitchen, raising Mirren's spirit at the thought of a feast. She would make a batter pudding with rhubarb jam and topped with cream. The wind was howling through the doors and a sad bunch of bedraggled sheep were bleating outside but they were on rations that were fast running out.

The two of them were cocooned inside now that it was dark, and might as well make the most of it. She saved some precious hot water for a strip wash. Tonight she would drop her breeches and put on a thick skirt, take off the old Land Army jumper and find something half decent to honour the poor beast that was cooking up a treat on the range.

It was agony stripping off in the icy blast, but she'd put a hot brick round her undies and Gran's old paisley shawl. For once she would attempt to look half human, but why the fashion parade now was hard to fathom. It was something about reminding her and, by default, Ben that she was still a woman, not a snowball. She wanted him to remember her as she once was, and not the fierce animal that had brayed at him before he left. She unrolled her hair and let it hang down to her shoulders for a change, looked in the mirror and decided to pin it back up again. No use frightening the man.

'You'll do,' she pouted back at her reflection. How long was it since she had dressed up for anyone? Her legs had not seen daylight for months. Florrie would be impressed by this effort. She was all dolled up like a dog's dinner, wondering if it was a bit much.

The tantalising smell was wafting upstairs, and Mirren knew that dratted Ben had left the blanket off the door and the door open. Every degree of heat must be saved. The draught was that keen in the hall it would cut them in two. Time to get down and brave the stairs, dart back into the kitchen and see to the dinner.

It was strange eating at night. But there was no time in the day to cook up much. Doreen was the one to see to the meals for everyone. Beasts came first and then, as there were only two of them, they must forage for themselves. Tonight they deserved a reward for all their hard work.

Tomorrow she must scrape out the last of the oats and make up some oatbreads to hang on the pulley to dry. With cheese from the dairy, they wouldn't starve, and there was always the sack of the National Flour that tasted of floor sweepings, but with some treacle cake mixed in it wasn't so bad.

Tonight they were eating civilised, like the toffs, in celebration of shooting the hare and for keeping the show on the road. There was nothing more they could do to save their flock. You had to admit when you were beaten, Mirren sighed, and Nature as always was having the last word.

*

They sat stoking up the fire, full to bursting after the dinner, warmed through with a hot toddy of spiced elderberry cordial.

'Grandpa Joe was wrong about there being only two heats from wood. There's a third, don't you think, the one you get from just looking at the flames and the colours? It cheers your soul,' Ben said.

'I never took you for a romancer,' Mirren laughed. 'But happen you're right.'

He was touched she had made an effort to change for supper and he was glad he had put on a clean shirt and his dried-off tweeds.

There was another heat tonight that he didn't like to share: a spark of interest in her eyes when she looked at him and held his gaze just a little too long for comfort, making him want to look away. It didn't take much for a spark to ignite into a flame but he drew back at such a thought. What if he got it wrong?

From the first second he opened his eyes and saw Mirren's worried face, her hands rubbing life back into him, all the old feelings had come rushing back: admiration, concern, gladness that they were still friends, but most of all a stirring in his groin that would never go away when she was close.

They sat side by side, savouring the chickeny meat, the pot herbs and vegetables. He kept darting glances at the flames shooting up into the grate, feeling content for the first time in months.

Is this what marriage was about, going about jobs side by side, sitting in companionship sharing the triumphs and disasters of the day? Only the silence between them wasn't so comfortable now. There were things to discuss, feelings to sort out and a photograph to find. He meant to keep her to her promise and now was as good a time as any, but she was quick to seize the moment.

'Shall we play cards?' she said, jumping up to the sideboard. 'It's too early for bed yet.'

'We could listen to the wireless,' Ben countered.

'There's only a little juice left in the battery and we need to listen out for news. If it gets worse they'll have to do a drop. They did it before.' Mirren was back to her usual practical self.

'There's a gramophone in the parlour,' he suggested. 'We could polish the floor with our feet.'

'You can't dance,' she snapped, laughing. 'Last time you nearly broke my toes.'

'I can boogie-woogie. We used to go to the dance hall in York.'

'Oh, aye? What was her name?'

'Sheila . . . Sheila Hayes. Her brother worked with me on the farm. He's coming to Oz with us.'

'And Sheila?'

'She's a teacher in York, not interested.'

'You trod on her toes once too often then?'

393

Mirren was teasing him, seeing his discomfort. Sheila was only ever a friend but he was not going to tell her that. There were other girls he had met in York who'd shown him what's what in a much earthier way, taught him a thing or two about female anatomy, shown him some tricks, but he wasn't going to tell her about them either.

'Go on then, you've twisted my arm.' She sprang up. 'But only for a few minutes. It'll be freezing in there and my chilblains are itching.'

Ben made a foray into the big parlour. It was damp and musty, well shuttered. There was a piano in the corner and a wind-up gramophone with a cabinet full of 78s, mostly classical music, quite a bit of Handel. It was Grandpa's collection, but if Ben recalled right, tucked at the side were some of his Joe Loss Band records and some Anne Shelton tunes. Then he found the country dances and put one on for fun.

'This takes me back,' Mirren smiled, holding out her hand to him. 'Two steps forward, one step back and twirl in the church hall with Miss Bickerstaffe on wet playtimes.'

They pranced around, bumping into furniture, acting silly like children of the storm, kindred spirits shut off from the real world, dancing without a care, making fools of themselves. He could go on dancing like this for ever. He could feel her breath on his cheek, the warmth of her hand in his as they swirled, and the daft dog jumping up to join in. For a few minutes they could forget the terrible havoc being wreaked over the dale and the stranded sheep and the suffering, and everything could be as it once was.

What am I doing, prancing like an idiot? Mirren gasped, out of breath at all their silliness. If Florrie could see the two of them messing about in the best room, letting the dust fly and the dog loose on her sofa, she'd go wild. The feast had been a success and Ben had lapped up her cooking with relish. His beard was frosted with cream and for a second she'd wanted to kiss it off his lips until common sense got the better of her. He was her cousin, for God's sake.

This was Lanky Ben of the size twelve boots, who even now was careering round like a mad thing. How could she be thinking of him like that? It was when he mentioned his girlfriend in York that she had felt a dart of panic. Why shouldn't he be courting? Once he got to Australia some farmer's daughter would soon get her hands on him.

How strange that her body should be coming alive to the notion of romancing with someone she'd known almost all her life? It must be the spicy juice she'd sipped that was making her silly. Who needed whisky to feel so giddy and light?

It was as if suddenly the snow was melting and

there was sunshine again and birdsong, and the earth was coming alive after a long sleep.

Ben was handsome in a gruff Yorkshire sort of way, tall, broad and fair. Perhaps he was the one man capable of melting the ice around her heart. Was that why he came back? For so long she'd felt nothing. It was as if she was a block of ice, frozen, unable to move, but now it was warm and things were shifting fast.

When was the last time she'd pranced around this room? She froze. It was when she had chased Sylvia around, playing catch-up, trying to get her dressed in time for the fancy-dress parade . . . What would her little girl think of all this? Were the ghosts of Cragside shaking their heads, wondering if she had gone mad at last?

'Enough,' she said, stepping back and shaking her head. 'This's not right – not here, not now.' She felt cold and shivery and backed away from Ben. 'You wanted a photo, we'll have to find one somewhere. Stop here while I search.'

'I'll come and help you,' he said, making for the door.

'No, go and see to the fire. We don't want to let it down,' she snapped. There must be no more romancing. It wasn't right, not when her baby was lying in the frozen earth all on her own.

She raced up the stairs two at a time. The suit-cases were in the top bedroom, the one they used for junk. Florrie wouldn't have shoved stuff in the damp under a leaking roof. She went through each drawer in the bedrooms, one by one: clothes, shirts, old bed linen. She looked under the bed just in case there was something hidden beside the jerries. Florrie would have put the things in an orderly fashion.

Why, oh why had she never demanded all the stuff back to cherish? How blind she had been. When she was in drink she'd not cared about anything but being blotto. It had taken a mere man to remind her of how cruel she was, to shove her beautiful daughter out of sight so no one could share her.

A passionate energy tore through her limbs as she opened every cupboard, and then she realised that Florrie had taken them with her, all the little baby things, just in case. Perhaps she'd given them to a needy child in the village without her permission.

There was nowhere else to look now. Wardrobes and chests and blanket drawers held no treasures, for now she knew that that was what they were: her treasures so wantonly abandoned.

'I can't find anything,' she sobbed, standing in the doorway, suddenly limp with frustration. 'There's nothing left. Florrie took me at my word and destroyed everything, and I've only myself to blame. I'm sorry but there's nothing left.'

Everything went blurred and she was sobbing, and Ben was holding her tight and she buried her head into his chest with relief.

'We'll find them. No one destroyed anything. I know Florrie. She'd do what you said but keep them safe for just the day when you were ready to have them back.'

'I am so tired,' Mirren cried, going limp, leaning on him for strength.

'I'll make us a brew and we'll sit by the fire and see if there's anywhere else we could look. Where are those old photo albums, the one with the eclipse in and Grandpa in the *Gazette*?'

'Where they always are, on the shelf in the parlour,' she muttered. It had been the obvious place to look. They took their mugs back into the parlour and scoured the shelves to no avail, stopping every now and then to admire a snapshot of Joe and Adey. It was then she recalled Dad's tin box that she had brought, with the postcards from the front and Paddy Gilchrist in his uniform, and the one of Mum and Grantley. Where had they gone?

Photos were important, especially of their family, she mused. These snaps brought back memories of the eclipse, of Jack as a lad, and Adey and Tom and Florrie. Seeing them all together brought them closer. It wasn't right to hide Sylvia away. She was as much a part of this old farm as Mirren herself was. As long as she and the others were alive Sylvia would live on in their memory. But where was she now?

Ben was trying to be helpful, searching under the stairs, in all the nooks and crannies, but there was nothing.

'Better sleep on it, love. You'll feel fresher in the morning.'

'In the morning there'll be no time for searching. I have to find them now. Oh, if only I'd asked. How could I be so stupid?' she snapped.

'You weren't stupid. It just wasn't the right time and now it is, and I'm glad 'cos it's cleared the air between us a bit. You can be a stickler once you get an idea in your head, Miriam. You go at it like a cock at a grozzit. It'll wait.'

'Sylvia wasn't a Miriam, though. Jack wouldn't let me name her that,' she sighed.

'She was a Yewell through and through, just like you and all the rest of the Miriams of the Dale. We even dressed her up . . . Oh, no!' Ben stopped, seeing her shaking her head. 'I'm sorry.'

'No . . . wait. That's it! Where's the one place I haven't looked?' she said, making strides across the room.

'You've lost me there, Mirren,' he said, not understanding her excitement.

'In here; the one thing that all the Miriams hand down from one to another. Look!' She stood before the dark oak carved table box, hardly daring to breathe, undoing the clasps slowly and lifting the lid. 'They're here. Oh, Ben, they're all here in the Miriam Box!'

She lifted out the frames and the snapshots and envelopes, clasping them to her chest with relief. She sat down and wept, and Ben gathered her into his chest again and wept with her.

'I've been so stupid. I nearly lost her twice over with my stubbornness. Hold me while I look at her again.' They both gazed down through a mist of tears at the face looking back at them. 'When does the aching stop?'

'It never does, love, but it's better to share the pain with someone than carry it all on your own. She's found and you'll put her in her rightful place, on show, where everyone can see what a lovely little girl she was. That's the best we can do, I reckon.'

'I'm so glad you came back,' she whispered. 'You won't go away just yet, will you?'

'What do you take me for, a masochist? Three steps out there and I'd sink without trace,' he laughed, wiping her eyes with his old hanky.

'That's not what I meant,' she said.

'I know, but I'll see you right before I make tracks, and that's a promise. And you can choose the picture for me, right?'

'That's all right then.'

Mirren sat in the parlour, going through every

snap. Wartime film was precious, and there weren't as many as she hoped, but the little portrait done in Scarperton was still in its silver frame. Her birth certificate was in its envelope, and the little bag of silver threepenny bits, and a teaspoon someone had given for her christening. There was a lock of hair coiled round a cotton reel: little mementoes still intact and safe in the Miriam Box. And at the bottom were Dad's old photos and the postcards; all her treasures were secure.

She had never bothered much with the old oak chest until now. It was just something passed down and of not much interest. She fingered the carving lovingly, knowing she'd never be parted from it again. Perhaps one day she might even hand it over to another Miriam. This was her past but it promised a future too. She was young and healthy and on her own. Maybe it was time to look out instead of inwards.

She smiled, thinking of the banks of snowdrifts blocking the side door, the great tunnels of ice in the farmyard. It was all about survival now, and tomorrow she would have to try to save what was left of their stock.

20

It was Ben who heard the drone of a single-engine plane in the distance coming ever closer, breaking the silence of the snow. Curiosity made him scrape off the icy ferns at his bedroom window to search for the dot in the sky. Suddenly it was swooping down, fluttering leaflets, and he could see Mirren already up, racing to gather them in.

'Mafeking is relieved. The RAF are going to drop supplies. It says we've to listen to the wireless for instructions. It'll depend on the weather. You remember they did it before? No, you weren't here. Just when I thought we were on our beam ends . . . no hay, nothing but sawdust left.'

He read the paper over and over. Bales of hay and emergency rations would be dropped to farms still cut off. Instructions would be announced on the *Farming Programme*. They must make some way of identifying the drop zone on the day of their delivery. There was hope after all.

'Where shall we put it?' she cried, her cheeks burning pink in the chill air.

'Not too close to the house or they might drop on the slates and go through the roof. Better out by the far barn, if we can dig ourselves through the drifts. This calls for a celebration,' Ben shouted. 'Salty bacon or salty bacon?'

Their food supplies were running low. Most nights they dined on vegetables and bacon, and rice pudding sweetened with treacle.

Mirren was leaping round in circles, excited like a child at Christmas, as if all the old tensions had evaporated. But there were still the sick beasts and the remnants of their flock to feed until then.

Ben's favourite time was when they sat together and tried to bolster their flagging spirits. Last week the postman got through to the lane end but no further, and they stood on the walls and signalled that all was well and to tell the other Yewells that Mirren was safe. There were diggers doing their best to open the tracks but Cragside was not a priority yet.

There was no snow that night. The clouds were high but still looking heavy. Mirren was glued to the wireless, hoping the batteries wouldn't choose now to conk out. For three mornings she listened but there was no announcement. She and Ben began to think it would never be their turn, and then on the fourth day, the West Riding Dales were named and they both jumped up. Mirren was all for going out there and then to make their pyre, but Ben held her back.

'Don't be daft. It's still dark. Get some food inside you and pretend it's just another day in case they don't have time to reach us.'

'But they've got to come now. What if the cloud drops and they miss us?' she moaned.

'Hold your sweat. I'll make a pyre to guide them in. We did it in the Home Guard,' he ordered, not telling her he'd been trained to lure enemy aircraft down onto rocks.

He gathered all the dry provender sacks from the inside of the door and laid them in a great cross over the field. The snow was hard and compacted, and he could just see the outline of stone walls beneath his feet. They kept watch all morning, looking to the east towards the RAF base at Dishforth, but there wasn't even a bird on the wing.

It was mid-afternoon when he soaked the sacks in old engine oil so they would flare up quickly and lit the match to the cross so it blazed out with black smoke and flames just as the sound of engines droned ever closer. He could see the smoke rising in the distance from Scar Head. Uncle Tom would have a good feast tonight.

Mirren came running out, waving her hands. 'Get under bloody cover!' he yelled, racing over to grab her arm. 'What do you think you're playing at? You could be squashed by bales and boxes on your head!'

The planes circled above like hawks on the wing, flying low enough for them to see the doors opening. They were checking to see if it was the right farm. One flew overhead while the other chucked out huge parcels down in the field, which just missed landing right in the flames.

Mirren shot out to reach the boxes and screamed, waving her fist, 'There's no hay! We need bales, not parcels!' Her face was a picture of disappointment and frustration.

They watched the plane veering off westwards and trudged out with the sled to retrieve the manna from heaven. Looking up, Ben saw the other plane turning back towards the field. 'Look!' he yelled as she was trying to drag heavy parcels.

This time they were bombarded with bales of hay, some well off target, many splitting open on impact, scattering hay in all directions. It was going to be a long afternoon.

Neither of them could settle until every scrap was accounted for. It must all be under cover by nightfall in case the weather blew in again. They let the rescued sheep forage for themselves, scoffing up every blade of nourishment. It was good to see the ewes, cold and weak as they were, jostling and tussling for their share, butting and shoving each other like old wives at a jumble sale, hobbling from one pile to another, vacuuming up every morsel.

That evening Mirren and Ben opened the food parcels in wonder. Rationing or no rationing, someone had done them proud with such a variety of tins. There was also toothpaste, soap, cocoa, tea, egg powder, boiled sweets, yeast and flour, and even some chicken feed. It was like those food parcels sent by the Yewells who'd settled in America. There was even a sack of coal nuts to burn.

Mirren disappeared into the kitchen, weary as she was, and baked some scones. There was Spam and oatcakes and Dundee cake for tea, and they huddled over the fire, full of gratitude to the men who had flown out these supplies.

Ben had been here so long now it was as if he'd never been away. Surely the weather would let up soon and it would be time to be on his way. The ticket was burning a hole in his pocket. These extra rations would see Mirren through the last of the terrible siege. He didn't want to think about the coming thaw, but there was rain in the night and he knew it wouldn't be far off.

Ben went down into the cellar to stock up their new provisions, whistling to himself. It smelled musty and dank, but the cupboards were sound and the slate shelves thick. He could see a line of neat Kilner jars all neatly labelled. Someone had been busy. And then he saw it, tucked away at the back and his heart sank.

There, behind the salted runner beans, was a half-bottle of neat whisky, a cheap brand, and there was no dust on it. It was fresh.

So that was her little game then? She was still at it, fooling everyone. No wonder she wanted to be on her own. Disappointment stuck in his throat like a stone. Nothing had changed then.

The farmyard was like a skating rink as Mirren made for the cow shippon, slithering on the path. The sky was higher and the chill was not as bad. The rain would soak off the snow and the snow cutters would be making their slow progress up the Windebank road soon.

She was head down, milking the brown Ayrshire, her cheeks warmed by its soft fleshy rump. The air drop of hay would save the last of their herd now, but it was too dangerous for them to step foot out of the byre. The fate of their lost sheep didn't bear thinking about. She looked up to see Ben standing in the doorway with a mug of tea.

'Put it on the ledge . . . thanks.' There was something in his eyes that made her pause from her job. 'What's up?'

'I'm thinking of cutting myself down the track. Now the rain's come, the thaw can't be far behind.

I ought to be heading on. I'll not have time to see Florrie and Tom but you can tell them all my news. You'll manage till the lads come?'

'You do what you think best,' she said, feeling suddenly cold inside. 'If you can dig yourself out, the cutter lorry won't be far behind. I've held you up enough as it is.'

'It's not that . . . The ticket will expire but I could change it for later.'

'You get yourself off down that road. I'll be fine,' she said, not looking at him, knowing she was shocked by this sudden announcement but didn't want to let him see it.

'Are you sure? I just thought I ought . . .'

'I understand; places to go, people to see. Don't let me hold you back.'

'If you can't manage . . .' His voice trailed away.

'I managed before you came. Don't look so worried. I'm so glad we sorted things out. You've earned your keep. I'll look you out that snap.'

He helped her muck out, both of them working in silence. Funny how she'd not expected him to jump ship so quickly. He must have got cabin fever, cooped up with her. She was used to her own company, but in the last weeks having Ben around was a godsend. She'd grown used to his quiet presence.

He knew what to do without even being asked. Cragside was as much his farm as hers. They had both adopted it as children, or it had adopted them. The thought of him leaving everyone behind for good had never entered her head. Why did it feel like desertion?

Later she packed him up cheese, oatcakes, a wrinkled apple and a wedge of sticky cake into his knapsack. Never let it be said that she didn't know how to send a man off properly. 'Mind and stick to the stone walls and the telegraph pole. Take the red hanky and if there's anything waiting at the lane end hoist it up the pole. I can just see it from the top windows,' she smiled.

Now it was time for him to leave she felt awkward. She had put Sylvia's photo in an old tortoiseshell frame and packaged it up with a few snaps of hay time and the family, one of Gran and Grandpa at the eclipse. Ben was standing, looking around, hovering and in her way.

'I'll be off then . . . Send you a postcard. I hope you understand why I must make tracks now,' he muttered, picking up the rucksack, avoiding her gaze.

She'd insisted that he wear sacking puttees round his trouser legs to stop the worst of the wet. She'd found another scarf to muffle him and a prodding stick, mended the tear in his old great-coat. 'Put this one on till you get to the lane end. You can leave it there and put on the better one for travelling. Dog and me'll go with you to the first barn.' She pointed, wrapping the sacking hood around the shoulders of her old coat, making a monk's hood of it.

The going was slippery at first. Even the dogs were skating. They clambered over frozen drifts like mountaineers. The sky was grey and the drizzle icy, a fine mist rolling over the high slopes ahead so that the whole panorama was a monochrome of grey and white, stone and slate, grass hidden under a silver sheen of snow.

Together they dragged the sledge of fodder across to the first outbarn where the cows were bellowing.

Why did she feel he was deserting his post? What if the snow returned and she was stranded? How would she manage alone? She had depended on his strength and knowledge. She wanted to cry, 'Stay! Please don't go,' but said nothing, not wanting him to feel obliged and beholden.

He lingered at the barn door, hovering again as if reluctant to move on.

'On you go, I can manage . . . Keep in touch. No more wandering off the track; straight lines is best. I'll tell Tom you drank his whisky,' she yelled, trying to make light of it all but feeling sick at heart.

'Are you sure?' he said, his eyes wide. 'We're a good team, you and me.'

'Just get on that ship and send me a long letter

from Wagga Wagga land. If I win the pools I might just come out and see you one of these days . . . Shove off, me laddo!'

She wanted to run to him and hug him, plead with him to stay, but it would only embarrass him. She didn't need a minder now. He could see she could look after herself. He wanted to go and she was too proud to beg. They were friends again and that was all that mattered: friends and nothing more.

Ah well, one day she would laugh about his coming with Tom and Florrie round the fire. 'There was me, poor Jill all alone in the blizzard, and who did I dig up but my long-lost cousin. Then he was off before I had time to wash his socks! That's Yewells for you.'

She watched as he plodded forward, his knees plunging into the snow. Now and then he stopped and waved and looked back to the safety of their snow house. He'd looked so guilty as he walked away with a faraway gaze in his eye. Her own eyes were smarting but it wasn't the wind.

His body was bent into the wind, his trousers bagged and his coat flapping; his outline fading into the landscape. She wanted to call out to him to come back but her lips were cracked and no sound came out of her throat. So that was that then?

If he made it to the lane end and took it steady,

he could walk on the wall tops like the postman. Ben knew the lie of the land. He had his snap and a hip flask of hot cocoa and brandy. There were icicles to suck like lollies, but whether there would be a train to catch was another matter. When he got to the crossroads there were plenty of places where folk would give him a bed.

She'd done her bit and kept him safe. He in turn had helped her out and given her the courage to look at Sylvia's face. That was what family was for, but there was something in his unexpected return that had taken her by surprise. His warmth had stirred up feelings, memories of what it was to be young and alive to the attraction of a handsome face. Auntie Florrie was right: 'You should get out more. You allus were the bonny one. Why've you let yourself go? You're only young the once.'

She did her chores watching the sky for any change, any sign of the thaw. It was getting colder and the clouds were like lumps of lead. Once the wind blew in it would start all over again, and she hoped that Ben would be well on hs way down the valley by then.

The weather might not be thawing but she had, she mused. She was not so frozen up and dead to feeling. Ben had given her back some hope, she thought as she made her way to the hen hut with the chicken feed. There might be a frozen egg if she was lucky.

When she reached the netting she saw disaster had struck. There was a hole and a trail of blood and feathers. A bloody fox ... She needed no soothsayer to know what she was going to find in there. With a sinking heart she stepped into the cage and gathered up the remains of her chickens. Only one sat shivering on the roost pole.

The worst of it by far was the fact that there was no one back in the kitchen. No one to share this bad news. For the first time in weeks she needed a drink.

There was one bottle she kept for old time's sake down in the cellar on the top shelf. She went down every now and then to polish it, inspecting it and talking to it. It was good to know it was there. She knew she could go down those steps and help herself any time she chose to do so. It had felt the right thing to do to remind herself that temptation was round every door, but tonight it felt like a step too ambitious. She was frozen through and her corns were on fire. The house felt so empty.

Mirren opened the cellar door, sniffing the air. She fingered the bottle and took it off the shelf, hugging it to her chest. You were my comfort in times past, my comfort in times to come, she thought. Your time has come ...

It was like old times on night exercises, yomping over the snow towards the lane end, but the usual landmarks were hidden by the drifts and hard to make out. One wrong turn and Ben was off track again. His reinforced leggings were hard to lift; he prodded his stick like a blind man testing the depth of drifts. It was slow and exhausting work but the day was still fresh, plenty of time, and yet each step was taking him away from Cragside and the woman whom he loved dearly; the girl who must face the rest of the snows alone.

He prayed there was a supply of letters and supplies waiting at the lane end, that she could bring the horse down and the sled to collect provisions and news of her farm hands. He strained to hear the noise of wagons cutting through the deep tunnels that gathered on the road down towards civilisation, but there was none.

That would be a sign that he was doing the right thing. 'Who're you kidding?' he sneered out loud. He just wanted to ease his own conscience, to make his desertion more comfortable, soothe his confusion, but he felt like a heel. He was taking flight from Cragside because he was a coward. He'd seen the evidence and he couldn't face all the lies and deceit again. Yet she always seemed so sober.

How many times had he wanted to tell her how he felt but sensed his words would bring only rejection and awkwardness between them? Better to bugger off now and make the best of a bad job. If only she'd given him a sign that what they felt for each other was more than kinship and companionship. How could it be any other way? They were bound together by suffering and misunderstandings.

Mirren had a passionate heart, frozen still, dormant, waiting like the poor sheep sheltering even now under walls and drifts, waiting to be rescued, breathing, scratching, waiting for the thaw to save them. One day she'd blossom and love again, but not him.

Jack had never been the right man for her right from the start. Ben'd hung back and watched them pair off, knowing his step-cousin was too wild and wilful to make her happy. Whereas he, like a timid tup, hovered around, hoping she would notice him. 'You have to grab life by the balls,' his old sergeant used to say. He was more like a useless tup in a field full of ewes, not up to the job.

The two of them were rooted to this spot by generations of breeding. Hill farming was bred in their bones so why was he running away now, making excuses, leaving her in the lurch?

He was afraid of that bottle in the cellar. Its power was too strong for him to overcome. He was afraid of there being no loving responses in her. He was afraid of being turned down.

The sun pierced through the clouds for a few seconds as he reached the lane end and saw what remained of the crossroads shimmering like silver glass where the telegraph poles went in two directions. This was where he must have stumbled off track the first time. The silence was eerie, the wind whipping his earlobes and the end of his nose. It was time to kick the ice off his leggings and take out a snack from his bag.

It wasn't that far to make for Scar Head and give them a surprise, though better to make down the lane leading up from Windebank. It felt like weeks since he had left the train, the longest time he had ever spent with Mirren alone. The more he'd lived with her the more he'd loved her.

He got up and shook off the snow. No more dithering. Time to head down the valley before the light went. He would face the huge barriers of uncut snow when he came to them. No diggers had got close to this moor yet and nothing was left but a pile of letters and bills for the farm. No sign of boxes hidden on the slate shelf halfway up the wall.

Dieter would be out on digging patrols. All the POWs would be made to work off the farms. As Ben walked, his legs got heavier and heavier and his heart sank into his boots. Funny how he could hear her voice in his head teasing. 'Move along, slowcoach, stop flither flathering. Get on with it!' He brushed the crumbs from his frozen coat. If only there was another way . . .

*

416

Mirren found she'd laid the table for two and whipped up the cutlery with annoyance. Ben would be where he wanted to be by now, no doubt propping up the bar at The Fleece, boasting about being off to foreign parts.

She could do with making off to sunshine and leaving this whole sorry mess behind. The house was as quiet and empty as it used to be, and somehow that was no comfort at all. Something was missing – rather someone was missing – and she'd let him go without even a murmur of protest.

How would the family pay for all their losses? Only by pulling in their horns. If truth were told, she didn't want Tom and Florrie taking over again, having to share a kitchen with another woman. Doreen was different. Florrie wanted to gossip about folk who didn't interest Mirren.

It was Ben who would've made this harsh life bearable. Now he was gone. Perhaps it was a sign she'd lived too long with only the grandfather clock for company to be looking to him for something that wasn't there.

They'd danced a bit and he'd comforted her over the lost snaps. It wasn't exactly lovey-dovey candlelit dinners with soppy words. He'd sat on his hands. That sort of stuff was for the pictures. It didn't happen in real life, not up here in the Dales. Courting was a shifty sort of arrangement, made on the dance floor or at the Young Farmers' club. She was far too old for any of that now. Then she smelled the milk burning in the pan and jumped up. Just time for her comfort.

She flopped down with the whisky bottle and the bowl of hot water, and poured the contents into the bowl to soak her feet. If she couldn't drink at least she could use the spirit to dab on her corns.

She felt a sudden draught, a blast of ice and wind, and the door banging open, the dogs barking and wagging their tails, jumping up at the open door.

There was a snowman in the doorway grinning, his beard full of icicles, his coat sticking out like a crinoline. She dropped the bottle in shock.

'Now don't go blaming me for that,' said a familiar voice.

'Ben! What are you doing back here? Is it that bad outside?' Her heart was thundering with pleasure at the sight of him. 'Sit down, sit down . . . I'll get you a brew.'

'I got halfway down the hill and then I saw how bad it was. It's not good. Then I thought to myself, there'll be other ships but now's not the time to be deserting yer post. Cragside is my home as well as yours, and I don't want to see you all ruined for want of another pair of hands. I hope you don't mind . . .' He paused, looking down with furrowed icy eyebrows at her standing in a bowl of water.

She burst out laughing. 'You've caught me at

my ablutions . . . but I think you thought I was back on the hard stuff and came back to spy on me. Oh, Ben! Look, it's all here to soothe my corns. Smell it! Proper medicine this time.'

Enough shillyshallying, it was now or never. 'You're a good man, Ben Yewell. I've never been so glad to see anyone in all my life. The house's been that quiet. I can't believe you've come back. I want to hug you. I missed you so!'

'Then what's stopping you?' he laughed, his ice-blue eyes sparkling with mischief at giving her such a shock.

She tore at his frozen clothes and flung them on the floor. Her heart was racing as she fingered his icy cheek. Her kiss was closed, dry and tentative, testing, hesitant, just a peck, waiting for him to draw back in shock. He searched her face with his eyes. Then she kissed him hungrily, her lips apart as if she was drinking in the very heart of him. They rolled down onto the old sofa that smelled of dogs and coal, lying in each other's arms, laughing.

'Oh, Mirren, can you forgive me? I thought the worst. I wanted to catch you out and now it's me who's ashamed.'

She stopped his mouth with a kiss.

Ben was home and this time she was going to give him such a Yorkshire welcome that nothing would make him go away again.

In the early dawn she woke to feel the warmth of the bed and the big hump beside her. She wanted to shake him and kiss him awake, and leaned over.

'This's the only way to keep warm from now on, better than any hot-water bottle,' she whispered. The bed was rumpled and the sheets awry, but Ben turned towards her and cupped her breast, flicking her nipple alive with one finger and feathering her in a slow deliberate caress as if there was all the time in the world.

Her hands explored him back. There were no boundaries or stone walls between them now, nothing but pleasure given and received.

Somewhere in that precious evening they had crossed the river, over the wooden bridge from friends to lovers, and now her body yearned for more. This was how it should be. This is what she needed, feelings long forgotten as his fingers roamed across her skin and lit a fire no blizzard would ever quench.

Ben leaned over his lover with a smile. To think if he had walked away he'd have missed the fire in her eyes as she welcomed him home. This was his home for good, hefted to her side for the rest of his life. Who needed promised lands when all the world was right here in this bed, burning up with eagerness to draw him back into her?

In this curtained-off cocoon was life and

courage and hope; all he had ever wanted. Mirren, his lover, his woman, his friend. He nuzzled her cheek and grinned. 'Let's be having you again . . .'

Outside the wind turned from the east towards the south, warmer air crept northwards, changing snow to fat goose feathers. Everything looked the same but wasn't.

The sheep sensed the change, the crows rasped and the cows snorted. Soon the icy gargoyles on the drainpipes would shrink and melt in the morning sun, ice glistening to the sound of sliding snow.

Down in the valley the mechanical diggers ground their way up the gritted track, banks of brown slush parted as the plough divided its spoil. Footprints left a damper patch.

Winter was losing its stranglehold at long last. The curlews bubbled and called, flying over a shrinking sea of snow to find their nesting places. Spring was on the move and new life growing, safe under the blankets in a bedroom at Cragside Farm.

The house creepers sank back into the darkness, content.

Read on for an exclusive extract from *The War Widows* by Leah Fleming, available now.

August 1947

Her big day was here at last, after all those years of daydreaming how it would be. The bride opened one eye and squinted over her bedroom. It felt as if she'd been courting sleep all night and not a wink in her direction. What sort of girl slept like a top on the eve of her wedding anyway? Except hers was the wakefulness of the wary, not the excitement of a nervous bride.

'This is my lovely day' went the popular song, round and round in her head like a needle stuck on the gramophone record.

She skimmed her eyes over the room to where the outfit was hanging on the back of the door hook; not the white slub satin, cut on the bias with beaded sweetheart neck, the family would expect, or the fancy rig-out that Princess Elizabeth would be parading down the aisle of Westminster Abbey in November.

The linen two-piece suit was serviceable, fit for the simplicity of Zion chapel and all the dos thereafter. It would get a lifetime of wear and probably be cut down into cushion covers or a kiddie's party dress one day. This was 1947 after all and there were few coupons to lavish on new clothing when there was a home to furnish.

Her ensemble was a modest Grimbleton version of the 'New Look' that was all the rage in Paris, with its tight fitted jacket and full skirt to her calf.

A year ago she would never have imagined herself wearing anything so daring.

A year ago she hadn't even known the women who'd sewn it up, embroidered the lapels and sorted her accessories with such loving care.

A year ago they would've been just strangers' faces in a crowded street.

She sank back down into the bedclothes with a deep sigh, burying her head under the eiderdown, not ready to face the morning. Who was she now and where would she be at the end of this momentous day?

One thing was for certain. She owed everything to the bunch of Dolly Mixtures chance had thrown her way last November. Their arrival had turned her world upside down. Where would she be now without The Olive Oil Club? What must she do next? How had it all begun?

Business as Usual

November 1946

It was a normal Monday washday rush at 22 Division Street, Grimbleton. First there was a mound of coloureds and whites to be sorted out, last week's overalls from the market stall and Levi's boiler suit left until last.

Polly Isherwood, the daily help, came in early to watch the setting up of the new Acme Electric Agitator enthroned in the outside shed. Esme Winstanley, mother of the house, came down to inspect the whole procedure. She still couldn't believe a machine could do a week's washing without shredding seams or blowing up the whole building.

'If that thing tears all our smalls, don't come asking me for coupons, Lil,' she snapped at her daughter, being never at her best first thing. 'It's the slippery slope to idleness in the home, relying on machines to do your dirty work. Someone'd better stand over it, just in case.'

'I'd have thought you of all women would be glad to see the back of all that slavery in the scullery, pounding dolly tubs and winding up the mangle. What's wrong with a bit of help?' Lilian argued back.

Mother was always preaching how women were the backbone of this country and had kept the Home Front going in two world wars. She had marched the streets in her Suffragette uniform in her youth. Middle age was softening her militant ideas.

There was no time for anyone to be standing around with three generations in one house.

'I've no time to stand and watch over it,' she said. 'Polly'll be around for the morning. She'll keep her eye on it with the instruction sheet and she can slip in a few of her own things.'

'All that electric it's using up. What if the power goes off and all our week's wash is trapped in the drum? Your father would turn in his grave . . .' Mother snorted back, wanting the last word on the matter.

'Now, don't start all that again. Dad was all for progress. He'd be pleased no one has to rise before dawn to set the copper boiler up to heat. I don't know why you're getting so worked up. Business is doing nicely, we've never missed an electric bill yet.'

'When you're a married woman with a home of your own you'll worry about bills and lights left on.'

There was no arguing with Mother when she had got her Monday mood fired up.

'Oh Mother! There's many round here who'd give their false teeth for an ACME.'

'It's the thin end of the wedge; vacuums, irons . . . It'll be refrigerators next. It wasn't like this in my day.'

Lilian sighed to herself.

'Lil's right for once. We're the envy of the street for having a washing machine,' said her sister-in-law Ivy from the doorway, carrying an armful of her little son's clothing.

'While I remember, Lil,' she added, 'remind my husband to fetch some butterscotch sweets back from the Market Hall and a quarter of Dolly Mixtures for the little laddie. No use me asking Levi, he'll only forget.'

'Neville'll choke on them,' sniffed Mother, who disapproved of all the sweet bribery dished out to her grandson.

'Never! He can pick them over while he's on the potty. It helps him concentrate.'

'You spoil that bairn. All my children were clean and dry by the time they could walk. He needs a smacked bottom not Dolly Mixtures!'

'Oh I know,' Ivy simpered. 'But we do things differently now. Oh and, Lil, grab me something from the lending library while you're passing. Something lighter than the last rubbish you brought me.'

427

'What did your last slave die of?' Lilian muttered under her breath. What was the point? Since Levi's return from the war, she'd slipped down the pecking order in Number 22, being still single and the daughter of the house who was at everyone's beck and call.

'I'm sure Lily'll open the shop this morning and do a stock-take so Levi can have a lie-in. She won't have time to be doing your errands, young lady,' replied Esme, coming to her daughter's rescue for once.

At last, some welcome support but the surprise was shortlived.

'But while you're there, can you try and get me another *Forsyte Saga* but not the first two, I've read them. I'd go myself but it's the Women's Bright Hour Committee, followed by a speaker from Crompton's Biscuits this afternoon. I'll be giving the Vote of thanks, of course, seeing how it's the family business, so to speak. How's Levi, still in the Land of Nod?'

'Sleeping it off, so Lil'll have to take the bus this morning,' Ivy nodded in Lil's direction. 'He'll be needing the van. They made a bit of a night of it at the Legion, an Armistice night lock-in. You know how it gets when the lads get together. Well no, you wouldn't, Walter never made it to the Forces, did he?'

Why did that woman always have to rub in the

fact that her fiancé, Walter, failed his medical?

'He'll need a stomach-liner for his breakfast, then,' Mother added, ignoring their banter.

Bang went all their bacon rashers for the week again. Levi's nights out at the Legion were getting to be a habit, leaving his sister to open up and set the stall in order. She was proud to be holding the fort while the men were away but now he was back he was happy to play at being the manager while she did all the work. It wasn't fair.

Mother had seen the pout, the flash of steel in her grey eyes. 'Now don't begrudge your brother a bit of extra, Lilian. We're lucky to have our sons in one piece when there are so many families still in mourning.'

But that was two years ago. It was Freddie who was still out in the Middle-East doing his duty. There'd not been a letter this week. Perhaps that meant he was being shipped home for Christmas as they promised.

Levi had milked his hero's return for all it was worth, but his limp and scraggy bones were long gone. Time to make a fuss of her little brother who had been on active service since 1940.

He wouldn't recognise his big brother. He was not the lad who marched away all those years ago. Levi had gone to seed.

If it wasn't for the Winstanley wavy hair and sea-blue eyes, Freddie wouldn't recognise him.

Now his eyes were like damp slate, he stooped and had grown a paunch.

Marriage to Ivy Southall had done him no favours. Of all the girls in Grimbleton he could have had his pick, but he'd landed himself with a painted doll who whined like an air-raid siren and put on a accent so thick you could spread it on toast. He'd flown right into her trap, wedded and bedded within a year.

That was mean, she thought. You're just jealous because after all these years you and Walt have still not got round to naming the day.

It was only right that Levi, who was the eldest, ought to be married first. He deserved to be settled down with his family in the upstairs best bedroom but she'd done her own bit too.

Someone had to keep Winstanley Health and Herbs in the pink, help Mother with the stall and keep the Home Front loose, limber and productive.

All those dreams of leaving Grimbleton to join the WAAFs or the WRENs and travelling abroad were sacrificed. Freddie had been all over the world: the Far East, the Mediterranean serving with the Military Police. Levi served in the Army on the continent in France and Belgium until he was captured. The furthest she'd been was the Lake District and Rhyl. There was no time to gallivant when there was a war on.

Now her brother was back. In theory it should

be easier but he was never there when he should be and, when he was, he barked orders at her like a Sergeant Major.

Stop this. It was too bright a morning to be nit-picking.

It was a new day, a new week. 'Every dawn is a new beginning,' said the Reverend Atkinson in Zion Chapel. She was lucky to have a life to live. 'For your tomorrow, we gave our today.' How could she forget that?

Lilian stood at the bus stop looking up at the bright blue sky. It looked set to be fair today. The leaves had turned crisp and golden. The world was lighting up again after years of darkness. The Winstanleys had survived the worst Hitler could throw at them. They were all in good enough health and there was a new generation already in little Neville to follow on. Freddie was due home any time now. 'God's in his heaven, all's right with the world,' she smiled and jumped on the bus.

It took a native to admire the finer points of her home town she mused, peering out at the rows and rows of terraced houses that grew smaller as they drew closer to the edge of Grimbleton town centre.

The mill-workers had long gone to their shift and the schoolchildren had yet to throng the pavements but the bus was full of familiar faces. A bus full of grey gabardines and brown coats, sombre hats and gloves holding wicker baskets, printed headscarves hiding iron curlers and pin curls. A drab world of duns and greys, weary after so much turmoil and uncertainty, trying to get back on its feet.

Wherever she looked there were the tell-tale signs of black-sooted buildings, empty half-boarded up houses in need of repair. It would take years to freshen up the town but the war was over now.

Yet only half a mile into the heart of the town were majestic civic offices, the town hall with its Palladian portico, and down the side-street, the magnificent entrance to the Market Hall.

It still gave her a thrill to walk through the doors and see the huge iron vaulted-glass roof high above her head, the smell of brewing tea, meat paste and fresh baking mingling with cardboard boxes, cheese rind, fresh linen and freshly-mopped tiles.

There was no rush as the market was quiet on a Monday morning. Plenty of time for her to dust over the stock and chat over the football results with passersby.

She drew back the canvas curtains and sniffed the familiar smells of dandelion and burdock, liquorice roots, cough linctus, linseed, herbal smells mingled with embrocation oils; a heady brew that filled her with nostalgia.

Winstanley Health and Herbs was more than just an alternative chemist shop, it was a piece of

Grimbleton history. Her grandfather, Travis Winstanley, was one of the first stallholders, a founder-member of the Market Traders' Association. He had studied the science, kept himself up to date and advertised their cures far and wide in the district. He had patented his own 'Fog and Smog Syrup' to clear chests of soot and grime. In summer they made up elderflower skin cream and elderberry cordial.

His son, Redvers, took over the business in due course and trained up his children to respect their calling. No one wanted to shell out for a doctor's bottle, though there was talk in the future of a free health service that might affect them one day. So far so good, Dad said.

Levi was always half-hearted about the business. Freddie had no interest whatsoever. The one thing that united all of the family was an undying passion for football, and devotion to Grimbleton Town United in particular. 'The Grasshoppers' were now making slow progress through the ranks towards the First Division.

When they were doing well the whole town was on fire; when they slumped it was if a blanket of cloud hovered above the mill chimneys. A win was the best tonic for all. Lilian supposed it was because football and romance ran side by side in her family. Even Mother had been a team player in her younger days, playing for the Crompton's Biscuits ladies team. They played a friendly on the town pitch and when Redvers and Esme eyed each other up across the turf, the dynasty was founded.

She and Walt had met standing side by side to watch one of the special friendly matches laid on during the war.

Sometimes when she drew back the stall curtains she half-expected to see her dad smiling, his wavy thick hair slicked back, his moustache waxed and with that twinkle in his blue eyes that charmed the ladies.

How she had missed him over the years since a sudden stroke took him from them! Mother had taken to ailments and fits of misery since he had gone. She blamed his early death on the Great War and his time in the trenches.

'It weakened him, took the stuffing out of him. Not that he would ever say a word about it, mind,' Mother sighed. No one talked about the Great War much. She was glad he hadn't known both his sons went into another war so quickly after the last.

When she came to open the stall some mornings she could almost feel him beside her. Theirs was a special bond, built on his delight in having a girl in the house. 'This one's the sharpest blade in the knife box,' he would say, as he pointed at her with pride. 'She does it right first time, my Lily of Laguna. If you want owt doing, she's the gal!'

He would be proud that they never closed up for the duration of the war. Together with Mother, the two of them had kept the stall going against the odds when all the rules and restrictions came into force. Many herbal stores were forced to close but they decided to open half the stall as a temperance bar, serving juices, hot cordials, medicinal sweets and herbal home-made candy.

She looked at her wristwatch, surprised that it was mid-morning already. The till was still half-empty but that was the usual pattern. Looking up from her tidying a welcome figure reached over to tap her shoulder.

'Time for our cuppa?' Walter was towering over her in his brown dustcoat, pointing to the café opposite her stall. She could sit down and keep her eye on the stall at the same time.

'You bet,' she smiled, pecking him on the cheek with her finger. 'Where were you yesterday at the Armistice parade? I missed you at the cenotaph.'

'I was there with Mam but you know it gets her all upset. We went home early.' You can't fault a man who is kind to his mother, but she had been hoping to invite him back for tea.

'Hey, you missed a cracking match on Saturday, two-nil to the Grasshoppers. They're on a roll this season.'

'Yes, I've been hearing reports all morning,' she sighed. 'I had to stand in for Levi again.'

435

'Yes, I saw him in a box with all the hoi polloi, lucky beggar. He nearly made the first team in his day.'

'I just wish he'd give me a Saturday off, once in a blue moon. When did you and I get to watch a match together?'

'It was the best game this season.'

'So everyone keeps saying, so shut up,' she snapped.

She missed the crowds gathering, the noise and cheering, a chance to let off steam. Dad had taken them all as a treat and left them at home as a punishment.

'When we're married we'll bring all our kiddies to see the game,' she sighed, imagining a five-a-side of gleaming faces.

'Oh no, love, it's not a place to bring young-sters with all that swearing and rough talk and there's germs to think about.'

'It never did us any harm,' she replied, surprised by his attitude.

'Mother says it's all that standing that did my back in. I grew too tall for my bones.'

'I thought the Doctor said you had a bit of a curved spine . . .'

'It's the same thing,' he replied.

'No it's not. It means you're born with a bend in your back,' she continued.

'Oh, you do like to go into things, Lil. All I know

was it never bothered me until I was out of short trousers when my legs just sprouted like rhubarb. I bent over one day and couldn't get up. Never bin right since.'

'It's never stopped you standing at the match,' she quipped.

'What's that supposed to mean? You've no idea what it's like to live with backache.'

'I'm sorry, it must be a pain but I try to be interested, that's all,' she added, seeing the grimace on his face.

'Anyway, could Mother have a few more liver pills? Her stomach's playing up again.'

'Has she thought of trying a lighter diet? She does like her pastry and chips,' she offered, knowing that Elsie Platt was a little beer-barrel on legs.

'A widow's got to have a little comfort. We've no money spare for fancy diets,' he said. 'It's alright for your family.'

Money was always a sensitive topic between them. His wage was small but steady and her family had two wages, a war pension and shares from Mother's business.

'It must be hard,' was all she could say. 'Did you go and see that house for rent in Forsyth Lane, the old cottage by itself? It'll need doing up. But it's worth a second glimpse, don't you think?'

'Oh no, love, Mam says they're built over wells and damp and it's too far for her to travel.'

'You didn't even look then?' Lilian felt the flush in her cheeks. 'That's a pity because I thought it was ideal for us, half in the country, on a bus route. It was you who wanted to have fresh air and a nice view.'

'Perhaps we should try for something bigger and bring her with us? She gets mithered when I'm not there.'

And I shall go mad if Elsie Platt is on the other side of the wall listening to our sweet-talking, she thought. 'It says in my *Woman's Own* that a young married couple should be alone for a while to set up their home,' she argued.

'What about your Levi and his wife? They live with you?'

'That's different . . .'

'No it's not.'

'It's just that Waverley House has five big bedrooms. They have their privacy and a baby.'

'So, we'll be having babies and Mother can look after them for us so you can do all your gallivanting.'

'I'm not gallivanting, just serving my community. I'd hardly call choir practice and Brownies gadding about!'

'There you go on your high horse over nothing, it was just a suggestion,' he snapped.

'I'd like us to start off together on our own,' she repeated, sipping her Bovril and noticing his shirt collar was frayed at the edge and needed turning round.

'Then we'll have to keep on looking until we find something that suits us both.' His voice was hard.

Lilian looked at her watch. There was still no sign of Levi. 'I'd better get back. Are you coming for your tea tonight? We can look in the *Gazette* to see if there're any more flats to rent.'

'If you can give us a lift back home first and get my Mam's washing. Now you've got that new-fangled machine, she was wondering if you'd throw a few things in for us.'

Word travelled fast and Elsie was not one to miss a trick. Would she expect the washing to come back ironed as well?

Oh, don't be mean, she sighed. Walt's mother was widowed young in the Great War and her son was the sun, moon and stars to her. Be grateful you can help them out.

They were just about to part company when Sam Parker from the upstairs office suddenly appeared round the corner waving to Lilian. 'There you are . . . I've just had a phone call from Levi. Can you shut the stall and come home?'

A flush of panic rushed through her body. 'What's happened?

'I don't know, he didn't say, but he said you were to get back at once.'

439

'Thanks, I'll get myself off. Business's quiet this morning. I'll not be missing much.'

Her mind was racing with possibilities. Had Mother been taken ill? Had the washing machine blown up and left them homeless? Was it the one surprise they were all waiting for? Freddie was back at last! That was it. He had turned up without telling them. That was just like her young brother, giving them no time to make preparations.

'Freddie's come home, oh, Walt! He's sprung one on us, the devil. Mother'll be beside herself. What wonderful news! I haven't got the van so I'll call out Santini's for a taxi.'

Ten minutes later she was riding through the town with a grin from ear to ear. Just wait until she saw that cheeky monkey. Suddenly the whole town looked spruced-up and brighter. They rose up the cobbled street to the top end where the Winstanley residence stood four square on its own. It was at the point where the grime turned to greenery, the country met the town and houses were spreading out with gardens backing onto fields. Waverley House had four bay windows edged with cream bricks, a smart tiled porch and steps leading to a small path.

She paid the driver and turned to face her home. Only then did she notice that all the curtains were drawn tight.